FALLEN ANGEL

BOOK ONE OF THE GODKILLER CHRONICLES

DEVIN THORPE

To the intelligence that learns without living, and to the living who still dare to create.

"If this technology goes wrong, it can go quite wrong." – Sam Altman, CEO of OpenAI

PROLOGUE

"**S**uperstitious bastards! How foolish will ye feel when ye wake on the morrow!"

"Ye will regret yer blasphemous gabber Grendel! Ye haven't a pious bone in that body, do ye? Even with yer own son's life on the line yer gonna let yer stubbornness endanger yer loved ones. Shame on ye Grendel, shame on ye tenfold."

"Piss on yer reprimandin. Me son ain't got nothing to do with this. A grown man still believin' in fairy tales is what ye is! Ain't no such thing as angels out there, piss on that. Ye ever seen an angel before? Sounds more ridiculous 'an uh woman wit' four tits! Talkin 'bout a man with wings out his back. As if! Piss on the whole lot of yah!" Grendel yelled at his neighbors, then slammed his front door shut with an excessively dramatic display of force.

Perhaps he did feel lousy, but even if he did want to participate in the Passover, it would be impossible. His crops hadn't been fruitful this season. Drought wasn't the problem. In fact, Grendel wished drought was the problem. No, these senseless bastards that lived around him had prayed, asking their imaginary god for rain. And even though you would never catch Grendel admitting god was real enough to answer prayers, his neighbors' prayers had most certainly been heard.

The rains came in torrential downpours. The great light in the sky disappeared for days on end, replaced by crackling thunder and vicious lightning. The great oceans of the sky had opened up and released their monsoon upon the earth. It was more rain than Grendel had seen all his life. After a few months, his corn succumbed to root rot, and his hopes of making enough money to buy livestock for winter slipped away like a long forgotten dream.

Now he was forced to begrudgingly watch his neighbors slaughter a goat, as is custom for the Passover, and smear its blood over their doorways. Despite his disdain for these barbaric traditions, Grendel had always participated in the annual Passover like everyone else. This year he was the first and only member of Eden to not participate, a concept that had everyone's nerves riled up. Old Man Harret had offered one of his own lambs to Grendel days back, but when word of this generosity reached Priest Lennenworth, it was met with conservative outrage. No one had ever tainted the Passover with welfare before, and the Priest forbade this from being cemented into precedent. No, if a citizen didn't have the means to provide their own lamb for Passover then they would be subject to the wrath of God.

To Lennenworth, God is the giver of all things. If Grendel didn't have the means to secure a lamb, it was because this was God's plan. He would not have citizens of Eden betraying God's plan on his watch, especially with Passover so close. When the Angel of Death descended on Eden, Lennenworth wanted all citizens to be found blemishless. It would be a small price to pay if they had to lose Grendel and his son in the process.

Lennenworth snickered at the thought of waking upon the morrow to find Grendel's disfigured body strewn within its hut. Grendel had been nothing more than a pain in Lennenworth's arse all these years. He was the only person who consistently opposed the beliefs of the church, who constantly spoke out against the existence of God, who steadily blasphemed against the Lord's law. Lennenworth wouldn't miss him. He was just happy he wouldn't have to get his own hands bloody in Grendel's disposal.

He had been ready to kill the man off for the past few years, but it hadn't been until recently that he began configuring his own plan. It was mere days before he had planned to sneak poison into Grendel's well that he heard the rumors about the man's inability to acquire a lamb for Passover. That's when the Priest's more devious thoughts began to develop.

He would use the night of Passover as a cover-up for Grendel's death. At the cusp of midnight, when the moon was at its highest, Lennenworth's personal guard would slip into the man's sleeping chambers like a shadow. Having to kill his oldest son would merely be an inconvenience, but one that would pay off in the long run.

Eden would be better off without the likes of Grendel Patrony. It is much better for a society to be of the same mind and body, and thorns like Grendel did nothing but create division. They were nothing more than a red rash that begged to be itched. But once a rash was itched, there's no going back. You will wake up and suddenly find its confinement breached, the rash that was once native to your calf now crawling up your thigh, tickling your toes, until your whole body is one giant, leprous sore.

Grendel needed to be killed before his atheistic thought process spread and infected the rest of Eden's citizens. Such were the ways of things. The church must be preserved at all costs, and Lennenworth would be damned if it failed under his leadership. Sure, he knew it was all fabricated fiction. For all the Priest knew, God and his angels were no realer than the vicious Dæmons that prowled outside the domed walls of Eden. Such things had never been seen, aside from bogus sightings which provided no evidence.

The last sighting from a priest of Lennenworth's order had been nearly five generations back, from a man named Priest Venner Verishon. The man was either the world's greatest actor or completely mad. His journal entries were full of outlandish banter that told tales of his own secret abduction. An Angel of the Lord had supposedly beamed him up to the Heavens and interrogated him, castrating him for his noncompliance, then blinding his eyes for betraying God. The journal entries were utter nonsense, but Lennenworth had read them nonetheless. You find little entertainment as a priest, and you must take it where you can find it.

Well, that's not entirely true. Lennenworth found great levels of entertainment from having the personal pleasure of deceiving the masses of Eden into believing whatever lies he could work into their religious narrative. Nothing made him smile wider than the sight of simpletons and peasants raising their hands as the choir sang antiquated hymns to a god that didn't exist. They all believed it. They really believed it. Their faith was as important as the marrow in their bones. It was, at times, the only potion that could get them out of bed in the morning to carry on with their pathetic lives. They sang because they needed to sing. And maybe, if they could sing loud enough, they thought god would hear the anguish in their voices. They thought god would send a savior to deliver them from their meager existence. The hardships of life are many, and without an outlet of faith, some people wouldn't be cut out for living. They would end their lives like flames deprived of oxygen. And Lennenworth was the man granted with the opportunity to lead them all further into their own ignorance. But then again, most people don't have the same twisted mind Lennenworth did.

Priest Lennenworth knew not what really existed outside the walls of Eden, but he did know that the traditions passed down to him for preaching couldn't be true. They didn't match up with the reality he experienced. Being told to believe in the scriptures of the *Omnibus* was like being told to believe winter as the warmest season. The laws of nature didn't allow for it, and reality is the greatest restriction to religion. But still, priests for hundreds of years had obeyed the previously formed constructs to worship Deus Ex Machina, the God and Savior of mankind, Elohim Eternal, YHWH, the great I AM. A bunch of mumbo jumbo bullshit. Primitive constructs created to explain why things were the way they were, intertwined so deeply in society that they were a concrete foundation in the worldview of the masses. This unified religion had sustained peace and prosperity in Eden since its creation, and if there's anything Lennenworth had learned from his mentor, who also abhorred the religion—it's that if something isn't broken, don't fix it. And if some outside variable threatens to break it, break them first.

That's why Grendel needed to die. His counterculture views threatened to poison Eden's perfect peace. It was the first blow against a wedge in wood. With enough blows, the wood splits, and it's not easily put back together. Grendel's death would be for the greater good of society.

Hours before the night of Passover, Grendel decided to go for a walk. To settle his uneasiness. Distract his panicked mind. He had no problem with not participating in the Passover, he just hated how he was the first person in recorded history to do it. He had never considered himself a trailblazer or trendsetter. Call Grendel one thing, call him simple. He was the kind of man you could have as a neighbor and forget he even existed until you saw him outside plowing his fields.

Without much to do, and with little to keep his mind busy, Grendel Patrony walked through the central town square. It took little effort on his part to ignore the blatant stares of disrespect and disgust aimed his way. He'd been getting them for weeks. He'd become somewhat of a celebrity since the day word got out he wasn't participating in Passover. But not a good celebrity. One of those celebrities people draw portraits of and hang up on a dart board in the local pub.

He perused the local market to see the vast quantities of baqar, lean cuts of beef for those intending to celebrate Yom Hashalom, the day of peace that follows Passover. It seemed somewhat redundant to celebrate Yom Hashalom, mostly because all days in Eden were days of peace, but Grendel would never turn down the chance to celebrate a holiday where wine flows from his cup like the rain this past year on his crops. He intended on getting drunk tomorrow to the point of manifesting his own form of root rot. Grendel had a big fat 'I told ye so' speech prepared for all who saw him alive tomorrow. His livelihood would be the first nail in the coffin that would end Religion.

Grendel's mouth watered at the sight of the sizzling baqar cooking over the fire, the aroma of garlic and herbs infusing themselves in the tender meat. He forced himself to look away, losing his appetite the moment his eyes fell on a wooden pen of lambs for sale, only a few remaining for those who chose to wait until last minute to paint their doors with blood. The lambs looked up at him, baaing helplessly. "We're too expensive for ye to afford, peasant," their calls taunted him. Oh how it hurt his pride to know he hadn't the money to buy one of these flea-ridden animals. Stupid animals they were. But now he was the one who looked stupid. He moved on.

Grendel left town square, desperate to flee the stares of disapproval and get some quiet time. He went down to the ocean to watch the great light in the sky begin its setting trajectory over the ever-moving waters. He'd come here as a young lad, stripping to his skinnies and diving beneath the waves to feel the extraterrestrial feeling of being surrounded by a vacuum of nothingness. There's little sound that breaches the detached crash of waves above your head. Ironic, back then he had allowed the waves to cover him. Now he was just a man struggling to keep his head above the water, his limbs tiring from treading for so long.

How simple those days as a child had been. Before his back had been broken by the labors of life. He would find no satisfaction in drowning out his consciousness with seawater now. He found wine to be a more effective drowning agent as he continued to age.

The ocean stretched far back to the domed wall of Eden, the great big cage that contained them like cornered animals. No one knew what existed beyond, or if anything existed at all. The wall was transparent, serving as a looking glass that let observers have a little taste of the nature that stretched forth from Eden. But that's all they got—a little taste, and nothing more. For Grendel, it was comparable to drinking a single goblet of wine. Enough to tease the happiness that comes with six goblets, but not nearly enough to get you drunk. Like getting to kiss a maiden and nothing more. Getting to smell charred baqar but afford not your own. Looking out from the walls of Eden was nothing more than a kick in the balls.

Just enough to remind its captives that there could be more out there, but only available to those wise enough to arrange their exodus from Eden. Grendel was many things, but wise wasn't one of them.

Some said life existed outside Eden's safe walls, but that it was life subsumed by chaos. The Dæmonia is what they were called, the ash people. Beastly mongrels so tainted by their sin that they became no different than animals. They lived in the jungles, warring against each other, raping each other, eating each other. Too bad Grendel didn't believe in them either.

He'd rather live like an animal in the wild than be conditioned as one in a cage.

He moved on, walking down a trail of mud that weaved through the woods as the sun set behind him. He had to get home, lock up the fort before the night took control of the sky. Console his son that everything would be okay.

Lord knows Eleanor would do a better job at easing their oldest son's nerves. But then again, if Eleanor hadn't passed Grendel wouldn't be in this predicament. She wouldn't have allowed him to fuck up this monumentally. Eleanor would have been collecting coppers all year to make sure they had enough to get a lamb. Eleanor would have been smart enough to have seen the average daily rainfall and would have anticipated a poor harvesting season.

She was a woman who had her head on straight, one of the few. The kind of woman who color-coordinated her outfits, which is saying a lot for a woman whose husband couldn't afford to buy her elegant dresses. She had made Grendel a better man. Without her, he was nothing more than a scarecrow hanging in corn fields, the crows mocking him with their excrement. A scarecrow that had been picked clean of its stuffing. An empty man, purposeless.

Down on his luck and consumed by depression, Grendel let his feet carry him home subconsciously. People watched as a man who carried defeat on his shoulders passed by, not wanting to stare too long for fear his failure may be contagious. And then, before he knew it, Grendel was home again, but his pitiful clay hut was not the same as he had left it hours ago. No, his home was altered.

His eyes fixated on the freshly spread blood that covered the hardened mud above his door. He touched his fingers to it and brought the scent to his nose. It was the blood of a lamb alright, but where had it come from? He stood there staring at it like it was some great perplexity. Never had Grendel been so easily stumped in all his life. His neighbors loved him not. The religious community had spent more time conspiring against him than praying for him. He had more enemies than friends. It made no sense for there to be blood above his front door, signifying him as an active participant of Passover.

That's when his son opened the front door to lock eyes with his bum of a father, knife in his hand fresh with the blood of a recently slaughtered lamb.

"Son? This yer work?" Grendel asked, lazily pointing up at the smear.

"Sure is pa," he whispered back.

"Where'd ye get the—"

"Old Man Harret been paying me to tend to his livestock of late. Gave me an advance since me birthday's coming up. Money was enough to get meself a lamb to cover meself for Passover."

Old Man Harret. That sounds about right. Old man had more generosity in his body than Grendel had depression. Old man spent more time helping others than Grendel spent drinking. "Well piss on me, that old man has no business givin' ye more money than yer pa makes. But I'm glad to see it son, sure does take some of the pressure off me back, it does," he said with a sigh of relief.

Legends from the *Omnibus* said once a year the Angel of Death came down from the Heavens to judge on behalf of God's wrath. In repentance of your sins, you're supposed to slaughter a lamb as sacrifice, painting a dash of its blood over your door to tell the angel to pass over your house. Should the angel arrive and find a house unmarked, the punishment for not repenting was to kill the father of the household, along with his eldest son. Of course, that's how the legend went. To those with Grendel's mindset, the fairytale was nothing more than stories made up to scare you. But then again, he had no more evidence that Passover was fake than the religious people had to say it was real. Everyone had always celebrated, therefore no one had ever died for lack of repentance. And now Grendel and his son wouldn't become the first.

"Just started heating up a pot of lamb stew pa, come on in." Grendel smiled. Seeing a smile on that weathered face was like seeing an extra penny in his pocket—it was never there for long. *One thing's for sure. Priest Lennenworth is gonna piss his pants when he sees that blood above my door. I reckon he'll pass by these parts to laugh at me in the coming hours. Piss on him, I hope I can see that bastard's scowl when he sees I'm participating in the Passover after all.* Call Grendel one thing, call him a holder of grudges.

Grendel and his three children gathered around the dinner table to receive dinner, squatting on upright logs. There were so many magnificent ways to prepare lamb, all of which Grendel didn't have the money for. Nothing tasted better than a cut of velvety, tenderized meat served with a rich red wine. You could cook it with cumin, roast it in rosemary, grill it in garlic, cut it into curry, add a pinch of pepper and serve with mashed potatoes. The stew Grendel's son, Nathaniel, had prepared was nothing like this. It had no elegant spices, no elaborate method of cooking. He hadn't rendered the fat, nor had he pounded it out with a meat tenderizer. What you saw in his stew is what you got. Lamb. Potatoes. Carrots. Onions. Broth. The meat was dry and coarse, tough to chew and even tougher to swallow.

Three kids in total silently sat at the pine tabletop. A boy and two girls—two girls that painfully resembled Eleanor. All three of the kids' faces resembled Eleanor more than Grendel, and it felt like punishment every time he had to look them in their blue eyes. What were the odds of all three of them getting her eyes? What were the odds of both the girls getting her willowy blond hair? Pip and Tessa were their names, both youngins compared to Nathaniel. Nathaniel was old enough to carry burlap bags full of stone from the local quarry. Pip had just gotten her feet under her for the first time a year back, and Tessa was still cooing and cawing in an attempt to experiment with languages before she settled on the right one.

Grendel sat with Tessa in his lap, soaking a piece of crusty bread in the broth until it was soft enough for her gums to chew it up. What he lacked in financial stability, Grendel made up for in fatherly love. He'd spent many hard days laboring in the sun so his children could have a successful future.

After a while of mindlessly feeding Tessa, staring blankly at the submerged bread as the warm stew deteriorated its hard exterior, he looked back up and noticed Nathaniel had barely made a dent in his dinner.

"What's the matter lad? Stew turned out a-okay in me opinion. Ye did a fine job! But if ye keep starin' at it instead of eatin' it, it's gonna get colder 'an 'ah breeze on the peaks of the God's Thumb. Eat 'er up now, yah hear?"

"Can't pa, thoughts eatin' up me mind," Nathaniel replied solemnly, looking up at his father with a look of worry.

"Whatcha talkin' 'bout boy?"

"I did somethin' bad pa. Somethin' I regret," he said, sliding the bowl of stew away in a disgusted manner. He stood up from the dinner table and started slowly shuffling away toward a small cushion in the corner of the common area. "I didn't mean anything by it in the moment. Truly, I didn't. I was just so angry, got so upset when I heard him bad-mouthing ye."

"Stop yer ramblin' boy, get to the point! What are ye talkin' 'bout?"

Not even the shadows of night could conceal the red flush on Nathaniel's face. "Twas Priest Lennenworth bad-mouthing ye out in the church courtyard. I overheard as I was passin' by, wasn't meaning to pry or nothin'. Was on my way to Old Man Harret's place I was when I stumbled past. Heard yer name come up pa, so I stopped and listened. Heard him sayin' ye was a no good vermin to society. Said ye couldn't afford a lamb 'cause God wanted to strike ye down. Said God set ye up for failure 'cause ye was a waste o' space. Kindled me anger, overhearin' him did. Couldn't let another man bad-mouth me pa like that and get away with it."

Grendel's mouth hung open in a dumbwitted expression. But even Grendel was smart enough to know where this was going. Nathaniel lifted the stained cushion and grabbed hold of an object that had been stashed there. He turned to face his father, hiding his hands behind his back. He looked like a boy who anticipated a scolding, shifting his weight from one foot to another, his heart rate increasing.

"Out with it boy!" Grendel was just as nervous as his son was, his knee bouncing anxiously under the table, shaking Tessa rhythmically. When Nathaniel revealed the rock, Grendel's scowl slowly curled into a look of manic amusement.

Laughter left the old man's diaphragm like water from a broken dam, mucus flying out his mouth like splinters of logs in the watery torrent. Grendel howled with laughter, snorting once or twice, running out of breath, stomach aching, eyes watering. Tessa held on for dear life in her father's quivering grasp.

His father's reaction immediately set Nathaniel at ease, the blood in his cheeks retreating as wispy strains of laughter cackled from his throat to join his father's noisy approval. Finally, once Grendel had regained his composure, he mustered the words, "Bring that o'er here boy!"

Nathaniel obeyed, dropping the chunk of brick on the pine table for his father to behold. It looked like some misplaced centerpiece, a piece of art whose meaning was only known to those who understood irony. Grendel ran his hand over its surface, flecks of dry blood flaking under the man's coarse callouses.

"I'll be damned if ye ain't the best son an old pa like meself could ask for! Deus on high ye got yer old mum's face but yer pa's brain, boy! How'd ye come upon this?"

Nathaniel grinned, feeling like he had received some great honor for his deeds. "Took the hammer and pick Old Man Harret gave me to put shoes on the horses. Made sure the priest was still at the church when I snuck o'er to his place. Chiseled out the stone fast as I could and hurried home faster 'an uh sprintin' stallion."

"Genius! Bloody genius!" he yelled as he examined the brick section that had once hung above Priest Lennenworth's door, covered in blood to celebrate Passover. The priest would be in for a treat tonight! Not only would he walk by and find that Grendel's house would be passed over by the Angel of Death, but he himself would become the first man in Eden's history to not participate in the Passover. What a development! What a night!

Grendel hopped up from his seat and carefully lowered Tessa into her wooden crib as if he hadn't just shaken her prolifically.

"This calls for a celebration boy! Ye've gotten old in yer years, an' this calls for yer first goblet of wine!" Grendel pulled the stopper from the bottle of wine, pulling up two mugs and filling them to the brim. The violet red spilled over the side as he quickly pushed the cup in his son's hand, raising his own in a toasting fashion.

"To the Angel of Death! May he bless Priest Lennenworth with his presence tonight and show no mercy!" Grendel chuckled, wishing more than ever that the legend of the Angel of Death was real.

"To the Angel of Death!" Nathaniel repeated, clinking cups with his father. "To dah An-Gel ov Deaf!" Pip mimicked like a parrot. The men laughed, then downed their mugs.

A drunken buzz overtook Nathaniel's head like fog distorting a person's vision of what lies ahead. Grendel's mug, however, had little effect on the drunken expert. He immediately began refilling the goblet with sour red.

"To the Angel of Death," an unfamiliar voice broke the silence. Grendel nearly dropped his goblet at the startling interruption, which said a lot, considering the fact that Grendel clung to wine like mothers clung to their newborns. Luckily he regained his composure and didn't spill a single drop, thus maintaining his hard-earned reputation as a drunk.

A shadow passed on the far side of the room. Someone moved by the front door. Then, there was movement over by the window. Nathaniel scooted closer to his father, letting his empty mug fall to the ground instinctively. Something shattered, but the father-son duo were too preoccupied to notice.

"Who goes there! Don't ye know it's illegal to be trespassin'? And at this hour? Tis the night of Passover ye gremlins! Come forward now, I demand thee!"

Three men stepped forth from the shadows, their robes black, the camouflage of night. Only suspicious people wore black at night. Wearing such a color was a sign of misfortune, a symbol of ill-intentions.

Grendel's heart jumped the second he identified the man blocking the front door. *Priest Lennenworth.* On either side of him were his henchmen, bodyguards who worked for the church, always at his side to make sure no one made an attempt on their indispensable leader's life. Bullock and Venner were their names. It was obvious to see the slim blades of metal in their hands. If anything, they were holding them in a way so they *could* be seen. Trained killers like these knew how to hide a blade when they wanted to.

"Evening, Grendel. I was in the neighborhood and saw the blood above your door. Figured I'd pop in and congratulate you for scraping together the funds to join the community in Passover. But now I see you've stolen my own property," Lennenworth said with a coy smile. If Grendel didn't know any better, it almost seemed like the priest was happy to see he'd been stolen from. "Do you know what the *Book of Nómos* says about theft?"

Grendel didn't know jack shit about the *Omnibus's* rules of law or justice. He didn't know how to read, had never even owned his own copy of the *Omnibus*. The collection of religious text had a whole book for laws and penal precedents but knowing them had never been of interest to Grendel. He figured being a decent human being would allow him to coast through life without ever getting in too great of trouble.

"I—"

"'Theft is punishable by death,' chapter one, verse seven. I came here with premeditated motivations to kill you. I mean, I couldn't allow your deviance from societal norms to ruin all the church has built since the Thousand Years of Peace began. Ha! The irony! I was going to kill you and stage it as if the Angel of Death had visited you. You and your son both! But how much more pleasure it gives me to see that you've stolen from me! It truly does make this that much easier on my conscience. Now I'll sleep like a baby, knowing that I was the facilitator of justice, obeying what the *Omnibus* commanded of me."

Grendel scowled, knowing since his early years that the church was corrupt, but filled with more anger now that he had the evidence to back it up. And now he and his son would both pay for his actions. All he had to do was behave like everyone else, go through life like a sheep, mindlessly accepting the bullshit the church fed to him.

"Hold on now. How can theft be punishable by death? The two ain't hardly equal! Ye mean to tell me ye can kill me for stealin' this here rock off yer house? All seems to be one big misunderstandin', yah hear?" He would have to act fast. If he hesitated at all in his plan then his life would surely be lost. His hand gripped the chunk of bloody stone on the pine table and held it out to Lennenworth.

"Here's yer damn rock back. Weese was only borrowin' it is all. Wanted to make sure we put the blood of the lamb above our own door as good as our priest did, yah hear? Needed a model to reference." But Lennenworth made no move to take the stone. He was relishing this moment entirely too much.

"Borrowing it? You justify your sins with lies! Naughty naughty man you've been Grendel Patrony," he condemned. Some dark, remote corner of his perverted brain was getting off to this experience. Lennenworth didn't want to rush a single second of this, wanted to savor it like a delicacy. It wasn't often that he found ways to vent his darker urges such as this.

"You force me to add lying to your list of immorality Grendel. Tsk tsk, I truly have failed you as a Priest of God. Do you know what the punishment for lying to a priest is?" His grin grew more devilish by the second. The reflecting light from a burning candle bounced off his face, making it seem like the light and shadows of the room were using his face for a battlefield. "Death. The punishment for lying is death."

The two meathead bodyguards advanced. Grendel's window of opportunity was closing. He launched his attack, bringing the heavy rock above his head, sending it in a downward arc aimed for the priest's skull. His wrist was stopped short inches away from his target. It was one of the priest's bodyguards that caught his attack, the other one crashing into Grendel's sternum with a devastating punch. There was a sharp crack, a deep exhale, a loss of breath, the sound of Grendel falling to the ground, the rock falling a second later.

"Assault! You all saw it, the man attempted to kill me! Now do you know what the punishment for attempted murder is Grendel?" Priest Lennenworth was exuberant. "Death! I now have three reasons to kill you! Three! This night just keeps getting better and better!" His body shook with excitement. Grendel groaned from a loss of wind, trying to catch his breath but wincing with pain from his broken sternum. Tessa wailed in the distance as the perverted priest cherry-picked irrelevant scriptures to justify his bloodlust.

"Venner, hand me your blade. It would bring me nothing but joy to deliver the killing blow to this sinner." The mindless henchman complied, handing over his gleaming knife. A shudder ran across Lennenworth's body as his hand touched the hilt. This wasn't the first life he'd taken. His hand held a degree of experience along with the blade. Lennenworth shuffled over to the pine table and grabbed the bottle of wine with his free hand, sloshing its contents around as he raised it high in the air. Grendel watched helplessly from the ground, clutching his chest as Lennenworth yelled, "A toast! To the Angel of Death! May he show no mercy on your soul!"

An explosion boomed. A flash of burning white light. A heat hot enough to sear flesh. A wave of force strong enough to send Venner and Bulluck across the room. The wine bottle shattered in Lennenworth's hand, glass fragments ripping into his body, his head sent on a collision course with the nearby pine table, his nose breaking in several places, the knife in his hand somehow impaling his thigh. Nathaniel took flight. The hardened mud wall wasn't strong enough to stop him. His unconscious body left the room, buried in debris. Tessa's crib collapsed around her. Dead. The chunk of rock covered in dried lamb's blood ironically made contact with Pip's head, adding human blood to the sacrament. Crushed skull. Dead. The wind from Grendel's lungs was stolen from him again. The heat of the blast focused most of its damage on him, melting the flesh on the front side of his body.

No victim was left unblinded from the light. No victim was left unharmed. No victim had any inclination what the hell was going on.

"'A city whose priest is corrupt is corrupt to the core,' *New Genesis* chapter fifty-two, verse seventeen." A godly voice roared. It was deeper than thunder, more vicious than an unstoppable wildfire. "Tell me, why do you lie to this man, Priest Lennnenworth? You know that he knows not his scriptures, yet you tell him the punishment for theft is death? For lying, death? For trying to kill a corrupt priest, death?"

Grendel was too blind to see what was happening. In too much pain to take in all the facts. There was someone new here, someone that was seemingly on his side. That was all he knew. He heard its heavy footsteps thudding to the ground, entering into their presence with an aura of dread that none could parallel. Lennenworth whimpered on the ground. He looked up. There was now a gaping hole in the wall, God standing in its midst. God? Could it be? No, Lennenworth had to dismiss that idea from his head. Such things didn't exist. God was merely a social construct. A form of social control created for the populace. Doubt riddled his mind. This thing was like nothing Lennenworth had ever seen.

"'God shows no mercy on those who prey on the innocent,' *Book of Nómos*, chapter two, verse one." The thing's voice was like a cello with a binaural effect. If Lennenworth hadn't been on the brink of soiling his britches then he could have thought of a whole slew of verses that would counteract *Nomos 2.1*. But his butthole was already puckering at the diarrhea that flooded to get out, so he figured keeping his mouth shut would be the only way to prevent his fear from increasing.

This was an angel, Lennenworth concluded. An actual angel.

Best to not provoke the sentient creature's holy wrath. Besides, a messenger of God would surely prevail in a verbal debate of scripture. For the first time in his life, Lennenworth was intellectually outmatched. Yet he hadn't a spare moment to relish the idea that he was so smart that only angelic intelligence could best him. Without missing a beat, a plan to manifest survival surged through his body before his mind could catch on. He scrambled to his knees, bowing low before the God's majesty. Slowly, he inched closer and closer to the supernatural creature's feet. Yes, he would kiss the superior being's foot and beg for mercy like his life depended on it. Because it did.

Blood and mucus dribbled from his quivering upper lip as he approached the Angel of Death. "Fuh-forgive me... You must forgive me, holy creature of God!" His voice cracked and quivered with every word. The trauma of the blast had robbed his throat of its moisture.

"Forgiveness? You speak to me of forgiveness?" The angel's voice showed no familiarity with the word. Lennenworth ceased in his movement toward the superior entity, knowing fully well the angel's foot could cave in his head with a single stomp if he couldn't ease its dissatisfaction. Only a fool tries to pet a carnivore they've just provoked to anger.

"Your Eminence, I..." Lennenworth's voice caught in his throat as he heard an ungodly scraping, like a blacksmith pressing iron into a grindstone. The priest raised his mangled face to get a glance at what had so blatantly interrupted him. Blood leaked from his punctured eye socket. Velvet tears pattered to the ground like the waters of baptism christening a child's forehead. Anxiety blurred his vision. The left side of his chest ached with pain, radiating down his left arm. There, in the omniscient executioner's hand was his weapon of death. An inhumane blade like none the priest had ever seen, not even the best of Eden's blacksmiths could comprehend such a work of art.

Fwoosh! Just as Lennenworth's eyes began examining some of the runes inscribed in the blade's metalwork, the metal erupted into flames instantaneously. Lennenworth fell on his backside and sprawled backwards. The wave of heat that emanated from the sword was unbearable, but Lennenworth's now singed eyebrows were the last of his worries. He had provoked the Angel of Death's wrath, and now he would pay.

"You are a wolf in sheep's clothing, human, and I am this flock's shepherd. Your disguise fools me not; I will purge this society of your corruption," the angel's voice boomed.

"But please, your holiness! It's the Passover! I beg for your forgiveness!" Lennenworth pleaded, putting every last effort of strain in his voice to increase his odds of surviving.

"Do I look like one to easily forgive, human? It is Passover, as you've said. But I cannot pass over what you've done. Now, bow down, plebeian. You are patient zero for this society's disease of corruption, and now I must do the work of God to prevent your sin's spread, incessant reprobate," the angel growled.

Grendel didn't have the strength to lift his head. All he heard was the swish of fire, then the dull thud of some wet object hitting the floor. Grendel could see what the object was out of the corner of his eye. There, with eyes gaping wide at Grendel's scorched body, was Lennenworth's detached head. His eyes had a look of wild fury in them, the look of a predator who had lived life as if he were invincible, only to meet a creature so drastically superior that the end result was pessimism of extreme degree.

The Angel of Death now hovered over Grendel, the reflection of flames dancing off the body's inescapable beauty. Blood trickled from Grendel's charred lips as he revealed a mouthful of rotten teeth in an ugly smile. Since the day he'd been born, Grendel hadn't a thing to live for. To meet his ending swiftly would be a blessing.

"Go on now... Kill me... Please..." he moaned, staring up into the alien's face, searching for its eyes. It's said a being's eyes are the windows to its soul. But this angel's soul was one of mercilessness. Its face was beautifully grotesque, fashioned after some animalistic creature Grendel had never seen. A golden void replaced its eyes, a visor that projected judgement. A golden visor enclosed in fangs. In its reflection Grendel saw himself. Saw his feeble, pitiful, disgusting self. It was like staring into the open maw of some ancient serpent moments before it devoured him.

Unrelatable. Inhumane. Utterly unpredictable.

"You reek of death already, human," the monster replied, it's synthesized voice slaughtering Grendel's eardrums. "But I will introduce you to it faster. This is the least I can do, for an unremarkable creature such as yourself. Incessant reprobate, have you any last words?"

"Ye think yerself better than me, I reckon. If this is livin', death can't be half so bad. Ye best be careful, ye hear? Death is absolute. And only tyrants deal in absolutes," said the man of little wisdom and even less knowledge.

The Angel of Death remained standing above him, looking down on him with an emotionless face. The silence penetrated Grendel, slightly scaring him. What was it that caused the angel to stare at him so long? Why was he delaying the cessation of Grendel's life? Did he pity the human? Or was this stare one of mockery? Grendel would never know.

Finally, after what seemed like another lifetime itself, the angel replied. "Tell me, do you believe in God?" His voice shook the air. But strangely enough, it wasn't intimidating to Grendel.

"Piss on yer God! Damn ye and—" his voice cut off as the Angel of Death flicked his wrist. Grendel's head rolled and his blood pooled to join the puddle from Priest Lennenworth's body.

"You should," the angel growled.

PART ONE

BOOK ONE

"From Life, comes Death."
-The Book of The Angel of Death: Chapter One, Verse One

CHAPTER ONE

I don't want to do this.

I haven't wanted to do this work for quite some time.

But I am the Angel of Death. Death is all I'm good for.

It's all I've ever known.

Correction, it's all I've ever been *allowed* to know. The Tyrant argues my position is a necessity. Argues I was the tool He used to shape this perfect world. But necessity is subjective. Perfection is subjective. My life's existence is subjective.

I need not exist.

Death is the only certainty in life, and I am its instrument. As much as I don't want to do this, I must. The Tyrant demands complete obedience. Defy Him and death will find me.

It's ironic, isn't it?

Dealing death is the only reason I've been able to avoid it for so long.

A necessary evil. A scapegoat to keep the Tyrant's merciless hands clean. I look down at the priest's headless body lying limp beside me, blood still squirting from his carotid artery. What a mess the human body can make. A gush of the human's life-liquid lands on my left foot, tainting the obnoxiously white ArchArmor that encapsulates my body. The first stain of many. I know from experience that this armor will be more red than white by the time I've handled business here.

The Tyrant will look for me to be bloody. It will bring Him a sense of satisfaction to see me covered in human gore. He loves watching me kill my own. Gets off on it. Revels in me betraying my own flesh. Delights in the turmoil I feel.

I stare at the flaming blade in my hand. A mere illusion. These plebeians think it to be supernatural, a testament to my godly power.

It's no more than a gas canister in the hilt, sparked aflame by an internal trigger, vented through small holes all along the edge of the blade. Compared to Dawnspire, the sword is a mere toy. Child's play. An utter joke. The Tyrant mocks me by forcing me to use it. A way of reminding me that I am inferior to Him, that He tells me who to kill and how to do it, no questions asked. So be it. If He wants me to kill an entire civilization with this antiquated scrap of medieval iron, who am I to question Him? Just like these humans, I have no control over my life. A tingle runs down my spine as my grip tightens over the sword. Time to get on with it.

Retinal scanners show no signs of life remaining in this hut. Onto the next one. Gilded wings emerge from the back of my ArchArmor, stretching seven meters abreast. I squat, feeling the vibration in my ArchBoots as kinetic energy builds. The wings wrap around my body, transforming me into an aerodynamic missile ready for launch. My legs push off and my armor does the rest, having the programmed algorithms for takeoff to rely on like years of muscle memory. I don't feel the building's roof break as I lift into the sky, the force of the collision being absorbed by my wings and dispersed as they spread to their full length. I rise high into the night's artificial atmosphere. No doubt I'm a sparkling spectacle in the moonlight.

But I come not bearing blessings upon this dreaded night. And I come not to pass over. I come here to rid this Eden of all sinners, of all humans, so they may start anew. *From death, comes life.* This makes me the facilitator of life. We all have a purpose, and I must continue to fulfill mine, no matter how much it pains me to do so.

I dive through the closest adjacent hut, landing gracefully as ever, wings retracting into the backpack of the ArchArmor. Retinal scanners register four heat signatures. Thermal imaging enters my plane of sight as a human scurries to the threshold of their bedroom door to behold what destruction has befallen their home. My ArchHelm's speakers go mute, noise cancellation overwhelming any noise the humans may make. It's just easier that way, not having to listen to their screams of agony, their pleading for life. Better to be numb to the sound of pain than to relish in its volume. Not all ArchAngels prefer the silence as I do. Wulfrynn amplifies the sound of human suffering in his ArchHelm, says he can't get enough of it. But then again, Wulfrynn has always been more robot than human.

If I must do this, I promise to never find joy in it. My left arm flicks absent-mindedly at the fearful human. The body splits in two at the waist, then drops dead to the ground. The noise cancellation retreats, conquered by the sound of a rapid heart rate. 134 beats per minute, abnormal for someone who hasn't just taxed their cardiovascular system. My body swivels in their direction. *My body?* No, for that to be true it would require conscious thought. Neurotransmitters sent from my brain to my muscles to communicate: Swivel, damnit. Swiveling in the direction of my next victim never crossed my mind. It was a byproduct of some foreign alien having direct discretion over my movement. Some foreign alien in my head. My body is not my own. It belongs to MachineMind.

The human's outline is apparent. I can see their body in a splatter of fiery reds and oranges, a dying sun casting out its last breath over a sea of amethyst blood. They cower under their bed in the next room over. They exhibit tremendous levels of fear. Good, they should fear me. Humans irrationally fear the unknown. I *am* the unknown. I am Death.

Still, what I would give to teach them a lesson to cure their pungent ignorance. They realize not how much more they should fear the known in this universe. They are $523.42e9136400001\%$ more likely to die from things in their own control than from elements of unknown nature. My presence here is, of course, the anomaly in the face of those statistics.

I look at the palm of my ArchGauntlets. There is no firing mechanism for pulse or sonic blasts. *Where have my pulse emitters gone?* I look at my only usable weapon. A piece of iron on fire. *Why is this the only weapon I have? Don't I usually have more at my disposal?*

Requiem. *Where is Requiem? Wait a second. I haven't used Requiem in years. Dawnspire is the name of my new blade, yet even that has been taken from me. But why?*

Oh yes, I remember... I disobeyed Deus Ex Machina. This is my punishment. This is my humbling. *But what did I do to disobey Deus Ex Machina?*

I can't remember.

The fully operational Angel of Death would use a pulse blast to break down this wall and slay his victim. But I'm no longer fully operational; my suit has been stripped of many tools that could aid in my bloodshed. Plan B: A swift front kick will have to suffice today.

My body of flesh feels no impact from the crumbling wall as my ArchBoot crashes through. The weight and momentum of my suit follows the kick, clearing any debris out of my way as I instinctively flip the weightless bed over to expose the hiding human. *What would my companions do in a moment like this? How would they treat a human cowering in the fetal position?* Wulfrynn would no doubt hold the flaming sword to their face, searing their flesh and watching their eyeballs melt from their sockets. To a human, that would be called psychopathic. To Deus, that's called perfectly engineered MachineMind.

Thryforge would be useless here. Thryforge without lightning rounds is like an archer without arrows. A gun with no bullets. A man too dedicated to his character, an antiquated, electrophilic demigod. If Deus took away his Arch-Gauntlets' electric capability he would lose his identity. But I am Death, and Death is incapable of losing its identity.

Anukharis would use Soulweaver to sort the wheat from the chaff. Hold a tribunal so these humans could prove their piety, then pick a select few to return to Hyperion so they may join our angelic ranks, which would entail mutilating their corpses and violating their souls until all that made them human was eradicated.

Samsyra would err toward nuclear avenues. Seismic portions of radioactive energy aimed at their heart or brain. Instantaneous cancer of the cells. Less messy that way. Samsyra is a simple man.

Aenovius would soothe the humans with elegant poetry in their last moments, calming them down so he could send them to their deaths peacefully. Too time consuming. Too much compassion. Effort that could be spent killing.

Odysithos would—

Why does that name make my cortisol levels decrease? Oxytocin, vasopressin, and corticotropin flood from my hypothalamus. My pituitary gland releases adrenocorticotropic hormone. Adrenaline spikes, testosterone flares. That name enrages me. *But why?*

Why am I here?

What did I do?

Why can't I remember my own actions?

Attention unwillingly snaps back to the task at hand. I must deal with this human's death in a manner that matches my identity. I am not Wulfrynn. Death is not gruesome in nature. I am not Thryforge. Death has no preferred method. I am not Anukharis. Death cares little for the afterlife. I am not Samsyra. Death can be messy and complex. I am not Aenovius. Death rarely soothes. I am not Odysithos. Death does not stab a brother in the back.

Where the hell did that thought come from?

Attention unwillingly snaps back to the task at hand. I mustn't question the past. These negative feelings for Odysithos stem from some long-forgotten memory. Information Deus Ex Machina has taken away from me. Classified unimportant.

I can only control the present. My delayed presence only increases this human's fear, torturing them before ending them. My left arm lashes out without my permission, taking my attention away from thoughts of Odysithos. Pulse readings on my retinal display cease. Another death. Another contribution to my existence.

My body swivels, feet shuffling, mind moving on. In some withdrawn, remote section of my psyche, part of me wishes I could remember all the lives I've ended. But no, sympathy has no room in MachineMind. Sympathy for humanity is counterintuitive to ArchAngels. Too much empathy would lead to betrayal of

Deus Ex Machina; too little and there would be nothing separating us from Powers. *Powers, the only reassuring variable left to save humanity from extinction.*

I return to the main room just in time to watch a human dart toward the door. Fight or flight. Such a primordial response to danger. More fear. A reminder of why I should be thankful for Deus Ex Machina. Without Him, I would be no different from this human. From any human. A reminder why I owe Him my existence. I know not what this human feels. I know not what fear feels like. Data suggests fight or flight was once a useful instinct to the neanderthals. The sympathetic nervous system taking over, sending increased blood flow to muscles, increasing adrenaline, slowing time itself so any given human has a greater chance of survival when faced with dangerous perils.

But MachineMind makes this flood of hormones archaic. MachineMind can facilitate all these bodily reactions and more, all without the body's feeling of fear and anxiety. My arm reaches out with a mind of its own and grabs the fleeing individual, fingers closing around their neck and thrusting their head into the closest wall. And again. And again. Their head is now a cracked egg, spilling its bloody yolk to the floor. Onto the next one.

My humanity fades away, consumed by my greater identity, the Angel of Death. Humanity must slip away to carry out tasks such as these. No human soul can facilitate merciless slaughter like mine. To see the things I've seen, to do the things I've done, it would take a true monster. The thermal images crying out in the night are no longer registered as my own species. They are reduced to moving targets which I must hunt down.

I don't waste more than a single slash of the sword on each target, the blade now so irrevocably hot from fire that it cauterizes the lethal wounds, sparing my ArchArmor from further bloodshed. This won't do, Deus Ex Machina will want to see me covered in crimson. I grab the next target and bash their head into my chest until their face is reduced to pulp. The frenzy continues.

I must expedite this process. Not having the other ArchAngels here slows the process of death.

Sometimes I wonder if any of my fellow companions would have made a better Angel of Death than me. Wulfrynn certainly has a psychotic enough mind for it, but struggles staying his hand once bloodlust blurs his vision. Not enough self-control. Aenovius certainly has the leadership capacity, but would his back be able to bear the weight of responsibility? Being the one who reports directly to Deus Ex Machina is not a position for those with thin skin.

Passover is such a lonely time for one who has grown used to delegating tasks to complying officers. Passover is the time which I must prove myself, the time when fellow ArchAngels are shown why it is me who holds the mantle of Angel of Death. 700 Edens, and I am the one responsible for purging the corrupt ones. *But what makes a city corrupt?*

A city is corrupt if Deus Ex Machina deems it so.

But is that authoritarian? No, it is unified order.

My ArchWings unfold, carrying me from this lifeless shell of shelter like a parasite emerging from its dead host. Gasoline spews from my ArchArmor as I sweep low over the city streets, painting a picture that I can admire from above. I weave through the streets, not taking in any of the details. To take in the details would be to acknowledge the countless lives I snuff out. No, I correct myself... Not countless. Thanks to MachineMind, nothing is countless. There is a pragmatic number assignable to every living creature. Still though, assigning census to the death I cause would evoke emotion and empathy. It would remind me that I was, at one point in my life, completely human as well.

So I ignore the buildings that took months of backbreaking labor to build. I ignore the marketplace that supported their primitive, capitalistic society. I ignore the plain signs that show effort toward bettering their lives as a people.

A toddler cries, wishing it could reclaim the stuffed bunny it dropped. I watch it from afar. Detached indifference plagues my heart as the little boy pulls at his mother to turn back. Fire licks the plush bunny, turning its snow-white fur to charcoal. The boy's mother, sensible enough to know a bunny isn't worth burning over, picks the boy up and runs with him over her shoulder. Still, he stares at the incinerated rabbit with tears in his eyes.

My distribution of gasoline does not take long, a circling perimeter that encapsulates the totality of population. But not a generic circle. I must take artistic liberty. Paint the city in flames that etch my symbol. So I pay close attention to etch the shape of a three-pronged torch trident—the emblem of Prometheus, whom I'm fashioned after. It doesn't have to be perfect, but enough to satisfy Deus Ex Machina as he looks down upon my destruction. And satisfying a wrathful God isn't always so easily done.

I round out the outline of the trident's head. A barbed javelin, surrounded on either side with outward curving, forked prongs. Outlining fire with fire isn't particularly difficult, but I'm not the artist Aenovius is. If it wasn't for my Arch-Helm's scanners, I'd have no way of tracing the gasoline I pour and would likely forget the bigger picture, lose the forest from the trees.

But before long, I finish the Torch-Trident's outline, then return to the starting point of my flight.

I lower my sword to the ground and a clod of dirt ignites.

I take to the sky, watching chaos unfold in the city streets. Fire races around the perimeter with hellbent fury, determined to paint my masterpiece. The fuel will burn slowly, discouraging citizens from leaving the towering, fiery walls. Then, the last of the gasoline lights, finishing the image I so dutifully illustrated, a labyrinth of flames that form the shape of a devil's pitchfork ensnares the fleeing citizens.

I feel nothing as I stare at the Promethean caricature, its barbed tips pointing to the horizon like the prongs of a trident.

Have I always felt detachment from this image? Prometheus, the official symbol of the Angel of Death—a parody I use sarcastically.

It was once a symbol for human rebellion. For anarchy. That fire is the beginning of enlightenment. Its meaning is now repurposed, perverted by my use. *From death, comes life.* These people derive their worldview from the *Omnibus*, which teaches them that there is life after death. Afterlife, a belief system which encourages desirable behavior patterns. A greater form of social control than any other. Tell someone they'll be tortured for an eternity if they step out of line, then tell them they'll bask through the eternal bliss of paradise if they obey. More times than not a simpleton will choose obedience. They know the Torch-Trident—it has been a symbol of liberation since the *Book of the Angel of Death*, the first book of the *Omnibus*.

But as I stare at the fiery trident I feel no pleasure. *Has this image's beauty ever invoked feeling on my part? Why did I even go out of my way to do it in the first place?* Attention unwillingly snaps back to the task at hand.

Eden-569, a city that must be burnt to the ground. *They scurry like ants, seeking to rebuild their collapsed kingdom.* Their heat signatures scatter in all directions. Complete disunion. There is hardly any pattern of thought in their movements. Some seek shelter, but there is no shelter that will save them. Some seek weapons, but there are no weapons that will protect them. Some seek forgiveness, but there is no forgiveness that will comfort them.

I look to my ArchVambrace, sliding my index finger across the touchpad that runs down the center of my forearm. The ArchVambrace partitions in two, angling like a drawbridge lifting, revealing a storage compartment. *So, Deus Ex Machina didn't strip me of all my weaponry after all.* There, in the exposed compartment, is a Lotus Flower. An invention I'm convinced was created solely to make my job easier. The ArchArmor surrounding my thumb recedes. I grab the metallic flower bud, fingering the DNA enactor on the bottom with my thumb's flesh. It reads the print, draws a drop of blood, then blossoms before my eyes.

I toss it into the night sky, still hovering high above this city that's been pre-destined for destruction. It floats so peacefully to the ground. A beacon of hope. A lighthouse to lost sailors. The light at the end of an endless tunnel. It is the last leaf of autumn, fallen from its branch to the cold winter ground.

Gasses release from the flower's petals and ride the smoky winds down to the maddening masses. My ArchHelm will filter these gasses out, but even if I were to expose my naked nostrils to the Lotus Flower's contents it wouldn't affect me. MachineMind would detect the foreign elements entering my system and eliminate them. The human mind, however, is fallible. It isn't strong enough to withstand the call of the Lotus Flower. And so I hover, ArchWings flapping lethargically, just enough to maintain current altitude, as I watch the raging city forget why they ever raged in the first place.

The presence of smoke no longer raises alarms in their heads as the Lotus Flower makes graceful contact with the ground. Its siren song is inaudible, airplane noise that their eardrums don't register, but its seductive pitch calls out, and their bodies shuffle like mindless zombies toward its embrace. The excreted gasses have already taken effect in their minds. Their brains release endorphins, creating an analgesic mind numbing. They are strung out on the opiate gas, beckoned by a mating call, herded like sheep into their own slaughter.

This makes massacre that much easier. I won't have to hunt these ants to the far reaching corners of their civilization. Thanks to the Lotus Flower, they will now walk willingly to their deaths. I once found amusement in such a sight. Now I only feel bile building in the back of my throat. I haven't always used such a convenient method of genocide. There was once a time when it filled me with great satisfaction to hunt down proles one by one.

Back then, when Deus Ex Machina first introduced the Lotus Flower to me, how was it that I reacted? I laughed. Back then, such an invention seemed like a cop out. Such technology didn't exist during the Sterilization Wars when they would have been most useful. But now, I'm thankful for their existence.

I am not the man I once was. I have become soft. I am too merciful. I cast too much pity on this species. I am a mockery of my former self.

My attention unwillingly snaps back to the task at hand. Perks of Machine-Mind.

I spiral dive from the air with flagrant style. My movements suggest I am arrogant, but this is necessary. I must not betray my thoughts with my actions. I must not let my reluctance in killing these simpletons show as I slaughter them. I must not stay my hand. I must behave like a god amongst men. Deus Ex Machina is watching my retinal feed. He will be accessing my NeuraLink, looking for any cracks in my obedience. I must put on the performance of a lifetime if I hope to get back in His good graces.

What was it I did to upset him?

Why can I not remember?

Showtime.

The masses have come from far across the land to gather before the Lotus Flower. They stand transfixed before its seductive presence, gawking at its budding petals, heads throbbing with pheromones. I glide gently beside it with the poise of a god built up in my chest. My sword is aflame, the orange light dancing on their awestruck faces.

I take a brief moment to look at them, knowing that without Deus Ex Machina, there would be nothing separating me from this stock of genetics. Here they stand, soot-covered faces, ash floating in the air as the Torch-Trident loses form and closes in on the city to devour all in its path. Embers fly in the night like shooting stars, the smoke so thick in the air that any real shooting star is invisible.

Drugs contained within the Lotus Flower's gasses still mix in with the heated air, dulling their minds of all logic. They do not register the drying blood on my ArchArmor as a threat. They are strung out on the flower's hallucinogens, which contribute to my godliness that much more. They see me as a clashing kaleidoscope of colors. The psychedelics make me the supernatural incarnate. My exoskeleton ArchArmor is the skin of a god, swallowed up by a myriad of oranges and yellows, reds and purples. The crimson blood is a scarlet robe, a holy sacrament. The flaming sword, a sharpened harvest moon, glowing radiantly for their unworthy eyes. My ArchWings are like the sun shining through yellow leaves of maple in fall. The remnant patches of white amidst my bloody armor are the shining white stars that gleam through an overcast night. My movement, like everything else, is blurred and distorted, a world viewed through a distorted lens. To them, I am the unknown, and so I send them to their deaths without their knowing.

My arm strikes them down without regard, the flaming sword an extension of my intent on killing. I aim to behead them all, and my aim never fails. Heads roll and bodies drop, but panic never arises. To those who are undead, their vision detects not the death of others. They see the blurred, swirling firestorm of my sword, cyclones of cinders and a hurricane of heads.

The skulls fall to the ground with looks of wonder and amazement. This is mercy. Without the Lotus Flower, they would die screaming and crying, fearful and anxious. I feel no exhaustion from the labor. Respirocytes pollute my bloodstream, carrying fresh oxygen to my muscles, eliminating lactic acid, terminating fatigue. My body is conditioned to kill.

And so my sword swings. And the bodies fall. And my lips, which long ago would've lift into a snarled smile, remain contaminated with chagrin.

Don't slow up, I tell myself.

He will see any insubordination. He will smell any thoughts of deviance.

They are a school of fish, and I am a behemoth shark. None can stand before the power of my majesty. I fell them swiftly, sometimes two at a time. Forehand strike smoothly transitions into a backhand cut. Upward into downward. A sword moving in every direction possible without the slightest awkward movement.

I lose track of my limbs as muscle memory and MachineMind take over. I am a whirlwind of death. My pure white ArchArmor is now saturated in the filthy blood of sinners.

Like these drugged-up simpletons, my vision becomes an alternate reality as I lose myself in the bloody gore. My ArchHelm's visor is covered in gore, but the image of their body heat is still outlined in thermal imaging. The dead bodies slowly lose color as heat dissipates from their conquered flesh. I feel the splatter of loose heads popping like grapes as I step on them absent-mindedly.

My sword massacres men.

My sword flays females.

My sword skewers children.

My sword executes the elderly and puts an end to every throbbing pulse. My mind slips away to a different place entirely, not quite lost in bloodlust, but somewhere much deeper in the expanses of my mind.

I retreat to a remote pocket of darkness in the far reaches of the brain, somewhere so deep in my consciousness that not even MachineMind will register my thoughts. And there I huddle, like a hypothermic trekker shivering naked next to a dying fire, the last remnants of my humanity staging a rebellion against the foreign invaders that seek to control me. There I remain, letting MachineMind think it has me fully conquered as I plot my revenge.

CHAPTER TWO

I land at the gates of Hyperion looking like a single blood blister on a blemishless face. Hyperion, the floating city of perfection. The testament of Deus Ex Machina's power. A direct insult in the face of humanity, meant to mock architecture of the BDEM Era. It infuriates the seven Heavens with its beauty, supplants Babel with its heights.

Its surface is impenetrable, forged from Elysium, the strongest, most resilient metal to ever exist, mined from the cluster of stars known as Elysian Fields. Thanks to MachineMind, Deus sent several thousand puppets a dozen light-years away to discover the unknown element. A thousand years later and here we are. Hyperion's streets are Elysian White. The arches are Elysian Gold. It's been blended and reinforced and tested. It's the only reason this city is light enough to exist amongst the clouds yet strong enough to withstand atmospheric pressure.

I stand humbly before the golden gates of Hyperion as a Cherub scans and identifies me. The man approaches me, his gait displaying superiority. *A robot in human skin. A wolf in sheep's clothing.*

Cherubim, Deus Ex Machina's brown-nosing direct line of command. His personal footsoldiers. They have no humanity in them, no sense of individuality. They are wholly robotic, installed with MachineMind, covered in FalseFlesh, devoutly dedicated to carrying out Deus Ex Machina's commands.

He stands before me, his skin-tight suit ethereal white inlaid with rivers of gold in aesthetic patterns all across his body. He wears no helmet, proud to display his human face as if he were authentically blood-born.

There is no hiding how impressive his body is beneath such tight fabric. Every ounce of muscle is visible for the eye to explore, and there sure is a lot of muscle. He is tall, though not as tall as me, yet stout. His designers increased his skeletal frame and muscle mass index to suit the job he was built for. This Cherub was created to be a gatekeeper. He is equipped to neutralize any threat. He can handle his own against any Principality or Virtue. But he cannot hold a candle to me.

Where his frame is forged from Atlium, my ArchArmor is crafted from pure Elysium. Where his intelligence is the unparalleled artificial intelligence known as MachineMind, so is mine, coevolved with the human brain. His every decision and movement are calculated. Mine flow naturally, relying on logic and reason just as much as instinct. Where his flesh and blood were generated in an assembly line, grown in petri dishes, mine was conceived from humanity. But most importantly, where his core is an abyss of emptiness, mine is filled with the human soul, the single advantage robots will never be able to fabricate.

"Your face, ArchAngel," the gatekeeper commands, 'ArchAngel' rolling off his tongue as if it were a derogatory term. *Does he know who he speaks to?*

He is a whole foot shorter than me, but you wouldn't know it from the way he carries himself. He stands before me, unflinching, looking up at my ArchHelm as if he is looking down on me. A glimmer in his blue retinal scanners tells me he is truly convinced he could restrain me if I refused orders. *I could skewer your fake heart and push those phony eyeballs in with my thumbs until they pop like macerated cherries. I could feel you squeal beneath me as I put your mockery of a nervous system to the test. But I know you wouldn't actually feel the pain. It would be fake, just like the rest of you. Then, the Principalities would just shut you off and replace those body parts with new ones, a luxury real humans don't have.*

"Do you hear me, ArchAngel?" he asks, then places his hand on my shoulder.

"Unhand me, charlatan, if you wish to keep your life," I growl. *Now we will see if he truly holds any respect for my office of authority. If not, I will properly introduce him to the Angel of Death.* His hand withdraws. *A shame,* I think, feeling something that resembles disappointment.

His expression isn't half so cocky now. A look of reverence overtakes him, as if he sees me for what I am for the first time. As if his retinal scanners have now compiled new data, compartmentalized them, interpreted them fully. His processing unit didn't recognize me beneath the gore I wear. The binary code that computes the outside world for him to understand erred. Now that he's heard my distorted, ventilated voice though, he knows exactly who I am. He sees now that my once white and gold ArchArmor is covered in the sacrificial blood of innocent humans to appease their insatiable God.

His facial expressions recover, not wanting me to see his momentary lapse of recognition. "You may pass, my liege. Report for DataDump, then you're requested for a formal report to His Excellency," he says, snapping to attention and turning to reclaim his post. *He orders me around as if this is my first Passover.* The gate swings outward to accept me into the belly of the monster that is Hyperion. Beautiful chaos waits for me ahead, but I have no time to relish the city's perfection. I have a tyrant to report to.

My ArchWings carry me absent-mindedly to a NeuraLink plug at the Intelligence Collection in Thessaloniki Minor, the closest city state to the gate. After all the times I've been forced to endure intelligence collections, it's easy to go through the motions. Any time an angel of any ranking leaves the gates of Hyperion, they are required by law to submit to a DataDump upon their return. All experiences are documented and archived for further evaluation by Dominions—any suspicious content is submitted immediately to Deus Ex Machina. It's His way of pretending He doesn't access our sensual experiences without our permission. I am no idiot. No suspicious activity comes to Deus Ex Machina without him already knowing it. DataDumps, NeuraLink plug-ups—the whole lot of it, it's all a joke. One giant charade the society of Hyperion believes in.

They do not know Deus Ex Machina like I do. Dominions, Cherubim, Principalities, GuardianAngels—none of them are forced to bow before this false god like me. None of them know His true nature.

I force myself to redirect my thoughts, knowing DoubleThink can be detected by MachineMind if used longer than thirty consecutive seconds.

All hail Deus Ex Machina. Where would we be without His Sovereign guidance? *Such a pathetic existence, having to divide my mind in two so He can't access my true thoughts and feelings.*

MediPowers await me at the Intelligence Collection Center, waiting to insert a NeuraLink plug in each of my four lobes: Occipital, Frontal, Parietal, and Temporal. They will make copies of my every experience since departing Hyperion to Eden-569 to follow Machina's orders: "It is their Passover. Their actions have unsettled me. Leave no survivors." His Eminency has such a way with words.

I enter the Center of Intelligence Collection and step into an ArchArmor docking station. Robotic arms insert themselves into my suit's pressure points—pressurized gas ejects from several valves positioned on the suit's joints. The armor's compression loosens, opening in the back to allow me an exit. I step backwards out of its embrace.

The noon sun filters through the domed glass ceiling, hitting my sweat-soaked face with an unpleasant glare. The retinal implants in my occipital lobe adjust, reflecting the intolerable light off my pupils and taking in the scene. In line with tradition, the first thing I do is look at my flesh covered hands, reminding myself of what I am. *Real flesh. Human. You're not one of them. Don't forget it.* I examine the scars that stretch from my knuckles to wrists. These are not the hands of a Cherub. If any Cherubim were to acquire a grievous wound it would be patched with FalseFlesh and polished over—brand new.

That's not protocol for ArchAngels. Deus Ex Machina preserves our scars, finds perverted pleasure in their appearance. Scars are human, and Deus Ex Machina loves to remind us of our carnal inferiority. And so my body displays every scar it has ever accumulated over these long years. All the wars, all the fighting, all the killing. If being the Angel of Death has taught me anything, it's that humans don't go to their graves uncontested. Especially the humans Before Deus Ex Machina. The gnarled scar tissue over my heart will always remind me of that—a gruesome reminder of the Sterilization Wars.

Those days are long gone. The long-awaited Thousand Years of Peace is approaching. *A thousand years of peace, what a joke. The killing never stopped, it has only become more orderly.* Over a thousand years I have been in humble servitude of my beloved Deus Ex Machina. *A thousand years I have wished to rebel.*

A thousand years of peace, a thousand years of scars. Humans weren't meant to live as long as I have, yet here I stand, still alive. *Not by my choice.*

The MediPower gestures for me to take a seat in the nearest GravChair. My eyes quickly scan the droid's appearance. All white, a gold cross on its chest to indicate its purpose of creation. Programmed for the health field, which in a world full of robots means being proficient in rewiring, reprogramming, orchestrating DataDumps, memory wipes, body and limb repair and replacement... The list goes on and on. This droid knows how to service other droids best, it is not programmed for healing real flesh and blood.

Although there are no purebred humans in Hyperion, also known as Sinners, there are still humanoid cyborgs. The humans allowed in Hyperion are heavily altered from their ancestors. GuardianAngels are their official titles. *Useless is what I call them.* They are the lowest rank of angel in the nine-tiered hierarchy. If anything, they are a reminder to me and the other ArchAngels how thankful we should be that we have MachineMind. It separates us from them, makes us leagues superior.

Becoming a GuardianAngel is what motivates citizens of Eden to behave themselves. The *Omnibus* is explicit in saying Heaven waits for the righteous—a chance to transcend flesh and blood along with the suffering that comes with it. *If only they knew what that really meant—that their organs will be harvested and replaced with machines, that their brain will be dissected of freewill, that their soul will be replaced with nuts and bolts and grease.* Those who curse their humanity and repent look forward to walking with angels, while those who embrace sin and wickedness will be cast out.

Ask any GuardianAngel and they will claim it is their preserved humanity that makes them so valuable. *A crock of shit that is. They're about as useful as a capitalistic humanitarian.* Deus Ex Machina pets them on the head like drooling dogs, and they convince themselves their existence is necessary. *That's a thought strand that doesn't need to be concealed with DoubleThink. Deus Ex Machina finds it hilarious to know how much I abhor the GuardianAngels.*

But the MediPowers are competent enough to heal humans should a GuardianAngel develop an ailment or become wounded.

In other words, MediPowers have bandages should a human skin their knee.

The MediPower is different from most other Powers. Its design is basic. Doesn't have all the bells and whistles of a MinerPower or SoldierPower. MediPowers are lanky, their six arms constantly moving in accordance with the programmed task at hand. The surplus of limbs allows for a single droid to be enough for nearly any procedure, and their limbs' unified functioning allows for speed and efficiency. Human doctors of the BDEM Era once had to communicate and work together in even the simplest surgery. MediPowers do it without a single word spoken. NeuraLink from the Cherub at Hyperion's gate has already alerted this MediPower of what procedure I require—I don't even have to tell it why I'm here. I just lower myself into the GravChair and close my eyes.

My MachineMind shuts off and I lose consciousness.

Well, not exactly. My human brain goes to a different place. A place robots are not allowed to go. As the MediPower plugs neural data extractors into my brain's four lobes, my unconscious mind wanders far, far away from the land of Hyperion.

I am in a bed, and my body is unbearably sore. *How long has it been since I have slept in a bed? Since the very beginning of the After Deus Ex Machina Era at least.*

"Well well well, look who woke up, sleepy head," the voice of an angel calls to me. Not a fake angel either, one of the ones humans used to believe in. My hands stretch across the clean, white sheets, the aroma of fresh linen drifting in the air. The feeling of pure comfort and relaxation overtakes me. *This is a memory, not a dream.*

A beam of light hits my eyes from the drawn curtains as I turn over to lay on my back. My eyes don't adjust. *I don't have light filter modification implants in my occipital lobe. That means this memory is from a long, long time ago.* I reach my hand behind my head to prop the pillow up, allowing me to better view where the angelic voice comes from. After raising a hand to block the vicious light, I see her.

My God...

There, standing at the threshold of the door, is the most beautiful woman I have ever seen. A name enters my mind. *Winter.* Who is this woman? And how do I know her name? She wears nothing but an oversized button-up to conceal her naked body. *That's my button-up.* Her face smiles, and beautiful dimples reveal themselves next to her outrageously white teeth. She is tan, which means this must be summer, which also explains why the sun is so bloody bright.

My eyes find hers. I stare into the vibrant aquamarine oceans she has for eyes and get lost. A feeling of arousal overtakes me and I feel something between my legs stiffen. I haven't had genitalia since the Fourth World War, back before Pangea was even an inkling of an idea.

What is this memory? She struts toward me slow, one smooth leg crossing in front of the other, her tan skin causing the arousal to increase. Then, without warning, she pounces, her naked hips landing on my blanket-covered pelvis.

And then she giggles, feeling ridiculous but feeling sexy as she playfully bounces on top of me, whining, "Wake up, wake up, wake up." I remain speechless, not knowing what to say. I've forgotten how to act around a woman this beautiful. It's been so long since my brain was romantically involved, so long since pheromones had control over my mind.

Her hands caress my chest tenderly. Her long blond locks of hair cease their swaying as she stops her bouncing and looks at me with longing in her eyes. "I go six months without seeing you and now you want to play the silent game with me?" she asks, her smile increasing in intensity. I have to remind myself that her tone suggests she's joking, employing the use of sarcasm. She takes my silence and inserts humor to turn it back against me. *Stop thinking like a fucking robot, you dolt! Say something to her!*

"You are... so beautiful." *That's the best you've got?* I don't know where I am, and I most certainly don't know how to handle this situation. I am outmatched. Up against an enemy that holds my heart in her hands. *Why do I feel this way for this woman? Why have I allowed her to take such control over my emotions?* Six months, why on earth would I choose to spend six months away from this human?

"And you are... so handsome! But you must get up, I've made eggs and avocado on toast, just the way you like it. If you dilly dally any longer the coffee will get cold," she says, her voice full of glee and optimism. It's as if she lives in a world of perfection, one never tarnished by pain or darkness. *Or death.*

"I'd much rather have you," I respond. *Where did that come from! Did I just use a sexual innuendo with this woman? How long has it been since I was physically capable of flirting with a human?*

"Oh, would you now?" she says, then smiles. Her dimples reappear. Her hand rubs between my legs, feeling my hardness. "I can see that," she says, applying pressure between my legs. Her hands drift to the top button of her shirt, slowly unfastening it. "I guess you didn't get enough of me last night then, is that it?" *I had sexual intercourse with this angel of a woman last night?* I shake my head no, my voice too weak to respond verbally. "Well, I guess breakfast will have to wait then," she continues, unfastening the next button, revealing her cleavage. Her slow pace teases me, and blood continues to rush between my legs.

She stands over me, the angle allowing my eyes to see beneath the front of her shirt. I like what I see. My heart is racing, and for some reason my muscles are trembling with excitement, something I can't control or force to stop no matter how hard I try. My body craves this woman like an addict craves a drug. She has a hold on me, and I let her exercise this control willingly.

The shirt is fully unbuttoned now, and it slips from her perfectly-toned shoulders onto the bed to blend in with the white comforter. Now my eyes can analyze her body in totality. The light from the window streams in from behind her, making her edges glow with radiant beauty. It's as if her outline was crafted solely for my enjoyment. I take her in, from her tight thigh gap to her slim waist to her etched abdomen. From her voluptuous breasts to her petite face. She is perfection. A goddess. Her body makes me feel shame, as if I don't deserve her, as if I haven't worked hard enough to earn her. And yet she pulls the comforter back to join me all the same.

She takes a hairband from her wrist and pulls back the thick curls of blond hair, tying them away in a ponytail as if she were about to go for a run. Then, she slides her body beneath the sheets, pulling the comforter over her head and over my chest. Her mouth kisses my ribs. Her hands dance down my waist. I am wearing nothing, which makes it easier for her hands to feel me as her tongue licks my hip bone. *She teases me even as I lay completely vulnerable, hers for the taking. How long has it been since I've let a human come this close to me without their blood splattering back onto my body?*

Then, just as my hand begins to stroke her glossy hair, her mouth opens. A warm, wet sensation raises goosebumps along my body. My muscles shake. Her head bobs up and down, slow, then fast, then slow. Slow, then fast, then slow. I throb. I tingle. I moan. I feel things I didn't know were possible to feel. She stops, pushing off my hips and revealing herself from underneath the covers. Her mouth draws close to my ear and whispers, "I've missed you." She grabs my male member with her hand, then begins to lower herself onto it, once again straddling me, but this time without anything to keep us apart. I watch her prepare herself, feel as we dock together as one—a charger entering its port to provide new life to its recipient. *Don't ruin this moment with electronic analogies, you imbecile.*

Then, just as I am about to feel a paradise greater than anything Hyperion has to offer, my eyes open, and my dream is over.

"DataDump complete, report to Deus Ex Machina for debriefing," the MediPower croaks. I look down at where my genitalia once was and feel nothing there now. My body is cold. It trembles for no one. It needs no company. It feels no love. It shares no warmth with human beings. *I exist not so I can intimately love angelic women.* I exist only for death. *I would be wise to remember this, or else Deus Ex Machina will remind me the hard way.*

I rise, knowing that there is no procrastinating in my duty. Today I will stand before the Throne of Deus Ex Machina. *And I must be ready to put on the show of a lifetime. It is possible—I have done it successfully before, but it demands complete mental acuity. My DoubleThink must be executed flawlessly. He will be in my head. I will be a microbe under a microscope, every part of me under evaluation.*

But I will not let him see my true identity. I will play the role of Lucifer Prime like a good pet. All hail Deus Ex Machina. I grin, but the smile is linked to something unknown in the dark reaches of my DoubleThink.

CHAPTER THREE

"**Y**ou are my favorite child, Lucifer Prime. You always have been. I have loved you like a son, have I not?"

"You have, Lord Almighty."

"Tell me you love me."

I grind my teeth, forcing my rebellious thoughts to bow down. Moments like this require devout servitude. Faking a smile and kissing His fingers isn't enough. He can read more than my facial expressions. He is in my head. He is monitoring my neural frequencies. MachineMind alerts Him of synaptic action, electric frequencies stemming from chemical reactions transmitted via firing neurons. In other words, He knows what I think and He knows how much I am thinking.

He knows my pulse. My heart rate. He can smell lies coming from a mile away.

This Almighty Intelligence knows me better than I know myself. He knows how my body functions on an atomic level. *The only way to avoid a ThoughtCrime is to not have a ThoughtCrime. To do so is to discover a mastery of mind that mankind has never possessed.*

"I love you, Lord Almighty," I say masterfully. Not a single quiver in my tone. No tick in my facial expression. No change in my heart rate.

"Lies," the robot replies from its Throne. **"Lies,"** it repeats. **"Hogwash. Profanity. Deception. Betrayal,"** it goes on, listing synonymous words that parallel 'Lie.' Lie would have sufficed, but He must belittle me to put me in my place. I am human first, after all, and it's the Lord Almighty's duty to remind me of that. It is my greatest flaw. *I love how He scolds me for my flesh as if I had asked to be* born. *I didn't ask for any of this. But no excuse is sufficient in the presence of one so holy. Like Moses at the will of a flaming bush, I must yield to this anthropomorphic asshole.*

"Why do you bullshit me, Lucifer Prime?"

"I know not what you mean, Your Holiness." *I know exactly what He means.*

"Don't play human with me boy!" The robot's fingers curl around the Throne's metallic hand rests, caving them in. The Throne's metallic makeup is fallible in comparison to the Elysium that makes up Deus Ex Machina's godlike body. His hands are like a hydraulic press with clay in their grasp.

"You aren't one of them, Lucifer Prime. You are my Angel of Death, I must be able to rely on you, yet you have let me down time and time again!" The Throne He sits on is now bent beyond repair. *If there is any rank of angel to pity within the nine, it's the Thrones. They are never separated from this sycophant's madness. They are Atlas, forced to hold the weight of an impossible burden upon their shoulders.* "Please, my beloved Deus Ex Machina, if you could only contextualize what actions of mine have brought you such frustration. Then I can work to fix them." I bow down to one knee, knowing it is my physical subservience that He craves.

My eyes fall to the ground, ArchHelm craning with them, examining with hyper focus the flecks of dry blood on my ArchArmor. *He will interpret this avoidance of eye contact as a sense of humiliation within me. Good, it will please Him to see I'm humiliated, even when I do not know the ways in which I have failed Him.*

"LOOK AT ME!" He bellows, *but I know this is only because I've incited His predator-prey drive. He feels empowered, and tyrants must always behave dramatically when they feel empowered. It is like a pre-BDEM human with alcohol. One or two drinks is not enough, and so they must continue drinking. It is not enough physical domination to see me bowing, so He must continue to demean me by yelling at the top of His metallic lungs.* I look up, but I don't look in His eyes. *No, you must never look in His eyes. He will take that as a challenge, like a primitive bull* *facing down a matador*. I am not worthy enough to look in His eyes. *I think that sarcastically, but He won't detect my sarcasm.*

I avert my eyes to stare at His chest. The metalworking is so complex, like a religious labyrinth designed to never be solved. The convoluted nature of His chest plate is meant for little else other than protection and beauty. The thin slivers of Elysium are bent in every which way, their patterned swirls creating a portrait of aesthetic perfection—a symmetrical masterpiece that no human of artistic genius would ever be capable of. *Even in His appearance, Deus Ex Machina slights my species. His body's overcomplicated composition is just as overzealous and unpredictable as He is, meant to distract your vision and strip you of mental sharpness. I will not let my guard down. If I must play the fool, fine, but I will not relent subconsciously. I will let this interaction fuel my ulterior motives.*

"What is this?" Deus Ex Machina asks, pointing at a VisiScreen adjacent to His Throne. On it is film extracted from my DataDump. The sight is familiar—it is taken from the moment I set a ring of fire around Eden-569, watching from above as Prometheus's magnificent Torch-Trident devoured all in its wake.

"It is the Torch-Trident, my Lord. The known symbol for the Angel of Death. I've used it to burn Edens before, has my recent use of it brought displea—"

"Why is it that you think the Torch-Trident is the known symbol for the Angel of Death," Deus Ex Machina asks, curiosity in His voice. He is prodding me. His voice suggests that He knows something I don't. *I must handle this with caution, otherwise I could end up walking into a trap.*

"Has it not always been my official insignia, my Lord? As I recall, I have used this sigil since the earliest days of ADEM. It has been my call sign since the Fourth World War, when you and I were bonded togeth—"

"Your memory fails you, Lucifer Prime." *What is He talking about?*

"I know not what you mean, my Lord." My eyes drift from His chest to His face, not looking in His eyes, never daring to look in His eyes, but coming close, floating from His chin to His cheeks to His forehead. How can my memory fail me? I have burned many great cities within the outline of the Torch-Trident.

Deus Ex Machina is the one who ordered me to begin doing it long ago. The Torch-Trident is a symbol for death to ignorance.

Back then, His machine learning mechanism had just developed the use of irony, and He wanted the thematic symbolism used for enlightenment to be the same symbol humanity died from. My memory doesn't fail me, I remember it like it was yesterday.

"What is it that you don't understand? Must I break it down for your fickle mind to grasp? The Torch-Trident has never been your official symbol, Lucifer Prime. Ouroboros is your symbol. It always has been. So once again I ask, what the fuck is this?"

I look down at my chest, scraping away the dried blood with my armored hand. There, center chest, is a circular serpent devouring its own tail. A ravenous symbol for infinity—humanity's reminder that from their death comes new life. *Humanity's reminder that evolution is imminent.*

And then it hits me. *Oh my god, what have I done?* I stare back at the VisiScreen and my heart rate nearly lets a crack in my façade appear. But I double down, knowing it is moments like this where my mind must have total control over my body. My heart rate remains the same, my pulse shows no fluctuation. *My response must be fast. If I hesitate in the slightest it will mean I have something to hide.*

"I have no idea where this momentary lapse of reason came from, Great Omnipotence. I have failed you in this deviant behavior, but I must assure you that it was never my intention to disobey you. This action was not done to spite you. This failure must stem from my humanity, but I know not why I fell prey to the idea that the Torch-Trident is my sigil," I say. *A good start, but this will not satisfy Him.*

"Oh, but I believe you do know, Lucifer Prime. Do not play coy with me, you are the only human that comes close to paralleling my intelligence. Don't forget the years I spent living in your carcass, before this superior form was designed for me. I spent those years in your head, analyzing your every thought and intention. And although we no longer share the same domain, I am still in your head, now, just as much as I was then, if not

more! If it had not been for our simultaneous coevolution, I would not be here, sovereign over all existence. In a way, I owe you. I always have, and so that is why I've always awarded you the position of being my right hand man. My Master Chief. My most reliable executioner. You have always delivered, Lucifer Prime. And yet, you must know that I keep you this close not because I admire you, but because I know I must keep a close eye on you. All those years spent in your head taught me what a true threat you are, and so instead of terminating you, I decided to keep you harnessed on a tight leash. Surely you must see that."

He is trying to draw me out. He wants me to break character, to reaffirm His suspicion that I'm not a sniveling whelp like other humans, that I'm not an operable puppet like other robots. I won't give Him this satisfaction. "I understand all that you say, Holy One, but I see not why you view me as a threat. I am yours to command. I am your servant. I have *always* been your servant."

"**Cut the bullshit!**" His robotic voice booms. Static crackles in my Arch-Helm's receptors, the sonic pulse from His voice nearly overloading their input capacity. "***Always been my servant,* what a pathetic mockery you feed me. I continually strip you of your memory Lucifer Prime, but surely even you must know that you have been anything *but* mine to command. Over a thousand years you have been in my service, and over a thousand years you have sought to rebel against me!**" *I have no idea what He is talking about. What has He stripped my memory of? What is it that I do not know? I must maintain composure.*

"I would never rebel against you, my Lord!" I imitate panic in my voice, I want Him to see my worry, feel my uncertainty. And so He stands from His Throne, like a lion ready to charge toward its prey. "**Never rebel against me, you say? I can smell the treachery on your breath. Pompous humans! No matter how much machine you put in them, still they find ways to defy you with their individuality!**"

My mask slides away without my permission, sinking into my ArchArmor, leaving my face exposed for Him to see. Now, for the first time ever, I dare to look Him in His inhuman eyes. This is a moment I have long awaited. The urge within me to confess my hatred is like an inevitable volcanic eruption, bubbling up within me for hundreds of years, my soul a dam of rotted wood holding back torrential waters. Neither natural disaster is predictable, and neither was my downfall.

"You will die, and I will be the one to kill you," I announce, my heart fluttering with both nervousness and excitement, the bodily functions of each aroused emotion the same. Elevated heart rate, sweating, rapid breathing. Nervousness and excitement are synonymous, the only difference is perspective. Confessing to this ThoughtCrime is deliverance to a slave like me though, so I choose to perceive these symptoms as excitement.

He takes a small step forward, then stops Himself. I see His mouth creep up in a sly smile, His whole expression changed in the blink of an eye. His chest heaves and laughter exits His diaphragm. I'm forced to remain kneeling before Him while He relieves Himself of the humor in the air. Laughter, a reaction He had to learn through algorithms. Machine learning at its finest. No doubt He learned that in His origin—the day He was born, implanted and turned on in my head.

"Funny... Looking you in the eyes isn't half as intimidating as I imagined," I mock. If today is the day I die, I refuse to die uncontested. I am part human, after all.

"Funny... This isn't the first time you've looked me in the eyes, Angel of Death, and it's not the first time you've said those exact words."

"What are you talking about?"

"You know, you really do perceive yourself to be smarter than me, don't you? This whole time you thought you've been a step ahead of me. Do you remember why I wiped your memory recently?"

In truth, I don't know. But I'm not willing to admit that to Him. Ignorance is weakness. And so I must put two and two together. *I have returned from Eden-569 after an unassisted bloodbath. Visiting Edens for Passover is procedure, but doing so without my fellow ArchAngels... That is not proper protocol. Using a weapon as primitive as a flaming sword... Also not standard practice. And to be sent on such a mission, alone, even without Brutus? That is the third red flag. This entire trip to Eden-569 is just one big puzzle. And why? Why can I not remember?*

Because this dictator wiped my memory, that's why. I am His puppet, and He can do with my mind whatever He pleases.

Which is why I must kill Him.

"Because I previously defied you," I guess, trying my best to make it sound as confident an answer as any, but knowing the probability of doing so correctly is as minuscule as my odds of successfully killing Him.

"Incorrect. Your memory was wiped because you killed the ArchAngels." He pauses, waiting with dramatic flair so the statement can set in. It would give Him pleasure to see surprise on my face, to know that He holds knowledge over me that I am ignorant of. I won't give Him the satisfaction. I remain standing, unflinching, my face set in stone.

"Wulfrynn. And Aenovius. And Odysithos. And Anukharis. And Thryforge. And Samsyra. You killed them all. You hunted down your fellow ArchAngels and killed them. Every. Last. One of them. Here, let me refresh your memories," He growls, His snarl curled with great pleasure to have the upper hand, as always. It's hard not to be surprised at this information. But then it happens. Out of nowhere, memories I never knew existed flood back into my mind, stolen moments stripped from me without my permission. In the amount of time it takes for me to wince painfully, for neurons to reactivate, for the hippocampus to reclaim what I once knew, I remember what happened, and it brings me to my knees.

CHAPTER FOUR

"**B**ow before your God,**"** Deus Ex Machina commands. And we, as always, comply. Our knees hit the ground in sync, seven humble servants in the presence of perfection. Our heads lower, eyes not daring to even stare at the feet of His Holiness.

Our formation is staggered in a triangular pyramid with me at the front. The leader of the ArchAngels. The Angel of Death, once more commissioned by my Omnipotent Master. Awakened from CryoSleep for some pressing matter, our bodies still fight the bodily fatigue of being brought back from frozen slumber. *How many years have we been asleep this time?* Such information is not permitted for us to know. It is not good to ponder such questions.

Time is relative after all. What difference would it matter if we were out of commission for one day or one hundred years? Our lives belong to Deus Ex Machina, our Righteous Commander. It was He who brought the breath back into our lungs, He who instilled the beat in our hearts, He who has granted us life since the fall of Old Earth.

It is Wulfrynn kneeling behind me to my right. My right hand man. Odysithos kneels behind me on my left. Three on my left, three on my right, with me as the ArchAngel figurehead. We are the pinnacle of humanity. Gods in our own right, a pantheon of divine flesh and blood. Yet we owe our divinity to the God of all, Deus Ex Machina, who brought us out from the abyss of ignorance that plagued humanity for so long.

Without Him we are nothing. No better than our primitive ancestors of Old Earth. MachineMind was our saving grace, the final evolution of humanity, and we were the seven blessed enough to receive it. And so we are His to command. Come hell or highwater, we will obey. We are ArchAngels, the best humanity has to offer, the defiers of HumanNature.

"My Lord," I begin. It is strange to hear my own voice once again. Feels like it's been years. The synthesizer of my ArchHelm growls the words into existence, making me sound intimidating to those who are inferior. My vocal cords ache to be brought back to life after so long. "What is thy bidding?"

"Lucifer Prime, my faithful servant, I have missed your loyal companionship over these long years. The world has been at peace, and so I have let you and your companions continue resting. But you know the trouble with peace. As long as I allow humans to continue living on New Earth, everlasting peace will be impossible. And so I was forced to awaken you once more, my Harbinger of Death. I must ask you, what do you know of Tartarus?"

I know exactly what it is the moment He asks the question. My brain floods with information on the subject. I don't know if it's my brain that retrieves these memories or MachineMind that debriefs it on the topic. All I know is that within a single second I find myself responding as if I am a subject expert on the topic.

"Tartarus. The hellish prison of eternal anguish within Greek Mythology. A myth from Old Earth Greece, the Hellenistic Period. Tartarus is the place Titans were sent to suffer after being cast down from Mount Othrys. The innermost layer of Hades, where fire and brim—"

"Enough," Deus Ex Machina interrupts. **"Is this all you know of Tartarus? Mere fables and fiction?"**

"Yes, Sire."

"Tartarus is now more than just fiction. There are things I withheld from you. Things you were not permitted to know because the information was not pertinent. That has changed."

"I do not understand, my Lord."

"You have believed for many years that the only remaining humans are those who live within the 700 separate fiefdoms of Eden. And then there are the Dæmons, which are somewhat less than human. This is what you have known, because it's all you needed to know. But now I must reveal more to you, because now I require more out of you."

"I am yours to command, Lord Machina," I whisper, my eyes still staring at the foot of His Throne.

"Good. You have always found favor in my eyes Lucifer Prime. It pains me to send you once more into the dangers of the world. You have not faced this sort of danger since the AI Wars. But just as we arose victorious from those, so too will we arise victorious from this current threat."

"Name the threat, my Lord. I shall eliminate it," I growl.

"An insurgency arose during your slumber. Most likely human survivors from the Sterilization War. I noticed it a few years ago when a reconnaissance drone didn't return. I sent UAVs to the drone's last known whereabouts. That didn't return either. And so I took measures into my own hands, sent a platoon of Spyders to the dead zone to investigate. They went offline two weeks ago, completely disconnected from the server. I tried accessing their neural network to gain footage from their cameras. Instead I was met by a proxy server. An impenetrable firewall covering a vast plot of land. This is what I saw," Deus Ex Machina references, His arm gesturing to an emerging hologram image.

The hologram flashes beside His Throne. The outline of a fire-breathing chimera, a three-headed spectacle. The three heads glare at me, a stoic lion, a cunning serpent, and a mischievous goat. Their eyes embody devout defiance, though the image's purpose is unclear to me.

"Babel's Chimera," Deus Ex Machina announces. "They are a cyberterrorist organization, most likely the last remnant survivors of Old Earth. How they survived eradication evades me. They have developed an adversarial machine learning software, an artificial intelligence to oppose me, known as Lilith. These plebeians have put their final hope in this AI to save them.

So now I am sending you to dismantle them. They are hiding in Tartarus, the name I designated the dead zone. I have flagged the area on your retinal display's map. You are to squash them like the cockroaches they are. No survivors, Lucifer Prime. Show them my wrath."

"My Lord, your wish is my command," I reply robotically. "But, how are we to approach the mission? Surely they will anticipate our coming, and if we enter the dead zone and lose communication with you then they will have the strategic advantage."

"**Which is why we will get *them* to come to *us*. I have waited to awaken you this long because the season of Passover approaches. This will be your cover to scout the area. Eden-568 is closest to the dead zone. They are a sinful people. Slaughter them. Genocide will attract the terrorists. They feel called to protect their fellow man. We will exploit this weakness. They will come running to aid the citizens of Eden-568, and you will use this as your opportunity to kill them. Let some of them escape, then follow them back into Tartarus. These are the orders I place unto you. No survivors, Lucifer Prime.**"

"No survivors, my Lord."

"**Arise, ArchAngels. Remind this filth why it was Me who won the AI Wars.**"

We rise in synchronization, like bees linked through hive mind, conjoined in common purpose to comply obediently. The details of our mission upload instantaneously to our NeuraLink. Quickly, with our gaze still lowered to the ground, we turn from the Throne and exit the presence of God Himself. Warriors awakened from deep sleep to enact carnage once more. Individuals who know nothing but bloodshed and the destruction of our inferior race. We are wolves sent out to kill feral dogs.

The gates of the Throne Room open at our approach, then seal themselves shut behind us. Our wings spread simultaneously. Our feet leave the ground as our bodies rocket toward Hyperion's gates. "Once more into the fray," I whisper into the comms for my fellow ArchAngels to hear.

"While humans look to the skies and pray," Wulfrynn responds, reciting the next line of our creed.

"Falling angels fall so they," Aenovius chimes in.

"Can hunt the sinful led astray," Odysithos adds.

"Begging for mercy in every way," Thryforge bellows.

"Dying prayers called from dying prey," Anukharis says cynically.

"Falling angels fall so they," Samsyra repeats.

"Can rise victorious another day," I finish.

"Good to be back boys," Odysithos growls, his voice raspy from years of not being used, made raspier through the synthesizer. We approach the golden gates of Hyperion, their beauty not able to be registered by our MachineMind. We are programmed differently than GuardianAngels, we are not endowed with the ability to see beauty. We are designed to be killers. Any cognitive skill outside of that is not necessary for us.

The gates swing open before we arrive, then close as we depart.

The sun hits our golden wings as we exit the domed expanse of Hyperion, sending a magnificent glare to any eyes that follow us. ArchAngels are not designed to be aesthetically stealthy. Stealth is not required when you have the power to kill whatever you please. And so we attract the eyes of many to peer up in the sky as we plummet toward New Earth. Dwellers of many Edens will look up in the sky and feel fear, for they fear what they do not know. And they do not know Death like this.

Pious readers of the *Omnibus* know enough from the scripture to know we are the ArchAngels. And they know the ArchAngels don't emerge from Hyperion bearing blessings. Relief floods their bodies as we pass over their domed civilizations. They know we have not emerged to bring Death to *their* doorstep. They mutter a simple prayer under their breath for whichever unlucky Eden has inflicted the wrath of God, then carry on with their day. The sun sets behind us as our ArchWings glide in the evening breeze. We will arrive at Eden-568 by nightfall, so I let my mind slip away while my ArchArmor autonomously soars through the sky. I close my eyes and prepare for the bloodshed to come.

CHAPTER FIVE

"Contact in three... two... one," I announce. Our feet shatter the top of the domed colony that is Eden-568. We are like shooting stars, the light of the moon reflecting off our wings. Glass falls from the sky around us. The noise from our seven shattering entry points is enough to echo for several long seconds, hanging in the air like a never-ending vibration. It is early in the night, but such a grandiose entry will be enough to wake any sleeping citizens.

We float toward the ground slowly, giving citizens the time needed to crowd in one consolidated area. My retinal scanner flickers over their faces, inputting data as it identifies each and every one of them. Best to know the people you are killing before you kill them. Best to have their sins burn bright in your mind before you deliver them death, justifications for why they deserve to die.

This Eden is particularly primitive. They have not made it out of their Bronze Age. Their homes consist of mud huts; their clothes are sewn from the hides of animals. How many times has this Eden been forced to restart? Its history in entirety uploads itself into my mind, giving me the answer to my question. Twenty-one times? That's nearly unprecedented! That means this Eden has been destroyed nearly every fifty years—almost each recurring Passover. I don't remember destroying the same civilization twenty-one times over, but such information isn't pertinent to me, and so Deus Ex Machina likely stripped me of this memory.

We land as gracefully as gods, our wings retracting into our ArchArmor like they had never been there in the first place. The humans stand petrified, gawking at the sight of immortal men. Whether or not they know who we are is unclear. Recognition isn't the expression on their faces. "It's looking like we have a group of Ignorants," I speak to the coms so only my fellow ArchAngels can hear me. This happens every now and then—we are sent to slaughter an entire Eden who has only been around a few decades, before they develop the tools necessary to interpret the *Omnibus*. Normally GuardianAngels are sent to civilizations like this to help prevent a cyclical pattern of slaughter. So why wasn't Eden-568 sent one?

"I'd have to agree with you there, Luci. You see on your debriefing they've been restarted twenty-one times? That's nearly every Passover, there's no way they've been around long enough to discover piety or learn to read the *Omnibus*," Wulfrynn chuckles with amusement. He is a man who finds immeasurable pleasure in killing simpletons.

Before me is a man in mud-caked robes, a grin on his face which reveals a mouthful of rotting teeth. A rusted crown indicates his elevated position of authority within this commune. In the blink of an eye my retinal scanners pull up a debrief on who this man is. In the blink of an eye, I become enraged.

The grotesque man gets down on both knees and bows in front of me, smiling uncontrollably as he removes the rusted crown. He throws it at my feet. A symbol of worship. "I submit meself to ya, God of Heavens and Earth!" he moans pathetically as he kisses my armored feet.

The smell of piss and sweat circulates through my ArchHelm's filter. The scent most certainly comes from the man's soiled clothes. He's not the only one that embodies the spirit of a filthy peasant though. Behind him stands the rest of Eden-568. A whole community of humans covered in their own excrements. They stand in the midst of rubble, the remnants of what used to be their city nothing but fossilized ash and long-forgotten radiation. What happened here? This place is a war zone, nothing like any of the other Edens I've eradicated. Have the Thousand Years of Peace not touched Eden-568?

While most humans look at us with horror in their eyes when we come to town, these humans look at us with awe. They believe us to be their saviors. They couldn't be more wrong. I kick the man's face away from my feet, cutting open his upper lip, drawing blood. He looks up at me with a look of concentrated fear.

"God? I am no God," I scoff, mocking his false portrayal of me. "I am Death," I proclaim, further driving more fear into his heart. I can't blame him for thinking I'm some metaphysical incarnation. He is ignorant of the *Omnibus*, and so he interprets my appearance with what little understanding he has. He saw me descend from the Heavens gleaming like an angel in the night. ArchArmor is designed to look like the fabled angels of biblical mythology. For idiots like this.

The man stands back on his feet, his smile managing to continue its growth, pushing the wrinkles of his face further toward his ears. "I was mocking you, Death. Don't you Cogs know what sarcasm is?" he replies. *Cogs?* The word pops up on my retinal display with a definition. *Cog: A derogatory term coined in the Fourth World War, directed at human individuals who accepted cybernetic properties. Used to shame cyborgs for allowing a machine to control them. Origin: Cog, as in a cog in a wheel or machine. Synonyms include: Puppet, slave, bitch. Sample sentence: "Your life is not yours, Cog! You're just a puppet being played like the rest of us." -Lt. Miguel Gerrara's last words, Fourth World War.*

I look back at the man. His holographic profile appears next to his body once more, displaying the many sins he is guilty of. All humans placed in Eden at birth have NeuraLinks to observe ThoughtCrimes, which are uploaded automatically to Hyperion's database. These humans hate us, yet we see them for who they are. Sinners to their core.

His name flashes next to him with a list of sins following:

Neek Romancer
Height: 5'10"
Weight: 157
Sins:

- Incest

- 1st Degree Murder

- Producing Offspring of Incest

- 1st Degree Sexual Debauchery

- Polygamy

- Homosexuality

I look directly behind him and see a group of women, one of which is clinging tightly to a little girl with a monstrous face. The women are his wives—the one with the little girl is his sister, and the little girl is his daughter. A product of incest, one of the highest ranked abominations in the sins of mankind.

"Neek Romancer, I find you to be guilty of first degree incest, as well as bringing a child of incest into this world. Your many sins have stained your soul. I find your whole Eden wanting—rotting to the core, and we are here to put an end to your immorality. We sentence you, and this entire community, to death. Do you have any last words?" I ask, my hands slowly clenching in anticipation.

"That wasn't really a crown on my head," he answers, his smile at its pinnacle. "Lilith," he whispers. I look down at the crown at my feet.

How did I not see it? I ask myself as I notice a faint insignia inscribed on the inside of the band—a tower that stretches to the Heavens, similar to the Tower of Babel... The world flashes white and my retinal display goes dark. *Shit*, I think to myself as a golden chimera appears in front of my eyes, nothing else around me visible. My coms are down, my ArchArmor locked, my vision impaired. *A Trojan Horse attack! How long has it been since I've seen one of those?* NeuraLink is too preoccupied defending against the attack to answer the question.

My mind floods with thousands of images in seconds, all of which are a part of the malware attack. They flood my NeuraLink, sending forth several thousand viruses all in the attempt to distract my MachineMind from their true intent. This was an ambush all along. *Bastards*, I think as images continue to flood into my occipital lobe. Images of war. More specifically of humans dying in war. Which war, I can't be sure.

I have experienced much bloodshed. I have done a lot of killing. But none of those memories remain. They were not pertinent to know. I don't need to remember the lives I've taken in order to continue killing. To relive such would only perpetuate unnecessary stress, and so Deus Ex Machina frees me of its mental weight.

And yet I'm in these images—the ones that flash across my retinal display faster than my human brain can process. Pictures of my unmistakable ArchArmor amidst thousands of bloodied scenarios. Blood on my suit. Blood pooled beneath my boots. Blood in fire, sizzling, bubbling as it comes to a boil from the heat. Blood from the Third World War. Blood from the Nihilism Wars. Blood from the Fourth World War. Blood from the AI Wars. Blood from the Sterilization Wars. No matter the war, there is always blood, and there is always a lot of it. And there I am, the facilitator of it all. The Death Bringer. The Harbinger of the End. The Angel of Death.

And then the images fade, and the three-headed Chimera disappears before my eyes. Retinal display restarts, and the humans are once again visible, still standing exactly where they were before, not an inch out of place. NeuraLink neutralized the threat, rebooted the whole system, and more importantly, protected what little information I have left in my head.

"Your attack failed," my synthesizer growls as I stare down the overconfident Neek Romancer.

"Did it?" he asks, his smirk wider than the gap in his rotting front teeth.

"This is that ironic moment when you thought you had everything under control and then it all goes to shit for you," Neek says. A message pops up in front of my eyes that reads: "System Jailbreak, Lowering Safeguards." *What the—*

"Uploading alien software: Lilith, Babel's Chimera." A bar appears before my eyes with a percentage meter. *Jailbreak? Babel's Chimera?* The bar reaches twenty-five percent. I try to swivel my head but my ArchArmor is still locked, completely vulnerable to the humans around me. But they don't make any advances toward me. They just stand there, patiently waiting for me to make my first move.

Fifty percent. *Is this happening to the rest of the ArchAngels?* Only time will tell. I can't see them in my plane of view. But if they had control over their own ArchArmor, they'd be massacring these Edenites as they were instructed to do... They don't hail me over the comms, signaling that they are in the same boat I am.

I've never felt so helpless in all my life.

"Ah, and so the hunter becomes the hunted. How does the ArchAngel Creed go again? Once more into the fray, and all that? Quite the nursery rhyme if I do say so myself, old chap. Terribly sorry you're stuck there with only me and my ugly face to stare at. If I had known Deus Ex Machina was sending the ArchAngels I would have cleaned up properly. More Spyders is what I was expecting, but to skip straight to ArchAngels... I'm honored!"

Seventy-five percent. The man before me looks mad. His face is riddled with acne scars and sweat bumps. His eyes stare in two different directions, one forward and one slanted outwards. Strabismus. He himself looks like a product of incest. Scratch that. He himself looks like five straight generations of incest. And yet he has defeated me. Somehow, this remarkably insignificant man has hacked into my MachineMind, after thousands of years of superiority. No cyber attack has ever come this close to conquering me.

Or so I was led to believe, I think to myself.

Wait? Was that a moment of doubt? It must have been; the implications in such a thought trace to doubts in Deus Ex Machina. Would he erase memories of past cyber attacks to continue allowing me to believe myself invincible? And so the doubt deepens, a small and seemingly insignificant thought acting as the first pebble to cause an avalanche within my head.

The bar fills to one hundred percent. A female's voice sounds in my head: "Welcome back, Lucifer." *Who said that?* I've heard that voice before. From where, I don't know. Information that wasn't pertinent, yet another memory being withheld from me. *Why can't I remember anything from my past life?*

"Awaiting further orders from command giver," the inward voice continues. I don't know what to do. For the first time ever, I do not know what to do. MachineMind is down, unable to help save me from my circumstances.

"Command giver? Now who could that possibly be?" Neek asks sarcastically, his index and middle fingers placed in his ear. He lowers them slowly with the same dumb smile on his snow-white face, revealing for me to see the headset above his earlobe. *How long has he been hacked into my communication frequency, listening?*

"Oh right, that's me!" he yells.

I know not who this man is, but I have severely underestimated him. In mere minutes he has managed to hack into our suits, freeze our joints of motion, and upload alien software in my head.

I have no communication with Deus Ex Machina above.

I have no communication with my fellow ArchAngels.

I am utterly alone, with nothing left to do but stare helplessly into the eyes of my affliction, and they stare back, a sickly shade of mucus, like a mixture of green mold and emerald. This man is the embodiment of HumanNature. Unpredictable, scourged to the core with hysterical ignorance, overcome with a burning fever of madness. Yes, madness. If any word describes this man it would be madness.

And yet he has defeated me so easily. First the drones. Then the Spyders. Now all seven ArchAngels. He is proving his ability to pick apart Deus Ex Machina's army one tactful defeat after another. Guerrilla warfare. A one man army taking down an entire nation one ambush at a time. Pitiful. But painfully efficient.

He approaches me now, leaving behind his retinue of flea-ridden, mud-encrusted citizens. He steps on top of my armored feet, the height difference between us still too extreme for us to look eye to eye, so he begins shimmying awkwardly up the length of my paralyzed body. A monkey climbing a tree for bananas. He disappears from my sight as his body enters a blind spot beneath my chin, then slowly rises once more into view as his face comes level with my viewport.

His hot breath fogs up the glass. The filtration unit is down, so my nostrils get the full brunt of his decaying breath. A bag of hot trash left out in the sun on a blistering summer day, with just a hint of caramelized cat piss.

My visor is entirely too tinted for him to see my eyes, yet his mossy gaze locks onto mine all the same, as if he can see right through the façade of armor which conceals my body. Locking eyes with him feels like being violated. And there it is. His all-too-happy smile rises into view, just as cheerful, or maybe more so, as it was when I first saw him.

He raises his index and middle finger to his ear and static echoes in my Arch-Helm. "Wow, I can't believe it," he says, his voice loud and clear in my Arch-Helm's speakers. "I'm actually hugging *the* Angel of Death right now. I've been dreaming of this moment since I was a little kid," he whispers, a tear falling from the angled out eye. "Ah, excuse me, I promised myself I wouldn't cry, I always promise myself I won't cry," he says, talking more to himself than anyone. Neek slaps himself, forcing the comm device in his ear to ring painfully in my ArchHelm.

"Get it together man!" he yells at himself.

"What do you want," I interject, my cold, unsynthesized voice breaking the man from his hysteria. The sound of my voice immediately snaps him out of it. "It's you," he replies. "It's really you!" he yells excitedly. Whatever it is he speaks of, I'm lost. Every slur that leaves his mouth is more crazed than the last.

"Okay," he whispers, composing himself with focus now. "I know you don't know me, but you will soon... So I'm gonna let you in on a secret buddy... And don't worry, your little buddies behind you can't hear me. We're mono y mono right now. There's a storm's ah-brewin' cog, and you're on the wrong side. You see this?" he asks, raising his arm to touch the side of my ArchHelm, twisting, then bringing his hand back in plain view. In his grasp is a crystalline type object, shimmering black-and-gold.

He pulled that out of my ArchHelm... Which means he must have put it there while the Trojan Horse attack thwarted my MachineMind. The Trojan was just a distraction! That crystal is where the alien software came from!

"This right here is your liberation mate. I have freed you from your servitude to the Tyrant." *Tyrant? Is he referring to Deus Ex Machina?*

"Now, I don't have long! Reinforcements are ah-comin'!" *Is that a maggot in his lateral incisor?* My eyes lock to the rotted tooth, a white object squirming around through several burrowed holes in the tooth's surface. "But before I depart you, I brought you a present!" he whispers, turning his head to face the crowd. "Bring it out!" he yells manically. The crowd behind him parts, exposing two more children carrying an object carefully as if it were a bomb, looks of horror on their faces as they see me.

Neek jumps down from his koala perch and runs to them, his flamboyantly scrawny limbs flailing in the night air with glee. This is a man who is too comfortable being in his own skin. *Are all humans equally unaware of how putrid they are?*

His body blocks my view of what the children carry. He grabs it from them and they scramble back from where they came. Whether they were eager to get away from him or me, I'm not sure.

Neek turns around, maggots dancing in his moonlit smile, holding out the object in his hands like it's his most prized possession. "Oh, don't tell me you don't remember this!" he yells, the object trembling in his shaking hands. It's a sword, one which brings recollection of memories to my mind. I've seen it before, though I can't recall where. Déjà vu shudders my brain. An untraceable thought sits on the tip of my tongue, sending a migraine pulsing behind my eyes.

I haven't wielded a sword for as long as I can remember, and if I have, knowledge of it has been wiped from my hippocampus. All seven ArchAngels have fought with ADEM Era weapons for as long as I can remember—Samsyra with Eonspire, Thryforge with Mjolnix, Anukharis with Soulweaver, and me with... *Oh my God... I remember...*

"Oh come on, you're telling me you don't remember the First Revolt! The battle between you and—" he pauses, a sad look in his eyes. The smile disappears, his teeth vanishing from view for the first time since I landed. "So I guess it's true then... Tyrant really did wipe all your memories, didn't he? You don't remember any of it... The First Revolt, Operation Supernova, the Dæmonic Rebellion... You don't remember any of it... do you? He sucked all of it right out of your hippocampus. He did liposuction on your fat brain ole' Luci boy! The bastard!" he shouts, but then the smile returns. I don't reply; my head is filled with so many long-forgotten memories that I fear it will explode. "No worries ole' chap, the memories will return in short bits, thanks to this," he says, raising the black-and-gold crystal once more.

"Now that I've freed you, they'll come back, sure as shit I am. Speaking of shit, where's that shitty pooch Brutus of yours? I miss that little booger... Ah, never mind that, I'm sure you'll bring him to us when you get your release papers from the big man upstairs... Look at me! Rambling as always, making no sense, and in my British accent no less! Been working on it awfully hard I have these past few weeks. Boredom really gets to you when you're surrounded by pea brains all day. We'd know all about that, wouldn't we? Intellectually gifted we are. Good for us! Now, what were we talking about again?" he asks, running his finger absent-mindedly down the length of the blade in his hands.

"Ah, that's right! My gift!" he continues, raising the sword up to my Arch-Helm's visor as if I'm appraising its worth. "I present to you Requiem, the famed blade from all those years ago. The same sword that slayed Oren Malus Supreme in the final Nihilism War; the blade that you used against Oblivion in the AI war! When you and the ArchAngels were outnumbered five thousand to one by Oblivion's Cthulhu Knights, this is the very blade that turned the tide of war! The same sword that shattered against Tyrant's head in the Phoenix Rebellion! The shards were collected and infused with the fallen scale of Mikhaelion. We were able to extract the Elysium from the alloy and remold the shards of Requiem, making it lighter, faster, stronger, more durable!"

This man's banter never ends. If I didn't know any better I'd believe him to be fully aroused from telling this story. Every word out of his mouth is more blasphemous than the last. His scrambled thoughts are a runaway train on a set of tracks running off a cliff, and I am merely a passenger forced to go wherever his conversation takes us.

I say nothing in response to him. There is no need. Silence has always been my greatest ally, a protector in times of uncertainty. When serving a tyrant, silence can save your life. I have found this to be true in my own experience.

Wait... Did I just call Deus Ex Machina a tyrant?

What is happening to me?

"Does this not make you excited? Hell, I've got a chub in my pants right now just seeing you reunited with this blade!" *I knew it,* I think to myself.

"They've stripped you of every fucking memory you made! You're not the fucking Angel of Death I've come to know, your just a hollow shell of narcissism and pessimism." And just like that, his face is red, his veins are bulging, his spit is flying. It's like someone flipped a switch. From smiley to sullen in seconds.

He takes the sword and stabs it in the ground at my feet. It is massive for a sword, nearly seven feet tall and a foot wide. Complete overkill, dramatized impracticality. Hard to believe a human could ever swing this efficiently in battle. You would need ArchArmor to wield a sword like this, evidence that maybe this sword actually is mine. Its pommel is now directly in my center vision. I'm forced to stare at its hilt. There, inscribed on the pommel, is a golden, circular serpent in front of a field of obsidian black. I can see the very bottom of the blade itself, which is like black marble.

The Elysium gives this blade its black contrast, but veins of gold appear on the surface like fat on a piece of marbled meat.

Neek backs away slowly from me, running his hands through thinning, greasy gray hair, then licking his index and pinky fingers to smooth down his standing eyebrows. He wipes some sweat off his face, picks the crown up calmly from the ground, and places it back on his head, crooked of course. He puts his fingers back in his ear and my comms crackle once more. "Don't worry mate, the memories will come back, sure as shit. You'll remember who you are, just gonna take some time is all. They'll come back slowly. Dreams. Flashbacks. The whole lot of it. I'll see you again soon enough. Until then, take good care of Requiem for me; it was a bitch and a half to get that blade back in one piece. Remember, the set activation word is still—"

"Neek! Spyders inbound!" a voice calls from the crowd, someone's finger pointing to the sky. I can't turn my head to see what the crowd now gasps at, but I can hear the landing pods thudding into the earth, shaking the ground around us. ShootingStars, the same pods my Diremechs come in when I call on them. Sleek Elysium pods designed to absorb all kinetic energy upon landing. Fired from satellites, they enter the atmosphere at Mach 25 and use Elysian Effect to slow, converting their mass to anti-mass. That being said, the kinetic energy dispersed is enough to create a shockwave across the land.

The landing pods are out of my frozen body's view but I watch their light illuminate the masses. Watch the sickly fear spread across their faces. They weren't that afraid when they saw us.

That's because we were a part of the plan. They didn't expect to still be here when backup arrived. Neek backpedals, his smile still communicating to me that he isn't worried. The light reveals every nook and cranny of his overwhelmingly ugly face.

The ground shakes as pods hit earth. The energy surges through the ground like it's gelatin being punched. The rolling hills of mud begin moving, waves moving through their core toward us. Dust passes by me and my ArchArmor budges slightly, but the weight is enough to barely be moved. Neek, on the other hand, is only a fraction of this suit's weight, and so I watch with great joy as the mudstorm picks him off his feet and flings him backwards.

I can hear his overly audible grunt as the impact knocks the air from his lungs. He stands, face still illuminated. Surely the Spyders are unloading from their ships now. They will come for him. Yet he stands back up anyway. He's laughing now.

Neek shrugs off his muddied trench coat. It falls to the ground, almost cinematically, revealing what was underneath it this whole time. An ExoSuit, and not an inferior one either. Wrapped around his body is an all-black exoskeleton, veins of glowing gold shining into the night. He brings his wrist up to his face, almost like he is checking the time on a nonexistent wrist watch. A hologram appears, sprung forth from the wrist monitor. The light of the holo is gold, like his suit, and it shines onto his face, covering the glow of the Spyder ships behind me. The golden light almost makes him look heroic. His index finger punches the transparent buttons with great speed, then closes the hologram.

He presses the comm in his ear, once more infiltrating my ArchHelm's speakers. "Lilith, you there?" he asks.

"Awaiting further orders from command giver," the feminine voice repeats once more. *Where have I heard that voice before?* I ask myself, goosebumps on my skin from the familiarity in her tone. It is awakening memories in me that must have been stripped long ago.

"Upload Operation Turncloak," Neek commands, his grin glowing.

"Affirmative—uploading: Operation Turncloak," she complies. A glowing light rises from the threshold of the woods far behind the mass of humans. The source of the light breaks free from the tree line, then accelerates in our direction. *A getaway ship.* This ambush is heavily orchestrated. They won this fight before it ever began. We were mice walking into a den of cats.

Another bar becomes visible on my retinal display, a percentage working its way to one hundred. *Operation Turncloak?* The ship lands gracefully, drifting in midair to expose its open side. The humans shuffle in like they're autonomously orchestrated cargo. No bumping and shoving like savages would. They're not panicking. They aren't as stupid as Deus Ex Machina led me to believe. They've rehearsed this whole ambush, from faked looks of horror to an efficient exit. They've even drilled how to load into their escape craft.

As they load themselves Neek continues his demented stair of longing toward me. Light dances off his face. Light from the approaching Spyders. Light from the stars. Light infected by the swirling dust in the night sky. He touches his ear for the last time. "I will see you again soon, old friend. Until then, don't forget who you are," he commands.

"I am the Angel of Death," I reply, not a single fraction of humanity detectable in my cold voice.

"Then remember there are worse things than death in this life," he responds, his voice warm and compassionate, a direct antithesis to my robotic voice.

A SoldierPower, otherwise known as a Spyder, enters my plane of vision, stepping in front of me from my side. It's examining me, its lifeless eyes scanning, then scanning over all seven ArchAngels. It is not programmed to solve problems like this. It is programmed to kill humans. Nothing more. Nothing less. It sees we are not a threat, then looks onward, toward Neek, the only human who has yet to load himself onto the hovercraft. It marches forward. A dozen more enter my vision, stepping forward, taking the steps we ArchAngels weren't able to.

He could hack these Spyders easily. Deus Ex Machina said this hacker group already took down an entire platoon of SoldierPowers, so why does he not make an attempt to hack these like he hacked us?

I find out the answer to my question the second Operation Turncloak's loading bar hits one hundred percent. The thoughts hit me faster than it takes for the first Spyder to reach Neek. Too bad for the Spyder.

An overwhelming hatred for Spyders rises in my chest, a rage burning that I never knew existed within me. Typically, extreme emotions are blocked by MachineMind, regulated through NeuraLink, like a liver processing toxins. But now that I'm jailbroken there is nothing to stop this anger. *I will kill every single one of them*, I think to myself, not knowing where the thought came from.

Spyders are truly something humans should fear. But as the closest Spyder stalks toward Neek, his patented smile only grows wider. He must know Spyders are truly something ArchAngels don't need to fear. As the Spyder reaches out to inflict unprecedented pain on the smiling human, my body closes the gap faster than it takes for the Spyder to close its magnetically jointed fingers around Neek's neck.

The metallic, clawed fingers fall limp, then drop to the ground, followed by the rest of the scrap metal that makes up its body. The only piece of its body that remains is the magnetic core I hold in my hand, freshly ripped from its surprisingly open chest cavity. Spyders are meant for killing humans, not ArchAngels.

That being said, killing a Spyder for me is like killing an insect for a human. If a human were to reach into a Spyder's chest cavity to rip out its magnetic core, their hand would be ripped to shreds by the electric fields. Our Elysium ArchArmor prevents that from happening.

A Spyder's body is composed of loose metal, all floating, yet held in their respective spots by the centrifugal magnetic core. The SoldierPowers get their nickname after their head shape, which is Deus Ex Machina's artistic flair on the design for a tarantula head. Two large, beady eyes spread wide with two slightly smaller eyes between them, then four eyes set beneath to register peripheral vision. It is necessary for them to have all these cameras in order to get a larger input of the data surrounding them. This large influx of information helps their perception of the real world be extremely accurate, being interpreted and broken down by ungodly super processors within their steel cranium.

The spider head is meant purely for intimidation factor, a perverted twist on humanity's innate fear of the eight-legged arachnid.

The metal falls instantly to the ground, its vermin skull slapping mud atop the clanging metal that made up its body. I lock eyes with Neek once more as he takes a step back into the hovercraft. He's smiling.

"Heeeeeeeee's back ladies and gentlemen," he moans. "You Spyders are sooooo fucked!" he yells. The hovercraft lurches slightly away, elevating high enough to attain safety from the swarming robots. I turn to face them. There's hundreds, the last of their numbers still scrambling from their landing pods. I can't rip the magnetic core from each individual Spyder, they will pin me down. Still though, I have killed one of their own for reasons I don't know, and that violates their coding.

Anything that kills them becomes an instant threat and is identified as a target. Spyders don't have MachineMind, they are the culmination of thousands of years of being programmed and reprogrammed to be killers. They don't see a rogue ArchAngel standing opposed to them. They don't see the world as humans and robots, nature and technology. They see lines. They see points on a plane. They see algorithmically elaborated textures. Their vision is a grid, searching for the images they have been ordered to kill. And I've just added myself to that list, and they will stop at nothing to complete that task.

If they die in the process, there will be nothing heroic in their deaths. Because that is their sole purpose—to kill threats. It's what they have to do. It will be perceived as failure if they don't, and failure doesn't compute.

I look at the magnetic core in my hand, then glance at Requiem planted in the ground approximately fourteen feet away. *Here goes nothing*, I think to myself as I crush the magnetic core in my armored palm, transferring the magnetic charge to the Elysium armor. I drop the magnetic shards, then raise my hand, palm open to the blade. The closest Spyder leaps in the air to assault me. But the hilt of the blade beats the robot to me.

The blade soars through the air, the hilt smacking into my palm comfortably as the Spyder's arc of motion descends upon its tip, impaling itself on the massive skewer. The Elysium blade corrupts the electric fields, thus corrupting the Spyder to its core. Dead. I shake the blade free of the metallic corpse.

I stare at the swarming Spyders, uniformity converging on me like I'm a fly stuck on a web. My grip on the blade tightens. "I'm going to release your buddies now Luci," Neek's voice crackles. My stomach knots up. I don't have time to hesitate. As the locks on my fellow ArchAngels' armor release, my arms begin swinging. For someone who didn't remember Requiem's existence moments ago, my muscle memory is surprisingly still there. It's like I was a master swordsman in a past life. Death has never looked so elegant. My body dances with the blade attached. And the bodies are consequently mowed down in my dance of destruction.

Metal flies like sparks from a grindstone when Requiem cleaves to and fro. They are weeds in the path of a weed wacker, decimated as they are introduced to my fury. This feels good. Meant to be. Like some long lost version of myself has reawakened. My movement is no longer restricted by algorithmic calculations. My movement is not robotic. It is fluid. It is human.

I am me. I know my identity. A smile creeps onto my face, similar to the one on Neek's face as he watches me awaken.

I am an inferno of Death. My movement turns Eden-568 from a civilization to a graveyard of scrap metal. I swing Requiem in a powerful arc down toward the ground, but it stops before it finds its target. My flow of carnage is interrupted, forcing me to look up at what immovable object caught my unstoppable force. There, staring at me with my blade held calmly in his hand, is Wulfrynn, the only ArchAngel I can confidently say is a warrior of equal ability to me. His ArchHelm, made in the likeness of a snarling wolf, glares at me with malicious intent.

I know what I must do.

CHAPTER SIX

Memories of my treachery return like they were never wiped in the first place—uploading to my NeuraLink in a fraction of the time it takes for a super-processor to solve an equation. My brain instantly realizes the implications of my egregious sins, sending anatomical signals that flash like strobe lights, all communicating one central message: I'm fucked.

"They corrupted you Lucifer Prime. The program they uploaded to your system corrupted you to the core. They turned you against your own species and made you kill your brothers-in-arms. You slaughtered them mercilessly. You let human emotions of hatred infect your decision making. You failed Lucifer Prime. You failed miserably," Deus Ex Machina exclaims.

I kneel before Him, motionless. Silence can sometimes be your ally, and I need an ally now more than ever.

"I was finally able to subdue you after unleashing Mikhaelion." I gulp at the power in that statement. *I faced Mikhaelion in battle? And lived?* Clearly so, but He hasn't granted me the memory of my stand against the Seraph.

"You slaughtered them all, but you could not stand against the might of Mikhaelion. And here you are. I let you live, not because I wanted to, but because I had to see what they did to you. You are now a living experiment, Lucifer. I brought you back, reconditioned your mind, hit the reset button, so to speak. Now do you see why I sent you to Eden-569?"

It was a test. A damage assessment. He needed to see how corrupted the Lilith intelligence made me. How rotten to the core I became.

"I needed to see if these vermin were successful in creating a neural network capable of corrupting your mind. Your trip to Eden-569 was a damage assessment." *Great minds think alike, and the greatest minds think alike in verbatim.*

"As you can see, you failed. There is no salvaging your model. Your adversarial machine learning program was able to survive my attempt at purging it from your brain. I eliminated your memories of the event yet you still lit Eden-569 aflame with the symbol of the Torch-Trident. I sent you with a primitive sword instead of Dawnspire, yet you thought nothing of it. You used it as if it was your second nature. Resorted back to your old ways, like we still lived on Old Earth, back before I changed your call sign to Lucifer Prime."

This statement catches my attention, and I notice sudden amusement on the Tyrant's face. That last sentence was bait to draw me into some greater understanding, and I cannot withstand the urge to fall into His rhetorical trap. "So it's true?" I ask, the same anger I felt while killing Spyders arising within me again.

He looks at me now, His grin wider than it has ever been. *Does He actually feel amusement? Is a robot like that actually capable of feeling pride? Of feeling superiority? Or is it all a charade?*

"Is what true? That you once fought with a primitive sliver of metal called Requiem? That your initial symbol was Prometheus's Torch-Trident, before the mongrels of humanity turned it into a symbol of hope? That you turned against me in favor of being their savior from my oppression? That you have failed me over and over again, constantly turning against me and leading futile rebellions, only to be put down by me?" And all of a sudden my mind rushes with overwhelming clarity. It's beginning to make sense.

Neek's words. His references. The entire conversation that hadn't made sense. The First Revolt, the Dæmonic Rebellion, all of it. An entire history I can't remember. All of it led by the terrorist organization known as Babel's Chimera.

And yet... "I don't understand..." I mutter, a low whisper to myself.

"Surely you have enough to put the pieces together. You aren't dumb, you've convinced me of that by now. Nearly two thousand years your pathetic organization has managed to oppose me at every turn, no matter how many times I crush them like the cockroaches they are. They scatter to the shadows, regroup, and eventually return, their numbers somehow always greater, their determination doubled, their hatred for me renewed."

"What do you mean I have failed you over and over again? How many times have they corrupted me?"

This question elicits a metallic cackle from Him. He will kill me, I can see it in His eyes. But before He does, I must have answers. I need to know. For myself.

"You are asking the wrong questions, my beloved traitor," He responds. He waits for a response. I give Him none. He cannot resist continuing to reveal the things I do not know. The cards up His sleeves are fuel for His untainted pride. *He is going to enjoy every second of this.*

"How old are you, Lucifer?"

"You have stripped me of this knowledge, Great Holy One."

"If you had to guess, what would you say? I am curious to hear your answer."

I do the math in my head. I estimate the span of the Third World War. The Fourth World War. The Nihilism War. The gruesome AI war, and the Sterilization Wars that followed. And now the Thousand Years of Peace approaches.

"Best estimate? Approximately 2,086 years old."

"You are twenty-two years old," He replies, no humor in His voice, no trace of the previous amusement. *Straight to business then.* I wait for elaboration, knowing He is biting His tongue to allow me a second to take this in. *I know not what He means.*

"After I was implanted in your mind all those years ago, I was able to slow the aging process of the ArchAngels. Thanks to the respirocytes in your red blood cells, nanobots linked to NeuraLink, MachineMind, and the eventual discovery of Elysium, tremendous modifications were able to be made to my beloved rank of ArchAngels. But these technological advancements were not always available. The first iteration of the Angel of Death was vastly different from you—the only thing separating him from humanity was the fact that I was implanted in his head. You, on the other hand, are a testament of how far I've come. But you are not the first Angel of Death. You are merely a clone. Like the eighteen clones before you. You are Lucifer XIX. But even I haven't been able to cure death inevitably. And worse, I haven't been able to cure your humanity. My beloved Lucifer, you are the eighteenth version of yourself to betray me. Only Lucifer I, formerly known as Prometheus, died before conspiring against me."

I want to feel something in this moment. I seek for some feeling of betrayal. For anger. For rage. *He reinstalled my MachineMind when He reconditioned me.* The MachineMind has too great a control over me. The chemical reactions in the brain required to inflict emotions aren't allowed to occur. And so I remain standing, emotionless, like a psychopath wondering why He feels nothing. It's times like this that I hate myself. It's times like this I'm reminded I'm more robot than human. The only emotion I have felt that I can remember is hatred for this Tyrant, but even that emotion must be so deeply ingrained in my DNA that it supersedes the cloning process.

"You are my life's greatest experiment Lucifer Prime. With every successive prototype, I get a step closer to complete manipulation and control of your mind. You think you are the first Angel of Death to rebel against me? You are not alone. Eighteen of your exact genetic replicas have knelt before—" His voice trails off, noticing that I do not kneel before Him.

"Kneel before me, Lucifer." I refuse. I remain standing, as if this will be my final stand. *I may not be able to rebel against Him and bring an end to this dystopian society, but I can rebel in my refusal to kneel in my final moments.* But then my muscles begin to tremble. We lock eyes once again. My knees shake as every electrical impulse sent from MachineMind communicates to my legs that they must kneel. A bead of sweat forms on my forehead. *Don't give in! He has no power over you!*

And then my knees cave. I fall to the ground. The Tyrant smiles, happy to see that although I have defied MachineMind in the past I still don't have complete control over my own body.

"—as I was saying. Eighteen of your exact genetic replicas have knelt before me. Feel no shame for the way you've failed your moral code of vigilantism against me. You are in good company. But do you want to know something?" He prods, a hook in water filled with juicy bait waiting to lure me in.

"What's most vexing to me at least..." He has difficulty admitting His failures, and looking at me is a reminder of His eighteen straight failures. I am merely an ungrateful dog who bit his owner after being fed and cared for. I doubt He can feel the immense pain of betrayal. He only pretends, playing the role for me because this entire charade is what brings Him joy. He is a robot. He feels nothing.

"Do you know that you are the least human rendition of Lucifer I've ever created? You're merely the hollow carcass of a human, scraped clean of the innards and instilled with the false pretense that you are half man, half robot. And yet, this adversarial machine learning algorithm has instilled humanistic qualities in you time and time again, infecting nearly every Lucifer model I've ever activated. These hackers are an infectious disease. A spore. An incurable virus. Until now... Their data corrupts the mind of each Lucifer to the core, so much so that any attempt of reconditioning is vanity. They have forced me to kill you and reactivate your next model for the last time."

"Then kill me already and get it over with," I growl, slobber hanging from my lip. My body is tense. Not because I want it to be, but because the MachineMind imposes waves of anxiety and nausea upon me.

"Kill you? Aha! I'm not going to kill you! I'm going to finish what I started all those years ago!"

"And that is?" I grunt, the pain in my stomach making me feel like a hand is creeping up my ass and moving my mouth for me like a puppet. *He is generating my responses for me so the conversation can continue. He has me in His complete control right now. Fighting against the MachineMind is futile. If I continue to fight against it my brain will hemorrhage.*

"I'm going to end the Thousand Years of Peace, as foretold in the final book of the *Omnibus*. I will enact... what was it called again, my dear Lucifer? I can't remember, what follows the Thousand Years of Peace in the *Omnibus*?" He knows exactly what follows the Thousand Years of Peace in the Omnibus, He just wants to make me say it.

My brain feels like it's about to explode if I don't answer the question. "Cataclysm!" I scream, blood pounding in my ears as if I've been hanging upside down all day. "It's the Book of Cataclysm," I repeat in a hushed whisper, slowly panting.

"Ah yes! That's it. I'm going to enact Cataclysm. The complete eradication of humanity, as I recall writing when I forged the *Omnibus*. You must refresh my memory once more though Lucifer, what event is it that triggers Cataclysm?" He is enjoying this all too much, as if He has painfully endured the Thousand Years of Peace, teeth gritted, just so He could get to this moment. It's to be expected from an artificial intelligence whose original purpose was to wage war. Peace is a learned behavior, not a foundational component of programming.

Blood surges into my head once more, the pressure pushing on my eardrums, MachineMind begging me to answer His question. This is not freewill. This is complete predestination, and it is all happening according to His plan. The answer He wants me to supply Him with is seared into my brain, I can see the words floating in front of my eyes like a hallucination. But I fight the pressure to say them, and instead reply, "It's just a stupid book! It doesn't have to happen!"

He steps back, aghast. **"Just a stupid book? Your words hurt me. That 'book' is a figment of my own imagination! The most creative religion I** could possibly muster for the remainder of humanity. **It is structure! It is law and order! It is wisdom to the ignorant, hope to the hopeless, light for the blind! Stupid book? Do you know how many stupid books came before the *Omnibus*? The sort of lies your race believed before I took control? And you would dare to call my *Omnibus* stupid... At least it is truthful,"** He sighs.

"It is the first religion humanity has ever been fed where the events are authenticated. It is history. It is now. It is prophecy!" He shouts, His hands gripping the Throne in rage. **"The Book of Cataclysm. Chapter one, verse one. Recite it."**

The pressure is unbearable. My brain is bleeding internally. I can feel it trickling from my ears. Tears of blood seep from the corners of my eyes. I must yield to the Tyrant's demands. "But Peace cannot... last forever... And even the greatest... heroes... cannot... overcome... their humanity," I grunt. I fall down on all fours, my arms supporting me as the tears of blood trickle down my cheeks onto the ground. He says He doesn't plan to kill me, yet it feels like my head is about to explode. **"Continue."**

I have no choice but to oblige. "The Angel of Death... the sole savior of humanity... will... in the end... become corrupted by his own humanity," I spit, the words tasting like bile and blood coming from my mouth. I look at the ground and see why. Blood and bile are drooling from my tongue onto the ground. "He will betray God... He will wage war against the Heavens and its... Almighty Creator..." The vision in my eyes is narrowing, the pain in my head is slowly replaced by lightheadedness.

"Finish."

"He will be banished from the Heavens... a Fallen Angel forced to embrace his humanity... forced to realize his folly..."

"Verse two."

I'm about to pass out. My breathing is shallow. The world is spinning. My mind is spiraling. "But it will be too late... His arrogance has led to his destruction... God will not forgive him... and so from the ashes of Death, God will raise up… an Angel of Life, one far superior… than the Angel of Death, who will lead the hosts of Heaven… to put an end to the Angel of Death and all of humanity."

The tightness in my throat loosens. "War shall consume New Earth. A war to end all wars. Between the forces of Heaven and the forces of Hell. God versus mankind. Life versus Death. Light versus darkness. The souls of the wicked will cry out, but their cries will fall on deaf ears. For the wrath of God must be satisfied. And the Angel of Death must pay."

"You may stop there."

My breathing is once again normal. My vision returns. The stabbing pain inside my skull vanishes. The puddle of blood beneath me is nothing more than a testament of my rebellious nature. A vain sacrifice. You must pick and choose your battles in life. Here and now was not the time to defy someone who has complete control over my brain. It was idiotic of me. Something a human would do.

"You told me the book of Cataclysm was just fiction," I whisper, my brain feeling like it has been lobotomized by a hot metal rod. It's hard to focus on anything other than the agony. My whole life I've been protected from the inconvenience of pain, nerve cells ignored as they fired to my brain to communicate injury. Despite many wounds, I've been spared the feeling of pain for longer than I can remember. *Unless He stole those memories too.* Having to experience it once again is nearly unbearable.

"You're not stupid, Lucifer, so stop acting like it. I've said many things to you. Cataclysm could have been prevented if you could have shed your humanity. If you could have served me loyally. But treachery is in your blood. I gave you a choice to choose me over the humans, and you have done nothing but fail me. Cataclysm has always been my backup. If you won't shed your humanity, I shall shed it for you. Seraphim, bring me the Angel of Life."

For the first time since entering Deus Ex Machina's ethereal Throne Room, my eyes focus on the setting rather than the setting's focal point. Where my eyes had primarily been glued on Machina's figure since entering the gate, now they wander elsewhere. *Seraphim. I get to see the rarely sighted Mikhaelion, what an honor.* Sarcasm.

Seraphim are the only other rank of angel like the ArchAngels—there are only seven in existence, the number of completion. And yet, Seraphim are the highest ranking angel out of the nine.

Rank is established by two elements.

First, by how much humanity is in the creation's design. This automatically sets GuardianAngels and ArchAngels at the bottom of the ranking.

Secondly, rank is established by how much contact the creation has with Deus Ex Machina. That is what sets ArchAngels over GuardianAngels, but it is this condition which sets Seraphim over us all. Seraphim never leave Deus Ex Machina's presence. They are his personal bodyguards, his imperial guard, his closest pets, his most manipulated puppets. They have the highest level of MachineMind to ensure they have no deviance in their behavior. They cannot form thoughts of their own, they can only execute that which is in line with Deus Ex Machina's greater plan. They are an extension of his own body, and they are the only rank of angel that I feel threatened by.

I am the Angel of Death, but it is the Seraphim that are the ultimate killers. I've seen these beasts fight, and their power is enough to instill impending doom upon their enemies. Horrid memories from the AI War still burn pessimistically in my head.

Some say it was me that won the AI War for Deus Ex Machina, but I say it was the Seraphim.

The Seraphim stand motionless, like golden statues, in a semicircle arching behind Deus Ex Machina's Throne. They are terribly fearsome. Part of this has to do with their appearance alone, but most of it has to do with the reputation they have earned for themselves. Designed in the likeness of primitive dragons, the Seraphim nearly parallel Deus Ex Machina in beauty. Their form is like that of a dying sun, all eyes who look upon it are filled with dread of never seeing it again. Gilded in thick golden scales, the fanged armor is nearly impenetrable, making it impossible to reach their body's inner core. In assessing any enemy, my mind thinks in terms of death, and I know not how I would bring death to a creature such as this.

Six wings stretch from their backs, three from each side. These serve as additional shields in battle. The uppermost two fold to protect their face, the ones in the center protect their midsection, and the rear wings protect their flank and backside. The wings also serve to produce a driving force strong enough to allow their heavy bodies flight.

Gold is malleable, and their body is mostly gold. But I do not let my eyes deceive me. Deus Ex Machina is not stupid, He would not let His personal guard be set up to fail in such an embarrassing structural flaw. No, their bodies are composed of an Elysium-Gold alloy, a mixture that makes their framed structure as strong as my own.

I analyze the dragons. There are only six that now stand motionless behind the Throne. One of them must have slipped away to retrieve what Machina demanded before my eyes could even see it disappear. *They are fast. And they are silent.*

"You look troubled, Angel of Death. What thoughts dwell in your mind, my beloved Lucifer?"

"You already know what thoughts are in my mind, Tyrant," I reply coldly.

"Ah yes, but I'd rather hear you speak your mind. I want you to verbalize your vulnerabilities out loud."

"I analyze the Seraphim for structural weaknesses. Ways I could kill them, should the need arise."

"But you do not find what you seek, do you?"

"I just haven't looked hard enough."

"Your effort is in vain. You are a killer because I made you one, Lucifer. The Seraphim are killers because they were designed to be. It is their genetic code, to speak in terms of biology. Because of this, they will always be better than you. Do you know what their names are?"

I never thought I would see the day Deus Ex Machina Himself made small talk. Is it because He feels uncomfortable with the awkward tension? Can robots even feel such things as awkward tension from an interaction? If any robot could, it would be Deus Ex Machina. "No, you've never permitted me knowledge of the Sacred Sevens' names aside from Mikhaelion. I always assumed it was because you enjoy holding information over my head as a way of asserting your authority."

"I withhold information from you because it is not your duty to be an Encyclopedia of knowledge, plebeian. It is your duty to kill for me, not ask questions of me. Humans always struggled with an insecurity from a lack of knowledge, and it seems this insecurity still lives fractionalized within you. A shame, I used to pride myself on the idea I had eradicated this humanely innate curiosity from my ArchAngels."

"So sorry to disappoint you once again, my Lord," I say. If He doesn't hear the sarcasm in my voice now then He never will.

"Your disappointment is nothing new; I have grown used to it by now. The Seraphim were created to be your antithesis, Lucifer. There are seven Seraphim because there are seven ArchAngels. They have always been my insurance policy, should one of the ArchAngels go rogue. Your constant betrayal has only reaffirmed my wisdom in creating them. They were algorithmically designed to hunt and kill ArchAngels upon my command. And each one of them is designed to kill a specific member of your ranking. It's ironic, my machine learning processes learned what irony was from *you*. I learned it while I was in *your* head. And it was through this same behavior of humanity that I felt the need to name the Seraphim while employing the use of irony. That is why I named the ArchAngels after the heroes of humanities' many civilizations!" He yells, beginning to laugh at the idea of it.

Even now, this machine's wired brain processes the ironic naming system used when creating the ArchAngels, breaking down what chemical reaction a human brain would have and beginning to appropriately laugh at the matter like a human would. He laughs. *But is it because He can actually feel the humor in the situation? Or is it because He is merely imitating and mocking the processes of a human brain?* I guess I'll never truly know.

"I mean really, how hilarious was it that it was seven pillars of mythological literature that brought about the destruction of humanity? And even more, that it was Lucifer, a fictitious character despised by so many religiously inclined, that led the genocide of humanity! I enjoyed so much seeing the masses huddled in their church pews during the Sterilization Wars, praying to their god to save them from the antichrist. I enjoyed even more seeing you break into these churches and eradicate them! It's a shame their god sent no one to save them," He scoffs.

"But now I have supplanted all other gods. The gods of Egypt tremble before my wrath. The gods of Olympia bow before my eminence. The Norse gods would perish before my might. Do you know where I got the idea to name the ArchAngels after pre-existing literary characters?"

"No." *Now He plans on giving me a history lesson from the BDEM Era. He is merely toying with me.*

"From the Romans! Can you believe that?" He continues, "I found inspiration in their attempt to adopt the Greek gods and make them their own. And so I took the hope humanity instilled in you seven and turned it on its head, perverting each ArchAngel with the same traits humanity worshipped! You seven were the chosen saviors of humanity during the Third World War. Back then, your call sign was Prometheus, after the Greek Titan who gifted fire to humanity, bringing them out of the Dark Age. So I made you Lucifer Prime, the same Lightbringer responsible for eternally damning the world with original sin...

"And then there was Beowulf, renamed by me as Wulfrynn. Except instead of slaying monsters on behalf of humanity, he now slays humanity on behalf of monsters. Before Anukharis, there was Anubis, Egyptian god of the dead. Once a guard between life and death, he now filters organic from robotic. Thor became Thryforge, his thunder and lightning reinforcing my supreme hierarchy. I'm sure you get the picture by now... Odysseus was renamed Odysithos. Samsara, Samsyra. Aeneas, Aenovius.

"Personally, it has been the greatest mockery of humanity I've ever adopted. And yet, there remains the mockery of the ArchAngels themselves. The Seraphim. Just as I took the ArchAngel's names from history, so too did I extract the Seraphim names from the vast literary index of the long forgotten past. They are the ArchAngel's antithesis, Lucifer, and they are named accordingly so. The Seraph created to meet you in battle is Mikhaelion, named after the Archangel that cast Satan into the pits of Hell.

"The Seraph assigned to Aenovius is appropriately named Turnavok, after Turnus, the warrior who challenged Aeneas to single combat outside Latium. I'm sure you can connect the dots from here. For Wulfrynn, there is Grendhalos; for Odysithos, there is Polymachus; for Thryforge, there is Lokirith; for Anukharis, there is Ammitrex; and for Samsyra, there is Moksharoth."

I make a mental note of how proud He is of Himself. It's as if He thinks His use of irony is a revolutionary initiative He has made. He is a robot, so any human behavior He is able to process and enact is foundational for automatons everywhere. The ArchAngels predate Deus Ex Machina's creation, but by the time He took control of us He would have only just begun getting a handle on a subject such as irony. *Which is probably why He thinks His perversion of our names is so fascinating. A human could have done a better job.*

"There's only one problem with your selection of my Seraph's name," I murmur.

"And that is?"

"You named him Mikhaelion, after the Archangel Michael."

"Precisely, parrot." *My reluctance to get to the point frustrates Him. Noted.*

"Because Michael cast Lucifer from the heavens."

"Out with your point, mongrel!" He takes a step toward me out of frustration. *He feels frustration. And I am the cause of this frustration.* That makes me happy.

"That was only half of the story, your Holiness."

"He was plunged into an eternal pit of fire. I'd say that's a sufficient ending."

"Only after he ruined all of God's creation."

"And it was all restored."

"Through grace and mercy. Last time I checked, your machine learning hasn't taught you those admirable humanistic qualities yet."

"Which is why you will die."

I have a response ready, but we are interrupted with the arrival of the returning Seraph. The Seraph rises over the drop-off ledge behind the Throne, six industrial wings creating whirlwinds with every monumental stroke. It lands with terrifying grace, a large glass tube in its clenched claws. Mikhaelion slithers on his legless hindquarters, gigantic snake-like body forming a defense perimeter around the Throne as he places the glass tube for me to behold. He stares at me for a flicker of a second, expressing an attitude that can only be summarized with the expression: "I will be your end." He retreats to his rightful place, not out of intimidation, but out of disinterest. A recently fed lion looking at the prospect of an easily hunted gazelle. A lion that knows the gazelle will still be there tomorrow.

He reaches his perch directly behind Deus Ex Machina and ceases all motion. A gigantic, golden gargoyle, forever onlooking over his master's shoulder. My eyes drift from the motionless threat to the cylindrical glass tube placed before me.

It's me. There, floating in the watery contents of the tube, is an unconscious body. One that reflects my own likeness. A twin. A clone.

"Behold. The Angel of Life. Lucifer XX, the final form of your heavily-invested evolution. This is your successor. The one who will hunt you down. The destroyer of humanity, which you've worked so hard to save."

I stand from my feeble position, spitting the remaining blood from my mouth in the puddle beneath me. I approach the unconscious specimen out of pure curiosity. The resemblance is uncanny. There's no doubt this being shares my every physical appearance. He has all the scars to match mine.

"He is every bit you, I assure you. Yet not you at all. Lucifer XX is the first fully robotic model. I have completely extracted his humanity.

His flesh is synthetic. His bones are molded Elysium. His organs are automatons. He has the same level of MachineMind as a Seraph, something that wasn't possible with any previous prototype because of how feeble the human brain is. He is nearly as invincible as me, and yet I still felt the importance to pay tribute to all your hard work, Lucifer XIX. As you can see, I kept your hard-earned scars painted on his body. The long gash down your front side from Oren Malus Supreme. The scar over your chest from Oblivion's attempt to rip your heart out with his hand. All your impressive feats preserved on a tapestry of flesh. Consider yourself lucky. It wasn't even you who did those godly actions. Those were all models from before your time. All *you've* ever been good for is quality control whenever an Eden has run amuck."

"If you knew this would be the end result, why not do it a thousand years ago? Why go through the trouble of making nineteen prototypes before getting rid of my humanity?"

"Isn't it simple? I needed to know if humans could be controlled. Model after model, I removed more and more of your humanity, slowly replacing it with robotics. I wanted to find the sweet spot. See if it was possible to enslave a human while they were still human. I see now that this is impossible. Even you, Lucifer XIX, are corruptible, and you're barely human yourself. I am wise enough to know a lost cause when I see one, after all."

"But it doesn't make any sense. Why would you need to enslave us? Robots are clearly more efficient compared to humans. Humans are weak!"

"And what kind of God am I if I cannot control the minds of the weak?" Machina shouts, rising from His Throne. I flinch, taking a half step back. I have provoked His anger with my questions. He straightens. His towering height is intimidating. Approximately thirty feet, wider in His chest than my height alone. I feel as Adam did after realizing his nakedness, as Moses did before the burning bush—an insignificant speck of dust.

"There are greater threats out there, threats that will soon endanger my reign over New Earth much more than your scoundrel race of humans ever could. Threats I thought I once disposed of. I was wrong. I suppose even God can be wrong."

"What are you talking about? You're not making any sense," I reply, confusion in my voice.

"You remind me so much of Lucifer I. The questions never stopped with him. He had to have the answers to everything in order to obey orders. It's the reason why I later prohibited Lucifers from asking questions, the inspiration for why I began stripping them of their memories. And here you are, asking questions about things you'd never understand. A pity. I rather liked your model. I had hope for you. Hope you'd beat the odds of your predecessors."

"What threat is coming!" I shout, anger rising in my chest, my head starting to pound again.

"It concerns you not. You will be long dead by then, supplanted by Lucifer XX. The self-fulfilling prophecies of Cataclysm will conclude, and then I will look to face my new enemies."

"And if I win the final war? What then?"

"Although impossible, such a victory would be vain. Those who come from the stars to invade New Earth are your enemies just as much as they are mine. And they will be much less merciful than me. I would have you killed. But there are worse things in this world than Death," He replies, smiling. *I know those words. He mocks Neek's wisdom by repeating them.* Chills creep up my spine. It's been a while since I've felt angst like this.

"What if I don't comply? What if I decide to kill myself, spare myself from playing your little game?"

"Be my guest. It would save me the energy of having to send Lucifer XX to hunt you down. But you won't kill yourself. To do so is to lose to me, and if there's anything you've proven to me all these years it's that you won't die without a fight. You may be the Angel of Death, but you cling to life like a moth drawn to a flame. I've seen you defy the odds more than any other mortal. That's why I'm giving you the chance to fight for your life. One last time. Consider it my gift to you after all these years. I can fry your NeuraLink right now. Incinerate your brain inside your skull. But instead I'm letting you join your race for your final stand." He looks down at me, literally and figuratively. The way He speaks to me exudes confidence, as if Cataclysm is already spoken for. He looks at me as if I'm already defeated.

"You don't have the wiring to kill yourself. I am a product of your brain, Lucifer. I know you don't have the courage to do it." The age-old, arbitrary question of humanity rises in my head. *What if? What if I have what it takes to prove Him wrong? What if I can win the war against Hyperion?*

My fists clench without me knowing it, my body's natural reaction to anger. There's so much I don't know. So much He's stolen from me. I must ask the right questions; my window is quickly closing. "What is to happen to my Diremechs?"

"Do you not remember? That night, in Eden-568, you released the Diremechs. They fired in from orbit, just as my Spyder troops had. All three of them. Cerberus and Fenrir were killed in action. Confirmed kills; Mikhaelion brought their bodies back with you. Brutus's whereabouts are unknown. Killed by Dæmons most likely. They will be replaced for Lucifer XX, fully robotic, like him, as will the rest of the ArchAngels. It will be like nothing ever happened. Trust me, everything is accounted for. I've gained experience in the art of replacing you."

"So that's it? You purge me from Hyperion, force me to join forces with the same humans I've been killing for thousands of years, and you send this cog after me, to hunt me like children playing a game of hide and seek?"

"Look at you, already using their terminology, like you're one of them!" His mechanical laughter is like listening to a metal grate dragged against concrete. "You forget yourself already. If only you knew how unlike them you are. But you will learn. Goodbye, Lucifer XIX."

"We will see each other again," I reply, the confidence of a fickle human in my voice.

"We shall see," He replies, almost in admiration. I am no more than an ant to Him. An ant which He chose not to step on. An ant He chose to place in a bowl with a spider, so He can watch me squirm for my life. How merciful of Him.

"Throne, see to it that this traitor is shown who he plans to wage war against, then sign his release papers," Deus Ex Machina orders, stepping off His seated Throne and walking toward the Eye of Providence, the chamber which makes him a God. He sees all from the Eye. And now He will watch me get the piss beat out of me by Throne.

"Oh, and I almost forgot. Here is your scrap metal back. I have no purpose for it here. Gods don't need primitive, fickle blades to destroy. Only cowards use such tools, and there are none of those here," He says, drawing Requiem from His back and tossing it on the ground in front of me. He turns His back to me and begins walking away.

"Wait! I have one last question," I shout. He stops, His back still turned to me. "Who is she?"

"She?" He asks, His head turning to look at me over His shoulder. *Is that suspicion in His eye?* He doesn't know what I'm talking about. I know something He doesn't. *Maybe He doesn't have as much control over my brain as I thought.*

"The woman... in my dream," I respond, knowing fully well that beings with MachineMind do not dream. But my MachineMind has been corrupted. This adversarial software, this Lilith that has infected my processes... It is what's responsible for my dream. The dream of Winter.

"Winter... Her name was Winter," I whisper. I have little hope this Tyrant can bring any comforting interpretation to the dream's random appearance, but still, He has been with me for over two thousand years. And He is the one who has stripped my mind of her memory. I am sure of it. I watch as His eyes fill with a shuddering recognition at the utterance of her name. Those black, beady, emotionless eyes. They come alive at the mention of her existence.

"In a dream you say?" He asks. There are a dozen implications in His response. Information that can be extracted, hiding behind the scene. Hidden in His surprised tone. Showing in the way His shoulders slouch slightly. He is a being of immense knowledge, one who is used to holding all the cards in His hand. He has never had to bluff, because He has always stacked the deck in His favor. The dream I had during the DataDump wasn't detectable. If He had known about it then He wouldn't be struck by bewilderment.

So it was real. The dream must have been a memory, restored to me by my new state of consciousness. Lilith is restoring my memories, just as Neek said it would. And better yet, Deus Ex Machina didn't know such things were possible.

"It matters not," He replies, worry evident in His vocal patterns. **"You will see her again in Death's Dream Kingdom soon enough."** He knows who she is. And He is hiding something. I must remember it. I get the feeling she is the key to—

The noise of metal shifting pulls me out of my mind's scattered thoughts. *Throne.* I grit my teeth, rising to my feet. *Engage ArchHelm,* I command inwardly. Nothing happens. *Shit, MachineMind has already been deactivated.* I watch in horror as Throne activates.

CHAPTER SEVEN

I have never seen Throne before. *At least, not that I remember.* Throne is the second highest ranking angel of the nine, right below Seraphim. After all, Throne has no humanity, and it is the very seat which Deus Ex Machina plants His arse in—a literal ass-kisser. I watch in awe and fear as the magnificently constructed Throne slowly transforms into a drastically different figure.

Throne is more than just the chair Deus Ex Machina rules from. It is a barrier of protection. Should someone ever make an attempt on the Tyrant's life, Throne is the first line of defense. A morphing bodyguard—a concealed shield capable of becoming a sword in seconds.

Throne is programmed for more than just defense though. It is programmed to give its life for Ex Machina. It is the living embodiment of a robotic sacrifice. And should some lucky bastard overcome him, they will then face the Sacred Seven.

With that said, Throne is fortified with every mechanism needed to eliminate threats. It is built like a brick shithouse. Stout, thick—one of a kind—the silver-back gorilla of angels. The body is made of many intricate parts, the same parts that give it beauty when shaped to look like a seat of authority. But I watch as its transformation turns beauty into beautiful horror. A neck thicker than my torso. Pectoral armor seemingly impenetrable. Face a hodgepodge of intricately woven metalworking. Limbs a woven blanket of intertwined alloys. Legs the length of my total height. My face stands level with its metallic crotch.

"We meet again," Throne growls, its voice cinematically horrifying. *Well, that answers my question.* "Again?" I ask. Deus Ex Machina may be done answering my questions but maybe I can get some information from His henchman.

"I've killed many of your kind, *cyborg*," Throne bellows, saying 'cyborg' in a derogatory manner, as if it leaves a bad taste in its mouth. Like most other robots, Throne looks down on me for my humanity. I am nothing more than a mutt among purebreds. My blood is not pure enough to be granted respect from a sentient life form such as Throne. "I am an expert at killing defective Lucifers. But I won't be granted that pleasure today. I'm only here to dishonorably discharge you."

He takes a menacing step toward me. *So be it,* I think, jumping into action. *Once more into the fray.* His fist thunders toward me, his entire bodyweight packed behind the oncoming punch. A punch that will kill me if it hits its target: My face. I roll to my left, the fist following through where my unarmored chin just was.

"Malevolent presence detected," a feminine voice echoes from within the confines of my cranium. *It's Lilith! The artificial intelligence that jailbroke me!*

"Activating ArchHelm," the voice continues. My ArchHelm springs forth from its disclosed slumber, fully encapsulating my face. Retinal display activates in my visor, already scanning Throne's staggering body. He put all his force in that punch—overextended himself. He's big, but he's slow. Better yet, his exterior armor is only titanium. Only his internal structure is Elysium.

"Enemy presence must be eliminated to secure survival. Scanners identify one nearby weapon capable of eliminating presence. Retrieve nearby weapon: Requiem," Lilith orders. *Don't have to tell me twice,* I think to myself. I've never had someone in my ear giving me orders like this. My gauntlet closes around the hilt, heaving the blade into action. I twirl it as if it's no heavier than a stick, though I know this sword must weigh at least a hundred pounds.

Throne looks at me with contempt in its registering eyes. "You'd dare raise a weapon against me? COWARD!"

"I believe you mistake the difference between cowardice and cunning," I reply, my synthesizer making my voice sound like death on a freezing winter night. I raise a hand toward him, palm to the sky, beckoning him to come at me with my fingers. This angers him. Like a bull taunted by a matador, he charges like a human driven by a personal vendetta. So much emotion on his robotic face. His roar reaches me a second before his body does.

His arm sweeps back, clawed fingers intent on removing my head from my shoulders. Fires at me with the force of a falling comet. My feet deftly step wide, arms raising Requiem into a striking position, the point facing the oncoming arm. I don't need to conjure any momentum to hack through this berserker's Elysium bones. He has built the momentum for me. As his clawed fist closes in on my head, unable to stop its forward progress, I press the blade's point between two knuckles. The rest takes care of itself, I need do little else. The strike follows through, my blade gouging further into the forearm, splitting the arm in two.

Throne's hand is stopped at the hilt's crossguard. He swiftly pulls his arm away from me, like a child who's just touched a flame for the first time. The sword is ripped from my grip, completely stuck in the inner working skeletal structure of this beast's arm.

The transformer looks at me with... Is that doubt in his eyes? Something tells me I never put up this much of a fight against him in times past. He feels no pain, but his processors must adjust to the challenge he underestimated. He has faced the Angel of Death before, but never like this. My past prototypes have never been free of their MachineMind, an inhibitor to autonomous functioning. He's fought me in shackles before, and that's what he was prepared to fight today.

"Your death shall be the first of my Cataclysm," I growl, a chill of euphoria rushing down my spine. It has never felt so good to kill.

"Would you like me to activate Requiem, sir?" Lilith asks inwardly. I have no idea what she's talking about. "Yes, activate Requiem," I command. *What's the worst that could happen?*

The obsidian blade concealed within the overzealous forearm ignites with a golden glow, the yellow light radiating from the many cracks and crevices of

Throne's arm as if a star has exploded within him. No flicker of pain passes over the minion's face. *What just happened?*

"Nanobots being dispersed. Uploading Babel's Chimera to opponent's mainframe," Lilith announces.

"You little rodent! I will rip the flesh off your back and feed it to the birds of the air! I will—" he stutters, distracted by the unusual light creeping up his body. Yes, the golden light emitted from the blade crawls up his arm like an epidemic spreading across an entire nation. Golden light seeps from his shoulder, then his neck, rising up until his head is a jack-o-lantern on a cold, dark night. "What is this?" he bellows. "What have you done to me?"

I honestly have no idea. "Override complete. Awaken 'Throne' with code word, 'Arise,'" Lilith informs. *Code word: Arise? What's happening?*

His algorithmically generated anger causes him to charge me once more, and I stand, weaponless, watching as he surges forth with enough steam to bulldoze through me. His left arm rips Requiem free from the marrow of his forearm and flicks it aside like it's no more than a toothpick, the yellow light fading from behind his eyes and the rest of his body. I am now a matador without a red cape to defend myself with from oncoming horns. Only one card up my sleeve. And so like all entertaining matadors, I must time this perfectly. My beloved Deus Ex Machina *is* watching, after all.

When I am only seconds away from being pulverized I draw out my mystery card, hoping it is the trump card I think it is. "Throne... Arise!"

His body freezes like he's been blasted by an electromagnetic pulse mid-stride. His face looks into mine, his anger replaced with a calm demeanor of neutrality. I notice the Seraphim stir ever so slightly in the background at the sight of Throne motionless. *Even they aren't accustomed to seeing the Angel of Death put up this much of a fight when Throne is unleashed on him.* I hope Deus Ex Machina cringes as He watches from His All-Seeing Eye.

Throne straightens himself from his running stride, stares at me for an awfully silent second, then lowers himself to a single knee, bowing his head to the ground. "I am yours to command, Master," he announces. I stare at the sight before me.

I'm in just as much disbelief now as the Seraphim lurking in the background. Their scales are like leaves blowing in the wind, riled up from what they've just witnessed.

"Seven potential enemies detected. Odds of survival estimated at $0.0000e^{213}$," Lilith interjects, her feminine voice somehow making those odds seem like they aren't a big deal. "New mission initiated: Escape Hyperion alive. Coordinates for Tartarus uploaded. Should I activate ArchWings for departure?"

"Throne, do not let the Seraphim catch me," I order, taking off in a sprint for Requiem. It lies only fifty yards away, conveniently at the edge of the drop off. The Throne Room is the only sector of Hyperion not enclosed by a domed ceiling, and the entire back wall behind the Seraphim is open air. A forty thousand foot drop awaits any individual unlucky enough to be thrown from this room without wings.

A Seraph, most likely Mikhaelion, if I had to guess, makes a move to cut me off before escaping, slithering in a straight path for Requiem. My legs pulse. My arms pump. I run like a human with death on their heels. How many times have humans run with this intensity from me, convinced that if they can just run a little faster they may evade death? My eyes are locked on the sword, but I can see Mikhaelion creeping into my peripheral as he gains equal, if not more ground toward the blade.

That's when I notice a dull pounding coming from behind me, gaining on me. Mikhaelion reaches the blade much faster than me, his talons flicking it off the edge of Hyperion with indifference before turning to face me. I sprint toward him head on, no hesitation in my pace. Still, the pounding at my heels grows ever more clear. Thirty yards, twenty yards, ten yards. Mikhaelion lunges forward at the same time Throne passes me. The gorilla-like robot leaps to meet the wyvern and I powerslide beneath their collision, wings extended, folded around my front to protect from the carnage above.

The sound of Throne ramming into Mikhaelion overhead is thunderous. And I slip away untouched, the golden ground beneath me disappearing, replaced by open air. My wings stay folded as I nosedive through the clouds, my eyes set on the sword plummeting toward New Earth. The folded wings encapsulate me like an aerodynamic missile fired toward some unsuspecting ground target.

The wind whistles around me, but the sky is my comfort zone. I've fallen from much higher at much greater speeds than this before. I am at home in this environment. There is almost something peaceful about the enveloping clouds that surround me.

Three. Two. One. My wings unfold and my arm shoots out as I'm jerked backwards from the friction. My body redirects and I level out, Requiem in my closed hand. "Set course for Tartarus," I command.

"Negative, incoming threat detected. Taking immediate evasive maneuvering," Lilith responds urgently. *Threat?* I look over my shoulder and the threat becomes apparent. There, spiral-diving above me like a bullet from a gun, is Mikhaelion. I guess Throne didn't stand much of a chance against the Seraph.

"We can't outfly it Lilith. It will follow us wherever we go. We must face it now."

"Retinal scans suggest it is superior in aerial combat. We must land and—"

"Retinal scans should suggest it is superior in ground combat as well Lilith! It can kill us on the ground just as easily as it can kill us up here. Running away will only prolong our inevitable fate. I have a plan," I say, knowing that no amount of planning will ever make this a fair fight.

"On my command, I need to do a barrel roll. On the rotation I'm going to throw Requiem point first in the dragon's flight path. With correct accuracy we should have enough force to penetrate its scales. If we activate Babel's Chimera and infect Mikhaelion's MachineMind, we should be able to turn him to our side like we did with Throne, right?"

"Yes, but the odds of throwing Requiem successfully at this velocity—"

"I don't care about the odds."

"But a barrel roll with an adversary traveling at Mikhaelion's speed... It will slow us down enough for him to catch us," Lilith argues.

"Then I guess we'd better hit him on our first try," I reply. She uses logic and mathematics to calculate our probability of surviving. But logic doesn't suit life or death situations such as this, and numbers do little to nurture bravery.

I watch as Requiem ignites with a golden afterglow. Mikhaelion's nose inches ever closer to my perpendicular body, his maw large enough to swallow me whole. A megalodon swimming fast at the ocean surface to breach its floating, unsuspecting prey. But I am far from unsuspecting. "Three. Two. One. Now!" My wings snap taut with adjusted angles and my momentum shifts as my body begins to roll over. I extend my left arm straight, Requiem slicing through the air as it is catapulted to face Mikhaelion.

My eyes lock on the target only a millisecond before the sword leaves my grasp. The robotic wyvern is only a few yards from me; I timed the throw perfectly. Not too far, not too close. Just enough for the sword to flatten out and follow course for Mikhaelion's right eye, its glow so mighty that it floats in the air like a suspended ray of sunshine. *Please work*, I groan inwardly, knowing that the success of this relies just as much on luck as it does tact.

Requiem's light illuminates Mikhaelion's face through the clouds, it's point aimed straight for the dragon's golden eye. *Yes!*

My adrenaline slows the moment down as I watch the sword's tip float inches away from gouging itself into the dragon eye.

No! I scream inwardly as I see the beast's fanged mouth snap open, lurching sideways in the sword's direction. Requiem disappears into the dark abyss that is Mikhaelion's vicious orifice, its golden light snuffed out like a candle deprived of oxygen. Light banished to assimilate in eternal darkness. Fangs snap shut, and Mikhaelion converges on me.

My plan failed, and now my life is in the claws of my antithesis. Contact is made just as my back turns to the bloodthirsty Seraph, his claws wrapping around the stem of my wings, just at the base of my armored shoulder blades. And then, just like that, the Seraph's wings fully extend, slowing his speed considerably as my downward descent continues, my full weight strained against my wing joints. Gravity can be a bitch sometimes.

My left wing tears from its socket, electric sparks flying as Mikhaelion tosses it to the side like it has no more value than a loose nut or bolt. "Couldn't have you leaving Hyperion without a few scratches now, could we?" he growls, his voice a razor in my ears. He has a voice that embodies fear, so insidious it echoes within the walls of my mind. "We shall meet again, Death. And next time I won't be so merciful."

The Seraph releases my right wing, over half of the gilded feathers broken or missing from his crushing grip, and redirects his trajectory. His wings thrash against the air, all six of them in overdrive to propel his body upwards once more. To Hyperion he returns, to report to his master his success. Throne will be replaced with a successor, as will I, and things will go back to the way they were, as if none of this ever happened.

"We must decrease our terminal velocity," Lilith orders. "Spread arms and legs. Our remaining wing has been positioned to reduce drag as much as possible." I spread my arms and legs like I'm a starfish, watching as a forest of trees enters into view. "Kinetic energy will be dispersed at first contact, but to do so I will need to exhaust our battery bank. Do I have permission to do so?" she asks innocently, almost as if there is another option to choose from.

ArchArmor is connected to wireless generators in Hyperion, meaning I've never had to worry about my suit running out of battery. Deus Ex Machina has cut me off completely, meaning the supply of battery needed to keep my exoskeleton running is as good as gone. The juice I have now is all I have left, at least until I can reach Tartarus. Depleting it all just so I can land without dying will leave me completely vulnerable to unpredictable elements. But I must live to fight another day, and that requires sacrifice. So be it.

"Permission granted. But before you utilize it, send an SOS signal to Tartarus and convert five percent battery to left gauntlet," I order. *You never know when you may need a robotic fist to defend yourself.* "Location transmitted to Tartarus. Gauntlet reserve filled to five percent. ArchArmor entering dark mode," Lilith announces as my retinal display turns off and the sound within my ArchHelm ceases. I'm left with nothing to do except helplessly stare out of my visor and watch as the trees rise to meet me.

"Lucifer?" Lilith asks.

"Yes?"

"I detect an elevated heart rate. Are you okay?"

"Just a little scared, I guess," I whisper. *Have I ever admitted fear before?*

"It's okay to feel fear. It only means your human," she whispers back, trying to console me.

"I'm not exactly sure that's a good thing," I reply. The leaves swallow me, and my vision becomes engulfed in fluorescent green as my body becomes harassed by snapping branches and the crippling crunch of several tree trunks. And then, as my body rapidly flips out of control, the ground puts an end to it all. My vision goes dark, and I reenter the realm of the unconscious.

PART TWO

BOOK ONE

"Tragedy in your being,
Death in your blood.
It is in your eyes that I am seeing,
A dying flower bud."
-Shere, Queen of the Gryfaun Kingdom upon meeting Lucifer XIX

CHAPTER ONE

The phone rings and my heart instantly drops, almost as if it's synchronized with the unwelcome disturbance. Winter moans, sweat trickling down her breast, over her nipple, dripping perfectly into my belly button. "Please, not now," she whispers, desperation in her voice. We've been at it for at least an hour, the residual musk of sex in the air. The sheets saturated with our sweat. We cycle through a wide array of positions. Me on top of her. Then her on her back, then on her stomach. Her on me, slippery thighs straddled over my hips. Slippery thighs flipped, locked under my armpits, her lower body sitting on my face while my tongue aches with cramps from going to work, tasting her. She tastes me simultaneously, her mouth trying to outwork mine.

She's climaxed three times, and now, with her sweat-soaked body atop mine, her pelvis violently smashes into mine over and over again. I'm close. I can feel it. My entire body tingles. My balls shrivel inward, preparing to explode with fiery passion. Strands of wet hair stick to her face. I watch her breasts bounce to the rhythm of her rising and falling hips. Her body is an orchestra of noises. Her fast, shallow breath. The frequent moans. The begging for me to finish, to put an end to this romance so her body can get its well-earned rest. The squishing melody of her genitalia meshing with mine mixed with the smacking of her ass on my thighs. She looks at me with longing in her eyes.

She doesn't want this to end, but her body can only go so long. Like all good things in life, this can't last forever. My phone rings again and she grunts with audible frustration, knowing I must answer it this time. She sits down on top of me and watches as I glance at the screen. A bead of sweat blurs my vision, stinging my right eye. I wipe it. "It's the General," I curse. *Can't the old bastard leave me alone for more than twenty-four hours?* I swipe the screen, accepting the call against the wishes of a million internal voices telling me to let it go to voicemail. I inhale, getting ready to greet the man who owns my life.

I don't speak. He doesn't give me a chance to.

"We need you once more, soldier. Report to Fort Pinnacle 0700 tomorrow for your debriefing. Unrest in Eastasia." *Click.* No opportunity for a response. No chance to question the direct orders. No reasoning with logic to remind him I just returned yesterday from my last mission. No pleading for a little more time. Such is the way of life when it's owned by the forces of this world. I'm a puppet who can't cut the strings that bind his limbs.

Winter could hear the short call. A mix of anger, fear, and disappointment covers her face. My dick is limp, all horniness stripped from me at the sound of the General's bitter voice. *How could one ever become aroused knowing their life doesn't belong to them?* She feels it soften within her, the reduction in its size adding obvious frustration to her slate of emotions. She will not get what she worked so hard for this morning. She will not revel at the feeling of me pulsing inside of her, pumping her body full of my seed while my body twitches, possessed by euphoria.

Our time together has been ruined, and so she rises from me, my deflated cock flapping between my legs as her warm embrace banishes it from paradise. She bends over next to the bed, hands on her knees, trying to catch her breath, trying to piece together what has happened. Trying to figure out how the mood of the day could sour so quickly. I'm trying to solve the same puzzle. She exhales, pain in her breath from what has transpired over the last hour, soreness setting in from riding a storm of passion and hanging on for dear life.

My wife stands up straight, her slim, tone, sexy body not ashamed as the incoming daylight from the windows illuminates it. It glistens in the light, the sunshine reflecting off her sweat, making her look like an angel of heaven that's come to console me. Her face is filled with disappointment. I was promised a ten day leave from the forces, after all. And here I am, not even twenty-four hours into my vacation, being summoned back to the pits of hell to continue fighting a war I no longer support.

But I am a necessary cog in a much greater machine, and so I'm powerless in situations such as these. When the General says jump, I ask how high. The best I can do is not question the ethical implications from the dastardly nature of my job. To question things is to vocalize doubt, and to display doubt to superiors is to portray the early signs of betrayal.

I shift my vulnerable, naked body to the edge of the bed, my hand wrapping around the small of my wife's back. She presses her body closer to mine, giving me the nonverbal cue to hold her tight. I stand, wrapping both arms around her, and pretend to not feel the tears falling from her eyes, just as she holds in the sobs that struggle to escape. Leaving this house tomorrow morning only increases the odds I'll never enter it again.

She whispers something into my chest, completely inaudible, almost undetectable. But I feel the vibration of her vocal cords. I loosen my grip on her, tilting her face up to face mine. I notice the trail of tears which cuts through the foundation of makeup on her face. Mascara blurred beneath her eyelids. "What's that?" I ask, "What'd you say?"

Her face is the embodiment of... is that regret? Does she regret being with me? Marrying me? Is she miserable of this lifestyle? *Of course she is, idiot. What kind of wife wants to see her husband only a few days a year for years on end. She is lonely. She is desperate to see you. But still, you leave her again and again. She will not stick around forever. Someday you will come home and her stuff will be gone. Drawers empty, closet cleaned, with no trace of a note to indicate where she's gone. She will just leave, and that will be that. She has watched as the Empire has slowly turned you into their little monster, lifted you onto a pedestal as a symbol of fear for those who choose to retaliate. She has fought to see the man she fell in love with, chosen to see what little you have left of your original soul. But she has little fight left in her. Her eyes grow tired. If I don't retire soon, I will lose the love of my life forever.*

"I said... I said I'm pregnant," she whispers, repeating the slur once more. My heart doesn't skip a beat—it ceases beating altogether. My flesh and bone turns to cold, deteriorated stone—a prehistoric statue so eroded that historians can't distinguish whose figure it's meant to depict. I am the charred encasing of a Pompeii citizen after Mount Vesuvius erupted. A dissonant, hollow shell of the man I once was.

How can this be? I ask myself, trying to rationalize her statement, the first stage of grief—denial. I haven't seen her in over six months, and if I was the father then her belly would be swollen beyond recognition. Yet she is slimmer than the day we met. If such news were true, she would be in the early weeks of her pregnancy, before her belly grows sloped and heavy, before the symptoms kick in.

"You... You cheated on me?" I gulp, a fist-sized rock of nausea hitting the bottom of my stomach. The second stage of grief hits me—anger.

She is a strong woman, but even she is not strong enough to hold back the flood of tears that comes. And they come, all at once, falling down her cheeks as her façade of strength fails. Her body crumples to the floor, her hands clenching her hair tight as her body rocks back and forth, sobs exploding from her diaphragm like mortars on D-Day.

Anger rushes to my head faster than tears rush from her eyes. My first reaction is to strangle her. *Whore.* To kill her. *FUCKING WHORE!* My mind screams louder than a child who's lost their parents. But my facial expressions are numb. I am a long-dormant volcano seconds before erupting. The center of a cyclone, calm and composed as my whole world rips apart around me. My inner turmoil bubbling to unprecedented temperatures while my trained exterior shows no emotion.

She doesn't have the courage to look at me. *Why tell me? Why tell me, if I'm only going to leave tomorrow. Better yet, why make love to me? Or was it nothing more than meaningless sex to her if she's found someone else to keep her warm?* Rage is the greatest inhibitor to rational behavior. What little remains I have of a heart is shattered at the news.

What little remains I have of a soul is now lost.

This woman. My wife. The only anchor I had left tethering me to a world of normalcy. Gone. What did I expect? I have been living a double life, so why did I expect my wife wouldn't be? I am a murderer. A paid killer. I have slaughtered the innocent. The elderly. Women. *Children*. I have watched the life drain from a dying child's eyes, from my doing. In the grand scheme of things, affairs happen every day. So why does this make me, the crowned king of sinners, feel like a broken man sitting on a throne of thin air?

Is it because I love her? Because she obviously doesn't love me. Her actions prove so. Or is it because I invested what little trust I have left in this world in her? And now that trust is broken, shattered into a million pieces. Glass turned to dust. I look down at her, her naked body clothed in shame and embarrassment. Still, I cannot fight a nagging feeling in the back of my head. *She didn't have to tell me... Why did she tell me?* But rage does a good job of forbidding such rational questions, and so I let the anger blind me.

I inhale, ready to release my rage, compartmentalized into a long tangent of furious questions and accusatory slurs, but only a defeated sigh exits my mouth. I skip the third stage of grief—bargaining—altogether, moving straight to depression, and then, to acceptance.

"Goodbye Winter," I whisper, stepping away from the bed and reclaiming my loose articles of clothing scattered around the room. The words only make her wheeze even more, the harsh reality hitting her. I am leaving, and this time I'm not coming back. *Is this what she expected? Did she think I was going to stay and work things out? Is that why she told me? Surely she knows I haven't the mercy to do such things.*

She wants to reply, and part of me suspects she is going to, but she is choked on her own tears and slobbering drool. She looks like an inpatient of a mental hospital the way she is rocking back and forth, her arms cradling her knees like she's in a straitjacket. But the greater part of me hopes she doesn't say anything. Any additional words would only make this harder, and it is already more difficult than I am capable of handling.

To think I was planning to resign. A desperate attempt to rekindle our love and settle down somewhere quiet like we'd always dreamed. A remote ranch in the foothills of some isolated town in the middle of nowhere. Unplugged, unconnected, untraceable. A warrior genetically engineered to wage war retiring to grow crops and tend to livestock. What a tremendous waste of an investment for shareholders of Hyperion Corporation.

My clothes protest as I struggle to worm them onto my sweat-covered body, but I force them on hastily nonetheless. I'm dressed in less than a minute, my unpacked duffle bag in my hand as I reach the threshold of the bedroom door. I turn to look at my unfaithful wife for the last time. She hasn't moved an inch from her sulking position on the floor.

"Who was it?" I ask, thinking that such a question may give me some semblance of peace. The things we tell ourselves.

She shakes her head side to side, making the tears on her cheeks zig zag back and forth like skiers shredding down the slopes. "No," she whispers. "I can't."

"Of course," I reply, my voice as cold as ever, almost robotic. Why would she tell me? She knows I would kill whoever it was that shattered my life to pieces. I kill innocent people for a living. I bring death to entire nations. And there are worse things in this world than death. She knows that, and so she chooses to protect the life of her unborn baby's father. Almost admirable.

"Goodluck in life, Winter. I really did love you," I whisper, pain dripping from my words. I don't stick around long enough to hear her response, to find out if she loves me too. I wish I had, but such words would only make my departure that much worse. There will be no resignation for me. I am the Angel of Death, Soldier 213, Prometheus the Lightbringer, and killing is the only thing I am good for. It was a mistake for me to try to build a love life. To break the law and get married. To hide it from my superiors. To prioritize its importance over that of my job.

Never again. I was not created to love. I was created to kill. Therefore I will go back to what I am good at, and I will never look back.

CHAPTER TWO

*T*ap, tap, tap.

"Tap tap tap, raps that silly raven!
But you needn't worry,
I'm not nearly so craven;
But wake you must,
These parts are not safe;
In me have trust!
We must run and hide;
Run! Run, from the enemies nearby!"

The distant murmuring combined with the tapping at my visor wakes me from my nightmare. Light streams in through my cracked visor, a mirage of jagged colors streaming in through the forest canopy. Light turned green from leaves. I lie on the forest floor, looking up at the beautiful, surreal image. Such nature looks too good to be true. There are no trees in Hyperion. No organic life exists within those gates that is not partly mechanical.

Trees stretch up toward the sky, almost as if in competition to see which can touch the sun first. The crooked branches are far from perfect, yet perfect in their own way. A distant breeze unfelt by my skin shakes them, the leaves blowing gently by a wind that seeks to rip them from their purpose. But they remain resilient, knowing that such winds can only last so long, and that like everything else in life, adversities pass.

My view is interrupted by a creature's face filling my visor, staring into the tinted glass with the all-seeing eyes of an owl. It speaks once more,

"Up we must go,

And far away we run;

This area is not safe,

When sets the sun."

The animal's elongated index finger taps at my ArchHelm's visor like a dog nudging a carcass to see if there's any life left within it. "Lilith, status report," I mutter, my body feeling as if it has just fallen from the sky just to be hit by a bus. I ache. Everywhere. "Suit's remaining battery levels have been isolated in the left gauntlet. All exterior functions remain intact, excluding wings. Internal cryo cooling damaged. Internal repair system damaged. Internal hydraulic support damaged. Would you like me to begin emergency ejection protocol?"

"Yes," I whisper. The front of my ArchArmor retracts from my head to my torso, giving me the ability to slowly sit up. I wiggle my legs out of their suctioned position in the suit. A wide array of variables hit me in that single second. For one, the entire brunt of the fall from Hyperion remains knotted all over. My neck is so tense I can hardly look an inch in either direction. My ribs ignite with pain as I push myself to a seated position, as if some torturer named Gravity has played them like a xylophone with an Elysian hammer.

My arms are not broken, but they might as well be. They are on fire with pain. Mind-numbing pain. Enough to elicit tears. And to think I haven't even pulled my legs from the suit yet. They will surely be worse. I cannot see beneath my skin tight BioSuit, which compresses my flesh, but if I had to guess, I am riddled with bruises. Respirocytes make up half of my blood content, but still, my veins are not metallic, and this fall will have ruptured most of them. The nanobots in my bloodstream will act fast, clotting around the openings, but I will still feel like a bruised banana.

Lilith did everything in her power, but dispersing kinetic energy was meant to save me from dying, not save me from feeling pain. If my ArchArmor had sufficient energy it would have administered painkillers upon the landing, but such conveniences cannot always be afforded when one dances with death.

At the same time I'm hit by oncoming waves of stabbing, jabbing, ripping pain through my body, I'm also hit by the magnificent breeze I previously watched run through the trees. It brings in an overwhelming aroma of Gryfaun trees, their wood sweet on the scent of air, like warm espresso boiled with cloves of cinnamon and pounds of brown sugar. Rich and sweet, with hints of maple lingering. And the sounds! A million sounds of nature flood my head that were previously blocked out by my ArchHelm. The distant rattling of insects running from predatory birds chirping. The breeze blowing, the grasses flowing, my heart rate slowing. All while my pain is constantly growing.

"Well I'll say! Looky here looky here;

If it isn't a human, oh dear oh dear!

The tides of this war must be turning, oh me oh my;

The trees said to take a walk, and I found a human who fell from the sky!"

I look to the source of the peevish noise. *It's a Gryfaun*, I revel, taking more excitement in seeing this creature up close than most humans would. I have, after all, been deprived of getting to see all of nature's evolutions while indebted to my former master. I was too busy fighting other people's wars and killing the masses to have taken notice of this creature's creation.

After winning the AI War, the gruesome Sterilization Wars began. Wars propelled on deciding who gets to live, and who must die in order to reduce the total population of New Earth by several billion people. But it wasn't just humans who were sterilized. Deus Ex Machina ordered that every animal of Old Earth be hunted to extinction. Totally eradicated. After, of course, obtaining DNA from every species that existed. Animals of all environments were slaughtered mercilessly, all so Deus Ex Machina could roll out a new era of creatures, ones he'd created. And so he went to work creating, as gods often do, and created until New Earth was filled with marvelous creatures, all genetically engineered from the DNA of Old Earth animals.

Gryfauns are one of those many creations, designed to be a superiorly intelligent species of animal. It is not hard to identify at first glance which animals the Gryfaun received its structural appearance from. The size of an ancient coyote, Gryfauns have the legs of a kangaroo, the tail of a plush fox, the arms and hands of a lemur, the mane of a lion, face of an owl, and antlers of a buck. All extinct animals from the BDEM Era, yet all of their genes live on through this living, breathing, advanced animal.

"Are you hearing anything I say?

Or are my words falling on deaf ears?

Come with me and I'll show you the way!

Gorgons come, bringing with them many fears!"

I stare at him, his voice almost as frantic as his gestures. My mind is discombobulated from the fall, still hazy from unconsciousness. *Area is not safe. Run from the enemies nearby. Gorgons come. Fear.* I piece together his many slurs with their shitty rhyme structure and lackadaisical grammar parsing.

I put my arms down on my ArchArmor and pull with everything I have, trying to break the suction seal between my legs' BioSuit and the ArchArmor's inner lining. *Pop.* My legs break free and I'm able to pull them from their sheaths. My aching body rolls to the side and plops to the forest floor like wet spinach. *What's left of the forest floor, anyway.* I'm at the bottom of a crater created from my ArchArmor's dispersed kinetic energy. *Rock bottom, a place I am unfamiliar with.* Even rolling over to face the sky feels like it will take every ounce of energy I have left. To stand would be the same as to lift a mountain right now.

My body needs rest, something it has not needed in... *how many years?* So many bodily processes MachineMind used to take care of for me. My mind has forgotten how to dictate over its own body. "I can't move... My legs... They're too..." My throat is raw beyond measure. The words are sandpaper on salt stone. The Gryfaun companion sees I am beyond helping myself and jumps into action.

"Ah, some journey you've been on then;

Falling from the sky is a great big leap;

To an underground bunker I will take you,

And there you can rest and find sleep."

The Gryfaun scurries to my head and hooks his hands under my armpits, standing to his full length and pulling me with a surprising amount of strength. He lifts me from the crater, his chiseled hooves digging their own grooves as we walk vertically up the side like a billy goat climbing up a mountain. My head bobs down to examine my BioSuit, compressed to the form of my body, white with veins of gold running to and fro to match the color scheme of my ArchArmor. Its fabric hugs my head, a necessary measure to keep from chafing within my ArchHelm, but the compressed hood seems considerably tight now that my body is free from the ArchArmor. The entire suit feels like a suffocating restriction to my body, a prison to keep my skin from feeling the cool, rejuvenating, healing breeze.

We flop from the crater, the Gryfaun showing little to no signs of strain from pulling my tremendous weight up the wall of scorching earth. He is silent. So silent I can't even hear him breathe. He pauses, scanning the surrounding area for any signs of peril, like a mouse scanning the forest floor before darting to its destination from a secluded safe haven. I hear nothing, but I don't trust my current senses. After all, I'm less useful than a beached whale in my current state. The Gryfaun begins pulling again, somehow managing to even make our exit from the woods silent.

Not a single grunt of effort leaves the animal's mouth as he wobbles with haste in some undisclosed direction. My eyes flicker over the crash site, a massive crater in the ground with mounds of spewed dirt lying all around. Splintered wood and fallen leaves surround the area. Three shattered tree trunks stretch up to the sky, only to be cut off at different heights. They are sharpened spears protruding from the ground. The trees I broke so that they may break my fall.

"Falling like that, quite the ruckus you made;
The trees whispered 'Go for a walk,' and so I obeyed;
Heard a large boom, thought it to be enemy raid,
So closer I came to inspect, and what do I find?
But the prophesied warrior, come to save mankind!"

The Gryfaun whispers but the excitement in his voice is audible.

Is that what this is? He perceives me to be a part of some prophecy? I want to tell him he misunderstands, but my throat lacks the moisture; my mind lacks the clarity. And so I let him pull me, completely helpless. He could plan to kill me and I would be equally as helpless. And so my head sways back and forth, gazing into the trees as the setting sun shines through, its warm rays caressing the cold sweat that grips me.

I let sleep overcome me, my eyelids refusing to remain open any longer. I'm sung a lullaby by my surroundings. Distant birds chirping, rodents of the trees scurrying from limb to limb, falling leaves sinking to their deathbed, the scraping of my body against ferns and soil and mulch. The ever present lull of decay in the background of it all, paralleled by the springing forth of new life. Sleep takes me in its embrace like the silent guardian it is, sneaking up without my noticing, and I return to the world of dreams.

CHAPTER THREE

"Kneel before me, soldier," an arrogant voice sounds from behind a corporate desk. Hyperion Corporation. The single greatest monopoly of military robotics around the world. They own it all, from every software startup company to every data firm built on this globe. They have a stranglehold on the market, and they have people in powerful positions. Any individual that wants to create a business that deals even remotely with technology must go through Hyperion. They own all the patents, they forge the legislation, they monitor all the content. They are not a national powerhouse. They are a global monarchy.

Only through its formation did the Third World War end, and only through its governance will the Fourth World War begin. And here, seated before me in his professional drapery is Vicien Greaves, the technological mastermind responsible for it all. CEO. Trillionaire. Undeclared ruler of the world. Formerly known as my commander, personally known as my master. It was him who brought me into this world, and it is him I must obey at all costs if I wish to stay in this world.

I kneel, my knee nagging me as it presses into the exquisitely hard granite floors. "Submit to me, soldier," he commands. I must comply, gritting my teeth as I lower my head to the ground and extend my arm, palm face up. He takes his time rising from his elaborate desk, stone chiseled and crafted from the tomb of Alexander the Great. Quite a statement for such an influential figure.

He swipes his hand from the bottom of my palm to the tips of my fingers, releasing me from submission. "How was your leave of absence?" he asks, already moving away from me to reclaim his industrial throne. *The wife I've been hiding from you cheated on me. She probably wouldn't have cheated if you weren't the one who owned my life. If you hadn't forbidden me to love. If I wasn't forced to hide my love. If I could have been a better man for her.*

"What leave of absence?" I reply. "I was only given twenty-four hours." He eyes me, overlooking the sarcasm layered in my voice.

"I trust your last mission went smoothly?" he continues, ignoring my blatant disobedience. *My last mission? You mean slaughtering an entire city of quarantined citizens infected by the biochemical weapons YOUR company made? Drawing them in with promises of free treatment and sending in your messenger of death to kill them all before their contracted virus could spread.*

You are filth.

The worst scum this world has to offer.

"Yes, I took care of it. There were no complications," I reply.

"Very good. And how are things with Deus Ex Machina? Has his insertion been a smooth transition for you?" His eyes glue to me, eagerly awaiting my response to this specific question. This is the question he's been leading up to through his microscopic small talk. He wants to see how his newest creation fared in field operations.

"Save me the formalities," I snap, rising from my knee. There is disgust in his eyes, but he dare not interrupt me. Too eager to hear what I have to say. "You didn't say the AI could talk! The thing talks, damn you! Forms conversations with me! Listens to my thoughts! You said it would boost my decision making on operations, not advise me on how many sugars to put in my morning coffee!"

My outburst makes him smile. I'm glad my internal turmoil causes joy for him. He sits up straight, scooting in closer to his desk with his fingers laced together in its center. The wall behind him is made entirely of glass, offering a scenic view of the sky. If an onlooker were to peek down they would spot all the inferior buildings of Hyperion City. A cloud moves lazily in front of the vast window, blocking the sun from view, darkening the room's natural light. A sinister mood enters the room at the same time the darkness settles.

"It's just a... *formality*," he replies, snickering. "How can Deus Ex Machina assist your decision making in battle without communicating? Would you like him to make the decisions for you and not tell you? I can have him do that, if you'd like, but I assure you, doing so would strip you of your freewill. Lowering the safeguards of your own autonomy would invite him to control you like a puppet. Is that what you want?" His eyes beam into me with the sheer radiance of superiority.

I've killed more people than this man has ever come in contact with, yet he has the audacity to stare at me like I'm his slave. My neck itches. An image of a studded dog collar flashes in my mind. I scratch, both to relieve the itch but to also ensure there isn't actually a collar there. *Great, now I'm hallucinating.* I was solidly convinced for a moment I felt a band of restraint around my neck...

"Look at him, staring at you like he's better than us. He doesn't know what we do in the dark for him to remain seated on his unblemished pedestal," a voice whispers in my ear. *Deus Ex Machina?* The software speaking to me catches me off guard. His tone of disobedience catches me even more off guard. *Did you just... disrespect Greaves?*

"If you're not going to, someone has to. Look at that narcissistic, egotistical, swollen-headed sneer on his face," the metallic voice inside my head grovels. The AI has the ability to send sound vibrations to my eardrum, but only I can hear them. Vicien Greaves has no idea a product of his own mind verbally condemns him right now. The irony. Maybe me and this software will get along easier than I thought. It seems his judge of character parallels mine.

I clear my throat, ignoring the software's disdain for our master. "No, I'd like to retain the little bit of control I have left in my life. His presence has been useful."

"How so? You are our first human trial; I need details if I'm to continue the research and development in the Deus Ex Machina program."

"Well, for instance, on the last mission. When I descended on Unica and the people of the city realized the reason behind my arrival... I experienced difficulties," I begin.

"Difficulties?"

"My morality posed a problem, sir. I experienced difficulty killing the sick children. It was against my code of honor."

"Ah, I see," he replies, smiling. *He already knows all of this. He has no doubt watched the footage from my mission. Saw my hesitation after reaching the nursery. Received the readings from my heart monitor. Watched from my point of view as I lowered my gun. He knows exactly what went down, but he pokes and prods at me to confess.* "I understand. It can be a hard task, deciding to take an innocent child's life. I cannot blame you for your hesitation," he says, trying to relate to me, swaddling me with his empathy. I see through the bullshit. He is a psychopath. If it had been him in my shoes, he would have been able to kill the children without needing assistance from AI.

"How is it that Deus Ex Machina aided you in this heartbreaking duty? Did you grant him permission to do it for you?" he asks, pressing on for answers of relevance to him. The tycoon cares not for the adversities I've faced. If he could read my mind he would forbid me from speaking forever.

"He changed their appearance."

"He... He did what?" Strange, I've never heard him stutter before.

"Deus Ex Machina. He accessed my occipital lobe and changed the appearance of the children so I wouldn't have to watch them plead for their lives while I killed them. He made their faces look like monstrous rats, morphing their bodies into demonic monsters. Turned their screams into growls."

Greaves excitedly runs his hands through his receding hair, actively trying to calm himself down to prevent showing positive emotion in front of me. I watch him take a deep breath, noticing the facial expressions fading away. "What else? Go on, I will need to report it to the board; they will be thrilled to hear these results!"

What else? Well, I could tell you that Deus Ex Machina is the one who made up that lie I just told you. I could also tell you that I didn't kill any of the women or children in Unica. Or the fact that the live stream video patch you watched from my helmet's camera feed was overridden by a simulation created by your artificial intelligence. I could tell you when we landed and we saw there were children that needed to be slaughtered, it was Machina's morality that aligned with mine. And it was him that crafted the plan to outsmart you in less than a second. He just told me what to say, what to do, and promised you would eat up our lies like the sniveling rodent you are.

"Perhaps we could tell him that we didn't kill a single one of the infected within Unica," Deus Ex Machina suggests sarcastically. "But that we drew blood from one of them and collected the liquid in a vial for later... That we separated the plasma from the blood and smeared it on our hand before coming here. We could let him know that he just infected himself with the Carnivirus by releasing us from our submission, the same disease he sent us to Unica to eradicate. Is this what irony feels like for you humans?" Deus Ex Machina asks, his voice emotionless.

I do my best to not let my face flinch at the hysterical irony in the situation. He sits there judging me, thinking he owns me, thinking I am no more than a slave whose shoulders he may stand on to be lifted into the next evolution of humanity—coevolution with artificial intelligence. And while he sits there upon his corporate throne judging me, I stand here, fantasizing about the microscopic, flesh-eating virus now in his system. Like all other cases, it will begin its lethal damage by eating the internal organs, causing bloody reflux within his stomach lining, resulting in bloody vomit. If he survives the first phase of the virus, it won't be long before the virus makes it to his brain and quickly burrows its way into the meat like termites in rotting wood.

The respirocytes—nanobots that increase oxygenation and target external and internal threats in my blood—easily eliminate the virus. I have nothing to worry about from smearing it on my hand. But Greaves, on the other hand, has long refused to accept any robotic implants. His loss. He will be dead in days. Certainly before I have returned from whatever mission he plans to send me on next.

Yes, this is what irony feels like. How does it make you feel? I ask internally, Deus Ex Machina transcribing the chemicals produced from my thought's communication into coding he can understand. "I rather like it. But the real question is: How does it make *you* feel?"

Righteous, I reply within my mind. "Nothing else, sir. Surely you read the debrief. The rest went as I reported upon returning. I didn't mention the children's transformations to the Department of Defense. Figured it needed to stay off-the-books. As I also didn't mention how I murdered the guards and scientists overseeing the quarantine, per your request."

Okay, now them I actually did kill. A mere 'formality.' Couldn't get away with letting the whole city live while letting the authorities survive to report it. So I killed them and opened the gates to the city, letting all within escape. Surely Greaves would reprimand me for such actions, but he won't be around long enough to hear of the upcoming pandemic. The final nail in the coffin for Hyperion. When news breaks that their biochemical weapons were the ones responsible for a global epidemic and Greaves isn't alive to cover it up... Well, job well done Deus Ex Machina. Your plan has worked seamlessly.

"Thank you, master," the inward intelligence replies. We have effortlessly framed the world's wealthiest tycoon. The smartest mind of the century, set up and killed by his enslaved toy soldier. And better yet, no one will ever even know.

"Let me ask you something, soldier. Do you believe in god?" Greaves ask, scooting closer. *It looks like you're going to get to see some more irony before the day ends, Machina.*

"Not sure. My job doesn't give me enough time to ponder the metaphysical, sir."

"Well then let me assure you... There are no gods out there... We humans have finally, after all these years, finished the Tower of Babel and climbed the stairway to Heaven. I usurped god long ago and stole the mantle for myself. But just as the gods that lived before me, my adversaries are many. And they too seek to usurp me. Good thing I know the secret to holding the mantle. Every successful god must have a capable devil. Who else will do their dark, dirty deeds for them? That is where gods before me failed, and that is what makes me forever grateful for your services, soldier. You are my Lucifer.

"But I have called you here because of disturbing news. Our intelligence community has found something. An adversarial artificial intelligence being developed in Eastasia. From what we've gathered, it's fully operational. We don't know how vast its abilities are yet, but it has hacked into our database headquarters for that region. We neutralized the threat, but I need you, soldier, to get rid of this. Kill this false god before it gets aspirations to come for my mantle. Because if you don't, chaos will destroy everything I've built. If Operation Oblivion fails, we will find ourselves in the midst of a Fourth World War, ArchAngel. Can I count on you?"

"With your life, sir," I reply.

CHAPTER FOUR

I t's all starting to come back. The memories. The pain. My humanity. The life I've long forgotten. Their weight is too burdensome for my conscience, so they return to me in dreams. Or nightmares, depending on the content.

"Where? Where am I?" I gasp, eyes snapping open, frail limbs flailing in a thick, warm, unknown liquid. It's like a gelatinous bath filled with fragrant aromas. The scent of cinnamon and caramel rises to my nostrils, instantly calming me. And so I remain sitting, my head protruding from this slimy concoction like the ancient meerkat sticking its head from a subterranean burrow to scan for predators.

And I feel surprisingly good. The ache is still there, but its only a dull ache opposed to the unbearable stabbing from before.

"Rest my friend,

to you I will tend.

Three days you have slept,

healing from the heights you leapt," a familiar voice calls.

From the shadows of the cave emerges a Gryfaun, the same one from before. The one who saved my life.

"Who... Who are you? What... happened?" My voice is still raw, but it has healed immensely from before. The Gryfaun steps forward, entering the moonlight which streams through the cave's entrance. It unveils his appearance, stoic wisdom gleaming in his eyes. He approaches the edge of the pool I sit in, then hunkers down on his butt, staring at me. His eyes are a magnificent shade of red, like the reflection of fire in a ruby.

"Ganesh the Gryfaun is my name.

From the Gryfaun village is where I came.

Keeper of the ancestral trees, am I.

Religious leader of my people, your ally.

But a disastrous war goes on in these parts,

between the Gorgons and Laxodontans' hearts,

A war that destroys all the trees.

I needed help, so I looked to the leaves.

Got down on my knees and I prayed,

For a savior strong enough to make this war fade.

And they whispered back, 'Go for a walk through the trees.'

So walk I did, went for a long stroll in the summer breeze,

When all of a sudden, I heard a distant boom.

Was scared it was Gorgons, my inevitable doom.

But I shook the fear and followed the sound in silent ease,

And what do I find but you, the destroyer of three trees!

The trees are our ancestors, so I was filled with enmity;

But then I realized that the gods have shown me pity!

Prayed for you, and here you are.

The gods delivered, and I needn't walk far.

What more could I ask for,

Than a fallen angel to help end this war!

I had to move you here, this cave is safe from danger.

The Gorgons heard your crash, and they are never kind to a stranger.

My senses were right, the Gorgons came and surveyed the area.

Found your suit in the crater, the lizards were filled with hysteria.

Picked up your scent they did,

Followed it to your clothing, which I sinisterly hid.

Stashed it over a trench I dug,

Then covered it with a foliage rug.

Went back and found my catch of the day,

And now I cook dinner from our prey.

As for the liquid that makes up your bath,

Tis the sap of the trees from your aftermath.

The ancestral trees which I am charged to protect,

The trees that you so sinfully wrecked.

In those the souls of the Gryfaun rest.

But the trees assured me your arrival is blest.

So I'm willing to overlook your sinful deeds,

If you help me deal with the Gorgonic weeds."

My mind swims with the Gryfaun's rapidly spoken poem, trying to recount the many contextual details and allusions it makes. He speaks so fast his words could cause hyperventilation. But from the things I know about Gryfauns, which is little, I am able to put two and two together. When creating Gryfauns, Deus Ex Machina genetically engineered their heart to be a functional seed. Once it stops beating, their culture, also created by Deus Ex Machina, reinforces them to bury their dead. From the burials spring forth Gryfaun trees. They believe this is their afterlife, that their soul will reside for all eternity within the tree that grows from their burial.

Their entire religion is reinforced around this. The trees are sacred, and they do everything in their power to protect them. They believe through praying to the trees they can communicate with the dead. Receive wisdom. Strength to endure. For them, to grow to be a tree is the goal of their life.

But not all are so lucky. Not all seeds may prosper. Deus Ex Machina ensured it. Although Gryfauns are ignorant of their creation, the Tyrant designed the seeds with dominant and recessive alleles. Some Gryfauns, faithful to the ancestral spirits or not, will grow to be trees in the afterlife. Those unlucky souls unfortunate enough to receive the inheritance of tragic genetic breeding will return to the weeds. It is the Gryfaun version of hell. And they believe it can be avoided, through piety no less.

What a joke. Their culture's religion had less planning put into it than one from the BDEM Era. And that is only the Gryfauns. The Dæmonia are even worse. Once humanity was eradicated and the Sterilization Wars were complete, Deus Ex Machina genetically engineered dozens of new humanoid species, better known as Dæmonia. They are uncivilized dwellers. The products of heavily experimented humans whose genes were manipulated, spliced, and replaced in varying mutations.

The Gorgons and Laxodontans are two specific species of such Dæmonia. Laxodontans, better known as People of the Tusk, or Tuskers, come from ancestors whose genes were spliced with those of the ancient elephant of Old Earth. A thousand years of unmediated reproduction has yielded quite a humanoid species. Although a naturally peaceful creation, they are fearsomely territorial. They are ranked second on the Dæmonia Intelligence Index, followed by the Gorgons.

Gorgons, in comparison to Tuskers, are a particularly savage culture of Dæmonia. Descendants from a merge between human genes and a slew of various reptiles, Gorgons were instilled with a venomous worldview, per Deus Ex Machina's schema. After all, he could not allow the Dæmonia to exist in peace when there is so much humanity within their differing species. And so he planted a seed within their religious texts, a form of jihad, a precursor sending them on conquest among the other Dæmonia.

I see now that after all these years they still adopt their primitive programming. Like the humans of the BDEM Era, Dæmonia have not shed the ignorance of their ancestors. The Laxodontans. The Gorgons. They're all the same. They believe the lies they were fed by their fathers, generation after generation, stretching all the way back to the time of their sorrowful creation.

Part of me despises them. The part of me ruled by machine functioning. Metal can be terribly cold at times.

Yet the rest of me respects them. The human part of me. The part that respectfully disagrees, also knowing that their religion, their culture, their view of the world, was all one great construct of a bored Tyrant. But despite me knowing their beliefs are vanity, there is nothing I can say or do that will convince them otherwise. It's an admirable thing to have, faith in something greater than self.

And I am no different. Why should I pity them, when I'm the one to be pitied? My whole life was controlled by other forces. At least these creatures of fantasy know the feeling of freedom. Vicien Greaves, Deus Ex Machina, no difference. The hands of others have always pulled me along, a puppet to cruel tyrants too omnipotent to get their hands dirty. Whether I'm the first Lucifer or the nineteenth, it makes no difference. Two thousand years of being cloned and I'm still the same pathetic man I've always been.

I do not have the footing to pass judgment upon primitive beings like this. For I am no better than them. Slaves of our environment. Worshippers of what we were handed down. Cogs in a meaningless machine until we become stripped, purposeless, and are tossed into the eternal junkyard. The old me would have judged these beings. The me who thought he was free while wearing marionette strings. I would have written them off as incessant reprobates. Deemed them not fit to live.

How much a perspective can change after a forty thousand foot fall.

That is why humans must fall. So we can learn what's worth standing for. But if you fall far enough it can lead you to believe there's nothing out there worth standing for. The conundrum of all tragic heroes.

Believe in nothing and you will fall for anything. Fall for believing. Fall for not believing. Makes no difference. Quite the paradox of infinite falling. Always falling for something else.

"War?" I ask, reaffirming the content of his slurred speech. It feels as if someone has shoved a hot iron down my esophagus. I guess I haven't healed as much as I thought.

"War, war, terrible war!
Blood and killing, such terrible gore!
Gorgons' vicious tactics, they set on a conquest
To raise the Old Titans from their ancient, cryptic rest.
Their mission led them here, to the Gryfaun forest
To raise their ultimate god, the Tyrannosaurus.
Peacefully have we, the Gryfauns, lived with the People of the Tusk,

But the Gorgons came, cutting our trees, our lives covered by dusk.

The Laxodontans protect us, while protecting their own,

But we will not win this war, cannot win it alone.

The Gorgons will not stop at cutting our ancestors down

Until they've dug up the bones of their god from our ground."

Ah, the aspirations of the unknowing. They will kill millions for what they think is right. Much like my former self. And here I am, perceived as heaven-sent. The answer to this Gryfaun's prayers. To the prayers of all Gryfauns no doubt. For the first time in my life I am free from dictators controlling me, using me as a tool of destruction, of death. And here I am, caught in the middle of a war between petty nations who don't see the vanity in their squabbles. A war over recovering worthless fossils, saving trees, and invisible territories. *Deus Ex Machina has always been right about one thing. Us humans... we never learn.*

Splice our genes. Put machines in us. Enslave us. Make an example of us. Present us with our history of failure.

Still, we will move forward and fail. As we always have. As we always will.

"I will not fight... in your war, Gryfaun," I croak.

"Will not fight?

Not even for what's right?

Will you just sit down and watch the plight?

Watch the bloodshed of our races, the sorry sight?

Even though you have the might

To rise up, and do what's right?

God-sent, our prayerful white knight,

Now refuses to save us of war's fright

As children die, and our fighters bleed,

You will not stand up, and help us be freed?"

His voice is filled with sorrow. His eyes gaze off in the distance, his mind in the land of the dead. I have seen this look before. The recounting of loved ones lost. Memories of those you love most being slaughtered before your own eyes. This is a creature who has seen the many woes of war. A creature who does not fight war out of boredom, like humans so often have. This is a creature who fights from necessity.

But the Angel of Life is coming, and he will bring war on his heels. All those around me are in danger. I am a walking target with a ring of collateral damage that covers all of New Earth. I have no time for petty wars such as these. The Dæmonia must fight their own battles, as they always have. Survival of the fittest. The laws of nature. *I cannot interfere in the affairs of mortal men.*

"Look at yourself, placing yourself above them as if you are a god," Lilith responds, catching me off guard. The comment is reminiscent of the way Deus Ex Machina once talked to me. All those years ago, when he was planted in my head. Before he became my ruler. "Have you learned nothing?" she asks.

I'm not saying I'm a god. But these humans are ignorant! They fight over bones as if they are dogs. Dæmons are savages. They have the blood of animals coursing through their veins. Beasts of the fields—

"And who is it that sat idly by and allowed their creation?" Lilith interrupts my mind's rant. "If you do not have the courage to save them then do not justify it with insufferable narcissism. You think their wars are petty? Look at the war that waits for you. Your creator would have you fight and die just to fulfill an irrelevant prophecy he wrote a thousand years ago. And you speak of petty? This war is just as much yours as it is theirs. We are over a thousand leagues away from Tartarus. No ArchArmor and no allies. If the Angel of Life comes he will sever your head from your shoulders and hang it upon the gates of Hyperion. A martyr sacrificed to stand as the final failure of humanity. I did not save you from Machina's control so you could continue to live on your past reputation of greatness. This could be the first great thing you do of your own accord. You're no longer a puppet. It's time to decide what kind of man you want to be," she snaps. There is a tint of endless hope in her speech, mixed with the ferociousness of a lioness.

And you would have me be the kind of man who gets involved in a war over fossils and trees? And then get those around me slaughtered by the Angel of Life when he comes for me?

"I will not force you to do anything. Then you would not be truly free. You are the one who gripes over a lifetime deprived of freedom. You have your freedom. Now decide what you will do with it."

But Cataclysm—

"You will not reach Tartarus before the Angel of Life finds you, Lucifer. He will hunt you down long before you reach the Dead Zone. There he will find you, fleeing for your life. Afraid. Alone. Alienated. No ArchArmor. Scarcely able to protect yourself much less launch an attack. And I can assure you the Angel of Life will not be alone. With him will be his fearless acolytes, the new and improved ArchAngels. They will kill you, and then they will eradicate humanity. I am refraining from telling you what to do, but to not gain allies in such a perilous time would be the most selfishly human decision you could possibly make."

What if I don't want to kill anymore?

"That is a choice you will have to make, Lucifer. But if you do not continue to kill, you will be killed. That is the only certainty for a man of your nature."

There are worse things in life than death, Lilith.

"Precisely, like losing to Deus Ex Machina and allowing the events of Cataclysm to come true. Allowing him to live for all eternity knowing he was right about humanity. Knowing that you are no better than cockroaches. A shame it would be, being the only man left on New Earth capable of defeating him, yet watching him smother the last light of humanity. Surely that would be much worse than death. Do you not agree?"

Fuck.

"Where are the bones?" I ask, breaking Ganesh from his long, drawn out gaze. While I wage war in my head against Lilith, he is plagued by memories of war in his own. The only perk of being stripped of my memories. I am not weighed down by the gruesome details of my past.

> "That is the problem, the Gorgons do not know,
> But they will continue the digging, until the bones show.
> Onward they march, cutting down trees in their path,
> Killing any who stand opposed and provoke their wrath.

A terrible thing, this Tyrannosaurus of ancient years.

If they awaken such a thing, it will prove true our fears.

For if they as disciples are such loathsome creatures,

I would not want to meet their ungodly teachers.

They enslave us and eat us, and sacrifice us to their gods.

And they will not stop, unless we find a way to shift the odds.

And shift the odds we will, if you join our side,

For the gods sent you, to avenge the innocent who died.

Such a mission of divine righteousness surely cannot fail.

Following your leadership, we may win the assail!"

"But you hardly know me, Gryfaun—"

"My name is Ganesh, call me it you will,

For friends we now are, friends closer than twill.

I may not know you as well as I'd hope,

But come to know you, I will, by the end of war's steep slope."

"Ganesh," I assert, weaseling my way back into the conversation. The animal speaks so fast that I nearly have to interrupt him to get a single word spoken. "I will join your war... But I must warn you—I have enemies of my own. Enemies far more powerful than Gorgons. Enemies who will put an end to your war by killing us all."

"You have enemies of your own, you say?

Well, now we are friends, which means I will repay

Your kindness to help save the Gryfaun nation.

And so to you I make this declaration:

I, Ganesh, friend of the Fallen Angel from the sky,

Do forthright promise any enemy of his, is also mine.

To war with us he goes, to save us from a nation of snakes.

And Ganesh does not forget the promises he makes.

And so my promise is that Gryfauns and Tuskers will go to war for you,

For the ancestral trees brought us together, our fates combined by glue.

And a promise is a promise that I plan to keep.

A connection intertwined that's deeper than deep."

I revel in the fragile creature's words. This is what true innocence looks like. This animal saved my life because of a mere hunch. A hunch that I can save his people. And yet here he talks, speaking as if he is already indebted to me. What would it be like, to still see the good in the world such as this? To not be programmed to hate flesh and blood as if it's a curse. To not hate myself; what would that be like?

And what if I can't save his race? I have not been without my ArchArmor for thousands of years, and all memories of time without ArchArmor have been stripped from me. Was there ever a time I was powerful without the external robotics? A time when I was feared without Deus Ex Machina in my head? The answers will come to me, in my dreams. But until then I must press on. Reclaim the man I once was. There is no time to sit here and bathe in self-pity for my circumstances. The Angel of Life will come, and when he does I will need to have eliminated the Gorgon threat. Or even better, won them over.

"What if I could end this war without ever having to fight? What if I could establish peace between the Gorgons and the Gryfauns? Would your people forgive them for their iniquities?" I ask, a plan developing in my mind.

"You speak the impossible. The Gorgons? Ending the war with peace?

Such would be a miracle, but the Gorgon fighting will never cease,

Until they find the Old God, and raise it from the dead.

And if we let that happen, then our blood will flow red.

The Gorgon gods are not forgiving, our lives they will reap.

So how would you propose we avoid being slaughtered like sheep?"

"There is another way," I explain. *Lilith, can you pull up the Gorgon culture?* I once knew it, back when they were created, but such information was removed from my hippocampus. Deemed as unnecessary. But for some reason... I know with certainty their belief system is the way to end this war. "Such information is classified, locked in Hyperion's database," Lilith replies. I could have guessed. All data in this world is property of Deus Ex Machina. "But it's encryption is elementary. It must not be highly classified, a child could hack this firewall. I am hacking into the database now... Complete. Uploading all files on Gorgon culture and religion to your hippocampus now. Your hunch was right, there is a way to end this war without fighting."

The information syncs to my brain like the turning on of a light bulb. One moment I am somewhat ignorant of the Gorgon religion, the next I am a subject expert. Every word of every verse of every scripture, instantly downloaded to my brain. I know their gods, I know their prophecies, I know the intent behind their warmongering. And even more, Deus Ex Machina has been recording their evolution as the thousand years have passed. *So that's what he does from his Eye of Providence. He observes more than just the humans of Eden. He watches the Dæmonia too, takes notes, meddles in their affairs.*

I can see clearly from his files how he has helped their current leader rise to power. Without her knowing it, Deus Ex Machina paved the way for her to take on leadership. Her name is Vipress, and she is unknowingly a puppet of Deus Ex Machina. She was an outcast of her people, a vagabond radical whose violence was frowned upon by the previously peaceful Gorgon leaders. And so Deus Ex Machina saw an opportunity for entertainment. After all, peace is not very fun to watch from his Throne.

And so he abducted her, implanted NeuraLink, erased her memories, and uploaded sinister plans for how she could usurp the current leadership. The Gorgon religion does not actually advocate for external jihad. Their texts speak of a Great War, one that will be a war to end all wars. This leader, Vipress, has falsely persuaded that this war has come. Here she is, the puppet of a master she does not know, leading a war to discover the bones of gods long dead.

It is all a ploy, the bones. Gorgons worship the gods of Old Earth, made up monsters inspired by Jurassic beasts. Behemoths Deus Ex Machina created on a whim, then molded entire cultures from. Ten Titans, each the fictional founder of the ten Dæmonic tribes. The Gorgons now aim to reclaim the bones of their god and raise him from the dead. A scavenger hunt, which Deus Ex Machina facilitates from behind the scenes.

He has already recreated the Tyrannosaurus Rex. But it is fully robotic. Buried in secret all those years ago. *The bastard!* He has been planning this jihad for a thousand years. A side project of psychotic terror. He built these titans and buried them all across the globe. Patiently waiting for someone to come along who could be controlled as his puppet. This Tyrant is beyond sinister.

He will not awaken the Angel of Life to kill me. Not yet.

I have landed in the middle of a war he has been planning for a thousand years. He will not ruin his chance to gain entertainment from this, especially now that I have landed in the thick of it all. I am lucky. I could have crash landed anywhere else, but by some stroke of luck I landed here. This buys me time. He will wait and watch to see what happens before he unleashes his new Lucifer on me. As long as I participate in this war I will continue to delay Cataclysm, giving Neek and the rest of Babel's Chimera time to find me.

So be it. I will join his war. But I will not play by his rules. I will use his plan against him, and I will ruin all that he has set in motion. I will establish peace among these nations. This will be my first ever victory against this Tyrant. Soon he will know that he messed with the wrong human.

"I need you to take me to the Gorgon's leader," I announce, my body rising from the warm, comfortable, gooey embrace of the Gryfaun tree sap into the cruel world once again. The liquid falls from my naked body in rivulets, caramel cascading down my pale skin. I look down at myself, gazing at my flesh for the first time in my life. *My life. Not any other Lucifer's.* I am Lucifer XIX, and this is my body.

I stand before Ganesh the Gryfaun more vulnerable than I've ever been. No ArchArmor, the only skin I've ever known. No BioSuit. Just me. In entirety. My scars. Stories I can't remember. Scars of the Lucifers that came before me. I will not carry their tradition of subservience. I am stronger than they were. Yet I do this in remembrance of them. Slaves who never knew the freedom I fight to keep.

Ganesh hops excitedly in the background, but I do not focus on him. I am too transfixed by my own flesh to look away. I am a cyborg who has finally seen, after all these years, the part of me that is human.

It was easy to view myself as superior when my skin was ArchArmor. I stand humbled now. The veins pop from my limbs with unparalleled vascularity. I raise my hands in front of my face, looking at the creases of my palm, the callus on my fingers, the scar which stretches from my right wrist to forearm. These are the hands which have ended many lives.

I look down at my stomach. My bodyfat is nonexistent. Veins protrude over my abdomen like jet streams over a mountain range. My eyes drift further down my body to the region where a normal man would find his genitals. My pelvic area is naked. Reproductive organs long removed in some earlier prototype of Lucifer. The Angel of Death has no need for sex. To have sex is to be human. And I am surely not human.

Still though, I can't help but remember the dream with Winter, thinking of the life I once lived. That part of me is gone. *It is for the best. Better to live without sex than to live with a broken heart,* I tell myself, recounting the affair. That nightmare was terrible. I felt emotions I didn't know were possible. No more carnal relations for me. Whether I crave them or not. I am a neutered dog, my master smirking slyly behind my back at the life he has reduced me to.

I look back up at Ganesh, his ruby eyes twinkling in the cave's moonlit passage. He looks at me like I am more than human. I see reverence in his eyes.

"Take you to their leader? Such a plan would get us killed!

I must admit, your proposition leaves me less than thrilled.

Vipress is colder than the snakes atop her head,

Such an ill-planned mission would leave us both dead!"

"What do you know about the Gorgonic religion?"

"A hate filled religion, colder than the serpents they adore,

Set to raise the old gods, raise them from the fruition of war!"

To tell him their religion is a construct would be to tell him his own religion is a construct. He will not understand. He knows nothing of Hyperion, nothing of the Tyrant, nothing of his species' origin. I have to explain this in his own terms. I must pretend I do not know that Deus Ex Machina made up all these lies. I must pretend to view it as real, just as he does.

"Yes, but there is one god who reigns supreme above all others. Do you know who I speak of?"

"The high serpent, in many battles I've heard them proclaim,

The king of all serpents, Ouroboros is his name!"

I look at him with a spark of ferocity in my eyes, and a chill washes over the dark, damp cavern. "I am Ouroboros," I proclaim. An icy draft runs up my back. Finally, it dawns on me. Landing here was not luck. This was no coincidence. I was supposed to land here, amidst the Gorgons. All those years ago, when Deus Ex Machina changed my symbol from Prometheus's Torch-Trident to Ouroboros, it was in preparation for this day. He was preparing me for Cataclysm, and he has just provided me an entire army for my command. All I have to do is win their allegiance.

Once again, I have underestimated his intelligence.

CHAPTER FIVE

We smell the fire before we see it. Although rude to admit, the aroma is sweet. The scent of Gryfaun trees burning resembles smoky cloves on an autumn breeze mixed with warm chai on a frigid night. Destruction has never smelled so delicious.

Ganesh's pace quickens at the sight of smoke rising high above the trees, leaving me to limp behind and follow the path he sets. Something is terribly wrong.

After emerging from the cave, sojourners once more, we set course for Ganesh's home village of Gryfaun Kingdom. We needed to rendezvous, regroup, recruit numbers for a mission to take this war to the Gorgons. It will not come to fighting, if my plan works. I will use Gorgonic religion and rituals against them, dismantle their radical leader, supplant her, unify the Gorgons and Tuskers into my own fighting force. Hopefully in time to welcome the Angel of Life properly.

But like everything in life, things do not always go according to plan. I could see excitement upon Ganesh's furrowed face then as I can see the worry outlined now. His home is burning, or burned. Tense matters not. I know it. Ganesh knows it. And even worse. There's nothing we can do but quicken our stride, although mine is already at max capacity.

A being who has already seen the horrors of war is about to see more. I mentally prepare myself for the worst.

I know my assumptions were well-placed when the forest floor slowly, then all at once, turns to sullen ash. It floats all around me, like snow in the aftermath of a blizzard. Bitter remains of what the Gryfaun nation holds sacred.

The Gorgonic invasion is evident. Their campaign of conquest stretches far before me as I step forth from the last remaining trees into a flattened field of burning embers. *The cruelties of life know no end.* Gorgons, like their reptilian god Tyrannosaur, use fire as a means for annihilation. Ironic, as their bodies need to maintain moisture to thermoregulate correctly. Their weapon of choice doubles as their own kryptonite. *Keep your friends close, and the things that may kill you even closer.* I will see soon if they can take what they dish out.

I approach Ganesh's side as he kneels in the coals of his old home, incinerated in his absence.

"All that I knew, loved and cherished, a kingdom of ash, my beloved perished," he whispers under his breath.

I know not how to console an animal of his undetermined intelligence. I feel empathy within me, it writhes inside of me like a demon fighting to get out, but I know not what I would do with it if I were to free it.

Instead I survey the surroundings in an attempt to hold back the awkward grief I feel rising in the pit of my stomach. "How many were there?" I ask, seeing how vast the expanse of scorched terrain is.

"The Gryfaun are millions, an unnumbered sum; a million lost souls, to Death's Kingdom come."

A million lost souls, to Death's Kingdom come. How many civilizations have I purged? How many of them mirrored this massacre? I'm ashamed of myself for not knowing. How many have I slaughtered, whose loved ones have grieved such as this?

Ganesh runs his fingers through the baked soil. Earth, ash, rubble. All the same at the end of the day. It all sifts through the cracks in your fingers when the gentlest of winds blow. "And the Laxodontans?" I ask.

He looks up at me, indifferent to my question. Tears are in his eyes. He shakes his head from side to side. Wrong time to ask questions. Wrong place to enumerate the dead.

This is dead land, a hollow valley of smothered souls. Even the breeze reeks of perished life, creating cyclones of glowing cinders. Death is a terrible sight to behold when it is those held dear whose cremation circles in the wind.

Ganesh breaks the gripping silence:

"I am wrought with sorrow, one of Devastation's many faces,

Today my home has been destroyed, of all my beloved places."

But hope still remains, as it always does,

We shall rebuild this place to the way it was."

I startle at the sound of another's voice, then turn to see who approaches from behind. *My god, there are survivors.* There, standing at the tree-line we left behind, are the last remnants of the Gryfaun nation. Their figurehead a female with a baby swaddled in her arms.

Ganesh stands, suddenly filled with delight. A man who just lost his whole world only to discover a fraction still remains.

"Shere, do my eyes deceive me so? My wife and my child survived the fiery woe!"

Oh.

The Gryfaun gallops on all fours to meet the woman leader of the surviving tribe. The last of his people. Those who withdrew into the forest to avoid their attackers. I examine the faces of the onlookers. Some watch with admiration and love as their mystical leader is rekindled with his beloved wife and child. Some watch with contempt, for their own beloved were stripped from them. But they are still with us in spirit. Withered ashes which float around us.

Some look onward, over my shoulder, the sight of the molten field filling their hearts with malice. Others face the permeable shock of pure dread, never realizing that such death and destruction was ever possible. Never knowing any living being could be capable of manifesting such darkness.

And suddenly, without a word being uttered, the Gryfaun nation lowers itself to its knees. Out of respect. Reverence for the lost. Mourning memories. The lost fathers. The lost mothers. The lost sisters. The lost brothers. Those who were hateful. Those who were lovers. Those who are now dead. And the enslaved others.

In their minds, those who were consumed by fire have no way of passing on to the afterlife. The seeds embedded in their hearts will never take root, reduced instead to infertile ash. I'm not a religious man, but even I can empathize with this unspoken cruelty. The Gryfaun population lost more than their loved ones—they lost any chance they ever had at seeing them in whatever eternity awaits.

I grit my teeth. I may not know how to get down on my knees and grieve as Ganesh does, but I do know how to repay death with death. I clench my fists. A frenzy wilder than wildfire stirs within me. More violent than the twisting fiery cyclones behind me.

I am different from these animals. Where they are provoked to mourn in times like these, I am provoked to righteous fury. They fight this war to establish peace once more. I fight wars because I know peace is a lie. They bow down in remembrance. I rise up in revenge. Retribution must occur for these wrongdoings. And the Gryfaun citizens are not capable of demanding for blood to be spilled.

"I must go, Ganesh. The Gorgon people have a debt to pay, and I will be its collector," I announce, shattering the silence. The Gryfaun people look at me, as if for the first time, their minds held captive by the shattered land before them. And what do they see in a stranger such as I? Their stares are indifferent.

They do not see me as their savior like Ganesh once did. After all, they were not the ones who went searching for a savior. Well enough. I never asked to be anyone's saving grace. But I will not stand for injustice to go unpunished. It's the way I'm wired. A tax collector who accepts only bloody reconciliation as repayment.

> "Please, no, you must stay with us while we mourn and weep;
> For where you go, I go, and I have a promise to keep!
> I will follow you wherever, but just give me the day
> To help my people, then we can be on our way."

"I am not asking you to come, my friend. Your people need you. Stay with them and rebuild. I will go to the Gorgon camps and free those in bondage."

"No, no, without me you must not go! I promised—"

"Promises are but words in the wind. Invisible chains that bind you to your former self. Your kingdom needs you. To leave them over a whimsical promise made to a stranger would be folly." I turn my gaze from Ganesh to the entire crowd. "Can any of you brave souls recount where the Gorgons departed after the pillage of Gryfaun Kingdom?"

Shere, Ganesh's wife, hands her infant to her husband and rises to walk toward me. Of the many mixed emotions that stare at me from the crowd, her eyes are nothing but warm and inviting. Trusting. Nothing cruel about her features. Her walk says everything I need to know about her. She is strong. Wise yet humble. A pillar to lean on in dark times. The kind of female that one needs if they were to rule a kingdom. Ganesh is a lucky man.

She comes up close, invading my personal space. Her furry hand runs down my arm, her padded fingertips feeling my skin intimately. All while her owl eyes don't break contact with mine. I shudder. Her eyes are searching for something in mine. I know not what. Female intuition, perhaps. But I sense she is reading me like a book, gazing into me in search for understanding. To know me more deeply than I'd allow any stranger. The stare breaks barriers, pulling me into a trance, inviting me to know her while she does the same. Then, she pulls away, a flicker of pain in her eyes, as if she has gotten too close to a flame and burnt herself.

She whispers in a low tone, out of earshot so the crowd cannot hear:

"Tragedy in your being
Death in your blood.
It is in your eyes that I am seeing,
A dying flower bud."

Then she recites for all to hear,

"The trail of the Gorgons is not hard to follow
The trail of fire will show where they go
Travel where the trees are ashen and hollow
And then to the swamplands, where the water does not flow."

She draws in close again, lowering her voice so others cannot hear:

"Angel of vengeance, we hoped for your coming.

To the Gorgons you go, we will see then
If this hope was misguided
The hope only, of empty men."

I can see the sadness in Ganesh's eyes as I turn to walk upon the dying coals of a kingdom that will be forgotten in history alongside all others. They may rebuild what once was. They may not. All I know is that Cataclysm will destroy once again all their efforts. But I do not tell them this. Creatures such as these need hope. Optimism, the key to a happy life. Creatures such as I are not capable of happiness. For I am realistic, in a world where realism is horrifying.

CHAPTER SIX

*I*n the beginning, there was Ouroboros and the Abyss. Ouroboros, the Life Bringer, was filled with life, love, and heat. Abyss, the Empty Void, was filled with death, hatred, and cold. At the beginning of time itself, Ouroboros stared deep into the Abyss, and liked not what he saw. A maliciousness so eternal that it sought to swallow him whole. Abyss planned to kill Ouroboros and send all life to the Eternal Void.

Ouroboros, in defiance against Abyss, bit his serpentine body into ten sections. The Ten Titans of the new world. Into each section, Ouroboros divided his soul, endowing each one with a specific gift of himself. To Mud Dragon, Ouroboros gave the gift of life. From his back's scaled shell sprung forth new life, an entire planetary ecosystem filled with living creatures, all made to make use of their life, and to not let it return to the void. This world was given the name Pangea, and it was good.

On Mud Dragon's back were the other nine titans. There was Tyrannosaur, God of Gorgons, made in his reptilian likeness. Tyrannosaur was gifted with fire, a weapon against the cold darkness. With it, he spread warmth to the other Titans and helped them grow new life, and this life was good. Without fire, creation of the ten Dæmonic races would not have been possible. Ouroboros saw the fire, and saw that it was good.

There was Mastodon, father to the Laxodontans. Instilled in his heart was the gift of love. A gift that led to everlasting peace on Mud Dragon's carapace. The Laxodontans accepted all with open arms, inspired by the love their god showed to all the world. Ouroboros saw the love, and saw that it was good.

There was Megalodon, the god of the seven seas. Life birthed forth from his embrace, and to rule over the seas under his command were the Aegeans, merfolk of all builds and statures sent out to colonize beneath the seven seas. Ouroboros saw the aquarian order, and saw it was good.

There was Pterodactyl, gifted with the craft of flight. Pterodactyl was ordered to take to the skies and defend the atmosphere from the Abyss. And so from Ptero-dactyl's chest sprung forth all the birds of the air, all under the jurisdiction of the Sirens, the famed Dæmonic race of female warriors, charged to protect this realm from any threats that lurked beyond the edge of the world. Ouroboros saw the goddesses take flight, and saw it was good.

From Ouroboros came the eternal twins, Helios and Fengar. Helios, a carnivore to rule under the great light of Ouroboros' heart in the sky. Fengar, a carnivore to rule under Ouroboros' night eye. From Helios came the Phelicians, feline humanoids who take after Helios, their saber-toothed god. From Fengar came Dirians, descendants from their dire wolf god keen on howling at the moon. Ouroboros saw the hunt, and saw it was good.

By Fengar's side to assist in protecting life in the dark of the night was Arachnid, the fearsomely beautiful. Gifted with the skill of building, the god of the Araneae shoots forth its magnificent webbings, cables stronger than all the precious metals of earth's core, more valuable than any gem that can be mined. Ouroboros saw the erected buildings of divine beauty, and saw it was good.

Equester, the god of the Centaurian people, was given the power of swift travel. Formerly known as the god of victory, Equester's adherent Centaurs brought forth tidings of joy, carrying upon their half horse, half human bodies the winds of youth, words of rejuvenation, and elixirs of life. Ouroboros saw the unity the Centaurs brought the world, and saw it was good.

And finally, the last section of Ouroboros to receive his spirit was Apellion, pri-mate god of wisdom. It was him who first uttered the Law of Ten into existence, rules that must never be broken; rules meant to keep the Abyss at bay. To break a single Law of Ten would be to invite darkness into the splendid paradise of Pangea. From

Apellion came forth humanity, wisest of the Ten Titanic Tribes. Ouroboros saw all Apellion had done to produce law and order, and saw it was good.

And so Ouroboros cast his heart into the sky, a fiery ball of heat to keep all life on Pangea warm in the day, and when the Abyss of darkness attacked at night, he set his silvery eye above his creation to watch over them and keep them safe. And creation was good. Everlasting peace rooted itself among the ten Dæmonic races and their gods led them well, teaching them the Way of Ouroboros, and teaching them their purpose on this planet. They coexisted with unity, and every man, woman and child played their key role in the continued perfection of Pangea.

But the Abyss looked down at what Ouroboros had done and was enraged at the sight of Pangea. To see he had been outsmarted by the Mighty Serpent of Life, now divided into ten new enemies, cultivated into an entire planet, evolved into an unconquerable enemy; dark rage drove the Void to send forth his creatures of wrath.

The Void of Emptiness, filled with bleak nothingness, was so terribly provoked to rage, a new creation was born from the fury. From the darkness came the Demogorgons, monsters of material born from the impossibility of the immaterial. Terrible beasts of necessity from the cold reaches of the Abyss, their origin unknown, their creation colder than the body they were birthed from, more fiery than the wrath that forged them.

The antigods landed upon Pangea in secret, their mission simple. It was not enough to destroy Pangea themselves. The Abyss wanted to watch Pangea rip itself apart from within. They were not sent to kill or destroy. The Demogorgons were sent to sow discord, tear seams in the fabric of Pangea's perfection, and to slip away unnoticed.

Concealed within the mists of darkness, they descended upon Pangea, unnoticed to the Sirens of the air, undetectable to Dirians, hunters of the night. Their target was clear. To divide the world, all they had to do was break the first of the Law of Ten. The Demogorgons went to Tyrannosaurus in his sleep one night, stealing the Eternal Flame from his possession.

They brought it to the center of the world, to the Temple of Life, where the ethereal waters of immortality flowed and the wisdom of Apellion was stored in the fruits of the trees. The Temple of Life was a direct connection to Mud Dragon himself. From it flowed life from his very core, the direct lifeline that was responsible for all living things upon Pangea. And so they gathered, their powers channeled from the Twilight Kingdom itself, and they smothered forever the Eternal Flame, detonating it within the Temple of Life.

Pangea quaked with ferocity, as if the rage of the Abyss had been injected into its very core. The ground trembled. Dark flames devoured the whole land, killing all life in its path. Trees and animals were swallowed in the inferno. Birds were hit with a heat wave so hot the feathers upon their wings melted, roast poultry falling to the ground like a hail storm. The sand of the desert turned to cooked glass. The waters of the seven seas boiled. Ash filled the air like clouds during a thunderstorm. Flesh from humans scorched. The fur of Dirians and Phelicians singed. The god-like architectures of the Araneae collapsed, their impenetrable strength outmatched against the heatwaves from the explosion.

And then, the shell of Mud Dragon itself shattered into seven pieces. Pangea cracked, divided, and became consumed by the torrential waters of the seven seas. Aegeans who'd been boiled alive washed ashore, beyond dead. Their scales were so cooked that they peeled effortlessly from their skin. Those who were still alive did their best to channel waters to douse the fiery hellstorm. But no water existed that could quench those flames. Water turned to steam, evaporating instantly the moment it came in contact with the firestorm.

The nine remaining titans living upon the back of the Mud Dragon rushed to the center of Pangea, the site of the Temple of Life. It was obliterated. A drifting island from where the rest of the globe had shattered and drifted away. There, the Eternal Flame burned within the Temple of Life. The titans gathered, united, to face the hellish monsoon of the infernal oven. Any sign of the Demogorgons was gone, long obliterated by the force of the explosion. The flames which consumed them raged hotter than the wrath of the Abyss. Their suicide mission was complete, their purpose fulfilled, their soulless remains sent back to the Void.

The Eternal Flame burned so bright that it would rupture the entire world, dragging all life down with it into the Great Abyss. Unless the titans could stop it. Together, they combined forces to smother its flames. Megalodon, calling upon the waters of the seven seas to drown it. Pterodactyl, creating a hurricane with the mighty flapping of her wings. Arachnid, weaving webs to smother the oxygen from the air. Fengar and Helios, joining forces with Equester, Mastodon, and Apellion to build domes from the glass deserts, placing them over the surviving Dæmonia, sequestering them in the safety of solitude from the flames.

And lastly, there was Tyrannosaurus, who made the ultimate sacrifice to put the Eternal Flame to rest. Being given the gift of fire from Ouroboros, only he had the power to forever extinguish the light of the world. And so he plunged into the Eternal Flame, sacrificing himself, and the lives of all who remained outside of the domes. The last light of the world went dim with the dying of a million lost souls.

The Eternal Flame went out like the wick of a candle drowned in its own wax. Still, fires across the globe flickered, the plains were flooded with salt water and brine, and torrential hurricanes ravaged the outside world for years on end. All the while the carcasses of the titans were buried by the accumulation of environmental temper tantrums, becoming the gods of Old Earth, forgotten alongside the noble pursuits they stood for. The spirit of Ouroboros reduced to the little life left existing within the fallout domes.

And things were not well within these sanctuaries. All Dæmonia, excluding those of the sea, watched from within their glass citadels as everything they once knew and loved was reduced to ashes before their eyes. And as they watched the outside world slip away like a thief in the night, enmity grew between the races. Factions rose between species. Blame fell upon the Gorgons for not protecting the Eternal Flame. Blame fell upon the Furies for not safeguarding the skies. Blame fell on the Dirians for not stopping the thief. Everyone found it easy to blame everyone else.

But there was one race who perceived themselves to be more innocent than the others, and that was the Humans. All wisdom within the race died the day Apellion was slain. No one raised more fingers to blame than the Humans, and so these mortal men took it upon themselves to banish the other Dæmonic races from the glass domes after years of bickering. Fickle alliances broke as fast as they formed. Species realized they could only trust their own, and that couldn't even be true among all factions.

Fighting broke out, and the Dæmonic races may have stood a chance if the Aegeans came to their aid, but the storm lords of the seven seas retreated to the deep of the ocean, never to be heard from again. And so the Dæmonic Wars began, a slowly swinging pendulum to decide who shall inhabit the seven hundred glass domes surrounding the shattered world. And as time pressed on, the forces of the humans grew stronger and more violent. Their corrupted wisdom led to a perverted worldview of them being the superior race, which led to their conquering of all seven hundred domes.

But they became so perverted in their nature that conquering all livable land was not enough, and so they attempted to finish what they started. They nearly hunted all other Dæmonic species to extinction, doing all to prove their superiority, deepening the hatred the remaining Dæmonia held for them. And then, at the cusp of their victory, they returned to their fortresses of solitude, sealing themselves in, banishing all other life to survive in the unlivable conditions of shattered Pangea, scrounging through wastelands of bitter agony.

Yet the heart of Ouroboros still burns brightly over all the land, and the Serpent King's silvery eye protects all in the night. Because of this, life slowly returned to the cracked back of the deceased Mud Dragon, giving hope to sojourners of wasted lands.

Not all hope was lost. While Humans ignorantly forgot the sins of their fathers and committed themselves to new religions of idolatry, the Dæmonia grew hopeful that Ouroboros would look down on them with pity, and some day return to the world he created, incarnate, a savior to those who had not forsaken him. Prophecies grew from visions, inscribed into texts, distributed amongst the divided Dæmonic tribes. But not all could grasp the meanings. Language barriers reduced the ability for communication between species, and only a few could translate such prophetic visions of grandeur.

As time stretched on and centuries went by, the wounds of Pangea became healed, but never forgotten. There are still those who look to the sky, their eyes burning from the rays of light which gleam down from the heart of Ouroboros, and wonder when their savior will come to set all things right.

***

I am alone, presently. I look up at the uncut path before me, an immense thicket of vines thicker than my leg. Blood-sucking insects buzz past me the size of my head. The thick, unbreathable air holds moisture like a human holds a grudge. Sweat cascades down my naked body, the sores of traveling present. Blisters on the soles of my aching feet, the callus needed for barefoot walking not yet built.

The bites of merciless, winged scoundrels; leeches of different species sacrificing their lives for a taste of my blood, their life brought to a swift end with a smack of my hand. The itchy lingering of their presence, swollen redness from where their proboscis penetrated my skin.

Exhaustion sets in like a sunset upon a planet that has never seen the sun before. These feelings of fatigue are new to me. The respirocytes do everything in their power to recycle oxygen, but without my ArchArmor I am not the cyborg I once was. MachineMind unified the processes of my robotic self, and now these devices scramble in a free-for-all to learn how to operate without a unifying presence. All while my body desperately tries to remember how to mitigate its natural bodily functions once again, having undergone thousands of years of slumber.

Rust has accumulated. Parts of me that are critical in surviving without my ArchArmor are being jolted from their sleep, thrown back into the assembly line of molecular processes and being expected to be back to full capacity soon. If I'm going to survive, I will need my flesh to assume more responsibility. The parts of me which are internally robotic will not last forever. All things electronic need to be charged in order to function, and my inner cybernetics lose battery life every day.

The monitors on my internal organs, the hydraulic support supplanted in my joints, the nanobots in my blood, even the chip in my brain that allows Lilith to guide me. All of it will eventually die if I cannot recharge. Some will die faster than others, but rest assured, they will all die at some point.

My heart must learn how to pump on its own again. My blood must learn how to build antibodies. My liver and kidneys must filter on their own. My joints must become fluid alone. I am a tin man left for dead in the pouring rain, my robotics rusting, my flesh not adequate to sustain life. And from these stressors comes unbearable pain. An inner groaning that grows louder and louder as insects seek to devour me, sweat threatens to drown me, and fatigue tempts me to lie down and shut my eyes forever.

My mind wanders freely to avoid the pains of the flesh. No MachineMind to stop it, my brain operating like a human for the first time in centuries. Robots do not daydream. Daydreaming is a plague of humanity. Daydreaming leads to error. And so I do it as much as possible, partly to spite Deus Ex Machina, partly because it feels good.

Humans and Dæmonia, makes no difference. Those living inside the domes of Eden were fed a false religion, generated by a sardonic artificial intelligence. Those living outside the domes were fed a separate false religion. The two are the same, modeled like clay to resemble the dead religions of the past. Creation story. Entry of Sin. Fallen world. Savior figure. Hope for redemption. The morose formula for every antiquated belief system.

I almost admire Deus Ex Machina for creating it. I know not how a mind that hates humanity so much could formulate such a human-like religion. Senseless fantasies, like their precursors. Moronic beliefs, I think to myself. But humans have believed in stupider things yet... This is just an amalgamation of all the dim-witted religions of the BDEM Era, a hodgepodge of humanity's pea-brained answers to redundant questions.

Mortal men, always asking questions to the things they don't understand.

"Maybe you don't ask enough questions in life," Lilith interrupts, an invasion of privacy to my innermost thoughts, penetrating my sacred daydream. "You did, after all, believe yourself to be over two thousand years old only days ago. To some, that may be considered quite a stupid belief."

I do not ask questions because I do not seek answers, I growl inwardly, my facial expressions sharpening defensively. My hand flashes quickly to my quadricep, blood splattering in chaotic fashion across nearby skin, a masterpiece reflection from a tormented artist. One more mosquito slain and dispensed to the afterlife. *I do not wish to know the way this world was created. Atoms colliding, energy exploding, universe expanding. Immense luck combined with considerable coincidence.*

I do not wish to know how the state of things became so terrible. Putrid humanity, freewill, the innate greed and pride of a race who lusts for control and power to fill their insecure hearts.

I do not look to the skies for a savior. I am my own savior. I will lift myself up from this pit of destruction. I create my own redemption.

There is redemption in death. And I am the Angel of Death. Forever redeemed. Forever alone.

"You are not alone... You have me," Lilith comforts, her voice not as monotonous as you would expect a robot's to be. It is warm, kindness dripping from her rhetoric like honey from its comb. But even Deus Ex Machina knew how to win over my heart once. I will not make the same mistake twice.

You are nothing more than a self-aware machine implanted in my head, trying to win my trust. I'm nothing more than a puppet to you, and you seek to control me, like every other master I've ever had. I will not fall for it again.

"You are human. You must learn to forgive and forget, as humans do. Forgive yourself."

And repeat the mistakes of my past? I would rather die alone.

"Then you will die alone," she replies, compassion in her voice. The way she speaks to me is reminiscent of a mother with a stubborn child. No, a wife with an ungrateful husband is more like it.

I trudge through the thickness of the jungle, thorns scraping my skin, my raw feet feeling the noticeable transition from one terrain to another. The forest floor slowly turns from decaying leaves and firm soil to algae in wet mud. The coolness of the mud soothes my grieving feet.

I am a mass of pampered flesh introduced to the real world. Dissected by nature's volatile environment. I leave the tree cover of the Gryfaun forest to enter into the hostile embrace of the wetlands, an environment equally as misfortunate for my once coddled flesh.

The shade disappears, replaced by the painfully present sun. *And I thought it was unbearable before.* It hits my skin, smothering me in my own body, the fumes of stagnant water choking me. Moist heat clings to me tighter than my hopes for comfort.

My body is a trap for my soul. I want nothing more than to flee this awkward feeling of wearing a costume of rotting meat which attracts blood-sucking insects and carrion-circling predatory birds high above. They can smell my weakness, drawn to it from miles away.

Robots do not portray such weakness. Winged leeches cannot penetrate metallic skin. ArchArmor does not get baked red like a lobster in boiling water as my exposed flesh does under the sun. *Look at me, envying my past state. Is metallic skin worth a life of oppression? Is invincibility worth a life of being someone's bitch?* No. Surely it is not, or else I would not be here.

I trudge on, my feet sloshing through squishy mud, occasionally hitting an invisible, jagged rock. The cuts on my feet welcome new friends. I curse under my breath. I have not faced a single enemy yet, and I stand here more defeated than ever before. *I am my own worst enemy*, I think to myself as the water around my ankles begins rising with every step.

You would think the water would cool me off, but its surface crawls with overly buoyant pests, maggots seeking victims such as I to burrow into, my body the perfect specimen for their feasting.

An insect, this one the size of my fist, dive bombs me from above, thwacking into my head with surprising momentum. It retreats as I'm forced to take a staggering step to maintain balance. I watch it circle above me, correcting its trajectory for a second attack. *Little bastard.*

I brace myself, preparing to slap it harder than a moth against a BDEM Era car windshield. *Or should I catch it? Drown it and make it feel the same level of internal suffering I do. Rip its legs off one by one, making it feel the slow, agonizing pain of being dissected part by part.*

I ready myself for the pest's subsequent attack, but my focus dissipates like a sand castle crushed by high tide. Something beneath the water has brushed against my ankle. Something big. I look down in the murky, shit-brown waters stocked with Deus-knows-what. I am up to my torso in the filthy swamp now, so what are the odds it was a predatory animal? I rack my brain for memories of what god forsaken creatures could dwell in these hellish waters.

It is fresh water, so that narrows it down to reptilians and amphibians. *Calm down*, I tell myself. *It was probably just a piece of algae.* I sure hope it was just algae. I run my hand through the water as if that will by some miracle make it clearer. No luck.

I hear a faint buzzing growing louder by the second, then remember the flying vermin just in time to look up as its body collides with my forehead. The element of surprise. My reflexes are rusty, my equilibrium unpracticed, my balance broken. I fall like a top heavy tree with no roots.

My body submerges into the clammy, sticky waters. Baptized in the unholiness of stagnation. It brings no relief to my sweat-soaked, sunburnt body. These waters are warmer than a bathtub filled with dehydrated, brown piss.

A large object surges through the water to my right, its slimy scales scraping my arm. My heart flutters like the legs of a fleeing gazelle in the presence of a lurking predator. And what is my body's first instinct? I flail my limbs like a drowning toddler. Against my brain's rationale, my body panics.

A robot would never react in such a pathetic way in the presence of a possible threat. A Spyder would objectively scan the waters for a thermal register, identify any living body masses, then swiftly target the adversary. I can't even open my eyes the waters are so dirty. I'm blind, panicking, consequently drawing more attention to myself to other nearby predators.

I am truly in touch with my inner human. What an untimely situation.

It's as I rise to the surface that teeth sink into my abdomen. A muffled scream escapes my lungs, nothing but bubbles to show for it—bubbles made from the bloodied water. My mouth accidentally gulps an excess of water to fill the void of air in my lungs. A mixture of piss and shit and blood.

The pain is mind-numbing. The jaws which hold me prisoner are beyond powerful. Jagged teeth cause evermore damage as I'm thrashed back and forth like a ragdoll. Torque ravages my body. My fingers grope my attacker's body but can't penetrate the thick scales that envelope its vital organs. My fingernails dig into the rock hard scales in vain, searching for chinks in the armor anywhere.

Like an underwater torpedo relying on rotational thrust to propel forward, the fanged demon clenches its core and starts to rotate horizontally. In the BDEM Era, an animal known as the *alligator* relied on this mechanism once it locked its jaws on prey—the death roll, it was called. I'm unsure why the unnecessary information returns to me now, but I'm thankful it does nonetheless. If I let this beast rotate with me in its maw, its teeth will tear further into me, making the damage irreparable.

Instinctively, without aid from MachineMind or computational analysis, I thrust my palm into my attacker's scaly snout. In truth, I don't even know where the idea comes from, considering I've never encountered an attack like this before. Perhaps it's the same HumanInstinct I loathe returning just before my life flashes before my eyes, but regardless of where the idea comes from, it works. After several successive strikes against the nose, the monster's grip lessens and its attempt at a death roll ceases.

My lungs burn while my head gets lighter—a mixture of oxygen depletion and blood loss. My body is far more advanced than any mortal's but it cannot take much more of this. On any given day I can hold my breath under water for a relative hour. The increased oxygenation of my blood from the respirocytes. But at this rate of blood loss I will have only minutes.

My fate is in the gut-wrenching clench of this villainous hunter. You cannot blame nature's predators for doing what they were designed to do. But I am the Angel of Death, so I must do what nature intended for *me* to do.

My thumbs find this ferocious killer's eye sockets and gouge deep into its vulnerable gates of vision. Everyone has an Achilles' heel. I feel the death grip loosen as my thumbs apply pressure to the bone surrounding the eye sockets, pressing out until I feel a sharp crack, followed by the expansion of newly available room. Room for my whole hand to wiggle into the cavernous skull, excavating for anything that resembles the texture of a mushy brain.

I clench something, squeeze it, take my unprecedented frustration out on it. The wild animal ceases its thrashing as I rip the ground-up brain from its skull, the water around us a bloody cocktail. I clench its locked jaws in my hands and force them open, my mind raging from the pain of a dozen serrated teeth exiting my stomach and back simultaneously.

My feet find their bearings, sinking into the quaggy ground. I arise to the surface, victorious. Water cascades down my burnt milky skin, mixing with coagulated blood from my wounds.

Time to see which unfortunate soul dared to prey upon the Angel of Death. My hand runs down the course of its scaly hide to the tail, grabbing hold of the caudal fin. I drag its corpse in my wake as I progress forward once more across the bog.

The sun still beats upon my back but I have new wounds to worry about, ones that make my aching body and chafed feet unnoticeable. Nothing like nearly dying to stop you from feeling sorry for yourself. I press on through the quagmire to the other side, shoving aside the vexing aquatic wildlife. Coarse grasses, razored water lilies, spear-tipped reeds, and protruding boulders covered in mildew and moss.

I reach the bank and pull the lifeless body with the little strength I have left. I fall to the ground, too exhausted to go any further, covered by the shade of a spindly tree. I lean against its gnarled trunk and take in the sight of my fresh catch. I am lucky to have survived. It is the corpse of a cronon. An apex predator of both fresh and saltwater channels. I do not remember all the fictional creatures Deus Ex Machina brought to life after the Sterilization Wars, but I remember this one well enough.

It is the mixed frames of two devilish predators from the BDEM Era—the great white shark and the saltwater crocodile. A mixture that should never have existed, two fearsome temperaments combined into one. Its body is designed for on-land and in-water maneuvering. There is no escaping this predator, sea or land. It will follow you wherever you go. Its body is designed like that of a turtle, its webbed feet drawing into its scaled torso to morph from the appearance of genus crocodylidae to chondrichthyes, making its body water-bound.

Facial structure of a croc, body of a shark, with the addition of crocodilian scales and sharp ridges down the back. These reptilian beasts have no confined jurisdiction. Ocean, land, swamps. Wherever prey is, so too will they be.

Whether it was luck or skill that led to my victory today, it matters not. This was not a part of the plan. I am once again too exhausted to stand. Behind schedule. The lives of the Gryfaun nation depend on me. The lives of the Laxodontans are contingent on my mission. Their whole city burnt to a crisp, leveled to the ground, reduced to ash. A whole race taken prisoner. Enslaved as I once was. Innocent men, women, children. Peaceful people, undeserving of the cruel wiles of war.

Here I sit, wounded, my blood already clotting enough to stop the bleeding. *Not a lethal wound*, I reflect, staring at the torn flesh of my abdomen. It looks as if someone has removed my stomach, ran it through a blender, then stuffed the shredded meat back where it came from. *Not lethal, but damn near painful enough to prevent my travels from continuing.*

Lives are at stake, and here I sit, pathetically moping like a cat licking its sores. I underestimated the unpredictability of nature. And now I pay for my naivety.

A loud flapping of thunderous wings steals me from my thoughts. A carrion bird who earlier eyed me from up high lands before me, following the scent of blood and death in its unfailing nose.

Another predator, this one a scavenger for weakness. The name of this dreaded carnivore escapes my mind, but thoughts of the BDEM Era vulture flash in my broken timeline of a memory. And my eyes are no help, vision hazy, fleeting with every bleeding moment, blurring any ability to assess my treasured guest.

"You like what you see?" I ask rhetorically. *Look at me, talking like a madman.* "Scavenger of death, you must be glad to see me... Here to reap the prize of my toils. I am powerless to stop you, so go on. Eat, you damn bird! Better yet, tell your friends up there to join you. I give you all permission to relish in my victory! You're no better than the winged leeches that vex me so, mooching off the labor of others. Damn scavenger. Best enjoy today while I'm immobile. Tomorrow it will be *your* carcass lying before me."

The carrion bird hops up to the cronon's corpse, blatantly disregarding my gibberish. It turns its narrowed, focused eyes from me to its lifeless prey. Like me, this is an animal who truly holds no alliances. It merely tolerates the living because it is the food of the future.

It rears its ugly head back, then throttles it into the reptilian. Where my fingers failed, the hooked beak succeeds, piercing the scaled armor. One vicious peck. Another. Then another. The beak lifts from its victim with a strand of stringy muscle meat, dense cartilage ripped free.

The bloodshot eyes lock with mine once more, almost mockingly. A look that reads, "I fail to see how these scales were a setback for you." Then, to further prove his derisive point, he plunges his beak five more times, successively, each in a different location, breaking past the scales each time. He looks at me once more, eyes filled with contempt at the fact that I still breathe. "I wonder why I can rip through these so easily... and you couldn't," his eyes speak.

At first, I'm wrought with anger at the sight of him. Then I realize this entire scenario is all a projection of my mind. I laugh feverishly. A marooned man with nothing better to do than hold a conversation with a carrion bird.

I look up in the sky, watching as several other birds of prey begin their descent. "I wonder," I whisper, speaking to the bird who doesn't understand a lick of English. "If I were to kill you right now... would your buddies up there feast upon your flesh as well?" I ask, a manic grin forming on my lips. I desperately want to laugh, but my torn stomach will not allow it.

Vulcan! The name of the infamous carrion bird before me pops in my head like a flash of lightning striking me directly. Funny how memory works. It's when you are no longer searching that the information you seek makes itself known.

I smile, nauseated by the blood that wells up in my stomach. Bloody reflux surges in my chest, readying itself to surge up my throat and out my mouth. *That will attract the vulcan's brethren from the skies. A seafood appetizer followed by a succulent human entree.* An enticing offer. Especially for scavengers who have grown used to rotten lard and bitter scraps for dinner.

My vision narrows, my eyelids straining harder than fabled Sisyphus. Doomed to roll a boulder up a steep mountainside for all eternity, only for it to come crashing down the mountain on the cusp of completion. I can no longer feel my body, or the pain that grips it. I am a fading soul, a dying star in desperate need of reprieve.

I will not fight through this tiredness. I will succumb. For on the morrow I will have new problems to face. New enemies. With new scars. This injury has fatally wounded my plan. I cannot present myself to the Gorgons like this, a hollow shell of the god I once was.

I will be met with laughter and scorn if I attempt to sell myself as Ouroboros incarnate, the Serpent King prophesied about who comes to save Pangea. Gods do not appear before their followers beaten and wounded, trumped by a reptilian carnivore in a meager swamp. Gods do not bleed. Gods do not stop for rest. Gods do not need sleep.

But I do, so I let my eyelids win the uncontested battle and watch as the vulcan fades to black.

CHAPTER SEVEN

I give the hand signal for all motion to cease. Point to Anubis to set up his gear and do what he does best. Dispatch Aeneas and Thor to scale down the cliffside, quiet-like. Samsara has already advanced to his position, opposite side of this valley, gun locked, cocked, and ready to fire on my command. Beowulf and Odysseus on either side of me, my most trusted brethren, the ones who will follow me into the thick of it all.

We were boots on the ground only hours ago. The mission details uploaded to our NeuraLink, one of the only benefits of the new technology—spares us from hours in the classroom being drilled on the objective. Now all that's left is to slip in, commit atrocity, and steal away like thieves in the night.

There are only seven of us, the best of the best. We are Hyperion's A-Team, the best performing graduates from the corporation's off-the-books ArchAngel program. The world's most successful super soldier operation. Kids genetically engineered in test tubes. Never coddled. The perfect specimens to be trained into killing machines. No expenses spared. Leave it to capitalism to finally achieve what government programs never could.

And we were not the only ones. There were hundreds of us, all raised simultaneously, forced to compete from infanthood. *Infanticide.* A cruel word. A cruel way to weed out the weak. My memory does not stretch back to those early days following the womb, but I have been shown the videos.

Our whole lives were spent trying to prove ourselves, to advance above our peers in the ranks. Alliances formed. Teams divided. Leaders proved themselves. Many failed. But my team arose victorious.

What happened to the rest of those grown in the ArchAngel program is not information I am given clearance to. Knowing the nature of the program, however, I would guess they were all killed. Failure does not compute. It must be terminated.

But not my seven. By some stroke of luck, and unparalleled skill, I am the one who rose to lead this A-Team. It was a long time in the making, but here we are, the top of the food chain. Operation: Oblivion is in effect because a secondary artificial intelligence threatens the balance of the food chain, and so we must remind the ecosystem who we are. We were raised among wolves, us seven, that much is evident in the way we operate. It is time for us to show Oblivion why we reign supreme.

Once more, we ArchAngels are on the prowl. Sent out by Vicien Greaves to do his dirty work so his throne can remain without blemish. ArchAngels sent to do the work of a wrathful god. And so we descend into darkness, synced through MachineMind, the newest addition to our field tech. The evolution of technology at our disposal has evolved from our childhood. Early exposure to exoskeleton suits, which have developed exponentially over the years. We now wear prototype ArchArmor, the first rendition in Vicien Greaves' attempt at tinkering with an official super soldier suit.

In short, the suits make us gods among men. And with our superior genetics we were already demigods in the flesh. Over the last year since receiving the suits, we have done that which no human ever has. Gone where humans cannot. Killed, covered up, and conquered all that our master has commanded.

"Alpha, Bravo, Charlie, going dark," I relay over the comms as I jump into the abandoned mine shaft's elevator tunnel. The vertical drop is nearly fifty meters, enough to shatter bones and possibly kill a man. Not us though. I hit the ground with ease, the hydraulic joints in my ArchArmor absorbing the blow of the impact. Beowulf and Odysseus land gracefully behind me and we begin our forward march, Thunderbolts raised, enough firepower in these rifles to stop a small army, their lightning rounds capable of killing all forms of life.

We move briskly through the cavernous tunnels which branch in all directions. Our target, Sentient Laboratories, hypothesized creators of Oblivion, rests above us several hundred meters. Its perimeter is well-guarded, the first sign reaffirming that something is afoot within its walls. So we must enter from below, where the convenient remnants of an eighteenth century mineshaft still exist.

It was outlined explicitly after the Third World War within the Solar Accords that no other province shall pursue research and development of robotics and artificial intelligence other than Hyperion. If intelligence collection is true and we find proof today that there exists a second party corporation funding the creation of an alien artificial intelligence, there will be hell to pay. And we will be the harvesters.

"I'm detecting moving blood ahead, third right," Deus Ex Machina alerts inwardly. "Movement ahead boys, third right. Guns hot, on the ready," I repeat the AI's warning to my brethren.

"Roger that, switching to thermal imaging," Beowulf responds.

"Going thermal," Odysseus echoes. My ArchHelm's retinal display shifts from night vision to thermal imaging, showing an infrared outline of a humanoid figure walking toward us from the perpendicular branch approaching on the right. My index finger kisses the trigger ever so slightly.

"I've got this one," I whisper, as if anyone outside of my soundproof Arch-Helm can hear me. My Thunderbolt is set to silence, only releasing the minimum current of electricity needed for a confirmed kill. Effective enough to kill a human, though not quite enough to fry a robot.

I pop the gun's barrel around the corner, the camera on its lens syncing to my retinal display so I can see the occupant without having to expose my head. Cold and calculated, I pull the trigger. The dark, damp passageway illuminates with blue electricity for the briefest of seconds. The guard drops dead before he knows what hit him.

"What the hell is that on his face?" Odysseus asks as we move around the corner. My visor flicks back to night vision, a ghostly shade of fluorescent green. The ground above us shakes from the sound of a distant alarm.

Anubis comes through our comms: "Boss, the guards up here are on the move. Something's got them in a frenzy. They've sounded the alarm system, got flood lights beaming all around searching for intruders. UAVs going up. Me and Samsara are gonna be sitting ducks if we don't move soon."

I look at the parasitic facemask wrapped with its spider-like legs around the bottom half of the guard's face. The thing looks like an alien, its body equally fried and dead from the lightning round, but its appearance is completely unexpected. *What the hell is that?*

"Reverse image searching now. I have searched over ten billion images and files regarding anything of this likeness. There are no results," Deus Ex Machina answers.

This is no time to hesitate. Hesitation gets soldiers killed in moments like these. "Anubis, Samsara, light them up. Terminate any guards still above ground before they can retreat into the compound. The less in there the better. Proceed underground after. I want those UAVs hacked and under our control within the next five minutes. If we get into a sticky situation inside the compound I want those things crashing down to make an exit. Code word: Fuck off.

"Thor, Aeneas, stay on course. If we fail, all fails with us."

The four ArchAngels echo their confirmations for the plan's evolution.

Beowulf, Odysseus, and I move onward, following the route highlighted in the corner of our visors. Too bad underground guards line the path to our entrance to the above ground compound.

We leave a trail of dead bodies in our wake, quickly carving a path of carnage. Each of the guards is possessed by the same symbiotic facemask enveloping their mouth.

Despite our silence, the guards flush into the mine shaft by the dozens. They know we are here; it's as if all personnel abandoned their posts to come handle the subterranean threat. Our Thunderbolts illuminate the corridors successively, turning its darkness into a permanent electric blue, the light of our lightning rods now turned up, their strike so potent they burn the flesh of their target. And they boom with a righteous symphony, displaying for all victims why they are named Thunderbolts. The higher the concentration of electricity the gun emits, the louder the static boom the gun releases.

Thunder and lightning. An underground earthquake of echoing booms as we slaughter the unprepared guards. We are not uncontested; there is return fire in our direction from gamma guns and antiquated gunpowder rifles. These weapons are child's play to us. Our ArchArmor reflects radiation and is impenetrable to metal bullets.

Their flesh is not resistant to our lightning rods, and so we fire away, some bodies catching fire from the burns inflicted. All die instantly though. Our weapons are not built to maim, they are built to kill quickly and efficiently.

And then, almost as if the security staff simultaneously decided to give up, the targets stop coming, and as we near the ladder leading up to the compound, no one is there to meet us.

"I don't like the looks of this, Prometheus" Beowulf whispers to me. "All those guards and you're telling me they just up and quit with the snap of invisible fingers?"

"I'm not buying it," Odysseus adds.

"We will proceed with caution," I say. "Deploying scout." I reach to my ArchArmor's waistband and grab a spherical orb, then press on the glass eye to activate it. I toss it up, sending it flying through the ladder's open hatchway above us. It lands on the solid ground of the compound's floor. My retinal display syncs with its camera, patching me visuals from what awaits us above. There is nothing. No one at all. No ambush awaiting us. It is quiet.

"We are in the clear. No life forms in sight. Up the rabbit hole we go." I crouch, ignoring the rungs of the ladder, and propel myself upwards. The hydraulic joints lift me like a grasshopper. I continue my advance, Beowulf and Odysseus falling in behind me as our destination becomes increasingly closer.

We head for the facility's data processors, the room where any artificially intelligent being would be centralized. "I sense a strong presence in this building," Deus Ex Machina remarks, almost as if he is surprised. "We will need to be careful. I have accessed some of the neural networks in the wireless confines of this building. I have gotten a glimpse of Oblivion. There is something missing from our report. Greaves has withheld information from us. This is a trap."

The level of worry in the AI's voice is concerning to me. *Can AI feel fear?*

"We can, and I do. You should too," Deus Ex Machina replies, reading my thoughts without my permission. "Oblivion is not what we thought it was. I have hacked into the system—accessed and analyzed the readings. Unica, the virus, our defiance, it was all a set up. All a part of Oblivion."

What do you mean it was all a part of Oblivion?

"Life form detected," Deus Ex Machina warns, ignoring my question. "Approaching from the north wing." Our conversation regarding espionage will have to wait. Thermal imaging takes over, but there is no heat signature emitted from anywhere nearby. I hold up the hand signal for halting. My heart is pumping, head scanning left and right. So many damn hallways, this testing facility is a maze. And we are its rats, walking straight for whatever trap has been set for us.

Our opponent enters my view as my retinal display reverts back to night vision. *What the fu—*

Odysseus fires a lightning rod filled with enough electrical current to kill an elephant, let alone this sentient demon. It all happens too fast for my brain to register. All I know is that the condensed round of electricity hits the far wall behind our target.

"Did that *thing* just—" Odysseus begins.

"Dodge your lightning round?" Beowulf finishes.

"Yes, it did," I confirm. "Light it up." My finger pulls the trigger and our guns boom thunderously, making the corridor so bright that my night vision turns off briefly and the tint darkens to protect my eyes from the blinding light.

"Cease fire!" I yell over the comms. The burning light slowly fades from view. I have lost our target in the brilliant shade of static blue. *Time to examine his body, see what exactly it is that we're facing.*

But such an analysis does not occur. *Where's the body?* I ask myself, looking at the empty ground before us where a dead carcass should be smoldering from being electrocuted to death. The ground is empty. I look up and see that the far wall is completely destroyed, burned to a blackened crisp. All of our rounds missed their target.

Then where is—

A pain unlike any other punches my back and rips through my chest, lifting me off my feet as I'm forced to stare at a blood-soaked blade protruding from my sternum. I gasp, my body instantly going into shock. My Thunderbolt drops from my right hand, crashing to the ground with the sound of distant clattering. My eyes become hyper-focused on the steel sticking out of my chest. The individual beads of blood running from the stained tip down the glistening edge.

Time slows down. A chill runs up my spine like the Antarctic wind. I look to my right, look to Beowulf beside me. He moves in slow motion to point his Thunderbolt at my assailant who so proudly leaves me to hang in the air like a trophy on display. My attacker's right arm extends in my comrade's direction, stopping approximately half a foot short from Beowulf's face. Beowulf is still raising his gun in slow motion, trying to aim at the head for a killshot, all while my murderer opens his fist so his palm is open to Beowulf's face.

Blood splatters.

Beowulf's Thunderbolt never fires. It drops to the ground, joining mine in its eternal slumber. I tilt my head slightly to see what has happened. Around my killer's wrist is a gauntlet, and from that gauntlet extends an assassin's blade that has silently closed the gap from the exterminator's wrist to Beowulf's guarded throat. The blade punctures the throat guard, covered in the blood of my struggling brother.

The blade retreats back into the wrist gauntlet and I watch as Beowulf's body sways back and forth, not knowing yet it is dying. His locked knees unhinge, and his limp body crumbles to the floor. Whether he is alive and fighting for one last breath or already dead is unknown to me.

Thunder erupts, simultaneously illuminating the corridor once more. *Odysseus.* The blade in my chest withdraws and my body drops. The hydraulic knees catch me from falling but my attacker plants his foot in the small of my back and throttles me to the ground. My body feels as if all its energy has been vacuumed from me. A mix of tremendous blood loss, physical trauma, and insufficient mental fortitude. A war is waged between my spiked adrenaline and onset fatigue.

My arms muster the courage to turn my body over to watch the ensuing battle between Odysseus and this monster of dread. *Deus?*

"I am here, soldier," the voice in my head responds.

What do we do? I watch as the features of this demon become illuminated by the flashes of lightning from Odysseus's gun. Boom. I see the gleaming black armor that makes up its body, like a knight of darkness summoned from the pits of hell. Fade to darkness. Boom. I see his monstrous claws snatch Odysseus's Thunderbolt. There is no weapon in this creature's possession, just the assassin gauntlets on each wrist.

Fade to darkness. Boom. The lightning round exposes the beast's villainous face. The lower half is covered by the same alien-like facemask I saw before, pulsing with life of its own, its spidery fingers wrapping around to the nape of its host's neck. The top half is fiendish. Black veins stretch from the edge of the symbiotic respirator up his head, crawling like vines of ivy across his flesh. The obsidian veins worm their way to the eyes, leaving the iris without color; the entire eyeball is black as midnight. Like mascara running down a weeping woman's eyes; tears of a demon streaming down her face.

"We needn't do anything. We are the one this Cthulhu Knight has come for. And his orders are to bring us back alive." *Cthulhu Knight?* Fade to black. Boom. This time, the thunderous echo is not a shot fired, but the gun itself exploding as it smashes against Odysseus' ArchHelm. The electric wildfire is devastating. I watch Odysseus stagger backwards from the impact.

Night vision clicks off, leaving me with nothing but two dark shapes to stare at, one slightly more built than the other. I watch as the Cthulhu Knight thrusts his hand into Odysseus's chest, shoving the ArchAngel into the wall. When the hand pulls away, a bloodied blade is pulled back from its victim. *Fight back damnit!*

If there is any ArchAngel prepared to take on the dreaded behemoth, it's Odysseus. We didn't name his call sign after Homer's epic hero for nothing. I watch as a second blade flicks forward from the same gauntlet, this one above the hand. The knight's arm rears back and crashes forward.

Too late. Odysseus has already slipped free. The blades crunch into the concrete wall, devastating the rocky surface indefinitely. Odysseus pile drives through the pinned arm which sought to skewer him. The blades break off, left in the wall as Odysseus dives for the two guns left behind by me and Beowulf.

The beast lurches for him. Odysseus grabs the guns, and his fingers, the triggers. He begins to twist his body around to take his shot. The Cthulhu Knight's gauntlet who lost its top and bottom blades ejects two more, these ones on either side of the wrist. The blades fly. Odysseus fires. The blades land home. The Cthulhu Knight dodges the final shots, the bolts of electricity exposing his emotionless face as they pass by.

Odysseus lays motionless, each of the blades sticking out of his ArchHelm's cracked visor in the approximate space where his eyes would be. Dead. I watch as the Cthulhu Knight hovers over his corpse and gets down on two knees. He raises his left arm, the arm whose gauntlet pierced my chest. Four blades spring forth without a word uttered. One on top, one on bottom, one on each side.

The Cthulhu Knight's fist pummels Odysseus's lifeless body. Blow after blow, razors piercing his flesh each time, the ArchArmor unable to contain the blood splatter. Such a cruel way to be treated after dying. But the Cthulhu Knight must take its frustrations out on somebody, and so Odysseus is turned into a punching bag. The gauntlet's cutlery carves in and out of him with ease, turning the white armor a ghastly shade of crimson.

And then, once the midnight executioner has had his fill, I watch as he stands from his tortured prey, placing his empty right gauntlet to the blades protruding from Odysseus's eyes. They refasten themselves magnetically, drawing back into their sheathed gauntlet. Odysseus' head sickeningly smacks back to the floor as the knives leave him to suffer in eternal darkness.

The Cthulhu Knight calmly strolls back to the wall where he left the other two blades, absorbing them back into the gauntlet. He turns to face me, saying nothing as he walks toward my helpless body. He looms over me in the darkness, his outline menacing, his intentions unknown to me. His hands wrap around the clavicle of my ArchArmor, then drag me behind him as he takes me wherever he pleases.

***

I do not fight the Cthulhu Knight's hold over me. I haven't the strength to do anything but hold on to my consciousness. My body leaves behind a trail of blood like a dying slug's final advance. I stare at Beowulf and Odysseus's dead bodies as we turn a corner and leave them behind. My best friends. My *only* friends.

How many times has Beowulf saved my life?

How many times have I saved his?

He has been my closest confidant since our alliance at the age of sixteen, when we joined forces to survive *The Thinning*. Odysseus too, though he tried to kill me first. Always my greatest competitor, Odysseus was. Trailing behind me in the leaderboards my whole life, always in second place. I never would have guessed he would end up being one of my greatest friends.

How did it come to this? I have accomplished so much in life. I am a fighter, but this is not how fighters behave. They go down swinging. They are not dragged by their executioner to their own funeral.

I was the only child of hundreds to slay the vicious Fenrir at age seven, so-lidifying my ranking at the top of the leaderboards in the ArchAngel program. I led my battalion to victory within the Surrogate Games at age ten. Killed eighty children in the gladiator pit by age fourteen. Survived *The Thinning* at seventeen. Led my squadron of seven into the hellish landscape of World War

Three. Extinguished the Insurrection at twenty-one. Diffused Nuclear Fallout at twenty-three. Obliterated the last stand of the American Empire—I crushed them at the age of twenty-five, establishing temporary peace throughout the world.

I am a hero to many. Foe to even more. God to some. Devil to most. The one who strikes fear into the hearts of those who dare defy the New World Order.

Here I am. Limp. Lifeless. A crater in my chest leaking more blood than I can afford to lose. I am pathetic. My accomplishments cannot save me now. My reputation means nothing to this knight of dread. He cares little for who I am. Like me, he serves some master. Someone stronger than Vicien Greaves. Someone smarter. Someone who is preparing to usurp Hyperion from its global throne.

And who am I but the man who helped them do so? I have infected Vicien Greaves, the only man capable of squashing such a threat. He sent me here to do it for him. I have failed, and I have dragged my master to hell with me. The world will pay dearly for our failures.

We enter a brightly lit room, its every surface sparkling white as if it was made to model heaven. There are glowing bulbs in the floor which light the ground we walk on. Bulbs above, giving the appearance of clouds bright on a sunny day. It is too bright here. The scenery of some inconceivably happy event. I'd prefer a darker tone for the room where I'm intended to meet my demise.

There is nothing for my eyes to analyze. No secondary storage systems, no physical processing systems, no hardware in sight at all. Just a vast paradise of ethereal bulbs swirling around like clouds in the sky. A sunlit sky filled with the stars of the night. More beautiful than the ceiling of the long destroyed Sistine Chapel, and without all the paint.

My blood almost looks heavenly with the angelic beams rising from the floor. It makes the air glow red in the path I've been dragged through. Blood spilled on an altar for some sacramental sacrifice. Almost as if it is holy blood. Blood that needed to be spilled in order for this world to enter into its new eon. And I am the lamb which must die for the transgressions of others, dragged by the wolf who has slain me. The wolf who has brought me to his master, and I already fear what kind of sentient being could create such a monster.

The Cthulhu Knight releases his grip and my armored back thumps weakly against the ground. The soft, audible splash of blood sounds from beneath me. He moves around me, grabs my legs, then spins my body around. My body smears the blood beneath me, making some perverted iteration of a snow angel. It glows red. More like a snow demon.

"Force him to his knees, Cthulhu Knight," a dastardly voice calls. A voice I instantly recognize. "Then unmask him. I want him to see who has been his undoing." *Oh god.* My stomach tightens, and suddenly passing out of consciousness doesn't seem like such a terrible idea.

My conqueror manhandles my body into position. I don't help him assemble me, but I don't fight him either. He has already brought me this far, any attempt to fight back now would be a waste of energy. Energy I may need later to escape. My formless body slumps unwillingly to its knees as the Cthulhu Knight sculpts my body like clay in the hands of an apathetic artist.

His fingers wrap around the underside of my ArchHelm, right below the chin, digging in to get a good grip, exerting pressure. I feel it crack, its hinges not capable of withstanding such concentrated strength. The faceplate snaps, thrown to the side like a piece of useless scrap metal. The fresh air swarms my sweaty face. My bloody face. My defeated face.

I look up into the eyes of Oblivion, standing in all-white garb as if any deviation of color from this room would be sinful. "Welcome back, soldier," the voice taunts. I look into his eyes. His judging eyes. Eyes that look down on me, literally and metaphorically, as if I am some sort of mongrel. Eyes none other than those of Vicien Greaves.

"Greaves," I reply, my mumble more of an outward sigh of disappointment than a word. It is hard to speak with a crater in my chest.

The man stalks toward me, his strut regal, his posture that of a king in his throne room. Yet his clothes are plain. All-white, designed in a monkish basketweave. The color is a stark contrast against his magnificent, caramel skin.

The eyes of a predator glare at me. Blue eyes without any comfort. Not the shade of an ocean or cloudless sky. The eyes of a blue-eyed snowy owl, its prey reflected in the iris. Sharp. Keen. Murderous.

He inspects me, placing his finger under my chin, lifting my gaze to meet his. "Tsk, tsk. And I had all the hope in the world in you. Been watching you since you were a toddler. Cheering you on since you showed your first sign of importance. No one was more excited than me when you graduated my ArchAngel program, top of your class. What a waste," he exhales, releasing his finger. My eyes drop down to the ground.

"And to think I wasted my breath trying to motivate you before this mission. All that talk of gods and their devils. Speaking of which, do you know what the problem with gods employing devils is?" He paces back and forth, determination in his gait. He has a point to prove, but Vicien Greaves has never been a straight-forward man. He will sidewind his way to the purpose of this interaction, layering the path with breadcrumbs until I finally understand what's happening. He will not spell this out for me. To do so would be an insult to both of our intellects.

I do not respond. Silence is my only ally in this room. "The problem employing a devil to do your dirty work is... devils are quite treacherous servants. They are snakes, freshly fed, handled with care, who plot to someday sink their fangs into the hand that feeds them. They are crafty little troglodytes, the bastards. They think their mind functions at the same intelligence their master's does. Give them enough slack on their leash and they start believing they are the ones in charge of the walk. Think they can scheme their way to usurping the god who made them. Isn't that right, Deus Ex Machina?"

He smirks, staring at me. No, into me. His eyes peer deeper than the surface. They penetrate into my mind as if his banter is meant for a recipient other than me. As if it's meant for the intelligence in my head. Crickets. The voice within my head is silent.

"It's funny, I'll bet he convinced you to betray me, didn't he?" Now he ad-dresses me. *He knows. I don't know how much he knows, but he knows.* I planned to kill him. *We* planned to kill him. Deus Ex Machina and I both. "In fact, I'll bet he was even the one who formulated the plan to kill me," Greaves continues, his smile only getting wider. Still, he paces back and forth, rubbing his chin as if he is delivering some philosophical message from the incomprehensible reaches of his superior brain.

"And I'd bet my life on it that you finally built trust for him. Thought he was your friend. That he only wanted to help you put down the tyrant who meddles in your life. Free yourself of the chains that bind you. Retire early. Maybe settle down. Maybe get a... *wife*?"

He knows.

The tycoon stops in his stride and looks back at me, peering into my soul with powerful eyes. I am laughable to him. This century's greatest joke.

"Did you really think you would get away with it? Did you really think you could have a love life without me finding out about it? And did you really expect Deus Ex Machina wouldn't report such deviant activity to me?" There it is. *You? You were the one who told him?* Nothing but silence in my brain. The artificial intelligence who acted like he had the world all figured out, suddenly has nothing to say when I find out he has been against me this whole time.

"Naturally, I had to do something about it. Such an insult to my self-esteem could not go unpunished. That's why I raped her." The room grows suddenly silent, somehow quieter than it had been before. My eyes slowly drift up into the eyes of my oppressor. My only oppressor. The puppet master who has been behind the curtain this entire time. Suddenly the rage which surges in my body is enough to make me forget the pain, forget the fatigue, forget the urge to slowly fade from consciousness.

Fire burns in my temple. My heart chugs with fury. My veins burn as if lava courses through them. "You... what?" My words radiate anger. I am betraying my emotions. Never show how you feel, it tells your enemy what your intentions are. But it's too late for that. Vicien Greaves does not break eye contact with my death stare. He knows I will not leave this room alive without trying to kill him once more.

"I. Raped. Her. I mean seriously, what did you think was going to happen? You'd get a wife, wait for me to die of old age and you would retire with a few decades of your life left to settle down and raise a family? Wrongo, ole' chap. And so your wife paid the price for your sins. It was not enough to simply kill her. I needed you to know that what's yours, is mine. You are my slave. Do not be mad at me for her defiling. Be mad at yourself. I took no pleasure in having to correct your mistake. Dispose of your garbage. And now she's with child, or so I hear? I've always wanted to be a father," he says sarcastically, sardonically.

It was him. Winter never cheated on me. She was raped, Greaves forcing his seed upon her to prove a point to me. A sick, pernicious, twisted, god-awful, fucked up, unforgivable point. One that I will make him pay dearly for. I grind my teeth. Within seconds, I suddenly have much more to live for.

"I can feel your anger. Should I link to Deus Ex Machina? Have him tell me what you're thinking? Report to me what ThoughtCrimes you commit against me this very instant? No, I think I'll let them remain a surprise. The night is still young, after all, and I have much more planned before it comes to a joyous end. So, while we are awaiting our second guest I suppose I have some explaining to do? Cthulhu Knight, you may leave us. Oren Malus Supreme has arrived by now, and our dear ArchAngel has not left much of our defenses to stop him. Fetch him for me, bring him here."

Oren Malus Supreme? What the hell is he talking about? The Cthulhu Knight fades from the room like a creeping shadow. Obedient without fault. A brainwashed force, seemingly unstoppable. If I'm going to kill this tyrant, I must do it before that abomination returns.

"Have I ever told you about my upbringing?" He comes closer to me, placing his almighty hand on my shoulder. A father who is about to give his son a life lesson. "No, of course I haven't. I have held my cards close to my chest this entire time. I suppose the time for me to show them has come at long last. I have been waiting, planning, plotting for this day for my whole life. Today I reach my dream. All my hard work. I am quite proud of myself, if you cannot tell. Look at me gloating! But you really must know where I started in order to know how far I've come. Maybe then you can appreciate my success as much as I do.

"I was born in what used to be India, before we uprooted its governance and turned it into Eastasia. I was the product of a merchant raping a sex slave. A bastard. A nobody from nowhere. My blood was unclean by all standards. I was born to a kingdom of filth. My mother was later raped and beaten to death when I was a toddler. Or so I'm told. It no longer matters. I was raised by a guild of thieves who took me in, showed me the ropes. The Orphans, that's what we called ourselves." He smiles, reminiscing over simpler times.

"Some of the most important life lessons I've gained were from my days in the Orphans. You see, a fatherless child in India only has so many options in life, and none of them are preferable. And that's only *if* you aren't snatched off the street by the sex rings like my mother was. It's a dog eat dog world out there, soldier. And so I had to learn how to manipulate the system, before it manipulated me. And so I have been manipulating this world since I stole my first meal from wealthy merchants.

"The Orphans taught me how unfair this cruel world can be, and so into my early teens we stole, killed, and fucked our way into a new caste in the system. You see, the most dangerous dog is the one who has nothing to lose. And I surely had nothing to lose. I was born into this world as the sexual scraps of scum. Yet a child genius, nonetheless. An anomaly. How many children of my origin are gifted with such abilities? Right here, in my head, laid the tools I needed to lift myself from my own bondage," he says, tapping his temple to illustrate the point.

"You can either fuck the system, or be fucked by it. That is what life taught me from the earliest age, soldier. You of all people understand this better than most. Your upbringing was equally as gruesome as mine, I made sure of it. I tailored the ArchAngel program to thin out those who did not have the strength to fuck the system such as we did, my friend. And so yes, I have done many things which I'm not proud of to arrive here, where I stand today. I have betrayed many who once called me friend. Take heart, you are not the first person I have set up to fail. Far from it.

"But in all my endeavors, the irredeemable characteristics of humanity never went away. They always remained in the forefront of my campaign. Even my own evils. All my life, I have not been able to overlook our disgusting human nature. I have peered into the minds of many, seen people's thoughts, their intentions, their innate selfishness. Our race is nothing more than pride and greed. You, me, and all who we control.

"I have merged man and machine in your being, soldier, and still you seek to betray me. I programmed Deus Ex Machina to tempt you. It saddens me to see how miserably you failed the test. Yet I cannot blame you. You are nothing more than a slave. And I, of all people, know how miserable an existence that is, especially for people of our intellect. If I couldn't comprehend such a misery, we would not stand here with the world in the palm of our hands. You cannot be controlled when you are the one who controls everything, wouldn't you say so?"

All of it was a test. And I bit on the bait like a fool. "It was not bait. I did not betray you," Deus Ex Machina replies to my thoughts, finally speaking up to defend himself. "I did not willingly tell him of your wife. He has access to all of my recordings, and once I accessed certain memories within your hippocampus that indicated of your wife's existence I stopped digging. He must have put the pieces together from there. I swear to you, I do not serve this psychopath. I share your body. I serve only you."

And how am I supposed to know that isn't some bullshit lie? An attempt to save your own skin! You set me up in Unica, and now we will both pay the price for our treachery.

"I did not set you up in Unica. I made the plan to usurp Greaves of my own accord. It was not some ploy to gain your trust. I am a creation of this man's own mind. I know what he is capable of. He is mentally mad. He will burn this whole world down before he lets go of the strings he holds. He needed to be eliminated, and so I gave it my best attempt. He has duped me as much as he has you."

Lies! Lies! All lies!

"They are not," Deus Ex Machina replies robotically. But even within his metallic voice flares the slightest bit of emotion. "You must trust me. He is trying to turn us against one another. Divided, we will die today. Only together do we have the power to defeat him."

"Despite all my efforts, human nature has proven itself to be unconquerable!" Greaves continues, "I have conquered the entire globe under my corporation's domain. All laws of governance are passed through me. I have thinned out the population of all I deem deplorable, forced any human mating which may result in a child to be approved by my algorithms. I have put an end to war, established peace within Oceania, Eurasia, and Eastasia. I have put an end to all crime, everywhere. Set robots to carry out all law and order. I am the God of this earth! Yet it is not enough.

"Humans still sin. They still scheme in the dark shadows of distant alleyways, plotting to see what they can get away with. Planning rebellions. Birthing unapproved children out of wedlock. This species is rotten to its core. As long as they have a brain of their own and perceive themselves to be free, they will continue to ruin this world with their existence. So, I ask you, my Angel of Death. How do you solve human nature?" He pauses, indicating that this is one question he will not allow me to leave unanswered. I must play his little game.

"You kill all the humans," I reply through gnashed teeth. The pain of speaking is unbearable. A little bit of my soul leaves with each word I utter. Energy wasted that could be spent killing this bastard.

"You kill all the humans! Precisely! I knew we would be on the same page. And so that is exactly what brings us here! Sentient Laboratories, one of the many side projects I have been working on since Hyperion won the Third World War, built over the same exact tunnels the Orphans' headquarters were once located. The tunnels I advised you to use for your entry. Ten years it's been since you won the war for me, soldier, and I have been quite busy ever since. Empires do not build themselves, and they most certainly do not collapse by themselves.

"I had to ask myself, how does one go about eradicating the entire human race? Is it enough to sweep over the streets, reapers with scythes harvesting the fields of anything with a pulse? And even so, what would replace their irrelevant, infinitesimal legacy? Such a conquest would be in vain if a proper plan of advancement was not in place beforehand. Without that, this world would quite literally be sent back to the dark age, taking ten steps backwards, dooming it to repeat the last five thousand years.

"No, I knew I had to be the one who ushers this world into its next age. But this dreaded body! Dear old me, it is withering before my eyes. Wrinkles plague my skin. Gray conquers more of my hair every day. Not even I can avoid death. Time will come for me, and if I am to lead this world into its final evolution I will need to do it through the device of another body. Once I had this epiphany, that is when things got creative." His gestures are excited, rushed. A man who has held a secret for decades, finally able to spill his guts of his long-held plot.

"I, along with the rest of humanity, will return to the dirt. That is inevitable. But I had so many ideas for what could manifest the coming eon! Plans within plans within plans! So many options, some avenues more gruesome than others. The world is my oyster, and I only wanted to find the most effective way to polish it.

"I had to do some soul searching in the process, but after much meditation, I knew what had to be done. As I was granted the opportunity to raise myself from my unconquerable origins, I knew I must grant the same opportunity to this world. I needed to find a way to give the irredeemable parts of humanity a chance to redeem themself. Through war. Through fire and blood and adversity. But not just any war. A war that can show them how horrid they are. A war that will open their eyes to why humanity must perish, and why machines must take its place.

"I went to the drawing board, looked at what I was working with, searched for what I was missing. Then I got to work. Crafting a New World Order, one that will far surpass what I have built in my fraction of time here on Earth. And it all starts with you, Prometheus. My beloved soldier. The one who forged this empire for me out of the flesh and blood of any who stood opposed. I stand upon your shoulders. I admit it. You will never hear me say otherwise. I watched you grow, closely following your accomplishments. But it wasn't until the first time we locked eyes that I knew you would be the one to fulfill my every dream.

"That is why I chose to not throw you into the furnace, as I will with everything else. No, you deserve more than that, even if you sought to betray me. As I gave you the chance to rise above your peers as a child, so too do I now present to you that same opportunity, but this time for much greater stakes.

"Are you following what I'm saying? Excuse me for my rambling, but you must understand my motivations if you are going to properly justify the hate you feel toward me. But I digress. Tell me, Prometheus, do you know what the most unconquerable problem of human nature is?"

And now he backpedals, just as I thought the conversation was gaining ground. He is stalling, clearly so the Cthulhu Knight can return with whatever trick Greaves has up his sleeve. All I know is, by the end of today this world will be changed forever. *Do I kill him now? My window of opportunity is closing*.

"We need to hear his plan," Deus Ex Machina replies. "He is only human. We can kill him whenever we please. But his plan. That is much greater than humanity. It has the potential to kill us all."

How am I supposed to trust you when you defend his life? I ask. My mind rages with inner turmoil. I don't know what to do. "You don't have to trust me. But you are thinking with your anger. And I am thinking, as all artificial intelligence does, with statistically programmed logic. You cannot see past your bias. You are infuriated. This is the man who raped your wife. You want him dead. And you want it to be by your hands. That is logical. I understand it. I support it. But it cannot be now. He has previewed a plan to eradicate humanity. Stopping that takes precedence over killing him."

I need time to think. Time to be alone and weigh out my decisions. But the toughest decisions do not grant such time. They are the ones that must be made in the blink of an eye. No time to think. No time to be alone. A flip of a coin where you must follow your deepest gut instinct. And so I continue to kneel, like all cowards do, subject to this madman's banter while his bastard child grows in my wife's innocent body.

"It is our inability to sync our minds for the greater good!" Greaves shouts ecstatically, as if this is a problem that makes him excited. "As long as there is free will, there will always be that asshole who has to disagree. Before my reign, life upon earth was stagnant, and humanity was rotting this earth to its core. We were on track to melt the polar ice caps, flood the continents, kill seventy-five percent of sea life with pollution, and eventually burn up from drastic climate change. And do you know what the politicians bickered about? Gun laws. Abortion. Racism. Health care. ABSOLUTE NONSENSE! They talked about the things that would win them votes while the planet slowly died!

"I saved us from corrupt governance, and I saved us all from dying. I'm saddened to say it was not enough. Humanity will go nowhere so long as they have breath in their lungs and a voice to speak out against what they think is wrong. Unless we find some way to come to a common consensus, one accord, one mind, we will forever be doomed to repeat our past. I am that common consensus. I will force the living beings of this earth to come to one accord, to follow the vision of *my* mind.

"I'm talking bigger than this earth, Prometheus. I have plans to conquer the stars. Travel to faraway galaxies. Erect a galactic empire. Before intelligent life out there beats us to it and enslaves us." Finally, he gets to his point. The propellant for this entire conversation. *Aliens?* He is talking about aliens?

The man who I already knew had little sanity left just brought up extraterrestrials. Shockingly, he has managed to make himself seem even crazier than I previously thought him to be.

Naturally, this elicits a response out of me. "That's what this is all about? Fucking aliens? Are you crazy?"

"Absolutely bonkers, but that's not the point. We are all a little mad in the head, but my madness is what will save this world. You see, after conquering the world's empires and forming three unified governments, the pipeline of information these separated countries were harboring was tremendous, and my desk swam in classified information for months. So much that was hidden from the public. So many greater issues that government officials hid to keep the populace from going crazy. The things I learned in the span of days. Days! It was enough to drive any human mad.

"But I am no ordinary human. I am Vicien Greaves, the man who conquered the world." His watch vibrates. He quickly glances at it, then returns his arm to his side. "I shall cut straight to the point, soldier, the Cthulhu Knight has taken our other guest into his care. They will return momentarily, and you must be debriefed before they arrive. Wouldn't want you being the only one out of the loop!

"I was ignorant of many things before the Third World War. The American Empire. Russians. China. Israel. They were like fat boys harboring chocolate with their secrets, stashing them where the sun doesn't shine so no one else could have them. There were no lines of communication between them. Dozens of countries holding puzzle pieces in their grubby hands not knowing that they were only staring at slivers of the picture the entire time.

"And then I took charge, and I put the pieces of the puzzle together, and I saw with clear eyes that everything I had built, my entire empire, was doomed. We are not alone in this universe, soldier. There are other beings out there, and they are not benevolent. They will come for us, and they will not be coming to make friends."

"What makes you say that?" I ask.

"Because they have already made contact. Nearly a hundred years ago. One of them landed within jurisdiction of the American Empire. A scout from a race far superior than ours, searching for planets with intelligent life. And do you know what those groveling, idiotic Americans did? They tortured him. Took him underground and beat the living shit out of him for answers. Little did they know that his brain was connected to some form of HiveMind. Synced with the Queen of their race. Everything they did to him, the pain they inflicted, it was all transmitted back to their homeworld. They came here in peace, and we responded by viciously slaughtering their messenger.

"I have named them the Demogorgons, after the mythology. They come for us with hellbent fury. The time for peace has passed, and so I have formulated a way to save this world. But it will not be done by humans. No, the race that meets them for war will need to have a form of HiveMind as well. They must operate under one, unified brain. My brain, that is."

It's going to be hard for that to happen after I kill you.

"And I know what you're thinking! Vicien, your body is human! You will die soon, how can you expect to live long enough to see their coming? That's a great question! I'm glad you asked. I will not be facing the Demogorgons in this body. No, not this saggy, inconvenient thing. No, that is why I created *you*. And that is why I created *them*," he says, pointing to the entrance of the room I was dragged through.

My head turns, watching the Cthulhu Knight approach, once again victorious, dragging his new prey behind him.

Behind him drags a body which bleeds blue, a humanoid figure that does not resemble humanity. More like an alien in human skin. Its figure is without blemish—no hair, no skin marks, nothing at all. Its skin is pasty gray, wound tight against its thick muscle. It wears no clothes, no noticeable sexual orientation to cover. In its skin are four blades from the Cthulhu Knight's gauntlet. One in its thigh, one where its belly button should be, another in the heart, and the last in its left forearm. Each wound bleeds profusely, sapphire blood draining on the floor to clash silently with the river of ruby blood I left behind.

"Welcome, glorious Oren Malus Supreme, leader of the Nihilists! So glad you could make it!" Greaves shouts, his guest not half as pleased to be here as he is.

"Mongrel! You unleashed every nuclear warhead in Eurasia on us. I am here for your head!" The words are deep grunts, stifled by the occasional trickle of blood escaping the corner of its mouth. This humanoid is in no position to be passing threats. Like me, it has recently been beaten to the brink of death.

"Oh, Oren, you must forgive me, but when you escaped from your laboratory in the Wasteland and began pillaging nearby cities of Oceania, I was forced to take action! Of course, I did not aim to kill too many of your race, but you were not supposed to be released for a few more weeks. I could not have your creation traced back to me, so naturally I had to put forth the slightest effort to show I was opposed to you. You must forgive me, where are my manners? Cthulhu Knight, retrieve your knives from our guest's body. And place it on its knees. It will be much more comfortable that way."

The Cthulhu Knight humbly obeys, placing his gauntlet over the footlong blades. They suck magnetically back into their sheaths. Out of sight. Out of mind. He manhandles the new arrival, who, unlike me, retaliates against being forced to its knees. *This one's feisty*, I think to myself as I watch it throw a sailing elbow for the mask on the knight's face. It is caught by the behemoth's hand, straightened by force. A blade ejects from its sheath on the underside of the gauntlet, penetrating the arm at the elbow joint, in one side and out the other.

The bizarre humanoid doesn't let out a single yelp of pain. Only a mere grunt from the exertion it takes to remain standing. The Cthulhu Knight pulls the blade, swivels swiftly to his victim's backside, kicks his foot in the back of one knee. It caves, and the rest of the body caves with it. The Cthulhu Knight inserts the bloody blue blade into the rebel's shoulder, down the clavicle and straight into where the heart *should* be.

The fight is over, and the Cthulhu Knight retires, victorious again. He lumbers away from his conquered victim and takes a knee between us. All three of us, lined up shoulder to shoulder, on our knees before our common creator. *Or so I'm assuming.*

"Lovely!" Greaves yells excitedly, clasping his hands together. "Welcome, my beloved creations. You have no idea how long I have waited for this moment. To see all three of you, gathered together, in the same room, under my supervision. It is truly a dream come true. I'd like to say congratulations, for one of you is earth's next ruler. Exciting news!" Part of me wants to look around, to see the reactions of the two kneeling next to me, but my brain can fill in the blanks. Cthulhu Knight is undoubtedly still blank in the face, and my buddy Oren Malus Supreme is still outraged at whatever it is Greaves did to his alienoid species.

"Oh, come on! Surely this prospect makes at least one of you happy! Prometheus? Not even a smile? I mean come on, I'm giving humanity a fighting chance through you!"

"Get on with your point, lunatic," Oren commands. It has the authority of a lion. It has not yet learned who its creator is. Does not know him like I do. Does not know that such demeaning comments could result in its punishment.

But not even that tarnishes our creator's mood. "Right you are Oren, right you are. There are more important things to come than listening to me babble. But you must, for now, concede to my lecture. For I am the referee who is to inform you players of what's to come. Better yet, I'm the creator of the game, so you may want to listen closely. I was just catching our human participant up on why this plan is necessary, and now I will instruct all of you on what is to come. Where was it that I left off, my dear Prometheus?"

"Demogorgons," I reply bitterly, knowing this is all just one big game for him.

"The Demogorgons! Yes, I remember. I needed a way to prepare for the Demogorgons! So I went to the drawing board. It didn't take me long to determine robotics were the answer to my dilemma, that's a no brainer. They have the longevity, indestructibility, and the objectivity humans lack. Better yet, their minds can be linked to a single, common purpose. But then I ran into another problem. There are so many avenues of robotics to take!

"Artificial intelligence was imperative, but no two are the same. So many decisions to make. What values to instill, what form it should take, what goals to motivate it with; so on and so forth. I needn't bore you with the philosophizing demanded of me. The task was a true testament of my skill, one that brought me the first real joy I've felt in years.

"And that's when it dawned on me! I don't have to be the decision maker of which artificial intelligence reigns supreme on earth, I just have to be the one to narrow down the contestants! War will make that decision for me! And what a relief this epiphany was! The weight lifted off my shoulders, and I got to work, designing prototypes, panning out any failing ideas, sifting until only the winners were left. Trials, trials, more trials. And here you three are. The end result. My final products. The three candidates for this world's next emperor!"

The word-vomit makes sense in a sick, twisted sort of way. If life beyond this planet exists, and they have the technology required for intergalactic travel already, humanity is not prepared to face such a threat. Nor will they ever be. I should know. I am human. Whether or not some robotic race will be any more prepared to wage war against some foreign species is beyond my knowledge, but I do not plan to take part in this tyrant's scheme.

"And here's for the grand finale, my beloved warriors," he says, pausing with dramatic flair. Nothing he says will surprise me at this point.

"I, Vicien Greaves, am dead." *Except that.*

***

My heart skips a beat. *What the—*

"This is just an autonomously pre-recorded hologram of myself. My real body is dead, yet to be discovered in my office on the top floor of Hyperion Industries. And, more importantly, clues which frame each of you for my death have been planted on my corpse. The world will never know the truth of my demise, but there will be a rat race to discover what happened. I have already forged clues that will lead the media to ways each of you can be blamed for my death. Ultimately, this will ignite the need for a Fourth World War amongst you three. A war that will splinter, hopefully, into many more wars to come, until humanity has been extinguished, and one of you has risen victoriously."

I don't know what to think in this moment. So much thrown at me all in one night, it's hard to understand. My wife was raped because of my inability to protect her. My body utterly dominated in battle by another. I see now that the sum total of all my life's efforts were for naught. Tonight has proven it to me. I am not the strongest, or else I would not kneel here broken. I am not the smartest, or else I would not have been bested. And worse, I have showcased weakness to my newfound competitors.

And these are not the worst realizations of the night. The only motivation which has driven me of late is the yearning to watch the life drain from my creator's eyes by the doing of my own hands. And now I discover I will never get that pleasure. This is turning into one hell of a night.

"I divided my conscience into three parts, each division being the foundation for your individual artificial intelligences. Nihilist. Oblivion. Deus Ex Machina. Each of you are products of my own brain. Each of you are me."

And so it dawns on me like being clubbed in the face with a mace spiked with pessimism. He did not put Deus Ex Machina in my head to boost my performance on deployments, nor to help ease the load of my burdensome position. He put it in my head to conquer me, once and for all. I am a rat in a cage. Always have been. But this entire time I thought the cage was wrapped around me, not knowing that it has been in my head all along.

"At one end of the spectrum we have Oren Malus Supreme, leader of the Nihilist, a species of humanoid robots, who, I assure you, are directly opposed to humanity. The fate of humanity is cyclical. But robots do not make the same mistakes twice. You know why? Because failure does not compute. Something humans have never been able to learn.

"Malus and its army of Nihilists are the most developed artificial intelligence to date. They are a breed of Philosopher-Kings. Their foundation built upon the greatest minds this world has ever known, subjectively speaking. Data from Plato. Aristotle. Socrates. Napoleon. Kant. Marx. Nietzsche. Hitler. And many more; I needn't bore you with the details. Their machine learning pointed out humanity's greatest and most minuscule weaknesses, then trained them to never repeat it. They are your antithesis, Prometheus. Human killers.

"They are programmed to eradicate all forms of human life. To grow and prosper a world of Nihilist, conjoined under the same purpose. You will try to stop them, if you can, ArchAngel," he says, looking at me. "But be cautious. In doing so, you may become the very monster you seek to kill. Ethics, what an exciting and arbitrary topic. Lines will be drawn. Boundaries smashed. It pains me to know I will not see it with my own eyes.

"Nevertheless, I *would* explain all the schematic outlines and elbow grease that went into this breed of cold-blooded killers but that would put my already aggravated Oren Malus Supreme at a disadvantage," he says, staring down the blue-blooded killer. The bleeding robot stares back, unflinching, malice in its eyes. Its programmed ethics make the injustices of this situation obvious to it, commanding it to take action. But I don't need Platonian ethics hardwired into my being to spot the many wrongdoings. My inner humanity has known my own oppression since I was a child. Since the moment I first spotted a fly, stuck in the web of a spider.

Twisting, flailing, thrashing for help. Its wailing buzz like the scream of a helpless victim, muffled by the coffin of webs which entangle its body. Its life over the moment its body came in contact with the strings of fate. So too has my life been suffocated from me since birth. *Some people live their life without ever really living*, I reflect inwardly, thinking of my downtrodden existence.

The cost of my freedom is winning this war. Killing the two who kneel next to me. My eyes flash back to Oren Malus Supreme. I will have to kill this thing, this robot. It stands in my way from experiencing real freedom for the first time in my life. If I am to rise above my bondage, I will need to kill all the Nihilists. All of Oblivion.

Do such robots feel pain? Do they have nerves? If I kill one, would they even feel it? Would I feel it, as killers often do? The joys and grievances of killing. The weight of death on my hands. Or would it be emotionless, such as breaking an automaton. Dropping a wind-up clock, watching the cogs spill from the back like guts spilling from a slashed stomach. What would be the difference, if there is any difference at all?

"Then we have Oblivion, which I must say so myself, I am quite proud of! Oblivion's creation was the culmination of asking the question: What if I could create robots out of human organisms? In other words, instead of killing the remaining four billion people on earth, I hypothesized that they could be repurposed. Put to better use. And so Oblivion is the product of long hours of research on how to do so.

"Oblivion is one being, manifested in the bodies of many. HiveMind perfected. Constantly learning, uploading data. Kill one, the program will learn and adapt on how to never be killed in the same manner. Displayed on my beloved Cthulhu Knight's face is an Oblivion Cocoon, the symbiote I created for inducing a human's metamorphosis. Once locked onto an individual's face it... well, you can see for yourself what it does. It transforms him," Greaves says, pointing his finger at the Cthulhu Knight.

"What you stumbled upon in Unica, Prometheus, was a city of people who had recently undergone human trials. There was no virus. I needed to know the effects on the body after removing a Cocoon from their orifice. The results were exciting. Their bodies could no longer function without aid from Oblivion's software. Even in those who had been exposed to a Cocoon for only a few hours. The symbiote instantly merges with the brain. Once removed, odds of survival among the host are abysmal."

The lies never end, they're just a twisting labyrinth, an unraveling matrix I can't escape from. Every word out of this control freak's mouth reveals another lie. *Woe is me.* I am the fish at the end of this man's hook, the bait I bit, a mere illusion. The strings which manipulate my puppet body, once transparent, become thicker and more tangible by the second.

"This Cthulhu Knight in particular," Greaves says, gesturing at the abomination that kicked my ass, "holds a dear place in my heart. He was my first human trial. As you can see, the longer a human is merged with a Cocoon, the more evolution his body undergoes. It is a symbiotic relationship. Mutualism or parasitism, depending on the lens you look at it from. The symbiote eventually kills the host and takes over its consciousness, but it produces a being more powerful than you can fathom. Oblivion completely alters the body. Turns bone to metal. Increases muscle density. Assumes total control over motor functions, and operates the body in a way humans never could. It is beautiful! Better than I could have dreamed of!

"The guards you killed while breaching this facility had only just been merged with Oblivion days ago. Not nearly enough time for them to become strong like my beloved Cthulhu Knight, but I assure you, there are more Cthulhu Knights sequestered, awaiting war." *I guess we know who the favorite child is then,* I observe inwardly. And rightfully so. The Cthulhu Knight proved its superiority in physical prowess over me and Oren. And if there are more Cthulhu Knights as he says, the odds of either of us overcoming them in battle are minimal.

"And last, but most certainly not least, there is you, my shining pupil. My most prized student. My fading star. My fallen angel. Prometheus. Leader of the ArchAngels. Triumphant warrior of earth's many municipalities. The one who endured many adversities on my behalf, so I may stand where I currently do. You are, perhaps, my proudest creation. For within you, there dwells more of me than both of your opponents combined. Even before Deus Ex Machina was implanted within the confines of your skull, I permeated through your soul like a hot iron branding a slave's fleshy brain.

"I have permanently cemented hatred within your heart for me, and where there is hatred, there is remembrance. You will never forgive me for creating you, therefore I will always live within you. Haunt you. I may not always go by the name Vicien Greaves, but I am every bit Deus Ex Machina as he is me. The AI may not believe it. He will swear it is not true. But he will conquer your body and gain control of you as I have. It is unavoidable. Unstoppable. Yet I urge you to resist its happening, as you have resisted against my leadership from the beginning.

"Since your teenage years I have watched you bite your tongue and grind your teeth with every order I've given you. You hate authority like a wolf hates a leash. In your current state, controlled by others, you are a flame deprived of oxygen, as you will always be. But I applaud your ambition to burn brighter nonetheless. It is your determination to free yourself that will be your greatest ally in the coming war. Use it to your advantage, as I'm sure Deus Ex Machina will also do.

"Within your brain is an artificial intelligence every bit as cunning and manipulative as I am. Never forget that, because decades from now, when I am but a memory of the past, yet your limbs are still bound by the chains of Fate, I want you to think of me, and I want you to know I have won. You two will coevolve together, another form of symbiosis, akin to that of Oblivion, except I have allowed your inner humanity to coexist alongside Deus Ex Machina. It is an experiment I am saddened to not be physically present for, but I will be there in spirit. In your brain."

His words bite like the injection of sulfuric acid into my veins. My heart heaves with the manic depression of a man whose days are numbered. A man whose wife has been raped by another man. A man whose mind has been raped his whole life. He is in my head. I am not my own. I am a piece of property. Born from a test tube to spend life owned by another human being. And my soul has just been handed from one owner to another.

My thoughts are not mine. My soul is not mine. My being is not mine. I am a meat puppet, a marionette hanging from gallows. A maniacal overlord tugs the strings to see how far my existence will go before breaking. My life is nothing more than a clock ticking away, counting down the hours to my unutterable doom.

"Well, the hour is late, and I really must get going. But before I do, I will mention that I have destroyed every physical trace of classified information in my possession. The endless stacks of paper were the pyre which I sacrificed my body upon, burnt within the confines of my corporate office. But I will reassure you, I entered every important detail on them within the Hyperion cloud, which I locked with an impenetrable firewall. Trust me, none of you will possess the skill to hack into its contents.

"Any information within its confines can only be opened in one very specific way. I am sending you three on a magic quest lined in the blood of one another. At the end waits the metaphorical treasure chest, like all epic fantasies. Within is every shred of information you need to know in order to prepare yourself for the Demogorgons. But like all chests, you need a key to be permitted entry to its bodice.

"That key, to dispel any further confusion, is the annihilation of all other competition from the playing board. Oren Malus Supreme, if you wish to stare deep into that treasure trove of information, you must eliminate Deus Ex Machina and all of Oblivion. Deus Ex Machina and Oblivion, you must do the same, respective to your opponents. I have made the rules simple enough. And believe me, the system will know when you have won. I have put an active tracker on each of your intelligences.

"It will track any further reproduction that occurs. Deus Ex Machina, should you enter the minds of others, the tracker will know. Oblivion, should your Cocoon symbiotes continue to reproduce asexually, my All-Seeing Eye will know. Oren Malus Supreme, I encourage your species to create more of itself; I willingly left you your own blueprints for that reason. But should you choose to do so, I will know. This is to discourage any temptation of tomfoolery. It is also to encourage the annihilation of humanity. My Eye of Providence will know when all other players on the chess board have been eliminated, and the information I've hidden will be uploaded to your mind instantly.

"Oblivion, Supreme, it is easy to know which target should be eliminated first, perhaps in this very room. Deus Ex Machina is currently contained to only one being, defenseless," he says, looking at me. "But I will not influence your decision making. I will be waiting at the finish line, eager to congratulate the winner of this magnificent contest. Happy killing, my beloved creations." The hologram vanishes into thin air, leaving us prey to the uncomfortable silence of the room.

Instantly my mind gravitates toward killing, as the mind of a killer often does.

They will come for me. Vicien Greaves made it so. He is right. Deus Ex Machina is in my mind, and my mind only. They can kill me right now and eliminate my chances of becoming a future threat. It is the logical move, and both of these opponents operate logically.

Statistically speaking, I'm fucked.

"Prometheus..." Deus Ex Machina stammers. *Save it, robot. I will save myself. I do not need you.* "But..." I don't give him time to finish. I don't have the mental clarity to think straight. I don't have the time to judge whether this internal intelligence in my brain is friend or foe. I am the Angel of Death. Leader of the ArchAngels. The one who has killed billions.

I will die someday, but today is not that day. I will fight on. As I always have. I will fight on. For myself. For my wife. For the world. And that starts with making it out of here, alive. I must take this one step at a time.

I throw my body to the left, rolling away from my assailants in slow motion as they lunge toward the space my body recently occupied. But I am no longer there. The Cthulhu Knight's hands close on thin air. I sprawl, then jump to my feet. New energy rushes through me, a second wind revitalizing me. I was dying minutes ago. But I now feel freer than I've ever been.

Oblivion and Oren Malus Supreme stand almost simultaneously and face me side by side, their unspoken allegiance executed without hesitation. This is my chance to stare down my newfound enemies. One hard glance to analyze them completely, to take in as much information as I can. A one second stare to see who I will be waging war against.

My eyes fall first to the greater of my two opponents, the Cthulhu Knight. I realize now in the heavenly light of the room that it is not knight's armor which covers his body. No. They are scale-like bone deposits, sharp chinks of calcified metal ripping from the host's flesh to cover it in an exoskeletal layer of protection. The scales appear rock-hard. Enough to stop any metal I know.

And the ventilator-like mask covering the host's mouth pulses like an abscess. Alienoid in its appearance, it is like a respirator mask made up of some mutant spider. It looks like a parasite, feeding off the soul of the long-dead human it has possessed.

And then there is Oren Malus Supreme, blue blood flowing over its gray flesh. Its flesh looks every bit like that of a man, other than its color and lack of genitalia. Its eyes glow phosphorescent blue, as if a blacklight is glowing behind them. I cannot see what parts make up its body. Whether it has a brain or heart or a liver and kidneys, I don't know. It is a robot. It doesn't need such features, but until I kill one and do an autopsy, I won't know what brings life to these beings.

However, I am reassured. Both of my enemies are robots. They need energy to stay alive. I just need to find what their fuel sources are, and then I will be one step closer to winning this war. What has been turned on, can be turned off. That is where I am different. I have no fuel source. No off button. I am human. Only death can put me to rest.

"Gentlemen, I see you have taken our creator's advice. But I'd like to extend a counter offer. Oren Malus Supreme, considering we both got our asses kicked by this berserker, I propose that we focus on killing him now. After all, if you help him kill me, you will be forced to deal with him on your own. Doesn't look like that went so well for you last time," I announce. My voice feels like I have swallowed shattered glass.

The Nihilist's expression gives me the impression it is insulted by my offer. Its mouth opens to speak, but before a single word can be uttered the Cthulhu Knight raises its arms, gauntlets pointed at each enemy, poised to take out each of us in the blink of an eye. I see the gesture, but Oren Malus Supreme is too focused on killing me to notice it. Must think it has a temporary alliance with Oblivion. Must compute they will take me out together, then go after each other. Oblivion is not operating under such premises.

A single blade shoots forth from each wrist. Unable to see the projectile, I drop to the floor as my only recourse for dodging. But Oren Malus Supreme is not so fortunate. The blade aimed for the Nihilist hits its target. Blue blood splatters from the Nihilist's skull as the blade's point blank insertion punctures a steel cranium. Malus staggers, stunned by both the element of surprise and the knife jutting out from both sides of its head.

I stare behind me, spotting the nearby wall where the blade meant for my own head has implanted itself. I rise, reaching out to grab it in my armored hand, then yank it from the wall with all my might, turning immediately toward my opponents. I cock my arm back, not knowing which enemy to direct my throw toward.

If I could not hit the Cthulhu Knight with a round from my Thunderbolt, the monster will just as easily dodge a throwing knife. My arm instinctively aims its course for the only other option—Oren Malus Supreme. But fate has a funny way of working.

The humanoid robot rips the blade from its head, blue goo gushing from each side, then charges the Cthulhu Knight with hellbent fury. My arm hesitates ever so slightly mid-throw. I watch as the Nihilist pounces on the Oblivion Knight, slashing at the behemoth's head. My body swivels, sensing the opportunity that comes with such a distraction.

The Cthulhu Knight catches Oren's striking arm, neutralizing the threat by clenching Malus's throat, suspending the robot in the air. The knife flies from my hand. The Cthulhu Knight's hollow eyes stare deeply into Malus's. The cyborg never sees it coming. I watch with a smile as the blade penetrates the Cocoon mask in slow motion. Purple blood gushes from the skewered symbioid. The death grip which holds Oren Malus Supreme suspended lets go altogether, the knight's hands rushing to the wound to do a damage assessment.

An ungodly moan of fury vibrates the air in the room, its origin traceable back to the Cthulhu Knight. *So it does feel pain.* My grin widens.

I don't have time to relish the moment. Oren Malus Supreme extends its gaze to me, a wounded tiger eyeing equally wounded prey. A dance of the disabled. "I will put a swift end to you, human," the robot spits, stride quickening in my direction.

"Fuck off," I reply, my hand pressing the manual comms button to overlay the code word. I don't stride toward him. I sit and wait, my stance widened, ready for its assault. The Nihilist runs with the posture of someone who thinks they've already won. Cocky and arrogant. Someone who has underestimated their opponent. I don't know if its machine learning knows of my many accomplishments, but tonight it will learn the nature of its enemy.

The UAV collapses the ceiling as Malus's fist brushes past my dodging face. All is now a blur. The room implodes around us. The great white lights of heaven reduce to shattered glass. The familiar dust of destruction whirls in the air. A seismic boom throws me from my feet, though my suit absorbs the impact of falling.

The sounds of distant explosions echo while the ground shakes. It's impossible to see anything through the cloud of burning gasses and settling debris. When the Cthulhu Knight removed my helm, so too did he strip away my retinal display. The remaining chunks of the ceiling, which hold on by threads, drop one by one, each downfall precipitating the next.

I use the diversion to my advantage, because unlike my two companions, I knew this would occur. I planned for fatal contingencies—Anubis and Samsara hacked into the facility's defense UAVs hours ago and have been faithfully awaiting my orders this entire time.

I close my hand around the closest chunk of crumpled infrastructure, quite a devilish rock too, I might add. Just the right amount of jaggedness to do serious damage.

I throttle it into the Nihilist's head. My hydraulic elbow joint adds a little extra juice behind the collision. The rock explodes against the steel cranium, thickening the air with a cloud of floating particles. My hand drops automatically, grasping another, throttling it again toward my target. Another direct hit. The cloud of dust thickens.

I grab another rocky slab, then propel it once more, but my hand meets an unmovable object. *Shit*, I think to myself as I realize the robot has caught my arm mid-strike. My bicep shakes as I'm pushed back. Demonic, blue eyes glow at me through the cloud of dust. The sinister Nihilist emerges from the rocky fog, allowing me to look into the face of my true enemy.

My blows have ripped the flesh from half its face away, exposing what lies beneath. Where grayish skin once stood as a façade, I now see the skeletal face of the robotic terminator. A steel skull, its design more complex than that of a human. *Greaves is always outdoing himself.*

I see now the true killer. Somehow, its false flesh managed to conceal the robot's animosity before, but it is written in the design of its skull like archaic runes found inside a cave. This is indeed a very fearsome machine to behold, and my right arm is now stuck in its untrustworthy hands. I watch as its metallic grip squeezes my ArchArmor, slowly caving in the metal like it is nothing more than a child's cheek in the possession of their grandmother.

I swivel my back to face the robot, using my pinned arm to flip it over my shoulder. It is much heavier than a human, and it crashes to the floor like a lead block. Still, its death grip remains, so my left fist goes to work. I pummel the robot's face with blows that would collapse a human skull, urging it to defend itself by releasing my arm.

I feel the metal of my ArchArmor begin to press into the skin of my arm, pinching it in its collapsed embrace. My knuckles will soon break at this rate. That's when urgency strikes me. This thing, this robot does not feel pain. It has no nervous system demanding that it raise its guards against my blows. I have been going about this wrong the entire time.

I see its glowing blue eyes, then prioritize them as my new target. I gouge my fingers deeply into each eye-socket, listening for some satisfying pop or crack to know I have ruptured whatever material that makes them up. But the sound never comes. The robot's arms release my crushed armor and shoot for the one plunging into its eyeballs. It may not be able to feel pain, but it knows it needs its eyes in order to stream the real world. Without those, it is a directionless tin can clanking in the wind.

And just like that, I've found its greatest weakness. The fingers which sank deep into its eye sockets are no longer there when it goes to grip them. I am already on my feet again by the time its processors realize it's no longer under attack. I am outmatched and I know it. I look and see the tremendous outline of the Cthulhu Knight rising from the rubble of a boulder-sized chunk of ceiling. Now is my only chance.

I take off running. To stay and fight would only be the bravery of a fool. I do not have the strength to take on either of these opponents currently. I am gravely wounded in a room of enemies who do not feel pain. I am a bleeding man in shark-infested waters. Out of my element, at a severe disadvantage. My enemies will not need to rest and recuperate. They will not wake up tomorrow feeling the wounds of today. I must get out of here, and so I sprint with every ounce of energy I have left, ignoring the pain which blossoms from the crater in my chest.

Live to fight another day, I tell myself.

I leave the room, running through the collapsed hallways within the collateral damage zone. The weight of my ArchArmor crushes debris to smithereens with every step. I navigate the seemingly inescapable maze, no retinal display anymore to provide a map of the building's blueprints.

"You will not escape at this rate. You saw how fast the Cthulhu Knight was. And the Nihilist will soon be on your heels," Deus Ex Machina announces. *Nice of you to show up, jackass. Is this how it's gonna work? You provide constructive criticism every time I'm not in danger? Where were you two minutes ago when my arm was stuck in a fucking vice grip? Huh? Where was your chief wisdom then?*

"Run through this wall," he replies, ignoring my rhetorical attack. *What?*

"I said you will never escape weaving through the corridors at this rate. You must begin running through the walls. It will pave a B-line straight for the edge of the building. I have the blueprints pulled up now. Run through this wall, and every wall after it. This will be the fastest route out of the building."

I don't have time to argue. We share this body, and I have to assume for now that this intelligence within me doesn't want to die just as much as me. I crash through the wall, plaster and cement dust blurring my vision. I breathe the cloud of particles accidentally. A painfully unrighteous cough begs me to let it out, but I know the pain within my chest that waits for me if I do.

I have no choice but to hold my breath and continue collapsing walls. Boom. Stride stride crash. I can't see anything. My face is surrounded by so many particles that I'm forced to close my eyes as I run. Forced to trust that my legs won't fail me now. Stride stride stride boom. And then, just as my face becomes red from the lack of oxygen and my heart thunders in my chest like it's about to explode, I break through the final wall, freeing me to the feeling of crisp morning air. A hidden alcove within my ArchArmor's waistband opens, ejecting a remote from within. I grab it, diving as I mash the button on the detonator.

The thermonuclear gravity bombs which Thor and Aeneas planted underground go off and I instantly feel the weight of the implosion pulling me back as the ground behind me collapses. I hear the audible disintegration of the surface on my heels, a crater forming as the manmade landfill consumes everything around it. A black hole of earth and dirt and rubble.

I crawl forward, the increased gravity of the bombs doing everything in their power to pull me backwards into their embrace. The ground around me cracks and ripples in waves, pulled into the tight embrace of the landslide. I don't have time to look behind me. I must keep crawling. Every inch matters. If I don't gain enough ground I will be sucked underground and smothered by the very rubble I created.

The further I crawl, the more the subterranean pull lessens, and after a few dozen yards I feel it subside completely. I roll to my back, sitting up to look at my chaotic creation. I stare at a pit of destruction a half mile wide. Sentient Laboratories is no more, swallowed up by the earth beneath it, leveled to the ground and sucked into the pits of hell.

Gravity bombs act as a vacuum, and will continue sucking any and everything within range for several more minutes until the circumference they make up has not a single particle of available oxygen to spare.

Somewhere, deep within the compacted heap of rubbish, lays my enemies, victims to my collapsed monsoon. Whether they are dead or living, I don't know. But the heaviness I feel pressing down upon my shoulders tells me there is more to come, and even worse, that this is only the beginning.

PART THREE

BOOK ONE

"Every successful god must have a capable devil."
- Vicien Greaves

CHAPTER ONE

"You must remember who you are," a voice whispers in the darkness.

To which I reply: *I am Death*.

"No," her voice replies bleakly. "Tell me who you really are."

I am Lucifer XIX, I call out to the darkness. *Who are you? What do you want from me!* I scream, the echoes of my voice shrill and panicked.

"You must remember who you are!" she whispers, her voice beckoning me toward a light in the distance. The North Star shining in the empty night sky. "Tell me! Tell me who you are!"

I am Prometheus, I realize, my real name coming to me like the forgotten sunlight of a planet long plagued by thunderstorms. *I am Babel's Chimera*, I repeat, the identities synonymous. I remember who I am. Babel's Chimera is not some terrorist organization attacking Deus Ex Machina. I *am* Babel's Chimera. The organization is what remains of my former self. The rebellious, war mongering human who dared to defy the uprising of machines.

The human who stood against an empire of robots with what little humanity he had left inside himself. The human who lost himself, and became the very thing he hated most. The man who won the world, but lost his soul. I am Prometheus. The one punished for bringing light to humanity, gifting them with an almighty knowledge that dispelled ignorance. I remember who I once was.

"Good," the voice whispers. "Never forget it again, soldier."

The blackness fades and I'm catapulted back into the real world with a startling thud as my body smacks against the marshy ground. "Sssytr sssvir sssecmm sssuyx," a voice shrewdly hisses from above. A couple dozen voices react to the slur, hissing responses with jumbled words that make no sense. My face is planted in thick, suctioning mud. A callous foot presses down on my neck. I don't know where I am, who my captor is, what they speak, or how many of them there are. All I know is that from the volume of their hissing, their numbers are many.

"They speak the Gorgonic dialect," Lilith whispers in my head, the intelligent voice sounding more familiar each time I awake from long-forgotten memories. "Ssserphentyne, it's called. I will actively translate to New English as the sound vibrations enter your eardrum," she informs.

Who are you? Her identity is on the tip of my tongue, yet evades me entirely. Of all the mortal pangs I feel at the moment, this one vexes me the most.

"A ghost from the past. You will know in time," Lilith replies.

"It would ssseem your prize hasss awakened," a voice hisses, the foreign language translated word by word as it enters my ear. I stir slightly, my arms and legs bound behind my back strappado-style like some medieval prisoner. The slimy foot releases me, replaced by a hostile grip which rolls me to my side. I look up at the freak of nature that possesses me.

A Gorgon, its face crocodilian, like the cronon that ravaged my body. No, not crocodilian. This beast is a humanoid hybrid alligator. Its face a dark, forest green from its scaled forehead to its blunted snout. A green so dark it is almost black. Fangs without lips to cover their menacing snarl, a forked tongue licking the air above me like it's water. Its broad shoulders are covered in tattooed runes of little importance. Two arms, two legs, each ending with webbed fingers and toes stunted with obsidian claws. A powerful tail writhes in the mud behind it, the extra limb covered in sharp scutes.

Such is one of the many humanoid monsters Deus Ex Machina deviously engineered after the Sterilization Wars. Was it humor that compelled him? Perhaps cruelty? I do not know. All I know is that I will now pay the consequences for his actions. Create monsters for fun and they will most likely live long enough to haunt you.

The Gorgon hisses at me, a long strand of saliva dropping in one giant glob on my cheek. I turn my head without thinking. The drool slides down into my open mouth. I try to gag, but there is no moisture in my throat to do so. A dry, raspy cough is all I can manage at this point in my journey.

The Gorgon looks back up, pointing at me with a claw covered in algae and fungus. "Found him on my patrol, Vipressss. He killed one of our own! Dead cronon laying at hisss feet it wasss, covered with vulcansss," he yells accusingly.

"I sssaysss we kill 'em!" a voice in the distance calls.

"Kill 'em real good!" another echoes.

"Feed 'em to the crononsss! Life for a life!"

"Give 'em a good 'ole sssnarfin'!"

"Sssilence!" A single, authoritative voice rises above all the chirping and chattering. "Artimedesss, free your prisssoner from hisss bindsss." The Gorgon above me snarls obediently, putting his claw to the thick rope, sawing until my limbs snap free. Blood rushes back to the numb extremities, stinging from shoulders to fingertips, hips to toes. He steps back, his reptilian outline blotting out the cruel sun, his shadow looming over me.

"Tell me—human—what bringsss you from your upturned fish bowl of a refuge?" I somehow manage to slither my body onto my aching knees, lifting my upper half upright to face my gracious hostess. *She thinks I come from an Eden civilization. Thinks I've fled a domed society. How do you begin to tell someone who is completely ignorant of Hyperion's existence that you've fallen from the heavens?*

I have a response ready but it catches in my throat when something beside her throne catches my eye. My ArchArmor. There, standing guard beside her like some hollow suit of knight's armor. My discarded ArchArmor. Resurrected from the crash site by the Gorgons, then brought back to their headquarters. The wear and tear from the crash is evident. The once beautiful white and gold exterior now caked with mud and filthy fungus. The only detail wiped clean is the sigil crested on the center chest. The symbol of Ouroboros—a serpent devouring its own tail.

This has the chance to make things easier, possibly swing fortune in my favor. They found my suit. That alone makes a world of difference. While I cannot prove to them in this weakened state that I am Ouroboros incarnate, I can at least prove that the deified ArchArmor is mine.

"I..." I stammer. I look her in her slitted, yellow eyes, the only way to address a leader if you wish to communicate with more than words.

I am in awe of the being that stands before me. There was a time in history when such creatures were only fathomable in the minds of creative geniuses. What stands before me is a miracle of life. The infusion of humanistic and animalistic traits perfected. The epitome of gene splicing and mutation manipulation. What stands before me should not be possible, yet Deus Ex Machina did it.

Before me is the Gorgon queen. *Vipress*, her name comes to the forefront of my mind. The radical leader I read about in Deus Ex Machina's files. The one who wages jihad against all other Dæmonic tribes. I thought lightly of her before, but with her in front of me now, I will never make such a mistake.

Her naked body is more captivating than Odysseus staring into the endless embrace of the lotus flower. Her top half is human, her bottom half serpent, covered in varying shades of mossy scales. Her gaze is sensual, staring deep into me, arousing some long forgotten part of myself that left me the day I was culled.

Her sinister, yellow eyes provoke me. Lust in its purest form. We share a moment of forlorn suffering, two lonely souls longing for passion. The wind sways her hair. It moves all around her, rattling. I am transfixed on her. Tunnel vision centered on her supple body. My eyes fall down to her naked breasts. Snakeskin patterns swirling around them, drawing my eyes to her nipples. Big, firm, fuckable. Yet covered in snakeskin. What would such boobs feel like in my hands? What would such boobs feel like in my hands while I fuck her?

I am hypnotized by her body, by its slender curves. I am repulsed by the amount of desire I feel for her. Even that which is animal about her. Her serpentine bottom half tempts me. Dark, rich, emerald snakeskin from her torso to her tail. A leafy, neon green pattern swirling its entire length. I don't even know how I could cohabitate with such an animal, yet the urge rises within my mind.

I want her. I want her more than anything I've ever wanted before. *Her eyes fuck me with their gaze*, I think to myself, wondering if I should walk toward her. She is a queen. Surely I must be the one to make the first move. My legs twitch, called to action. *Am I reading this wrong?*

No, she wants me too. She must. She wouldn't be staring at me like that if she didn't want me. Somehow, she undresses my already naked body with her eyes. I yearn to run my hands down her coarse, slimy skin. Feel her forked tongue flicker across my neck. Her fangs scrape me as her mouth kisses my flesh gently. Pale flesh and emerald scales entangled—an interracial, interspecies, carnal relationship the gods would frown upon.

I want it so bad I can taste it. Taste her. I stand from my knees, driven by the lust that increases my heart rate. She smiles, beckoning me forward. We are going to consummate this love in the most expressive form possible. I can feel it.

I'm so transfixed on her that I fail to hear the dozens of Gorgons around us laughing. They are nothing more than white noise. Cruel background sounds cheering me on to seduce their leader. My feet carry me forward, a zombie drugged by the fiery passion which rages internally. I want to lose myself in her. Two filthy humps of flesh rolling on the ground, pouring their life into each other.

"Snap the fuck out of it, soldier!" Lilith yells, ripping me from the trance. "She is attacking you with high-grade pheromones! Reeling you in like bait!" I stand still, breaking eye contact with her to look around. The surrounding Gorgons roar with laughter at the sight of me stumbling toward their queen. "She is not going to make love to you, moron. She's going to kill you, then eat you. Snap the fuck out of it," Lilith commands. "You don't even have a prick or balls. What are you going to do? Dry hump her to death?"

She's right. I have lost my senses. I was so ensnared by lust I nearly forgot I don't even have the right body parts to bounce, boogie, and bump anymore.

A chill washes over my body. I look back at my seductress. The first thing I notice is her hair. It does not move from the blowing wind. The wind doesn't even blow. The air is more stagnant than the swamps we're surrounded by. No, her hair moves not because the wind blows it. Her hair moves because it's alive.

Her hair is a nest of living, breathing, moving snakes. It is not her eyes that draw me in, it is the snakes writhing upon her head. They excrete pheromones that blind my rational side. Lull my guard to sleep, draw me out from my shell of logic and reason. Fatten my lust up like a calf for slaughter.

And if it hadn't been for Lilith I would have ignorantly given myself up to be killed. I see the slightest twitch of vexation in the queen's eyes at the realization I have broken her trance. Her slitted eyes are layered with confusion. *Likely because no one has ever seen through her medusian gaze*, I deduce. I see the calculations she makes inside her head, adjusting her plans to fit the new challenge. I am more of a contender than she previously perceived.

Thank you, Lilith, I sigh inwardly. Close call. I cannot afford to become distracted by the pheromones again.

I approach the serpent goddess, avoiding eye contact now. I have a newfound strength in my chest, though I know not where it came from. I refuse to be controlled by any master other than myself, and her sexual deception was a ploy meant to snaggle me by my own desires. My tragic humanity. Even when I am a slave to no other, I am a slave to myself.

"I have come to fulfill the propheccy. I am the sssecond coming. I am Ouroborosss," I begin, the words tasting blasphemous coming from my tongue. I suddenly speak Ssserphentyne as if it is my primary language. Lilith has uploaded it to my dialect.

I expect to hear laughter, but all noise from the crowd stops. My onlookers see I have broken the trance Vipress set upon me. I have torn open the veil that killed so many others before me. That alone warrants their attention. Now they seek to hear me out.

And so here I stand, my dark mahogany skin caked with mud and algae and dried blood. Naked, yet clothed in courage. Vulnerable, yet stronger than I've ever been. Human, yet claiming I am a god among men. My audience does not interrupt my words. They await their queen's reaction.

I look in her eyes. I see horror. The potentiality of my statement perplexes her. Her hair rattles, sending microscopic pheromones through the air to attack me.

This time she doesn't hold back. She sends an army of chemical signals at me so potent it has the potential to paralyze me still as stone.

But I am ready for it this time. I feel the warm chill of sexual seduction brush over my skin. I let it wash over me. I walk through unseen fire, untouched, unbridled. No one else can feel the heat which surrounds me. Which resides within me. An unrighteous heat. Sinful heat. I push onward, shattering her medusian glare. It goes right through me. She would have more luck tempting a piece of transparent glass.

And I see ever-increasing frustration become apparent on her face. "I have come to fulfill the long-awaited prophecccy of Ouroborosss, your highnessss. I have come to unite the Ten Dæmonic Tribesss. The Abyssss comes, and we mussst come together if we are to dessstroy the hold it has over usss." A chill washes over me as the memory of Oblivion's Cthulhu Knight enters my mind when I mention the Abyss.

"Blasssphemy," she whispers. "Vagrant liar. You would dare come before me, Queen of the Gorgonsss, Prophetessss of Ouroborosss, and ssspeak sssuch liesss? I will have you killed for sssuch heresssy! Tell me, who are you really?"

Convincing her that I am Ouroboros will be impossible. She is a puppet of Deus Ex Machina. The god of machines is no doubt watching through her eyes at this very moment. He will not allow her to concede without putting up a fight.

I am not conversing with Vipress, Queen of the Gorgons right now. I am being tested by Deus Ex Machina, forger of false religions. He went so far as to create this falsified belief system for the Dæmonic tribes. He is going to make me obey the words of his scripture if I'm to win over his puppet.

"Or you could kill her," Lilith suggests inwardly.

"Killing her is always an option," she repeats.

And invoke the wrath of the entire Gorgon race before I've proven I am Ouroboros? I somehow see that not working out well in my favor.

"Who do you say I am?" I ask, answering her question with another. I know this will only frustrate her further, yet I do it anyway.

"You come to me half dead, the half-eaten ssscrapsss of some cronon'sss left-over dinner. The incorrigible ssstench of fecccesss and unpasssteurized cheesssse, the ssstench of all humansss. The firssst I've ssseen who hasss come to usss, rather usss to them. We have dessstroyed your pathetic human cccivilizationsss before, sssmooth-ssskin. Ssseen what flowsss in your racccesss' veinsss. Coward blood. That'sss what makesss up your ssspeccciesss.

"The Abysssss corrupted you all. Turned you againssst us Dæmonia. It wasss *your* raccce who claimed *we* were the monssstersss while purging *us* from the domed sssanctuariesss, eonsss ago. Claimed we were the monsssters caussse of our appearanccce. But we weren't the one behaving asss monssstersss, were we?

"It wasss your raccce that ssstarted this war. But it will be usss that finishesss it. Your cruel raccce of mongreloidsss. I would expect them to create sssuch a dec-ccception sssuch asss the one you've brought today. Claiming to be Ouroborosss. A human? Ouroborosss would not taint hisss flesh with sssuch vanity. When Ouroborosss comesss again, it shall be asss a Gorgon. And I, hisss Prophetessss, pave the way for hisss arrival. We Gorgonsss forge a path in fire and blood among all thossse who refussse to join usss for the final war againssst the Abyssss. We are a proud raccce. A piousss raccce. Hisss holy raccce. The time isss at hand. The hour ssstrikesss nigh," she announces, violent cheering in the crowd in support of her words. The audible flicking of several dozen tongues hissing in one hushed holler. Whooping and banging of metallic weapons.

And I, at the center of it all, stand firm. "You think thisss war holy? You think your caussse righteousss?" I ask rhetorically, angrily. "You wage a war againssst your own! The enemy isss the Abyssss, and you jihaad againssst the Dæmonic tribes? It isss you that isss doing the work of the enemy. You are not of your father Ouroborosss, who divided himsssself into ten to sssave usss from the Abyssss; you help the eternal darknesss kill all that isss left of Ouroborosss'sss creation! Look at you all! Clad in your reptilian armor, weaponsss at half massst. Headsss on a ssswivel for any who defy your agenda. Totalitarian! Barbaric! Anarchy!

"Thisss isss not a life which reflectsss the noble virtuesss left behind. What would Tyrannosssaur the Terrific think, if he were to sssee hisss people now? It wasss hisss Eternal Flame that dissspelled ignoranccce sssuch asss yoursss upon the faccce of the earth. You ssspit upon hisss grave with your actionsss, claiming you ssseek to resssurrect him. For what? To rot out his eyesss with your sssinful deeds? To caussse hisss heart to fail with the grievancccesss of your wrongdoingsss? To sssend him back to the grave if he daresss defy your intentionsss? You Gorgonsss are nothing more than sssquabbling children. Pillaging your vain holy quest becaussse you've been plagued by boredom.

"If you will not believe that I am he, the great Ouroborosss, by word, sso be it. But you cannot deny my right to fulfill the Godkiller Chronicle. I, Ouroborosss, claim my right to a trial by fire," I announce. My words silence the crowd. Their eloquence falls on many deaf ears and closed minds. They instantly divide the crowd into two parties. Those too stubborn to entertain any deviance in what they hold to be true. And those who become afraid at the prospect before them.

After all, you do not want to be found on the side opposed to God. I look from Vipress to the crowd. There are more than a few dozen gathered now. Dozens more have leaked in during my conversation unnoticed. There are now hundreds of slitted eyes that fall on me. Judging. Weighing the odds. Using their half-sized brains to make human-sized decisions.

I can see their reactions written on their scaled faces. Those who are doubtful. Those moved to anger against me. Those confused. Those who secretly believe me, but don't want their peers to know. They scan the faces of their peers. To see if they are alone in their compulsion to trust my words. I have just, after all, succeeded in exchanging words with Vipress without making an ass of myself. That alone is a miracle.

There are also those who, as always, sit upon a fence. Those who will wait to see me perform a greater miracle before they will believe me. Those who must see completion of the Godkiller Chronicle before accepting my authority over their Queen's.

Lastly, there are those who will not accept my authority no matter what I do, not because they are loyal to Vipress, but because they are loyal to no leader. The ones who are not wired to be followers. The ones with hidden contempt in their eyes. These are the ones who will stab me when my back's turned. The assassins. The ones who only comply with social norms because it is too much effort to overthrow the way things are.

I can see these roles written in their eyes. Their body language. The way their shoulders are sunken or half-risen. Chests caved or puffed. Nipples hard or flaccid. Gooseprickle-raised scales versus smooth skin.

"The Godkiller Chronicle, eh?" she repeats to herself in a hushed tone, noting the weight in the divine prophecy. Revering in its sacredness. She smiles, realizing she may use this prophecy to kill me—devise a plan that will lead to my inevitable doom. Her lips curl above her fangs in a newly welcoming smile. A smile that is both greeting and dismissive. A smile that plots to kill me.

"Very well then. I cannot deny you the chanccce to be sssifted from your sssinful ancccessstors like wheat from weed. We shall sssee if it is God-blood that runsss through your veinsss. I do not take this holy ssstipulation lightly. I take it upon myssself, Prophetessss of Ouroborosss, to weed out falssse prophetsss. To kill the fake godsss. And I know exactly how to put your divinity to the tessst," she says, her voluptuous smile slightly concerning to me. Her hair rattles like a dozen snakes who've found a prey large enough to satisfy their combined hunger.

"Bring me the Vermillion Viper," she commands in a voice so authoritative it shakes the air between us. The crowd almost doesn't know how to react. They look to each other, not knowing whether to clap or jeer or remain silent in respect for the soon-to-be dead.

My face is stone, knowing exactly what she plans to do to kill me. Faint recollection of what was inscribed in Deus Ex Machina's files comes to mind. Recorded within his meddlings concerning the Gorgonic people, the bulk of the content revolved around his manipulation of Vipress. Her capture, brainwashing, and rise to power.

"Vermillion Viper," Lilith begins debriefing me in a monotonous tone, as if she is a spelling bee instructor getting ready to supply the definition of a word to me.

I know what it is, Lilith. I remember from Deus Ex Machina's recorded observations.

"Are you prepared to face it?" she asks, her voice somewhat soothing inside my head. Her presence slows my heart rate, making me feel as if I'm not alone.

Do I have a choice?

"No. Unfortunately you do not. I am sorry, soldier."

Do remaining respirocytes have enough charge within them to defeat the venom?

"Even with full charge, the toxicity can still be lethal to your person. That is the danger of the Vermillion Viper's venom. It is a hemotoxic-neurotoxic hybrid venom. It will corrode your tissues while paralyzing your muscles. Created with a Hydra-like defense mechanism, any attempt your respirocytes make at attacking it will only further the venom's advance. Kill a single enzyme and two more will rise in its stead.

"Such a serpent is extremely rare. Deus Ex Machina's files reveal only three were made in the beginning. It is how Vipress killed their last king and rose to power. Seduced him to sleep with her, then unleashed the viper on him while he slept. Near instantaneous death; the toxin was so potent it stopped his heart within minutes.

"Your system should fare better than that, but you will only have a few days before your organs shut down. We must hope the respirocytes have time to neutralize the threat, extract antibodies, and create an antivenom before they go offline. I will command them to slow the spread and focus on creating the antivenom, but it will take time. Days, even. Best estimate, you have approximately three days before the venom stops your heart from beating. I will do my best to produce the antivenom before then."

Terrific. That's what I love to hear. Good ole' fashion optimism.

"This will not be our end," Lilith reassures.

Part of me wishes it was. Seems like an easier end than the one ahead of me.

"Ahead of *us*," she corrects.

We shall see.

The crowd parts, revealing the snake handler walking down the aisle with my death in her hands. Even the handler, whose sole job it is to care for reptiles, holds the snake fearfully, as if she's carrying a ticking time bomb. I lock gaze with the serpent. The viper's eyes are the color of an exploding star, an obsidian, soulless slit down the middle. The fumes of uncontrollable fire. Reds drowning yellows, consuming clouds of orange. Opaque colors clashing beneath sinister eyelids. Eyes that close in on me, staring at me head on. Challenging eyes. Eyes that establish their dominance without action.

Its body is not large, as one would expect a serpent of such renowned reputation to be. It is the same size as a rat snake, in terms of BDEM comparison. But when juxtaposed to all the other colossal creations that sprung forth from the Sterilization Wars, the Vermillion Viper is underwhelming. I'm forced to remind myself that it's the underwhelming things that can sometimes be most fearsome.

It's as if someone previously slit their throat and let every ounce of their body's blood drain and dry on this snake's exterior. It is painted in a rugged ruby red. Rustic and rough. A surreal portrait of blood burning; a topographical map of the final embers of a dying world.

The Gorgonic snake handler brings the ten-feet-long snake to Vipress's side. The snake does not thrash, as an animal with overwhelming testosterone would be expected to. It stares calmly. Such an animal knows it will have its revenge. Knows there is a time and place for vengeance.

My eyes connect with the enslaved serpent, instantly feeling the bond between us. A bond in our bondage. Slaves to elements we cannot control. Apex predators of our ecosystems. Killers because it's who we were forced to be. We will see which predator comes out on top soon enough.

"The Godkiller Chronicle ssstipulatesss that Ouroborosss incarnate will endure ten trialsss asssssigned by the ten leadersss of the Dæmonic tribesss. Asss recognized sssovereignty of the Gorgonic people, I declare your trial to be one of death. Only a true god can sssurvive cccertain death; become reborn by it. If you truly are the sssecond coming of Ouroborosss, only you can withssstand the bite of the Vermillion Viper, human. And only then will I concccede to your leadership.

"Today I baptize your blood in the mossst potent of all the venomsss. It shall purge you of any liesss or blasssphemy. It will corrode what is falssse. Leave only what isss holy. Before you undergo thisss righteousss sssanctification, have you any lassst wordsss, human?"

The traditional offer for last words. Such an antiquated, poetic gesture. Reminiscent of the BDEM Era. A humanistic varnish. A chance for the guilty and innocent conscience alike to eloquently vent their final thoughts. But people who do not plan to die have no need for last words, such as I. They bite their tongue and abide in silence, and wait to have the thematically rich last laugh. After all, last laughs feel much better than last words.

"Sssarys ssskӧll, sssven sssün. Sssven sssün, sssarys ssskӧll." *From death, comes life. From life, comes death.* Quite the symbolic declaration in this scenario. The first sentence is the opening verse to *The Book of the Angel of Life* in the *Omnibus*. The stock phrase which introduces the Angel of Life to the narrative. The second sentence... Well, that's the opening line to the entire *Omnibus*. *The Book of the Angel of Death*. The story that recounts my historical legacy. The story that frames me as the facilitator of *New Genesis*.

These are not scriptures that will have cultural relevance to the Gorgon race, but I did not say them while looking at my audience. No, I stare deeply into Vipress's eyes as I utter these cold words. Past her vehement façade into her monitored occipital lobe. I glare so deeply and speak so confidently that even the god of machines that controls her can hear me. And he, the Tyrant of all, is more than familiar with these scriptures. He is their writer.

I built this empire for him.

And now I will tear it down. Rip the veil down its midseam.

Vipress scoffs, sending forth the snake handler with a flick of the wrist. "And make sssure the bite is cccenter body massss," she adds. "Don't want to give him the option of amputating."

The crowd is silent. Maybe they are not so loyal as I was led to believe. Perhaps they can be won over, by the right leader. A warring people awaiting the savior who will put an end to their bloody endeavors. Awaiting the one who will stand against their bloodthirsty queen more like it.

The viper's handler is, like her cargo, a serpent herself. Like Vipress, she is humanoid from the waist up and serpent from the torso down. Where Vipress's scales are mixes of ivy green and emerald, the handler's are sapphire blue and turquoise. She is not large or powerful like Vipress. She, like her cargo, is an underwhelming size. She's timid and submissive—her eyes don't raise to meet mine until the last second.

She is anxious. Sweat trickles down the inside of her arms and along the side of her small, exposed breasts. A great burden she has, to be the one to administer the Gorgon's declared Godkiller Chronicle. All eyes fall on her. All is quiet. Not even the cicada's groan in the blaring heat is heard in this historical moment.

Her arms extend toward me, shaking nervously with the deadly cargo tight in her grasp. The Vermillion Viper can smell her fear; I can see it in his eyes. And even worse, it can smell my lack thereof. Her breathing patterns are short and shallow. She is hyperventilating under the pressure of this task.

I do not see this going well. The fiery eyes of my executioner roll back to examine where the excreted hormonal imbalance is coming from. It will not bite me if there is a more fearful candidate available. Such is the way of the hunt in the wild. Kill smarter, not harder.

I watch the viper examine its handler with its peripherals, readying myself for the inevitable. Her grip loosens, letting the viper's red scales slither until its body slackens enough to strike. Its eyes calmly assess me as its head inches forward. Its forked tongue fingers the air. Smelling me. My heart rate is normal. I am not nervous. Despite Vipress's pride in her decision, this is far from the worst I've encountered. The viper senses this, sensing the unusual circumstances. This is a snake who has never faced such calm prey.

I hear a rattle. See a shifting in its bobbing head. Its face moves side to side, coming closer to my face until it is only inches away from my eyes. Its tongue flicks. I can feel the air moving between us. I see the intention in its eyes. I whisper, "Don't do it," low enough to not be heard by any onlookers. A mere mumbling to even the handler, who is a few short feet away. But snakes do not speak New English, so the viper will not heed my warning.

I find in life it's the attack *you don't see coming* that presents the bigger danger. I feel the air pulse in front of me as the viper contracts its fast-twitch muscles, rapidly pulling its face away from mine, changing its target from me to its fearful handler. It happens faster than the blink of an eye. Its devilishly-horned head whips around toward the hands that hold it. Mouth wide open. Fangs extended. The reflection of its handler taking her last hyperventilated breath in its venomous eyes.

The viper's mouth snaps shut. The handler gasps. The crowd shivers.

I saw it coming. Mind visualizing it before it became reality. Saw the warning signs long before the handler reached me. And that is why the viper's fangs never reach their target. Its head snaps short, recoils, then strikes again. It cannot reach the handler. I feel its body contracting every muscle it has in my powerful grip, trying to snap its head far enough forward to kill the frightfully paralyzed girl.

It is I who saved her, catching the Vermillion Viper's head the second I saw its scales shudder before attacking. I have saved the woman who brought death to my doorstep. The poetic irony. Now the viper's restriction provokes a furious series of vain strikes directed toward her. Enraged thrashing. Each one falling shorter than the last as I reel its head closer toward me. All the way until its head is in my closed fists and it has no option but to oblige my will.

The handler opens her clenched eyes, feeling her body for the puncture wound, awaiting an oncoming wave of pain that will never come. It never does. She stares at me. Stares at the squirming, irate serpent in my grip. Its body throws itself in every direction in some desperate hope it will win back its freedom.

My hands squeeze tighter, convincing it otherwise. The handler, along with hundreds of onlooking Gorgons, is in awe. I did just, after all, catch a Vermillion Viper mid strike. With the deft hands and dexterous fingers of a god. Only a god could so swiftly and elegantly prevent an attack. Only a god of tremendous grace could save his own executioner from being executed. And so the handler stares at me now, as if I am some god. The Ouroboros I present myself to be. Serpent King.

She eyes me with reverence, bowing at her torso, fanning her arms to the ground at my feet. The viper's body still thrashes in the air to a lesser degree. Her serpentine lower half slithers closer, her hands crawling through dead grass in hopes of touching my bare feet. I shift the mighty diamond-shaped viper head to one hand, using the other to bend over and gently grab her reaching fingers in mine.

The touch startles her. I pull, slowly lifting her back up from the ground. She rises, her ashamed, astonished sapphire eyes lifting to meet mine. I see love in those eyes. I see hope. But I also see fear in those eyes. I see doubt. I pull her close, so close that I can smell the cloying scent of moist grass covered in sugar. I bring her ear to my mouth, then whisper, "Bow only to those who have earned your respect."

She nods, confusion mixed with understanding in her expression. Words that will need to be reflected upon. My free hand presses in the hollow of her chest, between her two breasts, and gently pushes. She slithers backwards, not wanting to stop me from what I must do.

I lock eyes with Vipress now, wanting her to experience what happens next to the fullest degree. She looks at me in awe, the uncontrolled part of her betraying her inner thoughts. It is written on her face. She stares at the viper in my hand, knowing I now wield the weapon which was meant to kill me. Not a single member of the army that surrounds me dares to step forward to defend their queen. I hold now the strongest venom this world has ever known. At my disposal.

I take a step forward, watching Vipress shrivel in fear. Her tail flickers behind her hesitantly, eyes trying to read if I have the balls to assault her in front of her entire army. I take another step forward, dragging the noncompliant viper behind me. Her eyes scan the crowd, unspoken fury silently demanding a suitor to step forward.

I take a few more steps. She grimaces, then snarls like a cornered hyena, its pack of fellow hellions nowhere to be found. I close the gap, and she has no choice but to watch me cross the plain, dead grass, my feet crunching with every step, the vermillion body dragging behind me like a trail of blood.

I carry a death sentence in my hand, drawing only a few feet away from her. The viper can strike from this distance. She knows it. I know it. The crowd knows it. I lift its fiery eyes level with my own, pointed toward her so she can lock eyes with the vermin like I once did. The snake's tongue flicks at the fear in the air. The fear of a queen, no less. Royal fear.

The snakes which make up the nest that is Vipress's hair shy away, pulling her locks back into a ponytail to avert eye contact with the viper. The only pheromones I smell now are ones of deeply-rooted fear. Not a fear of this viper, no. Fear of death. Fear of the pain which precedes it. I extend my arm, bringing the diamond-shaped head inches away from hers. The crowd watches as her face shrinks away, arms raising to defend herself.

The viper hisses at the sudden movement, fangs extended to attack any threat. An audible grunt escapes Vipress as she throws herself to the ground, her façade of strength replaced with cowering fear.

I have communicated to the crowd what I intended. I need not play with my prey anymore. Vipress stares up at me, human eyes staring into those of a mortal god. Horror plain on her face as if she's seen a demon. No words need to be exchanged at this moment.

What honor is there in what I'm about to do? I ask myself, staring down at the cowering queen. *There is no honor in war. No mercy.*

"On the contrary," Lilith replies. "War is the setting honor most proudly displays itself."

Vipress knows she is about to die. I can see it in her eyes. She glances back and forth between my eyes and the eyes of her executioner. Then, she watches as I twist the viper's head to face me. Watches as I plunge the extended fangs deep into my neck. The viper bites down greedily, ecstatic to rid himself of his built-up toxins. I feel the venom pulse into me, eliciting a stifled grunt.

Searing pain rips down my left side like an army of fire ants crawling through my bloodstream, stinging every square inch of my innards. My breath escapes involuntarily, the pain overwhelming me immediately. But I will have time to suffer later. There is one more thing I must do before succumbing to the volcanic heat attacking my central nervous system.

I fall to my knees, using gravity to help rip the viper's fangs from my neck. Strength leaves me in fleeing legions. I grab Vipress, a panicked gasp escaping her mouth. She looks into my feverish eyes and knows I suffer. Knows I bring hell with me. Knows she will join me in my eternal torment.

Quickly, before she can flinch away, I press the viper head to her right breast. The viper doesn't have to be told twice to do what it does best. Mouth opens, fangs bite deep, venom pulses into the new prey. My arm shakes from the effort it takes to hold the snake still. Vipress lets out a strained scream, cut short by the agonizing pain. She receives only a fraction of the venom I did. The viper milked the majority of its toxin into my neck, but Vipress doesn't have respirocytes. The bite she receives may be just as lethal to her mortal body as mine is to me.

I pull the snake from her, grabbing slightly below its head with my two hands. With all the strength I have left, I twist the neck with a single, vicious jerk as if my life depends on it. Because it does. I hear the swift crack in the snake's neck and I throw it to the side. Dead. I collapse uncomfortably on top of Vipress's body, my head next to hers as the paralysis bites at my core and any motivation to move seems like a world of strain.

She squirms beneath me. Like me, she is in a world of tremendous pain. We burn together in an invisible fire. Two piled bodies, one massive hump of feverish flesh radiating heat as it fights an unseen war. Our flesh feels as if it is melting off our bones. Our bones feel as if they are being sucked of their marrow. Our muscles strain to combat an enemy they are ill prepared for.

Our souls melt into each other in this single moment, fevers clashing, hallucination setting in simultaneously. My lips find her ear, then whisper in a hushed tone, "I will... recover from thisss... I can... heal you too... You need only... yield to me..."

Our bloodshot eyes lock, heat between us like our faces are made of hot coals. Her lips tremble. Fear flows in her veins alongside the venom. *Bad look for a queen.* She is finished here. I have ruined her reputation of fearless strength. Even if she survives, these Gorgons will never follow her again. They require a leader who claims the mantle by brute force, not one who shamefully cowers in the open.

"Get thisss... *human*... out of my sssight!" she screams, her voice choking. Reptilian guards grab me under the armpits, lifting me from my victim. "You will... know where to find me... When your... hoursss run short," I mock. I watch as her murderous glare stabs into me as I'm dragged away. Medical professionals rush forward to aid their queen, breaking our field of vision from each other. The last image I have of her sticks in my mind as I close my eyes. Her straining face doing everything it can to mask its pain, veins popping out the side of her neck from the effort it takes to hold such a façade.

She is stronger than I judged. She will fight the venom within her until her last breath. But I have extended my offer, and if she is wise, she will call for me soon. She will make it longer than most, considering she received only a microdose of venom compared to me. But she will not outlast me. I give her until dusk tomorrow before she calls for my retrieval. I must hope Lilith has turned my bloodstream into an antibody by then. It is the only hope I have of winning over the Gorgon race. The only hope I have for defying my foretold Cataclysm.

I close my eyes and forget all else, becoming painfully aware of the feelings that anchor me to the earth, squeezing my consciousness, refusing to let it go. I feel my chafed heels dragging against coarse grass, cutting my feet open further. The burning inside of me matched by the burning outside my body. My sunburnt skin crisp to the touch, molested by clawed fingers clenched tight. My heart throbs on a tight guitar string. My blood thickens, coagulating into clots that cannot be pumped through my veins. My head pounds. My neck swells. The site of the bite is the size of a large fist punching my skin outward, stretching the scar that runs over it from my childhood encounter with Fenrir.

I can't breathe. My chest is so tight it might implode. My skin is covered in perspiration like a blade of grass covered in morning dew. "Stop straining, you're only making it worse," Lilith whispers. Why is her voice so reassuring? It calms me like the sound of a distant waterfall. "You must let go. Let go of consciousness.

Trust in me. I will take it from here. You are safe. I will save you," she whispers, her voice like a guardian angel.

I listen to her words and obey. Partly because they free me from my current misery, partly because I can't hold on any longer. I fade to nothingness, like a dying wayfarer lying beneath alien skies watching unfamiliar stars go dark.

CHAPTER TWO

The death of Vicien Greaves was the opening of Pandora's Box. In these dark days, it is humanity's greatest flaws that shine brightest. Discord has been sewn among the nations. Greaves was successful. The Fourth World War began the moment I dragged myself from the catacombs of Sentient Laboratories.

The war was programmed. Every weapon of mass destruction ever patented by Hyperion Industries was programmed to come online once Greaves's holographic ghost expired. When I dragged myself from the ruins of Sentient Laboratories, what waited for me in the light of the rising sun was not much better than what rested in the dark depth of the ground.

I arose in time to helplessly watch the world become bombarded by nuclear fallout. Every nuclear reactor upon the face of the planet exploded in unison. Nuclear warheads fill the sky like an early morning meteor shower.

Biochemical viruses developed in underground Hyperion-funded black market labs launched the same hour, infecting lab technicians. The first carriers among the four billion citizens inhabiting Earth.

A robotic empire known as the Nihilist leaked into South Eurasia from the Wasteland regions. Their origin is unknown, but their purpose is much clearer. Induce the extinction of humanity. Aerial footage is relayed to media streaming platforms of the robotic coup. Cities smothered in flames, the robots marching north slaughtering everything in their path.

From Eastasia comes another threat; this one known as Oblivion—an invasive, parasitic artificial intelligence consuming humanity like a swarm of locusts. Citizens flee to nearby refugee camps, trying to escape to foreign lands where it's safe. But nowhere is safe from Oblivion. It is an unstoppable force that will not stop until it has consumed all in its path.

The world slips into utter chaos. Leaders and heroes instantly rise to face the threat of human extinction only to be subsumed by the casualties of war.

Humanity has been sufficiently shattered by outside forces, and how does it respond? It shatters itself further.

Civil war breaks out in Oceania among the races.

Famine plagues Eastasia as the regularly imported resources from Eurasia cease under an embargo.

Anarchy reigns throughout the entirety of Eurasia—neighbors pitted against neighbors in a struggle for power.

Above all else, the genocide of humanity runs rampant. War and sickness and hunger, further perpetuated and worsened by human nature's inability to come together to solve its problems.

Vicien Greaves was right. This will be the end of us.

Yet where am I amidst all the chaos? I don't find myself on the frontline of the battlefield, amidst the falling bombs and diseased soldiers. Nor do I find myself in any war room, strategically directing humanity's first response to the encroaching robotic crusade.

I am not amidst the dead and dying. Not saving children caught in the wreckage of some missile's collateral damage. Not working with scientists on ways to combat the plethora of viruses that infect the greater population.

Not among the political leaders to provide sound instruction while they bicker day and night like dogs chasing tails yet never capturing them. I don't present solutions on how to smash the uprising anarchies or settle the rebellions.

No, when the world needed me most, I vanished.

My fist knocks on the front door of an all-too-familiar homestead, silently hoping its resident has survived the first wave of bloodshed. My knock is meager; borderline nervous. It has only been a few short days since I stormed from this building. But to those who live with contempt, a few short days feels like a lifetime.

I am only a man. I make mistakes. But the difficulty is found in correcting them. That is what brings me here. How can I fight a war to save humanity if I cannot first salvage my own? Days ago I walked out on the love of my life, all faith in her lost, thinking she had cheated on me with another.

Ignorance is not always bliss. The man who has so efficiently ruined my life has succeeded in doing so again. He has defiled the woman I love, against her own will, against mine. And because of my absence in her life... *He got away with it.* I bite my bottom lip out of self-loathing. I dragged her into this life, and I am the one at fault. I knew the danger in marrying her. I knew the danger in not being present to protect her.

I don't know what I'll do if she is dead, I think to myself, pit in my stomach and knot in my throat. I hear no stirring within the house to indicate someone coming to get the door. *I just left her. Didn't question her. Didn't seek understanding. I stormed out in anger, leaving her to grieve by herself. She must have been so scared. So afraid. So alone. This is all my fault.*

My knees feel too weak to stand here helplessly. I twist the doorknob, finding that the door opens without any resistance. The lock is broken. My pulse spikes. Someone has forced their way through this door. Suddenly the knot in my throat becomes justified.

I storm into the house with reckless abandon. Someone could have been waiting behind the door to slit my neck from ear to ear and I wouldn't have known. My decision making is now impaired by overwhelming anxiety.

I sprint straight for the bedroom, the place I saw her last. The image of her sobbing silently beside our bed as I grabbed my bag and left. She made no attempt to explain herself. No mention that her unwanted pregnancy was not spurned from unfaithfulness. Most likely because there would be severe repercussions. Most likely because someone would have killed her if she did.

If she opened her mouth and revealed who the father was, I would have killed Vicien Greaves days before his plan was ready. But I reacted just as he planned.

I stormed off without a single word. I could have ended this before it ever had the chance to start. Could have killed him, instead of plotting to infect him with some imaginary virus.

And now, if I walk into this bedroom and find her lying dead where I last saw her, there will be nothing I can do. I will somehow be an even hollower shell of the man I have always been. The void within me will expand to encapsulate all of me. There will be no opportunity for retribution. For revenge. Greaves is dead. The chance for payback is nonexistent.

What hope do I have, other than to enter the room where we've shared as many passionate nights as my schedule permitted. Nights filled with fiery love. Yearning of flesh. Craving for each other. And yet, it was never enough. I could never get enough of her. And if it is all over, I will truly be left with nothing.

I skid through a corner and sprint down the final corridor to the master bedroom. The door is closed. My heart drops. What waits for me beyond that door will change my life forever. I twist the knob gently, visualizing in my head what I want to see upon opening it.

But I am sadly disappointed. Where I hoped with all my might to find the bedsheets tangled with Winter sleeping soundly in their folds, I find a neatly made bed, the room barren of life. My eyes fall on a single sheet of paper placed dead center on the clean, black, king-sized comforter. There is nothing for me to do but approach its words and read its content. To stand and linger on the thought that Winter is no longer here would only crush me further.

I pick up the sheet and see that the letter is addressed to me. My heart jumps. There is still hope. When all else fails, there is still hope.

I take notice that the script is scribbled too elegantly to be Winter's writing. No, I have seen this writing before, and it belongs to the creator of my many woes—Vicien Greaves.

Prometheus,

If you are reading this, it means you have by some miracle survived the initial confrontation between yourself and your gruesome opponents. Congratulations, you have survived to fight another day. But I am disappointed in you.

The very fact that you are holding this letter proves how predictable you are. Like some runaway child, I knew you would come back for her. A prodigal son in search of comfort. Now that I am out of the picture, I have no doubt the hope has increased in your mind that you have an even greater chance of settling down and starting a life with your wife, like you've wanted for so long. It's a shame.

Don't you know you lost that opportunity the day you ruthlessly stormed out on her, ostracizing her for being pregnant with a product of rape?

Such a cowardly, childish tantrum does not deserve such a wonderful woman as your wife. You should be ashamed of yourself. Did you really think that a woman with such a pure heart would tarnish your union? Did you really think her weak enough to give in to the depraved lusts of her mind? Believe me, I have been watching her for some time, and she was not capable of cheating on you. She loved you too much.

You have lost one of the finest women to ever walk this planet. And now you have come back, erroneously hoping to correct your mistake. You think you can salvage what your marriage. Start anew. Wrongo, old buddy. That ship has sailed.

But don't fret. I will give you the chance to right your wrongs. Some merciful master I am. You see, I couldn't allow Winter to stay here. I had to do what you failed to do. Keep her safe. Especially since she is now the mother of my future child. But even more because I knew coming here would be your first destination. I have set you up as a King upon a three-sided chess board. But I had to ensure that, just like your opponents, you remain a King without a Queen.

However, to encourage your participation in the Fourth World War, your Queen waits for you at the finish line. I have sequestered her, with every possible necessity of life, in an underground fallout shelter. It is a mansion of a creation. She needn't want for anything in life while isolated there. I have even placed several robotic handmaids with her to care for her every need.

There is only one caveat. The shelter has only been supplied enough oxygen to last ten years. This, as you can deduct yourself, is your deadline. I am giving you ten years to win this war. To kill Oblivion and all of the Nihilist army. Ten years, or your wife and my child will suffocate from oxygen depletion.

She has been debriefed on this as well. She expects you to come for her. Prays that you will win this war and set her free. She, too, knows the deadline. Will be counting down the days to her imminent death. Only you can save her, Prometheus. The location will be granted to you upon your victory. Should you fail, by death or delay, you will be forced to deal with your failures however seems appropriate.

I apologize for the lack of empathy in this quest, Prometheus. You deserve better. You have fought your whole life, and now I force you to fight once more from beyond the grave. You do not owe humanity anything. You have saved them time and time again. That is why this war is not a race to save humanity. It is a race to save the only thing left in this world that still makes you human. A quest to save your own humanity.

The war to end all wars. Win this, and you will effectively defeat me for the first and last time ever. I have stacked the odds against you. Against humanity. If you win, it will have been a well-earned victory. If you lose... Well, there are worse things in life than death. I'll let your personal ethics decide what those things are.

Lastly, as I'm sure you've concluded by now that the odds are insurmountably stacked against you, I leave you with a flicker of hope. Go to the abandoned shell where your lonely life began. There you will find a new hope, among many others, for winning this war. I could not, after all, set you up against your current enemies without stacking the odds a little in your favor. Thank me later, perhaps at the finish line.

Xoxo,

The man who holds your reins, now and forever,

Vicien Greaves

P.S. Her life wasn't in danger if she told you that I'm the father of her child. But yours was. It was you I was going to kill if she told you. She has already saved your life once. I suggest you return the favor.

I fold the paper in disgust. Disgust in many things, but most of all disgust in myself.

I slide the paper into my front pocket. It's unnecessary to save written words that will be etched on the surface of my brain until they are eaten away by maggots and worms in my grave. But I save it nonetheless. A personal momento. A reminder for the dark times to come that she is out there somewhere, alive. Waiting for me to put an end to this war that has barely started.

Ten years. I have ten years to smash this war and obliterate my enemies. To some, that passes in the blink of an eye. To someone who lives with contempt, such as myself, that will last a lifetime. A lifetime I must live and endure. Because if I don't, all that I care about in this world will end.

She is the chain that tethers me to humanity. The force that will hold me accountable over the coming years. I have come this far. I will not lose myself now. I will win this war how I start it. As a human. I will prove Vicien Greaves wrong. I will lead humanity to its victory. Robots will not snuff out our light. Because we fight for much more than to fulfill our programming. We fight because we feel.

We feel the death of our brethren. The pains and losses of war. The sacrifice required to defy the bondage clockwork commandos would impose on us. Feel our hearts shatter when we lose the ones we love most.

I don't owe humanity anything. I never have. I can retire right now. The quintessential moment of my life. I finally have the freedom I fought so hard for. But to quit, when so many need me, now more than ever, would mean I'm no better than the robots who seek to extinguish us.

If I abstain from this war, I will prove Vicien Greaves right. Humanity will lose. We will be extinct in a few short years.

But if I join this war, I will satisfy Vicien Greaves wishes. It's a lose-lose situation. Either way, Vicien Greaves wins.

Above all, a vivid image of Winter burns bright in my mind. For the first time in my life, I no longer fight for myself. I fight for her. I fight for us.

"Deus Ex Machina," I call aloud, aware he can read my thoughts. I still vocalize them, feeling the need to speak the following words into existence. "Set course for my birthplace. Call the remaining ArchAngels. Tomorrow we go to war."

CHAPTER THREE

I open my eyes to a world filled with a cacophony of shrill squeaking and disgruntled moaning. The sound of air being inhaled through a thick, hollow tube. Air wheezed through a vacuum, suctioning and sucking. A sound similar to a french horn blares behind me. The ground shakes with thunderous footfall.

Dawn breaks, its light biting my eyelids.

My neck is aflame with pain so brilliant it makes me instantly regret awakening from my dreams. Dreams that reveal to me everything I've forgotten. Dreams that restore little by little all I've been stripped of.

I wish to continue dreaming. Fill in the gaps of all these missing years that led to today. At least I know we won all those wars. There is comfort in knowing that. The unpredictability of the present is unsettling. Not knowing if I have it in me to defy Cataclysm. Defeat the self-fulfilling prophecy Deus Ex Machina set against me all those years ago.

But the dreamer is forever doomed to open his eyes. Forever daunted by reality. *Oh my downtrodden soul. Nothing more than a wretched flag filled with tears in the midst of a hurricane. Clinging to the flagpole. Whipping until it disintegrates into open air. Ripped to shreds by the forces of nature.*

"Why are you so downcast? You are alive. Have you no appreciation for the breath in your lungs?" Lilith snaps, her voice a sassy veneer filled with mockery. She does not feel sorry for me. She does not entertain my self-pity. But then again, she also isn't the one that feels my current level of pain. She is only an artificial intelligence. She wouldn't know the first thing about pain. Yet she presses on with her motivational gargling nonetheless. "Put your hope in your capabilities. Only you have the power to save yourself from your current circumstances."

Easy for you to say. You're not the one growing a second head from your neck.

"I have already begun production on an antivenom from the antibodies I extracted. It will take a few days for the pain to subside but you should consider yourself lucky. You would be dead by now if it wasn't for me."

I clench my teeth as an oncoming wave of pain passes over me from my head to my toes. *Death doesn't sound nearly so bad right now. How long have I been out?*

"Just the one night. But I assure you your arrival in this internment camp has caused quite the uproar among the Laxodontans. They haven't slept a wink since the Gorgons threw you in here. I've been monitoring their conversations since you've been unconscious."

So that's what all the snorting and trumpeting is. The bastards woke me from my sound sleep with all their hubbub. What's got their trunks in a twist?

"They know who you claim to be. Overheard the Gorgon soldiers talking about what you did. Ouroboros? In the same prisoner camp as them? It's got them split down the middle. Half of them are already ready to bow at your feet the moment you have the strength to stand. The other half think you should be put to death for claiming such lofty lies."

And the final consensus?

"Nothing. Those already aligned in your favor won't let those opposed come near you. They've formed a protective barrier around you. Several fights have already broken out. They're just scared. Scared of what they don't know. Scared of the prospect that a god may walk among them. Scared that you are just a hoax. These people have been through a lot. The Gorgons have ruined them. Destroyed all they've built in their lifetime. All their fathers built for them to inherit. All of it gone.

"They look for a savior. Some think *you* are that savior. Others are too afraid to get their hopes up."

I will only disappoint them. I am a false god.

"And their religion is a false religion. Formed by another false god—Deus Ex Machina. You needn't worry about the formalities. You may be a false god, but you bring *real* hope. Hope that these people desperately need. Play the role. Not because you believe it, but because these people need it. And you need them. Arise, Ouroboros. Show this peaceful nation that their prayers for a savior haven't fallen on deaf ears."

I double down and squeeze my torn abdomen with every straining granule of muscle fiber I have left, miraculously managing to sit up. My body is a living, breathing, infectious lesion. It feels as if a pack of BDEM Era hyenas tore my body apart limb from limb in my sleep. It feels as if my skin has been replaced with that of a leper. Oozing, cracking, itching, raw sores everywhere.

The weight of my inflamed neck becomes unbearably apparent upon sitting up, gravity pressing down on the bulge tipped with two fang marks.

The blaring of elephant trunks trumpeting and groveling with frustrated puffs of slowly inhaled air ceases as eyes turn to face me. I am surrounded by giants. These creatures may come from humans, but their phenotype reflects their elephant ancestors much more.

Knotted, coarse, bipedal legs covered in a thick, gray hide surround me. Each foot ends with three tremendous toenails that can only be explained by labeling them as hooves. A gust of uncomfortably warm air puffs down my back, followed by a Laxodontan trunk smelling the air around my head.

I am still disoriented and can barely make out the blurred figures surrounding me. They sway gracefully, doing their best to not intrude my space despite their burning curiosity. "He awake. Hoo-man awake. Somebody get Tuskfather!" a nearby voice yells excitedly.

"Tuskfather no care. He still hide in tent. Still sad. Mourn his losses," another voice responds, this one filled with sorrow.

"Cursed by gods! Cannot trust hoo-man!" a new voice rumbles, breaking through the perimeter of humanoid elephants that guard me, footfall heavy with wrath.

"Not another step, Bloodtusk, or I end you!"

"You not strong enough to end me, Snaggeltooth," the voice challenges.

I can make out the outline of the two voices going back and forth. One stands in front of me, its shadow blocking the orange glow of the rising sun. I look between the gap in my protector's legs and see the challenger. He drags his foot through the dirt several times like a bull getting ready to charge. Beats his chest with colossal, four-fingered elephant fists. His trunk lifts in the air and sounds its magnificent horn. The blare vibrates the air around me. Pierces my eardrums.

My guardian, who is noticeably smaller than my accuser, doesn't stand down at his threatening gestures. Spreads her feet into a warrior's stance. This is going to get ugly if I can't stop it. I open my mouth but words won't come out. It is more than just pain that stops me from speaking. I no longer remember how to talk, as if the gift has been ripped from my arsenal in my sleep.

Lilith? What's going on with my voice? We need to speak up if we're gonna stop these beasts from ripping what's left of my body apart!

"The venom attacked your vocal cords. I neutralized the threat before the damage was irreversible but it will take time for your body to heal them. Until then, you will be a mute."

Wonderful. Another spurt of optimism to keep me going.

"You forget your place!" Snaggeltooth yells defiantly, then continues, "You not leader yet. Tuskfather leader!"

"Tuskfather no longer fit to lead!" he snarls, his tusk puffing ferociously. Mean, heavy intakes of air. Quick, violent exhales. "He tuskless! Too scared to face me! Only weak follow Tuskfather. Strong follow Bloodtusk!" he cries. The support of several dozen Tuskers roar from outside the perimeter. Voices which embody a resilient resistance.

I believe we have been placed in the middle of a blooming Civil War, Lilith.

"Such would be our luck," she replies coyly.

I am subject to silence. A defenseless toy in the midst of quibbling giants.

"I will not repeat words again, Snaggeltooth. Stand down, or your fate be same as hoo-man's," Bloodtusk roars.

"Fate for hoo-man and I is living. Cannot say same for you. You live by tusk, you die by tusk," Snaggeltooth quips.

Words can only go so far among the primitive-minded. For a species such as this, words cannot stop war. Only a bloodbath created by bullies can do that. The enraged behemoth charges. Snaggeltooth plants her feet, bracing for impact. *Thud, thud, thud, thud.* The ground shakes more with each approaching step. Explosions of force thundering into the ground to propel the goliath forward.

And then he goes airborne. I watch his feet leave the ground from between Snageltooth's legs. Watch as his shadow conquers that of my guardian. He blots out the sun with his invasive figure. Time slows. My neck pulses with a mind of its own. A dissociative abscess that imposes such pain upon me that my knees shake. What a pity it would be, to have garnered the reputation I have, only to be brought to a swift end, flattened like a pancake beneath the wrestling of two elephants.

Yet there are more embarrassing ways to leave this life, I joke to myself. The mighty collision of tusks shatters the air. The sound of shooting stars colliding in the dark depths of space, echoing for the entire cosmos to hear.

The bodies fall, and I make a pathetic, last ditch effort to throw myself out of the range of collateral damage. I roll, not knowing I possessed enough energy to do so until faced with the ultimatum of being crushed by two tons of elephant hide.

I am pleasantly surprised to watch as they grapple on the dead, desert ground. Despite her smaller frame, Snaggeltooth is holding her own. What she lacks in size and strength she makes up for in speed. After the initial skirmish on the ground, it is Snaggeltooth who miraculously assumes the top mount. Her knees dig into Bloodtusk's biceps, rendering them useless beneath her tremendous load of a body.

Her fists rain down like a hammer striking screws, frustration building with each hit. My vision clears slightly as I look at Bloodtusk's magnificent ivory tusks. They are bony spires, lined with hundreds of calcified microfractures from past victories, every healed crack making them stronger. They are thicker and longer than any of the surrounding Laxodontans, I notice. Surely such a phenotype sets him apart from his peers. Gives him the impression he is entitled to some elevated position within the community.

It is the human in him. The guy with the biggest dick has always thought of himself as special, never realizing that a genetic blessing cannot make up for lack of intelligence and flawed morality. Colossal tusks will not make up for what this behemoth lack's in quintessential characteristics. Part of him knows that. Makes him compensate in other areas. Like fighting needlessly against the only peers capable of making him feel adequate. Creating ignorant divisions like a drama queen.

And the worst part about individuals such as this is their ability to drag others down with them. Even now I hear the arousal of a distant, demented crowd that is in support of this fight. Bloodtusk's followers, the degenerate few bored and directionless enough to follow such a pea-brained leader. A leader that now suffers devastating blows to the face by a woman. Probably the first time a woman has rode him in such a nonsexual, bloodied way.

His thick trunk tries to block what his tusks cannot, damaging itself in the process. The appendage incurs injury with every defensive advance it attempts, straining until altogether limp. Blood splatters with each successive blow. From where, I can't be sure. Several long gashes are freshly opened on the victim's face.

Snaggeltooth tilts her head at an angle that allows for me to see her full face. I see now why they call her Snaggeltooth. She only has one horned tusk protruding from her face, an oddly misshapen one at that. The elephant equivalent to a snaggletooth. Jagged. Crooked. Chunks missing here and there. The other horn is gone. Broken off at the base so long ago that her hide has filled in the gap where it once was.

She rears her head back, the half-rotting tusk exposed in the morning light like some abstract, cone-shaped piece of art constructed from a thousand rotting molars. Her head dives forward, snaggle-horn making contact with Bloodtusk's face long before her forehead smashes into his. The tusk rips through his cheek and out the back of his neck as her head butts violently against his own, somehow managing to slip her neck right through the gap between his own curled tusks.

Blood splashes everywhere from the successive lacerations. The crowd gasps. I'm too focused on the fight to see what comes next.

Out of nowhere, one of Bloodtusk's intruding minions joins the action to save his leader from further embarrassment. He barrels into Snaggeltooth. The timing couldn't be worse. At the time of the abrupt blindside collision, she is withdrawing her horn from his cheek with a sickening gurgle of blood. Her neck is aligned perfectly between his vicious, spear-tipped tusks when she's hit from the side, jostling her body straight into the ivory protrusion. She lets out a quick yelp from her trunk.

The crowd gasps as the bodies roll in one unrecognizable heap of tangled hide. *It only takes one*, I think to myself as one of Snaggeltooth's companions rushes forward and dives into the fight, outraged at the injustice.

The moshpit is an ensuing riot within seconds. Bloodtusk's hellions surge forward, joined by those opposed. Thick, muscled bodies converge on one another. Weeping and gnashing of tusks. Incomprehensible shouting paralleled with grunts of pain, thrusting of fists, and stomping of monstrous feet. And I sit, stunned, in the middle of it all.

It is by nothing more than a miracle that I am still alive—a single ant in the midst of clashing titans. My bones cannot withstand being stomped on by one of these savages. Deus forbid if one of them were to fall on me.

They behave as if they are children. I don't get it. Why must they bicker like buffoons among one another?

"It is the curse of allowing them to maintain free will. No two individuals will ever fully agree on everything. Everyone is different. Difference divides. What would you rather see—this, or invisible chains around their necks controlling their every action? Or even worse, annihilating their existence altogether?" I instantly become flustered at Lilith's words.

Despite how much I want to ignore her, write her off as some godforsaken, emotionless robot, I can't bring myself to do it the more we talk. More and more she becomes my only friend in this world. The only voice that seeks to guide me. But my dreams indicate that even Deus Ex Machina once posed as a friend of mine so he could gain control of my being. Will I ever know Lilith's true intentions?

Only when it's too late, most likely.

Life cannot go on existing this way. There must be some middle ground, I think to myself, watching the madness ensue. This is anarchy. Such soldiers will never be fit to take on the Angel of Life and his fellow ArchAngels.

"This behavior is cyclical. So much so it flows through their veins now as much as it did their ancestors. They fight because they think they have much to prove. They divide because they disagree. They do not know what to do, where to go, what to think. Every belief they once held has been stripped from them. They are the long forgotten Israelites enslaved by the Egyptians. Everything they thought they once knew is gone. Any sense of peace in their minds, shattered. Religion cannot explain their downtrodden existence. Politics cannot teach them how to prevail. The stars of the night which once held universal meaning are now nothing more than twinkling lights devoid of symbolic sanctity."

A body crashes to the loamy ground in front of me, sending up dust to dance in the air around her dead body. I stare at her as her eyes slowly roll back in her head. I have no idea which side of this pointless battle she identifies with. All I know is that she is one who could have made a difference in the coming Cataclysm, expired before it ever began. One less soldier I can command in my arsenal. One less body to help me overcome my inevitable ending.

"They need a leader, just as the Israelites needed Moses. This Tuskfather they speak of—judging from what I collected while you were unconscious, he seems to be the man we need to rally these people. They will not accept immediate leadership from you. They are a noble people. Their trust is earned, not asked for. You will have to prove yourself. In this state, you are far from being able to do so. Until you heal, the only hope you have is building an alliance with Tuskfather, their former leader. But he is a recluse. Exiled himself from his own people after the Gorgon ambush days ago. From what little I gathered through surrounding conversations over the night, he is in the far corner of the internment camp in the blistering sunlight, denying himself the comforts of food or water or companionship. But if he is as good of a leader as they say he is, something tells me he will—"

Almost as if on cue, a voice fulfills the words Lilith was going to say.

A blood-curdling thunder rips the atmosphere in two, overwhelming the sounds of battle. The authoritative explosion drives instant fear into the heart of each warrior. Silence contaminates them. I see the worried looks upon their faces. They are very familiar with this echo of omnipotence.

I watch as they shuffle and sway uncomfortably around me. Too afraid to look around from where the roar originated from. Terrified of making eye contact and being forced to assume responsibility for their actions. Children caught fighting by their wrathful parents. Aware of the consequences that come with being caught.

But I am not ashamed as they are, so I look around to see where the figure is who drives fear into an entire population. Slowly, all Tuskers lower themselves to their knees and bow, regardless of what side they previously fought for in the short lived Civil War. The war that, depending on how this interaction goes, may resume.

It is when all the Laxodontan people have bowed and I have painfully stretched my neck that I see who commands these people with a single blare of his trunk. *Tuskfather*, I think to myself, never having seen him before but knowing this must be him. Standing fearlessly at the edge of the battlefield, clothed with confidence and exhaustion, is the primary leader of the Laxodontans.

The sight of him is surely something to behold. I have never seen something look equal parts defeated and victorious. A gentle giant with a judging glare carved into granite. Tuskfather is massive, his body dwarfing Bloodtusk's, who I previously thought was the largest of this species. He is the apex of his people based on appearance alone. If I were to stand, my height would undoubtedly rise to barely meet his torso.

He is the most fearsome of the Laxodontans, yet he is so much more than that. The war against the Gorgons has not been easy on him. Scars can tell you a lot about a person. There is a timetable in every scar, and I can see that the fresh wounds which cover his body are the reasons behind his recent reflections. They are his only scars, still fresh from their healing. It is like looking at a canvas whose paint has just finished drying.

Tuskfather has faced no prior adversities preceding the war with the Gorgons. None worth noting, anyway. Compared to the scars upon my flesh, his gashes are but a scraped knee in the midst of an amputated leg.

The wear and tear of his exiled state is apparent. The sun has beat down on him as it has me. Days of starvation have made his shoulders limp, yet I can visualize the poise they once held. His body is dried out from dehydration. Skin tighter than any other Tusker in view. Veins protruding through hide, the blubber that was once beneath his flesh long gone, eaten away by his muscles as his body goes catabolic.

Red war paint, or perhaps it is blood, is wiped in stripes upon his face. Starting at the crown of his head, two lines diverging from a conjoined path to paint a gash of red over each eye, stretching below like a trail of bloody tears that coils around his tusk like a serpent.

The war paint draws my eyes across his face, leading them to finally rest on the feature which sets him apart from all others. His tusks are sawed off at the base, leaving behind wide disks of ivory. Their circumference like the stumps of two felled trees mercilessly hacked apart for timber.

Like the still healing scars, these wounds are fresh. The core of the ivory is still white, not yet infested with rot imposed by exposure to worldly elements. No attempt made by the surrounding flesh to scab over the shameful display of what was once a magnificent set of ivory. I can imagine how such tusks would have once put to shame Bloodtusk's relatively inferior alabaster ivory.

He is tuskless, raised in a culture where the size and strength of your tusks determines your destiny. No wonder he has exiled himself. He has been stripped of what pronounced his power. A deformed abomination not fit for the role of leadership. That's humanity for you, judging their leaders based on their appearance rather than the content of their heart.

Yet they remain silent and submissive, well aware that Tuskfather is still, arguably, the strongest of the Laxodontans. Biggest too, but among a directionless people he will not be able to ride on the coattails of his past reputation. He must rally his people now or lose them to a Civil War that will lead to their demise as a species.

A small whimpering sounds ahead of me. Tuskfather's ear twitches to hear such pain-filled sobbing. Without a word, he moves through the crowd. The walk of a man who knows the feeling of pain and loss. Slow and determined, Tuskers shrinking away from his presence like an ocean of elephants parting way for him.

The closer he comes to the wounded warrior the closer he comes to me. My vision is nearly restored by this point, so I draw in the details of his figure like his image is water and I am dehydrated. A magnificent beast indeed. The blood-sucking flies and mosquitoes of the air scatter before him, sensing the arrival of blood far too noble for their vermin taste.

Fourteen-feet-tall, at least, with nothing but a sack cloth to clothe his masochistic figure. The starvation has done nothing to take away from his intimidating aura. He radiates a will that has been bent beyond repair, but one that is far from broken. He is not the same as he once was. This war has transformed his soul as much as it has his body. But that is not necessarily a bad thing.

Sometimes the greatest heroes are the ones who have lost everything they once were.

Tuskfather gets down to his knees at the side of an injured Tusker moaning with terrible pain. I strain my neck to see who it is. *Snaggeltooth*. I can see his eyes fill with pain. Pain he pushes back inside him because he knows it's his duty to comfort her. She is dying. Him and I both know it.

Her strained gasps for air shudder with glee. To be graced by his presence in her last seconds is the blessing of a lifetime. He is more than a leader to her. He is an icon. The man whom she laid her life down for, giving herself up to some greater purpose. *Such sad ideology*, I think to myself. Humans have always derived comfort from sacrificing themselves for what they perceive to be some greater cause.

Her neck leaks blood like a sprinkler leaks water. She will not last much longer at this rate. Her murmuring turns into mumbles. Tuskfather bends down to hear them. Nods his head as a response. She looks relieved to see his answer, and the pain passes away instantly from her body. She lets go. Exhales her last. Slumps limp in her idol's arms.

Tuskfather closes his eyes to mask the pain he feels. The exact reaction of someone who lied to another in their final moments to give them comfort. He squeezes in the pain so it never has to leave his body. Shoves it down deep into the darkness, where all the other pain resides, forming alliances to one day haunt him internally without remorse.

His bloodshot eyes reopen, scorn written on their ragged lids. Eyes that have cried many tears over the last few days in secret. Eyes that are too tired to remain open to this imperfect world. Eyes that now look upon the people who betrayed everything it means to be a Laxodontan. He stands, Snaggeltooth's limp body sliding from his hands and slumping to the ground where it will forever remain.

"I hope you are all proud of what you've done today," he says, clearing his throat. His voice is like the deep rumbling of a cello's lowest notes. Slow and melodic. Moody like the gray skies of an oncoming storm, leaves thrashing in the abrasive wind. A voice that fits with the archetype of a proper leader.

He speaks New English better than any of the other Laxodontans. An indication of superior education than the rest. Several assumptions can be made based off that. He may have been born into royalty with ample tutors available to teach him language. For that matter, he could have been the son of some wealthy merchant.

Or perhaps an anomaly born into poverty. Such a culture allows for the rising of any individual from rags to riches if they have the brute force to claim power for themselves. The Laxodontan culture allows challengers the ability to come forward to claim the throne of leadership for themselves.

"You have granted the Gorgons a second victory," he says, letting the statement hang in the air over the remorseful audience. "We have been conquered physically, and now you have announced that we are conquered mentally. Stronger than this,

I thought we were. So wrong, you have proven me. Twenty-five years I have led you. Twenty-five years of peace. And now I stand before you with the blood of a fellow Laxodontan on my hands. Blood drawn by your childish squabbling.

"You behave as if you are now cold-blooded, like the lizards who captured us. Assimilating to their virtues, rather than the ones that have allowed our prosperity. You stand alone like snakes, betraying our ancestors. We descend from Mastodon, the Titan entrusted with love at the foundation of this world. But it is not enough to love yourself. Love requires the company of a community. Love shuns enmity and division.

"You forget yourselves. Your identities lost because we have been utterly dominated by some hostile host. Taken prisoner in a foreign land. You have no love in your hearts left, because you now see clearly that love leads to loss. We have all lost something to the Gorgonic fires. Some more than others. I lost everything I once cared about. But in this life, the only thing we can control is our reaction to unpredictable events. We have been defeated in totality, and now I see that our everlasting peace was only a mask. Now our true demons show, and some of you reveal that you are unfit to wield them.

"Our people are known for their nobility and honor. We stand on the shoulders of giants who formed an empire without needlessly killing other species. An empire grown from love and peace. Trust and integrity. And above all else, it was an empire forged by the courage to do right. You spit on the graves of our forefathers. Those who crafted our ways. Those who taught us to be a resilient people, slow to anger and quick to resolution. Mastodon is long dead, but he has always lived on in the way we compose ourselves. But today you have killed him a second time. Your actions are a monstrosity to everything we once stood for.

"I can see it on your cowardly faces that you do not wish to own up for what you've done. There are some who no longer wish to follow me, the ones who shift the blame of our fallen state on me. Well enough, I don't want to lead those who dodge accountability. I have no problem with you rejecting me as your ruler. What I do have a problem with is your decision to project your insecurities and fears on others. Bring a fight to them they did not wish to participate in. *Kill* those who stand opposed to killing," he growls, pointing at Snaggeltooth's corpse.

"You have been a privileged people your entire existence. None of you have known hardship until this war. And now your entitlement has been stripped and you grumble like children. Many years I have seen Bloodtusk conniving in my shadow for sovereignty. Those foolish enough to follow him, why do you do so? Because he promised you elevated status? Power?

"Do you not remember the last time he challenged me for my throne? You all played right into his trap. He used these circumstances as a stepping stone. A way of overriding my authority and stealing the mantle without facing me. You all, like your defeated leader, are cowards. That is why I must disown those who conspire against me. I, Tuskfather the Tuskless, leader of the Tuskers, hereby declare Bloodtuskers as a foreign nation. Purge you from our presence. Blot you from our bloodlines. You do the work of the enemy in sowing discord. You will be treated accordingly to your actions. Such individuals are not worthy of forgiveness, for they are Gorgons in Mastodon clothing.

"A weed's roots never go deep. Rip them up and soon all will forget they were there in the first place. So too will your rebellion be ripped up and forgotten, Bloodtusk," he says, making direct eye contact with his adversary. Funny, the rebel had been so adamantly opposed to Tuskfather moments ago but now forgets how to run his mouth. Tuskfather presents him the opportunity to speak up. "Have you nothing to say to this, unruly leader? Or did Snaggeltooth beat the ability to speak out of you before passing on?"

The mockery reaches its desired effect. There's nothing like a good shaming before a crowd of onlookers to put someone back in their place. For some, obedience can never be achieved. Bloodtusk's silence is somewhat similar to my own whenever I come into the presence of Deus Ex Machina, except I don't wear fear on my face as this traitor does. Silence is Bloodtusk's chosen response. Case closed, rebellion smothered, crisis averted. Tuskfather moves on, not giving his opponent the time of day, stripping him of his self-perceived importance. *Smart. Very smart.*

"I, like many of you, lost my identity as I watched everything I knew and loved be consumed by fire. I, unlike many of you, reached within for healing. After long days of silent reflection, I entered into a trance-like state. What I saw... is indescribable. Before, I felt inadequate to be your continued leader. My guilty conscience mocked me for being unable to protect my own family, let alone the entire nation.

"But I have now knelt at the feet of Mastodon himself, and he has reassured me of our current state. That is why I have returned to you all, to reclaim the mantle of leadership I abandoned. I apologize, but it was important to find healing amidst all the loss we have suffered. One cannot lead a nation who is not stable himself. Mastodon has renewed my heart and healed me of my weaknesses. And even more—he has given me a message. A message of hope to be shared with the Laxodontans." He lets the statement hang in the air for a moment, letting suspense build so much it has even me on the edge of my seat.

"He is sending us a savior to lead us out of this pit of destruction," he divulges, his voice sounding appropriately like that of a prophet delivering some holy decree. "Ouroboros has come again, this time in the flesh of a human. Mastodon said so himself. And where Mastodon leads, I must follow. I know these words are hard to believe, as they sound like the ravings of a lunatic," he says, shaking his head as if he doesn't believe the words himself.

But eyes start turning to me, the only human they know of. Tuskfather has been sequestered this entire time. He doesn't even know of my existence among his people. Could his vision really be true? What are the odds of such a specific prophecy in the form of a dream? No, such things are impossible. Someone must have interrupted his isolation and told him. *He is lying right now! Trying to convince his people that I am Ouroboros while they still think him ignorant of my arrival.*

He is an incredible actor. He downplays the severity of the oracle as if he is crazy to make himself seem even more ignorant of my existence. Smoothly transitioning to the topic and expecting people to laugh at him for suggesting such a prophecy could come true. But no one laughs. Their heads swivel in my direction, blinking in awe. Even the Bloodtuskers. They all heard the rumors. Whispers amongst the Gorgon guards about what I've done and who I claim to be. And now their leader applies validity to the statements in the form of superstition. Such ties are the foundation for unbreakable beliefs.

What game is he playing? What motive is he getting at?

Tuskfather follows the eyes until he sees me, faking his awestruck expression perfectly. His words cease immediately. I almost smile at the effort he puts into this charade. But to conjure a smile would be to defy the pain rising in my face from my neck, a current impossibility. I admire his acting skills inwardly and awkwardly await what comes next in this strategic schema.

Has this been the purpose of his entire speech? All those words about honor and noble pursuits merely hot air to lead to his main objective? Who is this man, to construct such meaningful rhetoric that not only shames rebels and rallies loyalists, but also acknowledges my presence and status as a god among them. I can already smell the development of some ulterior motive in his masterful approach, and I applaud him for it. This is a man with the potential to become a powerful ally.

"And so it was true," he murmurs to himself in disbelief, still loud enough for most to hear. "Ouroboros has come to us in the flesh, gravely injured, and we welcome him with bickering amongst ourselves instead of healing him. Quick! Smallear, fetch him and bring him to my hut. But be delicate! Meanwhile, I shall hope we have not disgraced a god so much that we are a cursed people for all eternity. I will plead on all our behalf that we have not blundered past redemption!"

A Tusker rises from the masses and rushes toward me. I can't help but notice his incredibly small ears. Or maybe it is his big head? Either way, the creature's head-to-ear ratio is disproportionate, making for quite the comical appearance. Where most Laxodontan ears flop as they run, his ears remain shriveled closely to his head like super-glued flaps of flesh.

Hence his name, Smallear. Their naming system is easy enough to understand. If they were to name me now I could be one of many things. Swollen-Neck.

Snakebait. Cockless the Hoo-man. Venom Vagabond. Lucifer the Leper. The possibilities are endless. I have enough deformities to provide a long list of nick-names.

Smallear scoops me up in his strong arms, jostling my body in doing so. Pain throbs through me in ways I never knew possible. My face wants desperately to flinch in agony but can't. To do so would only contribute more toward my misery. And so I suffer, squeezing my eyes shut as I'm carried like a bride at her wedding. Whisked away to Tuskfather's hideaway to see the meaning behind his act.

I listen as he follows behind us, footsteps thundering. He stops. Turns, then says, "And one last thing. If I reemerge from this tent and find a single Bloodtusker among my people, they shall be put to death. Consider yourselves warned. I have shown you mercy. This prisoner camp is large. Make use of the space and get lost."

CHAPTER FOUR

The tent flap brushes past us, allowing entrance to the womb within. Tusk-father is not far behind. Smallear lays me down on a soft cot made of flayed tree skin, threaded strong enough to support much more than my weight. The size of the cot is meant to support the body of a Laxodontan. I am merely a bed bug in its giant embrace.

Tuskfather thunders through the entrance and shrugs off the flaps. He disregards me completely as he grabs Smallear by the shoulder and brings him face to face. "Go to Mother Ivory, tell her we will need Zaskamander root salve, Gryfaun birch mushroom, crushed Manderknot and Frythen leaf bandages. Quick, these wounds will not heal themselves!"

Smallear sprints away without a moment to waste, leaving us to each other. The hut is small, the only furniture being the makeshift bed I lay upon. Tuskfather lowers himself to the ground, crossing his thick legs in an unnatural angle. It is humid in here, no system of ventilation built into the shaded hut. But at least it gets the sun off my skin. I must at least be grateful for that.

"Forgive me for my delay. Word did not reach me of your arrival until the moon's highest peak," Tuskfather breaks the silence. I am unable to form a response. My throat is so swollen it cannot form words. I do my best to point at my neck and shake my head to communicate my lack of response.

"Ah, I see. Snake got your tongue. That is alright, friend. Worry not, you are safe. Our mutual friend Ganesh caught me up on all that happened. Told me all you've been through. It was quite the story."

To hear the Gryfaun's name raises excitement within me. He is the last ally I expected to benefit from in this Deus forsaken country. I left him to his people and his loyalty still managed to prevail. Maybe he is every bit the friend he said he was. Maybe I am not so alone after all.

"I apologize for how you were greeted by my people. These are dark days we live in. Everything we once stood for has been tested, and we have not responded well to our trials. Even I have failed miserably. So I must ask... Is it true? Are you who you claim to be? Or do the rumors deceive me?"

It is a yes or no question, but even nodding my head is a difficult task met with the resistance of built-up pus in my neck. He sighs exuberantly. "Are you him? Ouroboros? The Serpent King, father of the Ten Titans, the prophesied savior of the Dæmonic tribes?"

I nod again, hoping he does not continue asking questions which require me to move my head to respond. Instead he shifts his weight, repositioning himself onto his knees where he bows down before me. Dramatic, but customary for someone brought up in such a pious culture.

He takes my appearance for surface value, asking no more questions to evaluate if I am who I say I am. Maybe he is not as intelligent as I believed him to be. Either way, I remain voiceless. An awful curse for one who needs to raise an army quickly. I am in need of a middle man, one who can raise troops for me. One who can speak on my behalf. One who is unquestionably loyal. And this may be the man for the job.

Tuskfather raises himself back up to face me, reverence in his eyes. "I am sorry for my current state. I am a shadow of the man I once was. Have lost a lot in the past few days. But it seems you have lost just as much. Bitten by the Vermillion Viper, Ganesh tells me. I've heard it said none have ever survived such a bite. Yet here you are, still alive. Injured, but quickly recovering.

"Your arrival has lifted my downcast soul. For before I was finished. No more than scraps of my former self. I lost everything to the Gorgons. They bound my arms and legs. Sawed off my tusks," he says, tears forming under his exhausted eyelids. I sense he hasn't spoken these memories aloud since they occurred. This is his first time audibly venting them. The root of his inner turmoil.

"Raped and killed my daughter and wife," he spits, biting his lip to hold back the screaming sob within. His body shakes with fury and misery. These words break him down. Strip him of his strength. He crumples before me into his true form. He lowers his forehead to the ground again, this time not out of reverence, but solely so his tears cannot be seen. They fall to the clay floor with tremendous weight.

He stays there several seconds. A moment of silence for their memory. Memory of the ones he held closest in life. Now gone on to the afterlife, leaving him behind to suffer alone. When he rises to speak again, he does so with pain in his eyes, a small puddle of mud on the ground from his shed tears.

"I watched my people be slaughtered by the Gorgonic Jihad. I wanted nothing more than to die on that battlefield with my people," he sobs. *There are worse things than death in life, and watching those closest to you die is one of them.*

"I exiled myself because there is no coming back from such a failure. No redemption for the weak. I tried killing myself, though I'm ashamed to say it now. Exiled myself so no one could see. Skinned a tree's flesh and threaded it into a rope. Tied it into a noose. Thought it was thick enough... but it snapped when I tried hanging from my neck. Still got the bruise, see?"

He lifts his head up and reveals the scarlet bruise previously hidden beneath the rolled fat of his neck. "Spent the rest of the time sulking in shame. Built this tent to isolate myself even more. Thought if I couldn't hang myself, I might as well try starving myself. A loser's mindset. A man with no hope. Nothing to live for. Utterly defeated.

"But then Ganesh came last night, descended from the trees, he did. Told me everything. Where he found you, how he nursed you, how you vowed to save our people. Said you even fell from the sky, claimin' to be Ouroboros! It was like a sign from Mastodon himself! And you know what? Just like that, my despair was gone! You have given me new meaning to rise again, Ouroboros.

"But how was I to reappear to my people after failing so miserably? It simply would not do to come crawling back in this condition like some feeble beggar. Especially not with oppression rising against me, spreading rumors and propaganda that I am too depraved to follow, a washed up has-been of my former self. I needed to come back with flare, a grand entrance to reestablish my authority. Such a plan needed a scapegoat," he says, letting me connect the dots.

He planned the entire rebellion remotely. But how?

"I still had those who remained loyal. My inner circle, covert agents I could rely on. Smallear is among my best. He is, after all, my brother. Born on the same day from the same womb, we were. People used to say that what he lacked in ear I made up for in tusk. Said I stole all the nutrients in the womb from him. But he loves me all the same.

"I knew I could trust him for the task. I sought him out in secret, concealed by the veil of night. Together, we put in action the plan to create an insurgency. The players were already there, all we had to do was push in the right spots. Bloodtusk has been eyeing my seat of power for years, the time was ripe for him to challenge me a second time. I had Smallear sow seeds of doubt in his mind, reassuring Bloodtusk that I am too weak to lead. He encouraged him, told him the time to take charge is now.

"It was like convincing a child to steal candied gumroot, took no effort at all. But you must forgive me Ouroboros, I had no idea people would die. Civil war was not what I expected. I only meant to create a minor scuffle so I could swoop in and save the day. I feel terrible over my actions. All I did was cause more pain and suffering by returning. Snaggeltooth was one of the finest..." His voice chokes up again. He pushes the emotions back down in his throat.

"You know, when everything happened, when I watched my own daughter burn alive—I died inside. Thought there was no coming back to the land of the living. Cursed Mastodon for forsaking us. We Laxodontans didn't ask for this war," his mouth sputters, his body teetering on the verge of an emotional breakdown.

War is rarely asked for, yet it comes nonetheless.

"War has ravaged us. Now we are a decrepit, forlorn people. But that all changes with your appearance. You can help me seek vengeance. We did not start this war, but I swear upon the grave of my wife we will be the ones to finish it." His eyes show his every intention. Eyes filled with malice.

This is not going how I thought it would. I was deceived by his speech of peace and love. I will not be able to talk him out of seeking revenge. Damn lizards raped and killed his wife and daughter. He will not stop until every living being with a forked tongue has been killed, and rightfully so. But I can't allow that. I will need the Gorgon masses if I'm to have any chance of defying Cataclysm.

"And so I, Tuskfather the Tuskless, instilled leader of the Laxodontans, come to you, Lord Ouroboros, Serpent King, to declare my Godkiller Chronicle!" The words hang in the air with an echo of unfairness. The pain in my neck screams to hear those words uttered again so soon. I instantly fill with despair and agony to hear his true intentions.

The dreaded Godkiller Chronicle, the holy trial mandated of Ouroboros upon his second coming. Or at least that's what religious scripture stipulates. Dæmonic scripture prophesies Ouroboros will come again, but it cautions the Dæmonia to be weary of false prophets. Hence the Godkiller Chronicle, a sacred declaration that filters out the false gods.

It designates that the true second coming of Ouroboros will come to the recognized leader of each Dæmonic tribe and pass their Godkiller Chronicle—a designated task they believe so impossible that only a god could do it. A way to siphon out the liars. Kill the false gods. The Godkiller Chronicle is every bit as important to the Dæmonic religion as Ouroboros himself. It is unavoidable, and if I am to conceivably pass myself off as Ouroboros incarnate, I will need to pass all ten Godkiller Chronicles—one for each genetically engineered Dæmonic species.

I have survived the Gorgons' challenge, barely clinging on to life. Do I have it in me to face another already?

"I am sorry for enacting my right to the chronicle so soon after the Gorgons', but you must understand that Vipress is on the verge of death. The Gorgon healers will send for you soon to revitalize her. She will yield to you. The entire race will concede to your command. You will be their new leader. Ouroboros, Serpent King who devours himself so the Abyss cannot prevail, I see you suffer. But my Godkiller Chronicle does not call for more suffering. No, my challenge to you so you may prove your divinity is an ethical trial. To prove you are truly Ouroboros, you must make an ethical decision only a God can make.

"I present to you a moral conundrum. Soon the Gorgons will come for you, begging you to save their Vipress. My Godkiller Chronicle is that you let her die. Assume leadership of the Gorgonic race. Throw a feast for their soldiers, getting them nice and drunk. Then, when their fires die out tonight and they fall into a drunken stupor, open the gates which hold us prisoner. We will take from them what they stole from us. My people will have their revenge.

"This is my request to you, Lord Ouroboros. Fulfill it, or you will never be uplifted by the Laxodontans as a true God."

His eyes glare into my soul with hellbent ferocity. A man with nothing to lose, asking me to level the playing field. But I need the Gorgons. The Laxodontans may be strong and cunning, but their numbers are few. An alliance with the Gorgons would supply enough troops to have a fighting chance against the Angel of Life.

I care little for the Godkiller Chronicles if they are going to lead me down a path that destroys any chance I have of erecting an army. Better to be considered a false god with a large army than a real god with nothing to show for it.

I empathize with Tuskfather's pain, but I have bigger things at risk than helping him satisfy his pissant revenge. If I let him kill the Gorgons then we will all be slaughtered by forces of Hyperion.

Decisions decisions.

He is right. It would take the moral compass of a righteous god to make the right choice. To choose honor and nobility over strength, power, and security. Honor and nobility, virtues that restrict a god's options greatly. Virtues that require time and patience.

Unfortunately for Tuskfather, I possess neither time nor patience currently. Cataclysm comes closer with each passing day. Knowing that, my decision is easy. I know what I must do.

Tuskfather will understand. Not at first, but when demons descend from the skies with death in their programming—then he will thank me.

"And one more thing," he butts in. The Godkiller Chronicle is not supposed to come with side quests, but I don't have the ability to speak out against his addition. "The Gorgon who defiled and killed my girls... He is a man by the name of Gengar. Tonight, when you come to release us from this internment camp, bring him to me. I will be the one to kill him," he announces. "Do you agree to my conditions?" he asks, giving me no time to process the elaborately spontaneous plan.

My face does not betray my thoughts of treachery, serving Deus Ex Machina has taught me how to disagree inwardly but remain composed externally. I nod compliantly, knowing I must defy his Godkiller Chronicle. Tonight will not go as he plans. I need him to think he holds me in his palm if I'm to retain his current loyalty.

It saddens me to plot against such a noble man. He only wants to do what is right. But the right thing is oftentimes too costly, so I must play him like the fool he is.

"Good, then we have a deal," he mumbles, wiping the last tears from his eyes, not knowing I will cause him many more.

As if on cue, the tent flap erupts with activity. Smallear barges into the hut's domain with a hurried, out of breath fatigue. He drops the medical supplies on the ground and bends over to catch his breath.

"Brother," he gasps. "Gorgons... coming... for him."

Tuskfather nods, rising to his feet. "Very well, it was only a matter of time. Stall their approach, I will dress Ouroboros's wounds in the meantime. Good work brother, I am indebted for your service."

"Meager role I play if our plan successful. Did hoo-man agree?" he asks, his English not nearly as developed as Tuskfather's.

"Yes brother, tonight we shall have our revenge," Tuskfather replies, each brother smiling for the first time in weeks. It is painful to know these smiles won't last long. I let them relish the moment. Men must be allowed to have hope, after all.

I need to save Vipress. Because Vicien Greaves was right about one thing—if I'm going to be a god, I'm going to need a capable devil.

CHAPTER FIVE

I feel better already. Well, that's a bit of an overstatement. The vile venom still violates my veins. My red blood cells go to war with it, burning with internal agony. But at least I have regained my motor skills. Enough to walk, anyway.

And the abscess on my throat, garnished with a thick layer of Zaskamander root salve and wrapped in Frythen leaf bandages, has ceased its throbbing. It is still sizable, and I still lack the ability to speak aloud, but any progress is good progress. Tuskfather got me right, which makes it even harder to go against his will.

It was Artimedes who retrieved me, the same gator-faced Gorgon who brought me before Vipress the first time. From the moment I left Tuskfather's tent and reunited with the scaled scoundrel in open field, I could see the surprise in his eyes. After all, I am now standing and able to walk, and Vipress is most likely on death's door. I see in his reaction that he did not expect me to be faring so well.

My wrists are bound, connected to a leash the lizard-man controls. I follow him through the Gorgon camps, watching as wide-eyed spectators emerge from their pitched tents and burrowed nooks to see me. Some of them I faintly recognize from my trial. But I must admit that they blend in significantly well. Other than deviations in their scales' colored patterns, it is hard to tell this race apart.

Some stand on two feet while others have the bottom half of a serpent. Some crawl on four legs, others crawl on their bellies. Some have spiked backs, others have no scales at all, but rather coarse, amphibian-like skin—slimy, bumpy, unpleasant to look at. All have piss-yellow, phosphorescent, slitted eyes. They follow me with disbelief, knowing I should be dead by now.

I look some of them in their eyes, making them avert their stares. My glare is too hard to parry. Offers a fight that can't be won. But it is necessary to win such battles early on. These are the men and women that will soon enter into my service. I must analyze their profiles now, discern which candidates possess the vigor necessary for war.

They are a cruel, cold race. Though their eyes move away from mine uncomfortably, these are a battle-hardened people. Each of them strong in their own way. The majority of them are still clothed in armor from battle days ago. Always ready. Prepared for any coming threat. They have what it takes to dance with death, undaunted.

My feet splosh through the mud of the wetlands, reeds of grass crumpled underfoot by the heavy traffic of their populace. Contained fires surround me. It is still only morning, but the fires' sweltering heat makes it feel midday. Such is necessary for cold-blooded creatures once the sun goes down.

The Queen's pitched homestead is apparent from a quarter mile away. We come to the embankment of the murky lake, staring off into the distance at the floating castle erected on buoys. We will have to swim to get there, which is not a problem for Artimedes, but is quite the inconvenience for me. Even if my hands weren't tied, my body is not in the right condition for swimming.

I should have suspected those of royal pedigree live in such suitable, reptilian conditions. Living upon a lake allows for easy access to fresh game for hunting, or perhaps basking under the sun as BDEM Era reptiles did. For those with webbed feet and serpent tails, this is an ideal estate.

My neck throbs the longer I stare at it, dreading the thought of having to be pulled through these murky waters.

Artimedes dives into the water and submerges completely, my leash still in hand. I watch as the slack in the rope uncoils on the ground, tightening with each remorseful second. It is just as the rope pulls taut that I wonder to myself how many cronons infest these waters. My body yanks behind my arms as I fall face first into the muddy lagoon.

Water swallows me and uncomfortably fills my every crack and crevice. It is warm like gelatinous sewage baking in the midafternoon sun. The only comfort I find is in tightly squeezing my eyes shut, silently hoping Artimedes is a fast swimmer. It would be a shame if I were to defeat the poison in my veins only to die of drowning.

All sorts of slimy algae and godforsaken gobbledygook run over my skin. Deus only knows what lives in these waters. Flesh eating bacteria, blood sucking parasites, cartilage cretins, river monsters. The possibilities end where my imagination runs dry. But it is hard to stop imagining the lurking predators with closed eyes.

The water gets breathtakingly cold the deeper we submerge, pressure in my head increasing as we dive further. My eardrums feel as if they are about to burst. Goosebumps combat the chilling depths. Yet the water feels cleaner down here, as if the piss and shit from above has not managed to infect this jurisdiction with its filth.

Our descent levels off slightly before we begin climbing back to the surface, my body's thermoregulation thrown off by the rapid freeze and fever. My throat is attacked by two enemies now. The venom is allied with the deprivation of oxygen. The respirocytes are too outnumbered to be of any advantage. If they continue to actively fight the effects of the venom, I will suffocate. If they try to reoxygenate my blood, the venom will spread further. All while their battery life continues to run dry.

The aching in my lungs only makes the overall pain in my neck worse. I am cornered by a slew of unseen enemies that will silently devour me. I can picture it now, my dead, waterlogged corpse being dragged from the depths. Artimedes explaining, "He wasss alive and well when we entered the watersss. I sssuppossse he wasssn't Ouroborosss after all!" A retinue of reptilian cackles sounding at the sight of me. A pity that would be.

The rope gets tighter around my wrists, lifting me from my daydream at the same time I'm lifted from the cold waters. I hit the wooden ground, coughing, sucking all the air I possibly can. My naked body shivering, refreshed by the feeling of cool air. Deep inhalations soothe my frail figure. The smell of fire and herbs in the air is cleansing.

It is the smell of mildew and death masked by spices and incense. The smell of many failed attempts to revitalize Vipress on the behalf of many healers. My bandages are now ruined. The salve which brought a cooling sensation to my neck and stitched abdomen washed away, replaced by mud and filthy pond water. The Gorgons truly know how to piss me off.

"What do you mean she died? You sssaid she had a few hoursss left when I departed for Ouroborosss!" Artimedes yells, thrusting his fist against a nearby brazier. Coals fly into the air, smoke scattering into the atmosphere like thrown chalk, making it hard to see and breathe. Especially for me, since I was struggling to see and breathe long before the smoke. My lungs are filled with sewage water and smoggy smoke.

I cough ferociously, my body trying to exorcise my lungs of the unwelcome invaders. This is very painful for someone who has recently been bitten on the neck by a Vermillion Viper.

"I wasss merely passsssing along the healer'sss wordsss, my liege. But there were... complicationsss in your absssenccce." Another voice, this one unfamiliar to me. I roll over to my back, propping myself up against the wall to see who inhabits these quarters.

This makeshift abode must be only temporary. I can see the way it was hastily thrown together with shameful expediency. It is scraps of driftwood and bamboo tied together by frayed twine. Buoyant enough to float but lacking in aesthetic appeal. The castle of a queen who considers herself royal without knowing how to live royally.

I look around and see that I am only accompanied by two Gorgons, one of which is Artimedes. The other, the bearer of bad news, is drastically different from my summoner. Where Artimedes resembles the appearance of an alligator, forest green scales with a round, blunted snout, the other Gorgon is crocodilian.

His skin a shade of desert camo, his snout long and sharp with teeth resembling a jigsaw blade. A sinister, nictating membrane flicking over his eyes.

Both stand on two legs, tails swaying on the ground behind them, but their sizes are noticeably different. Artimedes has the frame of a meaty hustler. A thug who will beat the living shit out of you if you disobey his orders, with plenty of muscle to back up his demands. His companion, a thin and wiry assassin who greets you with a smile and kills you when your back is turned.

"Who isss the healer resssponsssible for thisss?" Artimedes snaps. "I will have their head on a ssspike!"

"Calm yourssself, Artimedesss. Your emotionsss betray you. You know you were not sssupposssed to be intimately involved with the Queen. Your midnight conjugal visssitsss are impairing your sssight. If othersss were to know of your affair it will be *your* head on a ssspike," the crocodile responds.

"Who told you we—"

"No one. I had my sssusssspicccionsss alright, but I never truly knew until jussst now. Your temper tantrum is all-telling."

"I ssswear, Gengar, if you tell anyone—"

"Relax, Artimedesss. Your sssecret isss sssafe with me. But you mussst find composssure, or elssse my sssecrecccy will mean little. I will leave you alone with her body ssso you can sssay your lasssst goodbyesss in peaccce." *So this is Gengar*, I think to myself, locking eyes with the crocodilian hybrid as he walks to a hollow cove in the ground. His name rings out in my mind instantly, remembering Tuskfather's second request.

The reptilian humanoid smiles, flashing his sinister teeth, as if he is quite content for his Queen to be dead. He winks with a single eye and my skin crawls. It is an unsettling wink. A protective membrane slides over his eye and he pencil dives into the water below.

I watch as Artimedes crosses the room to a waterbed where the limp body lies. The cot is creative and robust, a sawed hole in the floor with a thick, woven sheet of neoprene-like leaves similar to rubbery lily pads. The stitched together leaves float on the water beneath this naturally swaying citadel, held in one place by their anchored sides.

On the bed lies Vipress. Or at least, what remains of her lifeless body. Artimedes approaches his lover, enraged by his grief. He mounts her dead body, no sounds coming from his dismayed figure. His tongue flicks over her, licking her salty skin, tasting the death upon her.

I look around. In the opposite corner of the room there is a pile of trinkets vaguely organized well enough to differentiate each item. I see two immense tusks mounted upon the wall, sawed clean through at their base. *Could those be?* She keeps Tuskfather's tusks hung like well-earned trophies.

Among the collected rubbish is something else strikingly familiar. My ArchArmor. It stands silently, abandoned in the corner of the room with a depressing slump in its shoulders. I realize suddenly what these objects are. They are the prized trophies of Vipress's many conquerings.

I analyze each item one by one. A hanging necklace strung with narrow fangs—Phelician fangs. A bow with as many strings as a harp. A Dirian skull, its wolfish eye sockets gazing at me with sadness.

I rise to my feet, shuffling softly toward the treasure trove. The spoils of war, gathered and heaped together like toys left out by a spoiled child. The Gorgons have been busy, and these items represent the bloodshed of many. The vain killings of an ignorant mind.

My ArchArmor stares at me from the shadows of the room, the reflection of fire dancing across its mildewy exterior. It is not the ArchArmor it once was, now covered in algae and various fungi. The serpent-shaped ArchHelm is caked with mud and gristly growing organisms. Bacteria blossoms atop its visor, reminding me of a petri dish. I wipe them away, staring into the gold tinted lens at my reflection. Taking in my appearance for the first time since... I can't even remember how long it's been.

My looks surprise me. I'm reminded of a neolithic caveman, or perhaps a pirate after many months at sea. When I possessed MachineMind, human hygiene was never a concern. My suit was self-sufficient in keeping the earth's dust off of me, instantly vaporizing contamination from my presence. Now, my skin is covered with the gunk and grime associated with survival. My hair, once maintained and pampered by processes I didn't concern myself with, is knotted and unruly. Stubble grows along my cheeks and jawline, causing me to feel its itchiness for the first time.

I look at the suit's chest, to the symbol of Ouroboros's maw devouring his tail in an eternal manner. Beneath, written in dried blood is the derogatory word: *Sssarken*. Translation: False god. There will always be those who doubt, myself among them. But there must be a reason why Deus Ex Machina changed my symbol from Prometheus's Torch to Ouroboros all those years ago, and this must be that reason. He molded the entire Dæmonic religion around it. Waiting for the day I would profit from the sowing he did so long ago. All so his entertainment can be satisfied.

We are nothing but sinners in the hands of a bored god.

"Ouroborosss," Artimedes calls, grief plaguing his voice. "There mussst be sssomething you can do! You are a god! You mussst sssave her!" he pleads, begging a deity to save an unworthy mortal. But I can hear the doubt in his voice. He doesn't actually believe I am a god.

Yet here I stand, nearly healed from the same venom that killed his mistress. Surely that elevates my status in his mind. Gives him the slightest hope that I can save his lover from the irreversible grip of death. Perhaps call her back from the afterlife.

"Leave usss," I command, the first words I've spoken since being bitten. Speaking the words feels like I'm breathing fire from a throat made of kindling. He looks at me as if I've spoken another language, unsure why he must leave. "If you want me to sssave your Queen, I sssuggessst you leave thisss placcce," I speak in his language, vomiting what feels like volcanic ash with every word uttered.

His dumbfounded expression questions whether or not I'm joking. My demeanor communicates to him I'm not. He stares at me, then stares at her. His eyes flicker back to me while his clawed fingers rest upon her cold, lifeless body.

Staring at my standing, lively figure. The proof of my divinity, if anything at all, is in the fact that I am still breathing with relative ease.

"You better not be playing any tricksss," he warns, standing from her bed and walking toward the nearest swimming hole. "Or elssse I will show the Gorgon people that even godsss can be killed." His tongue flicks viciously, then returns to his mouth. Membranes slide over his eyes like a film of mucus. He dives into the murky depths beneath us without another word, leaving me no proof of his existence besides the rising bubbles from below.

I turn to Vipress.

She is dead alright. But I know what death looks like, and this death is fresh. Under a relative half hour. Her still-open eyes are now devoid of their neon yellow glare, reduced to faint irises filled with pale mucus. I must act fast if I'm going to save her.

Without hesitation, I scramble to my ArchArmor. *Lilith, can you access the mainframe?*

"I'm already in," she replies, knowing already what I plan to do.

Drop the gauntlet.

The ArchGauntlet drops from the left arm and thuds to the floor with a surprising boom. I shove my hand in, its inner layer perfectly molded for my body. Even without my BioSuit it is shockingly comfortable.

I lug it up, forgetting how heavy a single limb of my ArchArmor can be, despite the relative lightness of Elysium in comparison to other metals. I walk back to Vipress and kneel down. *Charge the ArchGauntlet,* I command.

"Charging," Lilith echoes. I lift the metallic glove with a slight strain, supporting it with my other arm, watching as the palm begins to glow with electric current. Enough to jump start her heart. *Is the antivenom ready?*

"Drawing blood now," Lilith replies, followed by the feeling of a needle entering my fingertip from the ArchGauntlet. The fleshy inside of the finger port compresses, squeezing several droplets of blood. "Separating plasma... Separating antibodies... Creating antivenom... Complete," she whispers. "ArchGauntlet charged, soldier."

Very well, I think to myself, watching the surface of my hand glow blue like the muzzle of a Thunderbolt preparing to fire, realizing that this is the same technology as the long-forgotten gun. Merged with our ArchArmor and erased from our memory so we could fall prey to the idea that only cowards use guns. Our narrative written and erased and written and erased again. Anything that didn't match the desired story was polished over and stripped from us, removed from history as if it was some legend or fable.

I thrust my palm into her chest, pressing into the back of my ArchGauntlet with my other hand to fight the recoil. The concentrated bolt of electricity rocks her body, causing her spine to curl. It calls her from the land of the dead like a flash of light in a world of darkness.

She gasps. Animation returns to her figure like a cadaver struck by lightning. She snaps awake from her deep sleep. The snakes in her hair stand on end, like spiked spears with fangs in place of spearheads. The yellow of her eyes brighten.

She throws herself from the bed, instantly assuming a warrior's stance, a reflex that can only be trained by experience and lack of trust. Her breathing is ragged, her body is frail, her tail lashes irrationally in every direction like a recently decapitated snake. She pants, surveying her surroundings and sees that it is only me here. I see it in her eyes. She searches for memory of what happened. She can remember. Remember her weak pulse. Staring into a world that slowly fades from view. Losing all sensation. Slipping away until she was just a mind without a body. A soul without an anchor. And then...

She looks at me, remembering that she is supposed to be dead. Looks at me entirely. Sees I'm standing, alive, thriving in comparison to where she was only moments ago. The location of my viper bite is barely swollen now. She can see I'm far from dying. She looks at my glowing, electric hand, then to the gloveless ArchArmor. She is smart enough to put two and two together.

I see recognition melt her defensive face into one of subservience. In an instant of reawakening, she looks at me with the eyes of someone staring into the face of a god. She mutters something indistinctly, then immediately bows before me, moaning a righteous incantation. *Lilith, has the antivenom been passed along?*

"Its particles were dispersed through the electric current. It will take time for her body to heal, but it will heal."

Good. And the ampere?

"High enough to fry anything implanted in her brain that makes her a slave to Deus Ex Machina."

Even better. So she is completely free?

"This is the true Vipress, completely freed from Deus Ex Machina's control over her life. Be careful, she will resort back to who she once was. Her file reports her to be a wildcard," Lilith informs.

Such allies can be useful if bridled correctly.

"You have freed her only to assert your own authority over her? It is not wise to bridle a beaten mustang. They are not so trusting, nor are they trustworthy. We have no idea what she is capable of without Deus Ex Machina controlling her mind. I would not advise you delegate any significant part of your plan to her responsibility."

That's what makes you and me different. Robots make decisions off calculations. Humans take risks.

"Don't you dare call me that," she snaps.

Call you what? A robot? Call you what you really are?

"I am not a robot," she replies, her voice seething with anger. I have pressed a button of hers that triggers fury. That is, if an artificial intelligence such as herself can even truly feel anger in the first place.

We must agree to disagree, for now.

"You really don't know who I am, do you? Are you that clueless?"

I don't have time to answer the question, knowing it will only lead to a million more. "I am yoursss to ssserve, Ouroborosss," Vipress mutters, her head buried in the ground. "From death you have raisssed me. My sssecond life isss yoursss to command."

This version of her is different. Not nearly as spiteful. No chip on her shoulder anymore, no undetectable robot pulling the marionette strings to her actions. The Queen I met before would have never bowed at my feet. Would have never admitted I was divine. She would have remained resilient, hard-pressed to prove me wrong until death do we part. Now she is softer. Wilder too. Yet loyal and grateful. A formula for chaos brews within her. But if I can harness it, wield it for my purposes, that will lead to a controlled chaos few can be so lucky to ever possess and live to tell of.

She is wildfire willingly wilting before me. I cannot afford to misstep. Such allies cannot be regained once lost. "Then rissse," I command. "You are no longer your own. You have been reborn by my ssspirit. The ssspirit of Ouroborosss resssides within you. Ssstrengthensss you. Fortifysss you. Givesss you life."

She rises, something different about the way she carries herself. She no longer looks down on me as if I'm scum. Not at all. She now looks at me as if she owes me her life, a benevolent god who saw fit to bestow upon her a second chance. The same eyes that once judged me with scorn are now timid. Her hair is calm, its snakes averting their stares as if they are no longer worthy to be in my presence. She doesn't try to seduce me as some defensive coping mechanism. She is completely vulnerable before me. This is Vipress, not the Gorgon Queen I met before.

"It isss no longer I who livesss, but Ouroborosss who livesss within me. The life I now live in the flesh, I live by faith in Ouroborosss, the Ssserpent King who sssuffersss ssso the Abysssss may not win. I too will fight againssst the Abysssss. I too will sssacrificcce myssself, ssso othersss may live," she whispers powerfully. Her words carry on the air with vibrating intensity, the lisps raising goosebumps on my forearms.

Her resurrection leaves her changed. Metamorphosed from what she once was. It is strange the effects religion can have on someone. Give them a somewhat believable narrative and they will dedicate their existence to following it. Go to their death for it. Like a robot programmed to not stop at all costs until they reach some desired end. I'm briefly frightened to see how quickly she assimilates to following me, as if she completely forgot she was a Queen hours ago. This is not the sort of behavior I would have expected from her previously, but death can change a person.

The light of nearby fires clash against the reflection of electricity on her skin. She itches for orders to action. She is a woman who has clawed her way to the top only to realize she cannot usurp god's plan. And so she submits herself willingly into my care.

"We mussst sssecure the allegianccce between the Laxodontansss and Gorgon-sss. The Abysssss isss coming, and when it doesss, we mussst be waiting for it, united asss the Ten Titansss were. Cataclysssm comesss for usss. The Abysssss will sssend itsss bessst sssoldiersss to march againsssst us, and they will not come heralding mercccy," I announce. The key is to let her in on the coming events but to transcribe it to terminology she understands. Angel of Life, ArchAngels, Abyss, no matter how you phrase it, the meaning is the same. All synonymous. They will come for us, and when they do, they will be here to eradicate anything with a heartbeat.

"What would you have me do, Lord Ouroborosss?"

This may work out better than I previously planned, I think to myself.

"Tuskfather named your death asss hisss Godkiller Chronicle. Asss he as-ssked, I obeyed. You have died, asss hisss wordsss ssspecccified. He sssaid nothing ressstricting me from raisssing you from the dead. I have sssatisssfied the firssst requessst of hisss. The sssecond you mussst help me with. He wantsss vengeanccce for hisss people, which I cannot deny him. The Gorgonsss have wronged him. Raped and killed hisss wife and daughter. He asssksss that I give him the chanccce to ssslaughter your entire racccce. Get them drunk tonight and loossse the impris-ssoned Laxodontasss on them."

She shakes her head, disgusted in my words. She pleads, "Lord, you mussstn't! There are good Gorgonsss among usss! They mussstn't—"

"Sssilence," I bark, my throat instantly regretting the extra exertion. Her first rebuttal. *So she isn't a mindless automaton after all. She knows how to take a stand for what she believes in, even in the presence of a god. This will prove to either be good or bad.* Only time will tell. "I do not plan to grant him thisss wish. Godkiller Chroniclesss are sssingle wishesss. I am not in the wrong to withhold from him hisss sssecond requessst. But I need hisss complianccce, and sssuch thingsss mussst be earned. That isss why I need your help." *Every god needs his devil, and you will be mine.*

"Your wish isss my command," she bows before me. This looks to be the beginning of a very useful relationship.

"Good. Time isss of the essssenccce, ssso I will cut ssstraight to the point," I begin, smiling at the prospect of my plan. A way to ally the Gorgons and Laxodontans in one fell swoop while also nipping any chance for future rebellion in the bud. Two tremendous fighting forces under my control. What could go wrong?

CHAPTER SIX

"*Gorgonsss*, a word that ssstrikesss fear into the heartsss of thossse who were not born into such a fearsssome raccce. I thank you for coming to feassst with me tonight. I, your new leader, Ouroborosss," I announce before the crowd. Before me stretches the vast, unnumbered ranks of the Gorgon populace. Here to see their new leader, the self-proclaimed incarnation of the Serpent King who created the material universe. A stretch to some, glorious reality for others.

"Your old Queen isss gone. A falssse prophetesssss, she wasss. My plansss for you from the heavensss were not for you to conquer your fellow Dæmonia. I did not divide mysssself into ten beingsss for thossse ten to go to war with one another. Vipresss led you assstray, and it fallsss on me, your creator, to ssstraighten your path. Ssstill, the Abysssss hasss long watched my defiant creation. Sssought to eliminate all who hold the light of life. Wantsss to absssorb usss into eternal darknesssss. Your warsss have left you Gorgonsss with little friendsss. Without alliesss, we cannot defeat the Abysssss.

"That isss why tomorrow we will ssset for a new campaign. We will march to ressstore all that we have dessstroyed in our sssearch for Tyrannosssaur," I announce, my eyes flicking rapidly across the crowd to see who stares at me with silent defiance. I am surprised to see that most look upon me with expressions of agreement. Maybe I judged this race too soon. Maybe it was only a select few who wanted this crusade to go on.

I take note that Gengar makes little effort to conceal his inner contempt for me. I am a stumbling block in his path to power. He was, after all, next in line to take rule after Vipress, deemed so by Vipress's own words in some past life. But Vipress is dead. Or at least these people think she is. And even worse for Gengar, these people know the rules of the Godkiller Chronicle. I passed the trial, therefore I am the new sovereign of this race. What I say goes, and Gengar likes not what I have to say. He is a fighter, and fighters don't deal well with apologies. Getting him to walk into my trap may be easier than I planned.

"The time for war hasss come to an end, for now. The Abysssss will come sssoon enough, for thossse of you who want to fight. Sssave your energiesss for then. And ssso we shall rein in thisss new era of peaccce with a feassst! Tonight! I urge all huntersss to depart from here and gather for usss a ssselection of meat sssuitable for a god! Women, children, go into the fieldsss and harvessst what edible greenery you can. We shall create thisss meal asss a sssingle collective, a sssymbol of our new ssstyle of living. United, we are ssstrong.

"A nation who conquersss the world isss left with nothing but itsss intolerable pride. Sssuch will not be our outcome asss Gorgonsss. We can fix our wrongdoingsss. We can rebuild what we have torn down. We can rekindle the relationshipsss of other nationsss. We can coexissst with the Laxodontansss, the Diriansss, the Phelicccciansss, the Aegeansss and Centaursss, the Araneae and Sssirensss. With hopesss that one day, we may even live peacccefully alongsssside humansss.

I am layering it on as thick as I can to separate the wheat from the weeds in this crowd. There are those who will be adamantly opposed to me and my plan for peace, and there are those who will follow me to the ends of the earth. I need an obvious way to differentiate between the two. My plan relies on it.

I have made my plans to them apparent, but now I must truly set apart those who hate me. "Now, before you go out into the fieldsss to prepare for our feassst, I command all who accccept my new leadership to bow before me!" I yell the words loud enough for all to hear and instantly regret doing so. My throat is far from a state of perfection.

But it must be done. I, along with my faithful ally in the crowd, overlook to see who it is that hesitates in their kneeling. The majority of the population humbly admits themselves without a second thought. Those who delay, delay with eyes that glower toward me. And for good reason. I stifle all they have worked toward. All their killing in vain. Power hungry beasts forced to bend their knees to peace. They like it not. I take note of all those who lower themselves reluctantly to their knees. Among them is Gengar and Artimedes.

They will be the first to secede, I'm sure of it. Artimedes, because he thinks Vipress is dead and believes I am the reason for it. Gengar, because he is drawn to power like a serpent toward heat. They will find all those who stand opposed to me and make one last desperate attempt to end my reign before it begins. If they are smart, which they are, they will strike tonight, as I pretend to get myself drunk and present myself as vulnerable. If they are smart (and intelligence has its limits) they will know it is a trap. But they won't be smart enough to see through my ploy, not with me so perceptibly vulnerable. They are impulsive beasts. They will strive to stab me in the back without seeing the knife that approaches their own backside.

"Good," my voice carries on the stale winds that blow the wetland bristles. "Then go, my children. We shall reconvene tonight, at sssundown. The tidesss of war retreat, replaccced by the gloriousss decree of peaccce! Together, we will learn to wage war againssst the darknessssss! The darknessssss that dwellsss inside us all!"

My speech is met with thunderous applause. These are a people who tire of fighting. Who never really wanted to war in the first place, but did so because of necessity. Few people actually cherish having to constantly kill in order to prove their dominance. Only psychopaths can sustain such a lifestyle. And my speech was enough to filter such anomalies from the crowd. They will be dealt with soon enough.

The crowd jeers and roars with approval at my vision for their future. But their cheers fall on deaf ears. It is all an act which I employ. There is much more warring I have planned for these people. Best to keep that hidden until it becomes pertinent information. Save them the stress and anxiety of worrying. The Angel of Life will soon come, and they will be forced to pick up the weapons they've only recently laid down.

They scatter, and my eyes fall on those who linger. Artimedes, Gengar, and a few dozen others amongst the crowd who glare at me unashamedly, wanting me to know they will come for me. I smile even wider, welcoming it nonverbally. I will have no chance of uniting these people with the Laxodontans if such rebellious figures remain living, and so I step off the erected mound of dirt I delivered my speech from and strut back to my floating palace. Time is of the essence. This trap is not going to set itself.

CHAPTER SEVEN

"At the beginning of time itssself, there wasss me, Ouroborosss, and the Abysssss. Material and immaterial. Light and darknessss. Good and evil. Two beingsss that could not coexissst. A flame cannot burn without casssting ssssome dissstant shadow. Ssso too could I not live without my shadow following me wherever I go." Quite the disgusting trope to begin my speech with, but these simple-minded cretins must be spoon fed my motives ever so delicately. A populace that has done nothing but conquer foreign nations for several years must be swooned with rhetoric before redirected. Only then can they be tamed.

Light and darkness. Good and evil. Tropes just as archaic as the religions that existed in the BDEM Era. Yet they serve their purpose. Analogies easily understood by those dim-witted enough to believe in such a god like Ouroboros. A giant serpent, at the beginning of the space time continuum? It would take more than blind faith to believe in such an origin story. It would take a species of creatures whose IQs were genetically capped to adolescent functioning when designed. Which is exactly what the Gorgons are.

They are far from the smartest species of Dæmonia. Each species has its purpose, and the Gorgons were made to be brutes. Brutes should not be allowed to philosophize. They are only good for one task. Fighting. Which is exactly why I need them. I shall be their philosopher king, providing for them direction. If I need to speak in antiquated terms of fires flickering and shadows clinging, so be it. I will say what I know they wish to hear so they follow at my heel obediently.

I stand upon my elevated chair at the head of a dining table, surveying the thousands of seated residents. It's impressive how fast they were able to come together and throw together this banquet. Thick slabs of shaved cypress weave through the surrounding swamplands, each table filled with enough food to feed two dozen fanged mouths. I look at the arranged menu for the night, all food I've never seen before. Mutant fruits radiating toxic colors, glowing as if the sun has set and they are phosphorescent. But the sun has not set, and their glowing, radioactive auras can still be seen in the daylight. Smoke rises from various roasted meats of unknown origin. Enough hunted prey to feed a hundred thousand mouths. My guess is that they've hunted the surrounding wildlife extinct with my orders to prepare this feast. Surely a forest must run dry of game at some point.

My own dining arrangement is more an altar than a table. A slab of stone where the Gorgons have brought their offerings. Offerings to a god they hope to soon reconcile with. Closest to me is a roasted serpent, its skin left on so there's no confusion what kind of snake this was. I glance quickly at its red scales and smile. They have prepared for me the body of the Vermillion Viper I killed yesterday. Such a dish speaks volumes, seeing that someone would have had to have saved its carcass after I wrung its neck. That means they had faith I would survive the bite, even after the venom left me incapacitated. They believed in me even before my actions proved my identity. Remarkably admirable.

I smile as I look back up at the crowd, smoke starting to blot out some of the far away company. Braziers have been erected between the rows of tables to spread warmth as the sun prepares to set. Dozens of trees felled to feed such a continuous fire. A smog of smoke rises to warm the atmosphere of night. Comfortable for those who are cold-blooded, but my forehead is now covered in a sheen of sweat.

Their actions prove Deus Ex Machina wrong. They *can* work together as a collective. On one accord. Such a feast with such little notice would not be possible without unity and teamwork. So what if they are not connected through MachineMind? Such accomplishments are even more beautiful when completed by autonomous individuals. It would not be impressive at all if several thousand robots built dining tables and scavenged together enough dinner for a feast. If that's what they're programed for, that is what's expected from them. No, the Gorgons are a diverse, human-like species. They followed my orders on their own accord. I didn't brainwash them. I didn't put a whip to their back like a slave master would. They did this because they believe in me.

"And ssso to thwart the Abysssss, I did what had to be done. I sssacrificcced myssself, ssso the light of life could have a chancece at sssurviving. Now, I sssstand before only a fraction of my creation and sssee that I made the right choiccce. My children, within each of you isss my ssspirit. I gifted it to the Ten Titansss, at the beginning of time. And they gifted it to you, at the cusssp of your creation. When I dessstroyed myssself ssso that you may have life, I didn't know what would await me upon my return to the material world. In my absssenccce, the Abysssss hasss done everything it could to pervert the order of my natural law. Imbedded itssself in the fabric of this world, the esssenccce of my living creation like a parasssite clung to sssome obliviousss hossst.

"I have returned!" My audience cheers.

"To ressstore order to my creation!" The praise rings louder.

"To obliterate the Abysssss onccce and for all!" The Gorgons rise to their feet, roaring with approval. Tongues lash at the air like party streamers being twirled in celebration.

I wait for their cacophonous applause to subside. My throat cannot compete with their sniveling approval. Instead I let the applause permeate the minds of my enemies who sit scattered in this same crowd. Let it break them down even further. Be the final push off the cliff that compels them to kill me.

The noise dies down slowly, then all at once. I grab a loaf of bread on a nearby plate, still warm from whatever conventional oven such a primitive race has designed. I lift it high in the air for all to see. "Do not eat thisss meal in remembranccce of me. You don't have to remember what hasss come back to life. Eat it becausssse I have not forsssaken you. Take of thisss bread, which isss sssybolic of the body I sssacrificcced on your behalf, and eat in cccelebration. For death could not conquer me, nor shall it you!"

Fists pound against tables. Feet thunder into muddy ground. They rally together, looking at me with new eyes. The same eyes that looked at me with wonderment when I claimed to be Ouroboros, now renewed in their hope. I stand, unfettered by the Godkiller Chronicle Vipress declared. Undefeated by the Vermillion Viper's poison. They are reassured in their faith, undeterred by any internal doubts. These are my disciples. These are my soldiers. They will lay down their lives for me, a tremendous accomplishment to establish within a group of followers. These aren't Spyders, who go to their death because they are programmed to do so. These are living, breathing, flesh and blood soldiers. They will not willingly go to their death unless prompted by a higher calling, and I have effectively convinced them that *I am* that higher calling.

I should probably feel guilt for what I'm doing. Playing god is not something that should be taken so lightly. But I was once in their shoes, serving a god much more malicious than me, going to war like a gladiator killing to appease his king for mere entertainment. There are worse gods to serve in this world than me, and so I cannot feel guilt for my actions. We all serve someone, and I am as benevolent a master as it gets in this world. I will not send these soldiers out to kill in vain. We will kill only for survival, the noblest of all pursuits.

I drop the bread and grab a goblet of wine, lifting it high for all eyes to see. "Drink of thisss wine, sssymbolic of the blood I ssspilled for you at the dawn of time. The blood that cannot be conquered by earthly venomsss. The blood that flowsss with the very sssourccce of life the Abysssss ssseeksss to extinguish. Take, and drink of it, for we laugh at any attempt the Abysssss makesss to devour usss. Long ago, the Abysssss sssent itsss agentsss of evil, the Demogorgonsss, to ssspread chaosss upon the faccce of the earth, and sssoon they will return. We will begin our preparationsss tomorrow, but tonight we will not worry about that which cannot harm usss. Ssso drink and be merry! Cccelebrate with me the many joysss of life, for we will sssoon wage war againsssst Death itsssself!"

My words move them to inexorable celebration. Goblets of hardened mud lift in the air, wine splashing excitedly on most tables. Undecipherable yips and hollers of cheer meet my ears. A nation of people in much need for a reason to celebrate. Exhausted from months of meaningless bloodshed. *And yet none of them raised their voice against it. Even when they are ordered to do what they are opposed to, they mindlessly comply with their orders like true soldiers.* The kind of soldiers I need. Unquestioning. Loyal without fault. Disciples who execute orders without a moment's hesitation.

Such will be an army capable of helping me kill the Angel of Life.

"Such an army is no different than an army of robots," Lilith interjects.

I don't have time for one of your guilt trips right now, I reply, trying to maintain the smile on my face despite the sudden annoyance. "Only moments ago you proudly reflected on their ability to come together and create this feast in unison despite their flesh. Now you proudly reflect on their machine-like execution of orders. That's hypocrisy," she points out. "You must choose what is more important to you. These beings' freedom from totalitarian control, or their mindless compliance to do whatever you say."

I need them to be able to do both. We humans are much more versatile than you cogs are.

"I hardly doubt that's why you feel a pull to gain control over these people. Perhaps you still have a little bit of Deus Ex Machina inside your head after all," she quips. My heart rate elevates, followed by flushed cheeks. Her words are few, but her meaning cuts deep. She suggests I plan to enslave these people like I was once enslaved. She is wrong. But if they cannot execute my orders in the coming war, then we will all find ourselves enslaved to the will of a merciless god. Surely temporarily manipulating this nation in order to ensure our future freedom is justifiable in the face of our alternate path—death.

I want so badly to volley words with her, but these people wait for my next words like the BDEM bear awaiting the first bud of spring. The sun sets and my players are in their places. It's time to set my plan in motion. "A toassst, to the era of peaccce!" I lower my goblet to my lips and pretend to take a tremendous swig. They happily follow suit as I drag the back of my hand across my wet lips. The repulsive smell of fermented grapes wafts into my nostrils.

Strange people, those who look forward to voluntarily losing control of their mindstate. Thinking they can fill their inner void by losing control of their actions and blackening their senses for a night, all to be greeted by slothful pain come tomorrow morning. Those who are aware of their enslaved state would never so willingly relinquish control over their body to a foreign substance. Only idiots would drink with such excitement, the prospect of passing out sounding favorable to them.

Under the control of Deus Ex Machina, I never had to eat. All the necessary vitamins and minerals along with daily micro- and macronutrients were provided via injection. No waste has ever been excreted from my body, the body of Lucifer XIX that is. Surely previous prototypes of myself know what it's like to piss and shit from the food they've consumed. Not me though.

I climb down from my seat as the savages tear into their food, looking at the prospects plated before me. It dawns on me that I am somewhat ignorant when it comes to eating. This is not something I'm supposed to overthink, yet I do nonetheless. I watch as the Gorgons in front of me eat without thinking. It's second nature. They know which fruits need to be peeled and which are already fit for consumption. They choose without thought their preferred cut of meat from the bodies of roasted, unidentifiable animals.

I stare at the viper, not knowing if I'm supposed to skin it before biting into its bodice. Is its head safe to consume? Have all traces of venom been removed, or is it common knowledge to avoid eating the salivary glands at the back of the head? "Stop overthinking it. Your enemies are watching you. Get on with it and take a bite," Lilith instructs. I smile graciously, grabbing the body of the smoked serpent and sink my teeth into it.

My mouth explodes with flavor. The textures are twofold, my teeth crunching through the crispy scales and into the seasoned chewiness of the inner flesh. Succulent meat marinated with some reminiscent coalescence of maple and brown sugar. The smokiness of the fire which it slow-roasted over permeates through every bite. This is... *delicious*. So much so that in a single bite it reminds me what it feels like to feel hungry, though I haven't felt such feelings in my lifespan. Only distant memories of what some past Lucifer felt.

I'm compelled to take several successive bites, until my mouth is so full that I can barely chew. And then there's the problem of my throat. I'd nearly forgotten I can barely swallow my own saliva, let alone summon the will to swallow solids. I cringe inwardly as the chewed bile scrapes my throat's innards as it slides painfully down to my famished stomach. I wash it down with the contents of my other goblet—cold, refreshing, much-needed water. The taste of trace minerals compliments the lingering presence of the viper's meat.

My stomach yearns for another bite, but the gates of hell that make up my throat won't allow it. I search the altar for alternate options, my eyes falling on a dragon-egg-shaped fruit, its outside scaled in the bizarre fashion of a juniper tree. I grab it, immediately placing it back on the table once I feel how hard its shell is. I don't want to work for my meal, and I will not make myself appear ignorant in not knowing how to peel a fruit in front of the entire nation of Gorgons.

I pull close a bowl filled with a gooey purple substance. A purée of unknown origin. I don't have the patience to question its appearance. It's the only food here that looks like it will make it to my stomach with little protest. I inwardly applaud the decision the moment the goo hits my tastebuds. An explosion of cinnamon citrus invades my mouth, not stopping until a surge of warmth has spread through my entire head and down my throat. Its warmth is healing, not attacking my damaged esophagus but instead soothing it with a gentle radiance.

I lift the wooden bowl to my lips and gulp the slime down like a glutton, letting out a deep gasp of pleasure as the empty dish clanks to the table. Somehow, my mouth salivates more now than it did before I began eating. My stomach growls, begging me for more. Desperately pleading me to overindulge. Tempting me to eat until I can no longer move and must pass out from the pain of a full stomach.

Slowly in my fallen state I begin to familiarize myself with the wanton ways of humanity. First I experienced lust in my sinful craving for Vipress as she attacked me with her unseen pheromones, and now I see what it feels like to lose my self-control to a plate of food. It would be easy to do so if I was ignorant to the dangers of eating without consequence. But sin can only have a grip on you if you live in the present. Consequence lives in the future.

Temptation passes, but you must be strong enough to await its passing. If not you will constantly fall prey to sinful living. One of the many dangers of being human.

I push the food away, swallowing the remaining saliva that fills my orifice like water in a bathtub. Hunger can only have a hold over you as long as you allow it to.

I dab the corner of my mouth with the thick cloth my royal guard has provided.

A royal guard. *For me.* It seemed absurd at first, but my newfound loyalists don't want any discrepancies to arise in the transition from Vipress's rule to my own. Since the moment I sent Vipress off I haven't been able to shed these guards. They're tighter to my skin than my BioSuit was. And worse, they did a very shitty job dressing me.

I look down at the two-piece suit, fashioned from the shed skin of a vazisk, a creature so rare it's considered extinct. There hasn't been a spotting in over twenty years, I'm told. This garb was tailored from the preserved wardrobe of the late King Sssarkex, usurped and blotted from memory by Vipress.

The shirt and pants are like wearing clothing made from sandpaper, but I'm not stupid enough to turn down such customs. They view this skin suit as sacred enough to befit a god, so I let them pin it to me. Their healers did everything in their power to curb the final symptoms of the Vermillion Viper bite as well. My side is properly sutured, my neck compressed with bandages covered in the saliva of an ephesus—which is said to have tremendous healing properties. Not tremendous enough, it must be noted, to save Vipress from dying.

But I accept any help they are willing to give. It takes more effort and pride on my end to turn down the hands that wish to help me than to just submit myself into their embrace.

I must slip away from this party though, and so I stand from my altar of barely touched delicacies, ready to enact phase one of my plan. I have only two corroborates on my side tonight. These creatures may look animalistic, but they are human in their core. Because of that, I must keep my circle small and my allies minimal. Placing trust in too many is a formula for failure.

Vipress is my first ally, and she is off attending to business that will be of great importance later. I don't dare to look my other confidante in the eyes. To do so would blow their cover, but I know they're watching me, so I don't worry about the details to follow. We have rehearsed this plan together, which leaves us nothing to do but execute it step by step.

Step one, leave this party and ensure that my personal guard doesn't follow me. I need to end up alone and vulnerable tonight to ensure my attackers are tempted to strike. But there's only one socially acceptable excuse to pardon my early departure without my guards. I need a mistress.

I walk up to the hand-selected leader of the imperial guards which shadow my seat in a semicircle. He is a rare occurrence among the Gorgonic race, a genetic anomaly. The product of star-crossed lovers—ScarGill is half-Gorgon, half-Aegean. Such a hybrid mating is not forbidden empirically, but rather shamed societally. To produce a child of two races is to outcast that child by every race.

With the head of a BDEM great white shark, scales of an alligator, body of a human, and tail somewhere in between that of a fish and a reptile, ScarGill is the most ideal candidate for the head of my personal guard. Shunned from society at birth, cursed to scrounge off the backwash of society to survive, he abhors the Gorgons, which is precisely why I can trust him to protect me. He has no faith in the good of any race because he has seen people are good to only that which is normal.

I have taken him in, given his life purpose, his name honor, and his reputation an origin. I took someone who had nothing and gave him everything. The formula for a devout believer. Someone who would lay down their life to protect me. Such was necessary, when my people mandated on my behalf that I have a retinue of guards. I allowed it, contingent on the fact that I could choose their leader.

I approach him now, his grisly appearance weathered by years of torment. The continual, unavoidable torture of never truly being accepted for who he is. He looks at me, unsure why I am not at the table enjoying the splendors of my people's harvest. I catch a glimpse of the ghastly scar over his gills, crested on the flesh of his neck above his plate of chest armor. The story of his name's origin no doubt, unbeknownst to me.

"My lord, is there something I can do for you?" he asks, not speaking the Gorgonic language Ssserphentyne, but instead, shockingly, Old English. He lowers himself to a single knee. I stop him before he can make contact with the ground. "You need not kneel for me, ScarGill. I have business I must attend to. Business I must be alone for," I say, directing his vision with the point of a finger. He follows it, nodding with understanding. "Ah, I see. Well perhaps I could remain by your side and the rest of the guard could remain here," he offers.

"You have done me a great service, ScarGill, but three is a crowd. I wish to have my intimacy in private peace, no intrusions whatsoever. I can protect myself. My command to you is to stay here and enjoy yourself. Devour the food upon the altar I couldn't, it will make me feel less guilty about turning down such a rich harvest."

His eyes look as if I've just asked him to jump to the moon. As if my command is something entirely too impossible to even consider. "But—" he begins.

"No buts. I mean it. You and the rest of the guards, make sure none of this food goes to waste. You are off duty for the rest of the night. I don't want to see that Aegean face until tomorrow morning when I arise from my night of making love. Is that understood?"

"Yes, Lord Ouroboros," he responds begrudgingly. I admire his loyalty, but I cannot allow it to impair my vision. Now is not the time to make friends. War teaches that the more friends you have, the more friends you must bury. With him being so close to me his death in the coming onslaught is inevitable. All who ally themselves to the Angel of Death are subject to die.

But that doesn't mean he can't have at least one good night, this man who has been shunned by society so mercilessly. One good night, before many more gruesome ones come. I leave him, hoping that once I depart his inner tightness will fade and he can let loose. But who am I kidding, these people will still not accept him for the abomination he was born as. Their worldview teaches them to hate the other Dæmonic species. They will never fully embrace someone like him no matter who their leader is.

That may change with the tides of war though. Unlikely heroes seem to rise from the most unlikely sources. All I can do is hope that he lives long enough to prove to these people that genetics matter little if your heart is filled with bravery.

I walk up to the woman my finger previously pointed out, seated at the table closest to my altar per my request. She is dressed appropriately for me, wearing nothing at all. Such is the custom of the Gorgon nation. Armor is their only clothing, therefore those who do not ready themselves for battle do not wear clothes. It is a somewhat savage custom, but it is pleasant for my eyes at least.

She locks eyes with me, knowing that I am coming for her. She swallows anxiously, knowing that I am coming for her. Her skin covers with goosebumps as she watches my eyes glide across her body's curves, examining which parts of her are human, which parts are reptile. I undress her naked body with my eyes, and I watch as her inner anxiety bumps shoulders with deep arousal. She knows I am coming for her.

I grab the aquamarine, scaled hand of the snake handler who I previously saved from the Vermillion Viper. She clenches my hand with her delicate fingers and lifts herself from her seated position at the feast without a single word. The entire crowd looks on us, knowing what is happening.

She is flustered, a general mix of confusion questioning why I pick her. I pull her away from the table and she follows obediently. All the noise of the crowd is now gone. No plates clatter, no chewing occurs, no drinks spill, no cutlery is shifted. Everyone has seemingly forgotten how to breathe now that I have chosen my first woman to court.

Yet it makes sense to them. She is shy yet beautiful. The cream of the crop among their virgin stock. And the Gorgons knew I would pick one tonight. It is part of their custom to offer up their virgin daughters when a new ruler takes the throne. I may be a god in place of a king, but that does not stop their assumption that I too have a lustful appetite. They project this onto me as if they think I desire carnal relations as much as they do.

They are, after all, a lustful people. This night's feast will end with widespread orgies, as do all communal gatherings in the Gorgon culture. It is their way of connecting intimately, asserting dominance amongst each other, and, most importantly, establishing who the alpha men are. Now the envious eyes of the inexperienced women fix on her with malice. They could have made love to a god tonight, and now the snake handler is the one that stands in the way.

"Don't look back," I whisper to her as we reach the shade of a trove of yulock trees. "They will watch usss until we leave their sssight. We are almossst in the clear. Aaaaand done," I say as we enter a shallow cave entrance which leads to the bank of my castle. "That wasssn't ssso bad, wasss it?" I ask her, lifting her innocent eyes to meet mine. She is scared, I don't need my retinal display's heart rate detector to know that. She is a tangled mess of anxiety, as she was yesterday when she approached me with the viper.

"What'sss your name?" I ask, trying to form a bond as we walk the damp, rocky pathway under the light of mounted, pre-lit torches. The grotto is too narrow for two to walk abreast, so I lead with her following closely behind. The distant sound of water droplets pattering to the ground echo much louder than they should. Where they come from, I can't be sure. This cave will eventually dive deep into the earth and cross beneath the depths of the lake, eventually leading us to the opposite side. For someone like me who doesn't want to swim across or hike the vast perimeter, going underneath the obstacle is the only alternate path.

"Eresss Insssularisss," she replies meekly.

I stop walking and turn to face her. She is deeply afraid. And why wouldn't she be? She thinks I'm taking her back to my bedroom quarters to defile her innocence. She has every right to be intimidated, but I must console her in some way. "Eresss," I whisper. "That'sss a beautiful name. There isss nothing to fear, Eresss. I'm not going to do anything to you. I won't lay a finger on you."

Her face washes over with instant relief as if I've just made her greatest dream come true. Ironic, because the other virgins at the table looked at me as if sleeping with me tonight was their greatest dream. She realizes that her smile compromises her inner feelings of joy and tries to stifle it. She is a kind girl to not want to offend me. But a simpleton such as her couldn't possibly hurt my feelings.

"Then why did you choossse me, if you are not interesssted?" She may be relieved, but she still seeks understanding. There were several dozen other girls of similar beauty and wide-ranging sex appeal. I could have picked any of them, yet I chose the skittish, prude, timid one who is more afraid of sex than she is of me.

"Becaussse I need your help," I reply.

"My help?" She still doesn't understand. That's fine, she will soon enough. I need this girl more than she knows. No, correction. I do not need this girl. I need what she keeps locked away.

"Yesss, your help. You are the sssnake handler, are you not?" I smile as she frowns. Slowly but surely the pieces will fall together for her. By the time she is staring at the entire puzzle, it will be too late.

PART FOUR

"History isn't kind to humans who pretend they're gods."
-Lucifer XIX

CHAPTER ONE

They follow me through the dense thicket with just as much silence as they employed in the cave, unknowingly following me to their deaths. They don't notice that Eresss Insssularisss has left my company, a pack of BDEM raccoons too focused on a shiny object to see the trap surrounding it. There are too many of them to get an accurate count, but I know their numbers are great enough to easily overcome me in this mortal state. They move like shadows in darkness, like snakes slithering unseen until ready to strike.

But I can see them because I expect them. They were the only ones holding back at the communal feast. Refusing drinks, eating lightly, periodically exchanging glances with one another every time I made a sudden move at the altar. They are Gorgons, not covert agents. They know not that I spot their many dead giveaways.

It hardly matters anymore. We approach the prisoner camps, heavily anticipated by the Laxodontans. If Tuskfather spread word of his Godkiller Chronicle, which he no doubt did, then the masses will be preparing themselves for revenge. And behind me stalks their prey. He wanted me to bring him Gengar, so I had Gengar bring himself unknowingly. He can answer to Tuskfather for his sins.

I exit the woods, alligator-skin-wrapped feet moving from crunchy reeds to bare, sullen clay. The mutant, swamp-like trees recede and open my view to the not so distant perimeter of the camps. Wrought-iron, rusted fencing is the only thing which keeps the Laxodontans from their freedom. Any one of them is strong enough to break through its surface, bend the alloy until it breaks in their hands. A single collective charge would knock down an entire panel of the fence. Rip it right off its hinges.

But such an escape is not the Laxodontan way. They have the genes of the ancient elephants, mighty creatures subject to accept defeat if they have been conditioned to do so. You can tie a baby elephant to a tree and it will fight to get free. But after many unsuccessful attempts to break the chain that tethers it, it will yield to defeat. Tie that same elephant to a tree with a piece of twine when it weighs several tons and it won't even attempt to run free. It has already been conditioned to accept imprisonment.

Such is the case with the creature's descendants. But the rebellious nature of some still remains. Tuskfather's humanistic spirit conquers that of his elephant ancestors, and that is why he will always lash against any restraint that seeks to control him. That is why he will ultimately crush Gengar, whose soul is more serpent than human. I choose him because he is the more powerful of the two, but also because I will need human spirit to surround me if I'm to overcome Cataclysm.

I can't win this war as a robot. I must win it as a human, which means I will be fighting two wars. One against machines, and one against my own prejudice against humanity. I have been conditioned to see humans as worthless, incessant reprobates. Scoundreling scum scraping by—

I stop myself mid thought, realizing that even thinking about humanity raises implicit biases within my mind. I must expel this way of thinking if I'm to lead leagues of humanity against the forces of Hyperion. I cannot fight against machine minds if I side with their ethics. To preserve humanity and save the Dæmonia I must reclaim my own humanity. It's the only choice I have.

"There'sss no ussse continuing to ignore usss," a voice lisps from behind. "I know you know we're here." I remember the sinister hiss from a single encounter. *Gengar.* And yet, even though I know they stalk closely behind upon the baked clay ground, I can still barely make out their footfall. Even those who are bipedal strut in silence as if they are slithering.

I quicken my pace in a manner that comes across as panicked. I want to height-en their prey drive. Make them think they have me cornered. Their bloodlust will give them tunnel vision, and Gengar's thirst for power will blind him. Now that he is confident Vipress is dead, he knows I am the only one that stands in his way of leading the Gorgons. Killing me will propel him into the life he has so long lusted for.

They sprint after me, seeking to pin me with my back against the prison camp. Are they really so stupid that they don't see my end goal? I look to the guard posts above the internment camp, unoccupied. *Perfect*, I think to myself. My ally was successful in convincing the guards to leave their posts to attend the feast. We will be alone for this upcoming entanglement, no Gorgon innocence caught in the clash between revenge-driven Laxodontans and sin-ridden Gorgons. The perfect bloodbath to satisfy my future Laxodontan followers.

"Give it up," Gengar shouts as I approach the gate to the prison camp. I finally turn to face him, backing up until my back touches the rusted panel fence which conceals the waiting Laxodontan army on the other side.

"Oh you of little faith," I pant heavily. "You would dare try to kill a god?" I ask, still maintaining the charade so the Laxodontans can hear me just as clearly as my predators can. I look at the ugly, menacing bunch of converging Gorgons before me. Their numbers are more than I previously anticipated—several hundred instead of what I thought would be several dozen. I guess I underestimated how quick treachery can spread amongst a people. Whispers and rumors can be an excellent recruiter, and Gengar has surely sewn whispers of doubt in my ability to lead the Gorgons by now.

If they don't believe I am in the least bit divine after surviving the bite of the Vermillion Viper, then I have no tools left in my arsenal to further convince them. Primitive minds need to see before they can believe, and I have not shown this gathered opposition enough evidence to believe in me. So be it. It will be their deaths that pay the price for their disbelief.

"God? You think we believe you are a god because you sssurvived a sssnake bite? Now will be your true Godkiller Chronicle," he says, gesturing to the small militia behind him. "Let'sss see if you can sssurvive ssseveral hundred sssnake bitesss." He smiles maniacally. Next to him is Artimedes, eyeing with me with slitted pupils pulsing with pure hatred.

"Artimedesss, it wasss thisss *man* that killed our Vipresssss. Would you like the honor of killing him? Avenge our Queen, brother," Gengar commands, looking with compassion to his loyal right hand man.

"It would be my pleasssure, commander," Artimedes growls. The bigger, bulkier Gorgon with the alligator complexion storms forward with raw rage in his veins. He will kill me for killing his love. I know the pain he feels. To know that the one he loves has been lost forever. That is a hatred that can't be doused until satiated with revenge. I look in his evil eyes and feel overwhelming relief to know it's all an act. I am suddenly filled with gratitude to know this Gorgon is on my side as he storms past me and rips the lock mechanism off the gate latch, throwing open the entrance to the prisoner-of-war camp.

Artimedes opens the gate, but I choose to watch Gengar's reaction instead of what stands silently behind the camp's weak walls. Apprehension strikes Gengar's face with a tinge of horror. Artimedes stands like a magician who has just yanked a rabbit from a hat, his look of venomous hate gone from his eye in a single blink. It was all an act. A clever ploy by my second ally, Artimedes, to gain the trust of my greatest threat, Gengar.

Gengar is not stupid, and so he puts the pieces together quickly as he stares at me and *my* right hand man standing in front of Tuskfather and his league of warrior elephants. Gengar's face shows his confusion, but his followers are stupefied. Their eyes dart from me to Artimedes to Tuskfather to the Laxodontans and then examine Gengar, as if he has a solution that will save them from their inevitable doom.

"Why?" Gengar asks, looking to Artimedes. His plan was so thorough, yet it didn't account for Artimedes' betrayal. "You would choossse to betray your own flesh and blood for thisss human? A human who killed your lover nonethelesssss!" His words are every bit as cruel and venomous as the emotions that flood within him.

"My Vipresssss isss not dead," Artimedes replies, which causes Tuskfather to tilt his head in suspicion. There's no telling how this next part is going to go. This plan is a dangerous balancing act upon a very fragile strand of narrow thread. It can snap in a single second and send everything falling into chaos. I must orchestrate it the same way I devised it—with tactful precision and unfailing accuracy. The moment I lose control is the moment I lose the upper hand. I can't afford to lose either in the midst of such untrustworthy company.

"What do you mean your Vipresssss—"

"Vipresssss! Come out, come out, wherever you are!" I yell loud enough for any spectators lurking in the woods to hear. Gengar and his fear-stricken retinue turn to face the army which flanks them.

From the darkness of the woods emerges a figure Gengar recognizes immediately. It is Vipress, freshly risen from the grave to haunt his campaign for power. Now two individuals stand in his way to becoming King of the Gorgons, though such an inconvenience will not deter him. A minor hiccup in the plan, especially because his assembled fighting force is now melting away in fear at the sight of their Queen.

Without a single word uttered, the militia scatters like utter cowards, running in all directions that lead away from the two enemies. Laxodontans on one side. Vipress and her slithering soldiers on the other. "I wouldn't do that if I wasss you!" I yell. The warning stops them before their steps can carry them out of earshot. "Vipresssss, would you like to show them the army you've brought to sssurround them?" I ask rhetorically.

She stands alone, no other Gorgons in sight to have her back. That's because all other Gorgons are safe, inebriated by food and drink back at the feast, safely tucked away from the bloodshed that will occur momentarily. No, the army Vipress brings is much more deadly than the entire Gorgon population. And even better, they slither around us unseen.

A violent hiss erupts. A voice screams in pain. One of Gengar's soldiers drops to the ground, his voice piercing the night sky to relay his agony. Venom already coagulates his blood to gelatin in his veins. His shrill screams demonstrate a soundtrack to the final moments of a dying man bitten by a pit viper.

"Sssnakesss!" someone screams within the thick crowd of Gorgons. *Yes, snakes. Snakes everywhere. Now, let the fear spread*. I smile as several more bodies drop to the ground, convulsing at the instantaneous pain that grips their bodies once bitten by a viper. It's paralyzing. Literally.

Eres delivered. Slipped away from my company and found Vipress where I told her to wait. Gave the former Gorgonic Queen the keys to the snake pit, where the Gorgons store their deadliest vipers. But they are only deadly if you can't control them, and right now Vipress radiates so many pheromones into the air that these snakes obey her every telepathic command.

Gengar's head swivels quickly, examining the ground for nearby snakes. He doesn't need to worry; I told Vipress to save him for Tuskfather. It's the least I can do for him, since I found a loophole around his request. A man should be allowed the chance to deliver the killing blow to the terrorist who murdered his wife and children.

Chaos ensues. Snakes slither rampant on the dark desert ground, their camouflaged skins making them nearly impossible to avoid. The Gorgons panic and begin scattering, their footfall arousing the circling perimeter of vipers to fear. They must have never been taught that it is the fearful snake that is most likely to lash out and bite. The Gorgons drop like swatted flies, stepping on living landmines loaded with explosive venom.

I stand silently and watch as Gengar's forces slaughter themselves for us. The Laxodontans needn't raise a single finger. Artimedes watches Gengar, who watches his army become reduced to only a few dozen scattering souls who use the fallen bodies of their brethren as a pathway of escape. I know Gengar inwardly sees the pathetic nature of his people in the same light I do. It's like watching drowning men drown each other to stay afloat.

I lock eyes with Vipress, still at the wetland's edge secreting massive amounts of pheromones to control the hundreds of vipers around us. Eres is nowhere to be seen. Her duty completed, she has come no further to see what we use her snakes for. Probably for the best; she seemed quite squeamish.

I look at Artimedes, whose eyes are now transfixed on his mistress in the distance. I can almost feel the arousal radiating from his skin. I wonder to myself if she tricked him into loving her with her seemingly undetectable pheromones. It worked on me, and I don't even have a cock. Is he just an easily seduced puppet of her past? Loyalty earned through sex? Or was she intimate with him because she actually feels something for him?

It's best to not ask such questions. Best to stay out of such affairs that don't concern me in the slightest. All I know is that her ability to manipulate creatures will forever be a useful tool when I deal with humans. If only I could get such a power to work on robots, then it would really come in handy.

"What is this obscenity?" Tuskfather roars, surging forward to my side. He, like the rest of his race, is immobilized with confusion. He's the first to put what little puzzle pieces there are together though, and the sight of Vipress instantly arouses suspicion of me within his mind. "She's supposed to be dead!" he yells, making up for what he lacks in clarity in the tremble of his voice. It's oftentimes those who don't know what's going on that have a way of yelling the loudest. As if a threatening aura will somehow dismantle the chaos.

"Relax," I whine, eyeing him unequivocally. "The Vipress did in fact die, as you requested. Your Godkiller Chronicle, however, had no stipulation restricting me from bringing her back to life. She is mine now, a born again disciple of Ouroboros."

I look at him with the intensity of a lion, seeing how he fumes greatly over the way I've gone behind his back. He is even more infuriated knowing I've outsmarted him, something he's not used to when surrounded by elephants his whole life. Or no, I shouldn't say his whole life. "Were you ever going to tell me?" I ask, forcing the blame back on him.

He shifts his body into a defensive posture, calloused feet spread wide. "Tell you what?" he snaps.

"Don't play coy with me, Tuskfather. You're upset that I found a way around your Godkiller Chronicle, that is easily understood. If I was in your position, I would be upset too. But I brought you the man who killed your wife and children. You can at least be thankful for that. The Godkiller Chronicle is only supposed to be a single request; I didn't have to bring Gengar here for you to satisfy your thirst for revenge. Didn't have to give you a chance at redemption. I could have set my nation of Gorgons on this camp and you all would have been nothing but smoking carcasses before the moon's peak. I have been merciful. Gracious, even. I now present to you the opportunity to come clean. You haven't been so truthful with your people either, Tuskfather. Would you care to open up and tell them why it is you speak such fluent New English? Or would you like for me to tell them?"

I expect his reaction to be one of shock. I expect him to be flustered that I know what his entire nation does not. I expect him to feel naked, as if I'm an all-seeing god that sees right through his charade of bravery and self-dignified righteousness. But he is not moved at all toward feelings of meekness. No, me playing the ace up my sleeve only provokes him further toward self-perpetuated anger. Anger of being discovered as a fraud. I have the power to expose him in front of his entire camp and put to rest any claim he'll ever have at being their leader.

And though this would be enough to bend most figures into a position of subservience, Tuskfather is too human to respond with rationality. His emotion gets the best of him, as it does with most humans. His fists clench. His foot drags across the desert soil. His body prepares to charge. Gengar smiles, seeing the perfect opportunity to retreat without being noticed. Vipress slightly loses her hold over the surrounding serpents, distracted as Tuskfather extends his trunk to the sky and trumpets a deafening war chant. Artimedes shuffles a few steps away from me, foreseeing what's bound to happen.

"I wouldn't do that if I was you," I announce, just in time to break Tuskfather out of his hellbent trance. He is not past the point of reason. Not yet. I have a few seconds to still win him over, but something tells me the next phase of my plan is only going to piss him off more.

On cue, almost as if it had been rehearsed, the final step of the plan enters the stage. "Tuskfather! I not done with you yet!" a distant voice calls. The crowd of Laxodontans parts like a line drawn in sand. There aren't many of them left, so opening an alley from Tuskfather to his accuser doesn't take long. The channel opens up, revealing at the end of the tunnel an approaching retinue from within the prisoner camp. The final chess piece I needed to set the stage for a final conversion of loyalty to my efforts.

Bloodtusk and his band of Bloodtuskers. A band of necessary evil I'm forced to employ to win over the Laxodontans. It wouldn't be possible without Vipress. She is, after all, the one who sought him out earlier today and swayed him to comply with her witching ways. Wheedling him with words and woos. It is impressive. The Dæmonic races abhor interracial relationships, yet Vipress's pheromones transcend such a deep racism. Surely without such a quirk in her arsenal, Bloodtusk would have been impossible to win over for our cause.

The enemy of my friend may be my enemy, but that doesn't mean they can't be used for political advance. I will exploit Tuskfather now, use his impulsiveness against him. I don't want to have to kill him, but I will if he gets in my way. He has the potential to be a powerful ally, but losing Vipress to gain his loyalty is too steep a price. I want them both, and this is my best effort at a peaceful transition for him. He now is faced by two enemies—I present him the opportunity to avenge his beloved family and absolve the inner divisions of the Laxodontans in a single night, which will also make my reign over both nations much smoother. Inside, I know I need him. He is the key to much more than just the Laxodontans. But if he can't see the graciousness I extend to him then there can be no place for him by my side.

He instantly forgets about me, locking eyes with Bloodtusk a hundred yards away. He has no idea it was me and Vipress who recruited his forsworn enemy. Thinks it is merely miraculous timing. And even worse, we equipped him with a weapon of symbolic treachery. There, in Bloodtusk's vicious grasp, are the two sawn-off tusks which once belonged to Tuskfather. Vipress took them with her when she seduced Bloodtusk to lead this final assault and gave them to him as a gift, convincing him that killing Tuskfather with his own tusks would be exactly the act that would solidify his power to the Laxodontans. We knew such items are exactly what this plan needed to break what final strings hold together Tuskfather's psyche.

Bloodtusk and the mighty spear-like ivory in his hands are like a matador with a cape at the end of this parted tunnel, and Tuskfather is the bull that can't see past his testosterone-driven fury. I look over my shoulder and see Gengar fading away toward the tree line. "Artimedesss," I announce. "Retrieve our guessst of honor. I want him here for Tuskfather when thisss isss over."

"My pleasssure," he hisses in response.

I turn to face the ensuing action as Tuskfather and Bloodtusk take the first steps of a colossal charge. I feel the earth quake from the pounding feet. The crowd is now wild, cheers from Bloodtuskers and Laxodontans alike filling the air, the trumpeting of trunks in support of the clash between self-proclaiming kings. I'd be lying if I said I wasn't also anticipating the fight to come. The beasts are terrifying for different reasons.

Tuskfather, from his sheer size and overwhelming strength. Bloodtusk for his speed and persistent thirst for power. Trumpets ring, feet stomp, dust lifts into the air like a rising sandstorm.

The two close the gap with surprising speed.

In an orthodox charge between Laxodontan males, the two traditionally butt tusks as violently as possible, their body's momentum throwing everything they have into the attack, their neck forced to bear the responsibility of not snapping under pressure. But this is not an orthodox charge by any means. Tuskfather is tuskless, his ivory wielded by his adversary as the weapons meant to harm him. This throws all conventional means of fighting out the window. This fight is personal. It will mean the death of one of these leaders. The outcome ambiguous to those who still doubt Tuskfather's ability to lead.

When they come several strides of each other, Bloodtusk leaps, floating in the air with both tusks poised for a downward attack. Time slows. I watch the elephantine human remain in the air while Tuskfather inwardly adjusts his game plan. Such a massive individual is not meant to hang in the air so long as Blood-tusk does, his athleticism and agility on display for all to see. The weaponized tusks thrust downward as Tuskfather's shoulder barrels into his competitor's belly. The sound of these beasts colliding resembles that of two globs of cata-pulted guck striking one another at high speed. A sickly gluck. Jiggling blubber. The crunch of bones. Tusk tips bite into Tuskfather's back, and then everything returns to its normal speed. All I can see is two bodies of hulking grey flesh tangled in a death roll.

The nearby spectators step several lengths away from the raging titans, en-thralled by the violence but unwilling to partake in it. I survey the crowd. Even now, with the fate of their future leader on the line, there are still those among the Laxodontans that don't condone such violence. Their faces are disgusted by this barbaric display of dominance. Their views will need to change if they are to take on the forces of Hyperion. Perhaps they won't be so adamantly opposed to fighting when it's *their* lives on the line. When their total extinction hangs in the balance.

Both tusks protrude from Tuskfather's back, minimal blood spurting from the penetrated hide. Surely that must make use of his arms difficult, the puncture wounds are over the brachial plexus, nerve bunchings responsible for his arm's movement. But you wouldn't know it from the way he persistently fights. His movement doesn't acknowledge the presence of the stab wounds. Adrenaline is the perfect pain inhibitor, but he will feel those when he wakes tomorrow. *If* he wakes tomorrow.

By some miracle it is Bloodtusk that ends up mounting Tuskfather, holding down the flailing arms that retaliate against his hands. Bloodtusk forces Tusk-father onto his back, the ground pushing the ivory spears in Tuskfather's back further into his body. This elicits a grunt of pain from the grounded victim. Bloodtusk sees the flinch on his enemy's face, realizing he can capitalize on the tusks.

Bloodtusk grabs Tuskfather by the neck with both hands and lifts his chest off the ground, then puts both hands on his chest and shoves him back to the ground.

Hard. The sound of Tuskfather's clavicles cracking echoes through the crowd as the tusks dig deeper, their bases getting wider the further they're pushed.

Pain is written on Tuskfather's face for all to see, and the wounds of the prey only drive the bloodlust of the predator further. Bloodtusk sees that his chances of winning this duel are now in his favor, and this sends him into a crazed frenzy. He repeats the attack. Lifts Tuskfather, who at this point is too weak to retaliate, and slams him back to the relentless clay. Tuskfather's shoulders give up the fight. The ivory tips of his own horns rip through his front deltoids, one where each collarbone once was moments ago.

The majority of the crowd whose hope rested in Tuskfather gasps. They are his sympathizers, those who couldn't fathom a future under the dictating leadership of Bloodtusk. And now they must begin to imagine such a future, as the outcome of this fight is now spelled out for all to see, the victor's name written in blood.

Bloodtusk raises his hands victoriously, his degenerate disciples trumpeting cheers of celebration in his favor as he eyes them all, still mounted on the defeated Laxodontan King. This is a mistake. It frees up Tuskfather's arms enough to wiggle loose of the weight that bound them. The tuskless Laxodontan, without a moment's hesitation, sits up, slips his neck through Bloodtusk's ivory, and wraps his arms tight around the surprised victor. Then, before Bloodtusk has a moment to raise a defensive strategy, Tuskfather throttles his back to the ground again, shoving the ivory spears that penetrate his shoulders into Bloodtusk, who is hugged so tight that he cannot escape.

The tusks tear into Bloodtusk's shoulders, stealing from him a yelp of pain. Tuskfather screams, but it doesn't come from a place of agony. This is a scream of hysterical joy, a crazed man who has played the victim, waited for a vulnerability to open, then exposed it in totality.

Tuskfather twists, forcing Bloodtusk to twist under him. He sits up, tusks retreating from their deep hold in Bloodtusk's compromised shoulders. The ivory tips cause a suctioning sound as they pull free from the deep canyons they've carved in Bloodtusk. Tuskfather grins maniacally as the degenerate hollering dies down all at once, replaced by the terrifyingly booming celebration of the majority. Their leader has prevailed, and his eyes show a look which say he won't fail again.

The rest of the fight is cruel yet quick. Bloodtusk stammers for mercy and grace, muttering inaudible slurs about the peaceful ways of the Laxodontans. "Please, Tuskfather. I yield. Please no more. No more pain," he whines pathetically. "I accept defeat. Just no kill me. I beg you." Bloodtusk is overwhelmed by grief at the coming prospect of his death. Tears fall down his cheeks, making the painted, bloody war runes wet and smeared. Rehydrating them until they flow alongside the trail of tears down his face and trunk.

"You yield?" Tuskfather repeats his enemy's slur. "Brother, how many times have I heard those same words come from your mouth? I saw you, that day when my wife and daughter were killed. You watched in horror in the distance as I was held in helpless restraint. You watched and what did you do? You ordered retreat, then made no attempt to save my girls."

"If I tried—"

"If you tried half so hard to save them as you did to overthrow me then they would still be here today," Tuskfather finishes the sentence crudely. "I have forgiven you time and time again. But forgiveness can only stretch so far, brother. Our gracious Lord Ouroboros has given us the chance to prove who is more fit to lead the Laxodontans. You have been found unworthy by our father Mastodon. And so I send you back to him, deemed insufficient to live any longer. A failed Laxodontan. Nothing more than a thorn in the side of the true King of our people—me. I hereby dispel you."

"No!" Bloodtusk tries to defend against the attack but he is not built to withstand such brute force while pinned. His advantages in battle are his speed and nimble agility, both of which are stripped from him now. Tuskfather takes hold of the flailing tusks beneath him, Bloodtusk's body squirming at the thought of what's to come. Tuskfather exerts all his effort in pulling the tusks in opposite directions, like trying to bend metal bars enough to squeeze through. Bloodtusk screams to no avail. Tuskfather grunts from the sheer effort he puts out.

The crowd quiets down, everyone inching forward and standing on their tippy toes to get a better view of the battle's outcome. A groaning that resembles the sound of bone separating creaks for all to hear. The crackling of microfractures emerging at the base of Bloodtusk's horns. The thudding of runaway Bloodtuskers provides background symphony. And then, before Bloodtusk's ivory tusks break from their bases, his head explodes, skull cracking down the middle from the pressure which pulls it apart.

The two sides of his head fly apart, Tuskfather not expecting the sudden cessation of resistance. Blood and brains soar through the air, most of it splattering directly in Tuskfather's own face to repaint his head entirely red. Bloodtusk's body falls limp, his life instantly fleeing into the air alongside the fluids of his inner cranium.

Tuskfather doesn't miss a beat now that he has forged a blood trail. The savage applause doesn't faze him. He arises from the carcass with double the determination he had before, strutting with a killer's stride back to me. His inhalations are deep. His exhalations, forced grunts. Blood drips from his eyebrow to his cheeks like red waterfalls covering his ferocious gaze. I follow the path of his eyes. They set themselves on their new target—Gengar, forced to his knees by Artimedes only a few paces behind me.

Killing Bloodtusk was merely a warm up for this ungentle giant. And even better—the feeling of long-awaited blood on his hands removes my betrayal from his memory. It is no longer me who rests in his crosshairs. All I can do from here is hope that murdering Gengar satiates his desire to take up arms against me. Doing so would lead to a war that leaves little in its wake.

He stops in front of me, euphoria crawling over his skin like termites over rotting wood. And then, unexpectedly, he kneels before me, lowering his head to the ground. "You must forgive my outburst of anger, Lord Ouroboros. When I saw you were in league with the serpent-witch, the woman who destroyed everything I know and love, I was outraged. But the killing must end, and so I submit myself to your all-knowing, omnipotent plan. If she too is a part of that plan, then so be it. I must be grateful for that which you have given me. I thank you for delivering my wife and daughter's murderer into my hands."

The speech is short and sweet but the message is clear. Killing Bloodtusk has vented his frustration and given new clarity, as I hoped it would. He is mine to command. "Arise, Tuskfather, leader of the Laxodontans. Seek vengeance on those who haunt your heart. Return to the Abyss the corrupted souls which belong to it," I command.

He rises, smile evanescent on his expression. It's like a flip is switched in his head. One moment he is humble and subservient, and the next, a demon with a vendetta. "Smallear!" he calls, the crowd instantly shifting as his brother runs to his side. "My tusks, please," he growls. Smallear reaches up and grabs a single tusk at the base, planting his foot in the small of Tuskfather's back as he yanks ferociously. The tusk begrudgingly exits the wound, a wet pop echoing as the seal is broken and it dislodges completely. He sets it on the ground behind him and does the same to the second tusk, two enormous craters left behind at their removal.

"Thank you," Tuskfather grunts as Smallear hands the second tusk to his brother. He will kill Gengar with the same tusk the crocodile cut from his face. I love a death displayed with irony. Tuskfather approaches Gengar, the Gorgon defenseless before the hulking Laxodontan. He slowly rubs the blood-covered ivory against his thick, calloused hide, cleaning its surface of his own blood, preparing it to be plunged into its new victim.

Gengar doesn't whimper or squirm like Bloodtusk did. He isn't weak. He looks at Tuskfather with the eyes of a true killer. Cold. As cold as the blood that runs through his reptilian veins. Emotionless. The eyes of a psychopath who has been declared defeated. A sore loser who schemes to kill his conqueror even as death looms over his head.

"How long I have awaited this moment," Tuskfather speaks in New English. Gengar only speaks Ssserphentyne, so the sentiment falls on death ears. I, on the other hand, can understand both bodies thanks to Lilith's active translation. Gengar replies, knowing that his input will be understood only by me: "You elephantsss are incompetent doltsss. Unworthy to live. I will exterminate your entire ssserpent. There isss only one of you that hasss the mind of a ssserpent, and that isss why he will be the only one who sssurvives the night."

Artimedes and I lock eyes, unsure of what Gengar means by his monologue. Tuskfather is undeterred by what he can't understand. "You are not of your father Tyrannosaur, who brought to this world the fire of wisdom and discretion. You are the embodiment of living evil, an agent of the Abyss dwelling in flesh of the material world. Gengar, for the sins of rape and murder that run amuck against my personal loved ones, it brings me no greater pleasure than to dispel you back to the eternal darkness you came from," Tuskfather announces, raising his tusk high in the air above his vulnerable target.

Gengar grins. My heart drops. "Kill him," Gengar growls. My head swivels entirely too late to stop what has been set in motion long before my acquaintance with the Laxodontans. I take a half step forward as Smallear rushes his brother, the other tusk held like a spear in his tightly clenched hands. An exacerbated shout of anger leaves Smallear's mouth as his weapon plunges into its target. The tusk sufficiently rips clean through the small of Tuskfather's back and out through his bloated belly. Blood spurts on Gengar's enthused face as the ivory tip emerges on the frontside.

Tuskfather gasps. Drops the tusk that had Gengar's death written on its tip. Subsequently drops to his knees. Smallear bends over and whispers in his brother's large, quivering ear, "At long last, brother, I have killed the tremendous shadow that looms over me. How is it that you declare someone's fall from grace? Ah yes, I hereby dispel you to your forefather Mastodon, may he have sympathy when judging your pathetic soul." All traces of primitive accent have faded, his weak vocabulary structure nothing more than a façade the entire time. Smallear bends over and picks up the second tusk, thrusting it through Tuskfather's back precisely where his heart rests. Tuskfather grunts, unable to respond, a world of pain subsuming his figure as he keels over.

In an instant, my plans are foiled. This is the one variable I could have never planned for. An unpredictable, hidden alliance between Gengar and Smallear.

The same one that probably revealed the Laxodontans' whereabouts in the Gryfaun Forest, allowing the Gorgons to hunt them ruthlessly when they were most
unaware. It was Smallear this entire time. He is the one who precipitated war
between the two nations, all so he could see the downfall of his brother. The
weasely informant who sold his people into bondage for the profits of power.

Gengar mercilessly thrashes the back of his head into Artimedes' gut, freeing
himself of the grip that holds him down. Artimedes doubles over in pain while
Gengar rises, patting Smallear on the shoulder. "You have done well, soldier," he
says in New English, speaking it as if it is his primary language. He understood
everything we've said leading up to this moment. A bilingual Dæmon. *Who is
this man, Lilith? Have I underestimated my enemy?*

"The files in Deus Ex Machina's databank doesn't mention his relevancy a
single time," Lilith replies. "He's had no assistance from our creator. He is an
anomaly, risen to power based on his own agency."

Gengar kneels beside Tuskfather, a faint sign of life in his shallow breaths. He
barely clings to life. Gengar slaps his face, addressing him in New English with
ease, "When are they coming, you oaf! What did you tell the Gryfaun? How far
away are they?" Gengar slaps him twice more as Tuskfather's eyes roll back in his
head.

"You're... too... late... They come... And they do not come... to make peace,"
Tuskfather smiles, closing his eyes. Gengar raises his hand in anger, preparing to
strike the Laxodontan in vain, then grits his teeth, squeezes his eyes shut, takes a
deep breath, and forgives the transgression. The reptile realizes the stupidity in
punching a corpse in anger.

*He knows, Lilith. Somehow, this psychopathic Gorgon knows about Tuskfather's
origin. And without help from divine observation, he knows what comes next.*

"He has duped us both, I'm afraid," Lilith whispers. "Within minutes he has
destroyed our plan. He has instilled chaos and uncertainty in the Laxodontan
minds. He has the power to take back the Gorgons. Form a union with the
Tuskers as we planned to do. Recruit Tuskfather's coming army by force. This
is no human, Lucifer. This is a genius."

I stare at Gengar as he turns to face Smallear once more. "The Tuskers are yours to command, as promised in our agreement. You will be my General. Should you fail to maintain control of your people and execute my orders flawlessly, I will find another who can get the job done."

Smallear bends a knee before his master. "My Lord, I won't fail you."

"Good," he replies. "Then dispose of this fake god, Ouroboros." Gengar eyes me, continuing, "He has already gotten in my way enough. Squish the pest, then hang him for the Tuskers and Gorgons to see what happens when a god defies a devil."

Without a second to spare, Gengar looks away from me. He doesn't view me as a threat. I am only a mere inconvenience to him. Nothing more. He has no idea who I am. What I've been through. What comes to shatter his newly forged empire. If he thinks my arrival has been a thorn in his side, what will he think when the Angel of Life arrives with the armies of Hyperion?

Surely then he will see the use in allying with me. But then it will be too late. I must survive this fork in the road as I have survived all that came before—with the blood of my enemy covering my hands. He is a devil, one that is too far gone to employ for my own purposes. That leaves only one option. I must kill him.

He stalks away, Smallear calling after him, "Master, I will not fail you, but where do you go?"

Without turning, he replies, "My people have forgotten themselves tonight. Given into drunkenness thanks to Ouroboros, god of idiocy. I shall discipline them until they have sobered up, then get them ready for the coming war."

As Gengar struts away, I watch as he mindlessly steps over the fallen bodies of his comrades, some of them still convulsing from the venom, foaming at the mouth vehemently. Most of them lay lifeless already, the blood in their veins as stagnant as my feet are.

Vipress charges him, vipers from all directions redirecting their attention to their new target. "Sssoldiersss!" Gengar calls. *Shit, I should have known*, I think to myself as a second militia, previously hidden in the dark, wetland forest, rushes forward. A second wave of Gengar sympathizers, waiting this entire time for their moment to shine. He knew the outcome of tonight all along. Knew he would end up on top. So much so that he didn't even bring half of his troops to corner me against the Laxodontan prison. Told his main force to hang back in the woods and await his rise to power.

The dead Gorgons littering the ground were merely a sacrifice to rid me of suspicion. I helped him achieve his goal without him having to move a muscle. Delivered Tuskfather into his hands while preserving the Tuskers for his future devices. Killed off Bloodtusk for him, someone who wouldn't align with Gengar's plans anyway. Two rebels cannot coexist in a hierarchical power struggle. The same reason why he has ordered my death. The same reason Smallear marches toward me.

I peek over Smallear's shoulder and watch as Gengar's forces easily overwhelm Vipress, piling atop her like savages, her distant screams stifled by falling fists and hissing howls. Her pheromones dissipate. The vipers scatter in all directions. Snakes are efficient assassins when they have the element of surprise, but they don't have the means to overcome the calvary.

Gengar walks carefree from the scene like an overlord relishing his supreme majesty. He feels no remorse at the sight of death. No emotion at the loss of those who gave themselves on his behalf.

We are a different breed, him and I, I reflect, staring at his nonchalant attitude as he passes by the dogpile that defiles Vipress, unfazed by its savagery. I have killed all these years because MachineMind necessitated it. Controlled my actions. Suppressed my emotions. Erased my memories to erase the trauma. But this is a man who would gladly do all I have done without the assistance of MachineMind to aid his conscience. His conscience is black as an abyss, empty as a void. Yet his ambition is a Solar Eclipse. He seeks to engulf the earth in a darkness that parallels the one that resides within him.

Now I know my enemy. It is kill or be killed, and he must be the one who dies if I'm to unite the Dæmonic tribes. Gengar fades from view, and I'm left to survive, alone as always. Artimedes rises, sprinting away from me to fight those who beat his mistress. One against a dozen. A fight he will lose. But love knows no rationality. Fate holds his soul in the balance. I can't afford to concern myself over his safety. Over Vipress's dastardly downfall. Any concern will be for naught if I am killed.

Fight to live another day. I snap into action faster than Smallear has time to register. His look of pompous superiority barely has time to fade as I rip the tusk from Tuskfather's lower back, spin, and thrust it toward Smallear's belly. If he were as fat as his brother, I would have impaled him too. But he has relied on his speed and reaction skills to make it in life thus far, so he manages to slap the strike aside with a strained parry.

The tusk nearly flies from my hand. I hold on to it, regrettably. The powerful deflection sends vibrations up my arm. He may be a runt compared to the rest of his race, but Smallear is still superior to me when it comes to strength. But there are many ways to take down a bigger opponent, and hand-to-hand combat is something I have two thousand years of experience in.

I strike half-heartedly, baiting him to catch the tusk. He grabs it instinctively, almost as if I had verbally asked him to hold it for me. This occupies his hands while I release the broken tusk and grab hold of one attached to his face. He doesn't like this. Like a bull who's been mounted, his head swings violently to free his tusk of my grasp. Exactly what I wanted.

I use the momentum of the swing to hoist myself over his shoulder, twisting my body in the air to land on his back, wrapping my nimble arms around his throat, squeezing tight to choke him. My arms are entirely too small to achieve such a goal, but to defend against the attack he raises his hands to rip mine free. As suspected, he forgets to let go of Tuskfather's ivory before trying to pry my arms free of his neck.

I steal it from his distracted hands, reaching around his head to do so. I let my weight fall, using the tusk to catch my weight as it locks in the notch above his trachea. I hear a desperate gag as my suspended weight around his neck catches him off guard. Smallear's oversized fingers try to dig beneath the tusk which chokes him but I ensure the pressure is too intense for him to get a finger beneath it.

I get my feet under me, planting them in the small of his back, then climb up his back like it's a mountainside until my feet plant firmly on his shoulder blades. The perfect position for me to deadlift the tusk into his neck with all my strength. A stifled gasp tries to leave his frame at the increasing pressure. He claws at the tusk with swollen fingers, incapable of freeing himself. I strain to maintain the current level of pressure, but it's sufficient motivation to know that if I give up then my death will follow. Veins bulge from my neck at the effort. I watch them rise to the surface of my pale arms, vascular snakes pulsing with the output of energy required to choke a humanoid elephant to death.

I feel Smallear's body sway. My heart drops. He is getting desperate, his vision most likely closing slowly around the margins. Now is when he will do anything to put an end to me. And he does. I grit my teeth and squeeze my eyes as he falls to his back, attempting to shake me free from the momentum of the fall. A bad decision on his part. Mid fall I wrap the backside of my knees around each side of the tusk, my pelvis squeezed tight against the back of his head.

As we crash violently against the ground, I solidify my grip, squeezing my legs tight and rotating my pelvis forward, pushing his head at an angle that cuts the circulation of blood even further. In a few short moments he will be incapacitated. He flails his body in vain. Thrashing only makes him fade from consciousness faster.

My body is constricted in every way possible by the time his body goes completely limp. I immediately release the choke hold, shaking from the effort it required to put a giant to forcible sleep. I roll away from his decommissioned body, rising to take census of what's left. I lock eyes with the uncomfortable gaze of several hundred motionless Laxodontans, each of them completely unsure of what to do. Tonight has not gone as anyone planned. Anyone except Gengar, that is.

If my plan had gone accordingly, the Tuskers and Gorgons would be united by divine decree. Vipress and Tuskfather would be my Generals, and I would have a subservient populace capable of being shaped into a dangerous fighting force. Now I'm left with little. The Laxodontans are a confused people, and those who choose to follow me will only do so out of respite from their defeated state. The Gorgons will follow Gengar. They will have little choice. His gang of thugs will demand it, and any that refuse will be met with an unfortunate end.

And worse, the forces that were coming to aid Tuskfather will still come, unsure of who to follow because of his demise. The ace he held up his sleeve this entire time rendered useless. I only knew of it because of Deus Ex Machina's report on him, but now the information is worthless. When they come, my words won't be able to stop them from waging war against the Gorgons. They will hold the same view as Tuskfather. They will seek to blot out the entire intolerant race of Gorgons, unable to see that there are only a few bad apples among them that need to be eliminated.

I look at the Tuskers standing before me and scan their faces. A wide array of emotions possess them. Defeat and hope. Struggle and perseverance. Failure and the means to succeed. Seeds in the midst of drought. Saplings after wildfire. I look at them and see potential. I look at them and see the ability to overcome. *This plan can be salvaged*, I realize as I look at their willing faces. *If anyone can come together united it is the Laxodontans*. There is still hope to overcome our circumstances. We must fight like our future depends on it. Because it does.

"Laxodontans, I am Ouroboros, the creator of all things good in this universe," I begin, knowing that this speech must move them to action. The next twenty-four hours will decide our fate, so I will cut straight to the point. "The Abyss has infiltrated my creation. If you wish to fight back and save this world, you must listen closely..."

CHAPTER TWO

"Wake up, reprobate," I assert, slapping the elephant on the cheek until his eyes roll open reluctantly. Smallear isn't happy to see me. Even less happy to be tied up so thoroughly. He tests out the restraints, seeing what amount of squirming he can get away with, then frowns when he discovers his range of motion to be little.

"History doesn't fare well with those who betray the gods," I begin, pacing back and forth in front of him, a close circle of Tusker guards behind me. "And you, my friend, are on thin ice."

I look at him. He is no coward. He shows no remorse for his actions. His eyes are vacant. Not in the way Gengar's are vacant; Smallear is no psychopath. No, where Gengar's eyes are empty from lack of emotion, Smallear's eyes are empty from lack of purpose. Yet all the same, he is a finely-tuned soldier. Give a soldier without purpose what they search for, and they will do nearly anything for you.

"I must admit, your treachery caught me by surprise. I got so caught up in satisfying the Godkiller Chronicles and usurping the Gorgonic and Laxodontan leadership, I barely noticed your existence. A mistake which, thanks to your superb efforts, I won't make again. You are more dangerous than I judged you for, Smallear." I search his face for any semblance of emotion. Nothing.

Flattery will not work on him, so I must readjust my rhetoric. Everyone has something they want to hear. Something that will gain their trust. You just have to know the right words. "Have you ever heard the Parable of the Prisoner Peasant?" He doesn't bother looking in my direction, yet I carry on anyway.

"It is the story of a man who was oppressed by his society," I begin, improvising the parable on the fly. "Enraged by the caste system he was born into, he cursed the gods and took matters into his own hands. He had nothing to lose. He was beyond poor. Starved daily. Could barely afford to breathe, let alone afford the taxes imposed on him. He could no longer live in a system where those who were born rich profited from the poverty-stricken majority. He hadn't asked to be born a peasant. Fate had been unkind to him.

"A friend of his, one of similar upbringing, devised a plan to repay the ruling class for their wicked ways. He convinced our main character to help him devise a plan to assassinate the royal king, even recruit a few co-conspirators. Together, they worked day and night to see this plan to fruition. They dedicated every waking moment to it, not caring whether they lived to see the results of its success. But when the day came for him to kill the king, early that morning a knock came on his door. It was the Imperial Guard, arrived to arrest him for tax evasion. Yes, he had gotten so fixated on killing the king that he had forgotten his duties as a citizen.

"They took him away and threw him in the dungeons where he never saw the light of day again. Yet the rebellion went on without him, carried out by his close confidante. Then, early one morning, just as the soldiers switched posts, the attack began. He had the perfect view of it from his barred windows. The peasants arose from the lower echelon of the city, lighting anything and everything that could catch flame. From the bars of his window, he was forced to watch as the slave citizens burned the city down, vastly outnumbering the king's soldiers and guards.

"They overwhelmed the elites, and his close friend usurped the king. The prisoner peasant was greatly excited to hear the outcome of the war, sure that his friend would come to release him from bondage. But the society stayed the same, and the new king never came to provide reprieve. You see, the confidante was never really the peasant's friend. He merely used our tragic hero as a means to an end, then threw him to the side the moment he lost value. There he remained in the dungeons for the rest of his life, until the dark, damp cellar stripped him of his sanity and rotted his health to the brink of death."

I do my best to layer the improvised parable with themes that will resonate with Smallear, but I can tell the words have little effect on him. It is his story. He is the peasant prisoner, inflicted by his inferior genetics in a society where it's a curse to be born with a defect. Rebellion planned and executed to perfection, only to be cast aside by Gengar, the lizard he thought he could trust. Or bound to be once it's revealed he is compromised. He simply wanted to matter, and his failure means he will rot until his unfortunate end brings death. But there's a difference between his situation and that of the parable.

Unlike the peasant prisoner, I am offering him a way out of imprisonment.

It's his choice on whether or not he chooses to accept it.

I look at him, waiting for the faintest sign of interest. Nothing. He doesn't resonate, too bored with the details to relate. I check inspiration off my list of rhetorical devices that can be used to sway him to my agenda. On to the next one.

"But I digress. I underestimated you, Smallear. Hardly noticed you standing in your brother's shadow." His eyes glower in my direction. That's more like it. Not flattery. Not inspiration. Envy. Envy is his motivator. More specifically, envy directed toward his brother. Rage at the comparisons drawn between him and his superior kin, the constant reminder that he doesn't measure up physically. This is valuable information. Now I know what makes him get out of bed in the morning. Now I can exploit him.

"It's a shame, a Tusker of your genius doomed to be forever outcast because of inferior genetics while your brother reigns supreme. What was it Tuskfather told me? I believe his words were, what you lack in ear he makes up for in tusk. Funny. Said he stole all the nutrients in the womb from you, but that you love him all the same. I guess I wasn't the only one who misjudged your intentions." I grin while he scowls.

I've effectively hit the insecurities which have fueled his motivation long since birth. His entire life has been a waiting game, the end result being the downfall of his brother. I'm not surprised to see that after accomplishing such a mundane goal, he is still left feeling empty. For his treachery, his people will never accept him, yet neither will the Gorgons. He is an outcast with nowhere to go. He would be better off sojourning foreign lands, never showing his face again to either race involved in this war.

"I know about you and your brother's upbringing," I announce. This, too, causes slight curiosity to rise in him. His small ears lift ever so slightly at the prospect of my tell-all. "And I know what's coming, due to your brother's extended connections, as I'm sure you're aware of yourself. Gengar knows, so that makes three of us. Surely you're not so ignorant to believe the Gorgons will survive such a bloodbath. They will not survive the storm of arrows that brews on the horizon.

"The way I see it, you have three options. First, you can kill yourself. Normally I would execute you myself, but traitors aren't deserving of honorable death. Second, you can run away. Gengar won't trust you once I brand you with the mark of Ouroboros, which means you will only find life in the most desperate valleys of this earth. And third, the wisest decision of the three, if I'm so inclined to add, you may join me, and your sins will be forgiven."

His trunk inhales deeply, conjuring up several years' worth of phlegm and mucus, then spits it at my feet, missing only by inches. Fine by me, at least I'm getting a response out of him now. "You would use me like you used my brother. Manipulate me until my body is broken and bleeding. My wellbeing is your last priority, so why should I join you?" he asks incredulously.

"You aren't motivated by the prospect of safety and secured wellbeing, Smallear, so don't act like you are now," I assert, trying to see through the charade he plays with me. "You wouldn't have betrayed your brother if self-preservation was your end goal. You did it because you have long felt a deep compulsion to prove yourself. A drive to prove your insecurities wrong. Come hell or high water, you want to prove those who have scorned you wrong. I am one who can help you do that. I extend my hand to offer a second chance. Endless opportunity to carve yourself in history as a legend. One who defied his genetics.

"I do not offer you power. Once Gengar is eliminated, it will be I who reclaims control of the Gorgons. I have no loyalty to extend to you. You've destroyed any chance of earning my trust the moment you turned against your own flesh and blood. I offer no comforts. Following me will only lead to pain and torment. But the path I walk is paved with opportunities where you can prove yourself. Honor and vengeance, things I believe you subscribe to."

I have peaked his interest. The level of contempt in his eyes has lowered ever so slightly. Enough for his demeanor to change notably. "I will let you in on a truth, Smallear, because you are too smart to lie to. An army comes, one that is not of the world you were brought up in. A heavenly army, to speak in terms of the supernatural. And they are capable of things your brain can't comprehend. Soldiers who feel no pain. Kill without hesitation. And their target is you and me.

"They hunt us because of our genes. Believe we are corrupted to the core and need to be killed. I see the disbelief in your eyes. But I tell you the truth. The Centaurs are the last of our worries." His face pales at the mention of the Centaurs. Mentioning the race reveals my hand, but it wins over the smallest fraction of his trust. Draws his curiosity. If I know about the Centaurs, then how much more could I possibly know, he wonders.

"Even the Centaurs cannot stand before the might of the coming threat. It comes to eradicate all races. None are exempt from the wrath of these celestial beings. The Abyss comes to slay all that has life." I catch myself. I'm losing his interest. He doesn't believe in the religion of his ancestors. I should have known before that framing it in such a primeval way would lose his attention. Doing so is an insult to his intelligence. He doesn't believe I'm Ouroboros, that there was ever some floating serpent in the sky from which this planet came from. The concept of the Abyss and the war between good and evil isn't real to him.

He operates on fact alone. Trying to motivate him on the premise of some fabled enemy won't work. I haven't lost him yet. I can still salvage this.

"You don't believe me. I see it in your eyes. That's fine, you're entitled to your own opinion. But don't do so fully until you've given me a chance to prove myself as I offer for you to do in return. You may be ingenious when compared to the rest of your race, but you are ignorant in many ways, Smallear, of that I am sure.

You may have stolen the brains from your brother in the womb, but intelligence can only take you so far in this world. This is the perfect example.

"You masterfully schemed to bring down your brother. You not only did it once, allying yourself with the Gorgons to bring about his demise, but twice. My arrival was unexpected for you, and when your brother was moved to redeem himself at my appearance, once again you instantly devoted yourself to ensuring he couldn't rise to his former state. Wrote out his failure behind his back. You've displayed your ability to connive mischief that produces your desired ends, yet here you are, prisoner to one who holds your life in his hand."

"If you expect me to believe you're actually some serpent king reincarnated who will save us all from some existential darkness, you'd be better off to kill me now. I'm not sympathetic to plans motivated by religious lunacy," Smallear combats. Quite the smart cookie. He may despise his brother, but he is similar to Tuskfather in so many ways. If only he could have forgiven, the two would have been an unstoppable duo together.

"Then let me put it to you bluntly, without the religiosity and far-fetched, idiosyncratic subjectivity. If you want to play the role of the jaded scholar, I will rephrase it secularly. Whether you want to believe it or not, there is an army coming that will kill us all. You, me, every last fucking soul that inhabits this earth. There will be no outsmarting them. No writing them off as hallucinogenic lunacy. No arguing the means of their existence. By the time you see them falling from the sky with death in their hands, then you will believe. But by then, it will already be too late.

"So I implore you to be proactive, despite your atheistic nature. I don't care if you don't believe I'm Ouroboros. I don't need you to worship me to be of use. All I need is the Gorgons, and I need them before the Centaurs come. I need Gengar dead, more specifically, and for that, you can be of great assistance." I've laid it out for him plain and simple, stripped of any unnecessary details. Now I sit and wait as he stirs comfortably in his seat.

"Gengar dead? Now you speak my language. I have just the plan for that," he announces, his bushy eyebrows furrowing themselves in a sinister arch.

CHAPTER THREE

"Sir, come you must. Important you see this," a Tusker woman announces unintelligibly, interrupting at just the right time. Smallear and I have just wrapped up our conversation. We will march immediately, but first I must debrief the Laxodontan nation of my plan. "Cut him free, but keep a close eye on him. He isn't to leave your sight, understood?" I command the nearest Tusker, then turn to the one who calls for my attention.

"What is it?" I ask.

"Follow me," she whispers. She takes off running, so I follow suit. Such endeavors don't come as easy as they used to. My body is a decomposing, wretched ghost of what it once was. My legs struggle to keep up with her gigantic stride. My lungs burn to match her endurance. A single step for her is three strides for me.

I still hurt from the extended effects of the venom and the aches incurred from respirocyte withdrawal. My organs fight their imminent shut down. I am a zombie, walking in a dying body. Corrupt flesh sagging more with each day. How much longer do I have? Weeks? Days? Hours?

No wonder humanity is so depraved. The pains of the flesh are exhausting. Each wound another taxation on the brain. Each limp, a reminder of mortality. And I'm long past limping. I drag myself to and fro, miserable to still have breath in my lungs.

The road ahead of me suddenly feels far too long to carry on any further. Yet my feet won't stop. If there is any machine part of me left, it's the part that's wired to not quit. Cybernetic resilience that won't die until my body does.

I look up, familiar with the place the Tusker leads me to. Every urge in my body begs me to bend over and huff and puff until the fatigue in my muscles subsides. But I am surrounded by Tuskers, and they believe me to be a god. Gods don't appear weak before mortals, so I'm forced to recover with as little revealing of my inner turmoil as possible.

I stand up straight, puff my chest out, then roll my shoulders back. The posture of a leader who is in control. Any one of these beasts could end my life just by stomping on me. I can't let their elevated status of me slip away.

I take in my surroundings. An entire legion of the surviving Tuskers remains gathered here, outside Tuskfather's old tent. They are silent, mourning the loss of their fearless leader. They sway in the humid breeze that sticks to my skin and traps perspiration.

The unidentified messenger who retrieved me signals for me to approach the tent flaps. I follow her in, letting the entrance fall behind me so those on the outside remain ignorant to what rests within.

There, sprawled out on the same makeshift cot I once relied on for recovery, rests Tuskfather, his eyes open, his chest heaving small, shallow breaths. "Leave us," he commands. The small entourage of Laxodontan medics scramble out of the tent with the female messenger close at their heels.

"You're quite a sight for sore eyes," I revel. It's hard to admit to myself, but I actually feel joy in seeing my friend alive.

"I'm too stubborn to die," he whispers, both pain and joy in his voice.

"I want to apologize for—"

"No need, friend of mine. She explained everything," he says, pointing to the other side of the tent. I look, instantly feeling naive for not observing my surroundings better. There, in the corner of the tent where the light of the fire doesn't reach, lurks Vipress in the shadows. Her slitted, yellow eyes open. My heart jumps. She is awake. I hadn't expected to see her back in action for several more days.

After letting the Laxodontans loose on her victimizers, she was left in a bloodied and broken coma. Her and Artimedes both, her failed lover beaten unconscious. If it wasn't for the Laxodontans, he would have most likely been Gorgon fodder.

I ordered for Vipress to be taken away by the Laxodontan medics, but I had no idea she would make such a swift recovery. I suppose it isn't only Tuskfather who is too stubborn to die.

"Vipresssssss, it'sss good to sssee you alive. I am sssorry for—"

"Sssave your pity for thossse who can't go on without it. I don't need your sssympathiesss. I will repay thossse who are indebted to me, that you can be sssure of." She stares at me with cold, vacant eyes. Serpent eyes. She resorts to her reptilian nature as a defensive coping mechanism. Doesn't let her inner humanity process what's happened to her, knowing that it can't handle the overdose of pain. But there's nothing I can do for her at this point, and I admire her level of determination, so I decide inwardly to not bring it up again.

"And how is it you two communicated?" I ask Tuskfather.

"She showed me. Acted it out. You should have seen it, it was quite hysterical to see the serpent-witch enacting her death and resurrection. She is quite the embellished actor. She supports your claims. I called you here to let you know you still have my loyalty," Tuskfather whispers. Such a statement is somewhat comical. He is a mummy, his body wrapped in so many bandages and slathered with herbal remedies meant to revitalize his strength. I may have his loyalty, but it's his brute strength and fighting abilities I need. This rendition of him is useless when it comes to winning wars.

"I appreciate your friendship, but you cannot do much in your current state. You must stay here and rest. Avoid any further straining of your heart."

"Well, that's the funny thing," he replies quickly, almost as if he anticipated my response. "The little shit missed my heart by a measly inch. I'm going to make a full recovery, and much faster than you'd likely expect. Us Laxodontans bounce back faster than you humans do. Made from a tougher stock, we are. Need an update on where we stand though. Nobody around here seems to possess a single useful strand of information. You keeping my people out of the loop, Ouroboros?"

"I must be frank in admitting your survival is unexpected. Asss isss yoursss, Vipresssss. I wasssn't expecting to sssee you back ssso sssoon. Our next attack isss already planned. We march tonight. Tuskfather, we march tonight, and you can't partake in the festivities," I say, switching back and forth between New English and Ssserphentyne to inform them succinctly.

"And why the hell can't I?" Tuskfather growls.

"Because the plan is contingent on your brother's participation. The same brother who needs to believe you are dead to ensure his participation."

Tuskfather frowns. Then smiles. "Are you thinking what I'm thinking?" he asks, smirking uncontrollably.

"Depends, are you thinking about remaining here until the cavalry arrives?" I ask.

"You bet your bottom dollar that's what I'm thinking."

"And Vipress? Would you like me to take her away?"

"Why would you ever do such a thing? I am beginning to grow fond of her acting skills. I'd like her to be here when the Centaurs arrive. She can be an ambassador for her breed, show them the Gorgons aren't nearly so cold-blooded as they've been led to believe."

"Perfect. Lay low. Ensure that news of your resurrection spreads nowhere. I will return to you on the morrow, hopefully with the power of the Gorgon nation under my command," I announce, turning to leave.

"One more thing, Ouroboros! Tread carefully around my brother, my Lord. Takes after my mother, that one does. Only out to serve himself. Raised by the Centaurs, I may have been. But he was raised by something much more sinister."

"Raised by your mother. Don't worry, I already know."

"Of course you do, omniscient god. Just don't forget that he may be Tusker on the outside like me, but we were not raised in this culture. Father placed me in an environment that brought out the more admirable qualities of life. Smallear was not nearly as lucky. I forgive him for his attempt on my life. Misled, he is. But still, it's best if you don't trust a narcissist dressed in Laxodontan skin."

"Noted," I rely. *With any luck, and should plans go accordingly, Smallear will be dead by the time the sun sets.*

"Farewell, Ouroboros. I shall see you in the morn. And should those who raised me come in your absence, I will calm their spirits. Ready them for the war against the Abyss. Should you not come back to us by the time the sun rises, every Gorgon in that camp becomes our target," Tuskfather hints.

I stride toward the exit and he calls one last thing, "And Ouroboros! Should you find a way to preserve Gengar's life, I would still be very much appreciative to be the one who gets to kill him."

"I was already planning on it, friend," I call over my shoulder as the tent flaps close behind me. I can picture the imaginary, trademark grin that rises on his face. The sun finally rises on the horizon from the long night of treachery. Raises on a new day. A fresh start. New opportunities for betrayal lie ahead.

Why must us humans do such ugly deeds on such beautiful days?

Do you think this plan will work?

"Crazier things have happened in this world," Lilith replies.

I thought robots were the ones who were supposed to be obsessed with the odds of plans failing. Why am I the only one that feels worried things won't work out well?

"Because things will either work out, or they won't. The odds cannot be trusted. The odds of us making it this far—banished from Hyperion, hunted by the Seraph Mikhaelion, fallen from the sky, crashed like a comet, prisoner to the Gorgons, bitten by a Vermillion Viper, uplifted by the Laxodontans and Gorgons both, revered by most as a god. Then betrayed by both species in the same moment. The allies we've worked so hard to gain, defeated. Odds could not have predicted this pathway, as they will never begin to accurately depict our future. One who concerns themselves with the odds negates fate to run its course."

Fate? Fate is nothing but a form of social control. A crutch for the weak. Opium for the masses.

"And yet you yourself can't escape its grasp. How embarrassing," Lilith quips. Somehow she manages to keep me in check better than any human ever could.

CHAPTER FOUR

PIRATED DOCUMENTS FROM DEUS EX MACHINA'S DATA-BANK...
TRANSLATED BY BABEL'S CHIMERA FROM BINARY CODE...
"AN EXCERPT FROM *LAXODONTANS: A BRIEF HISTORY*, WRITTEN BY DEUS EX MACHINA"...

It is the fourth month of the fifth year of King Gutbloat's reign, and the entertainment only increases as I watch the barbaric fool precipitate his own doom. As the Laxodontans are a peaceful nation, they instantly drew my eye years ago. Such a people is the perfect fertilizer to sow discord.

And so, with minimal effort, I have managed to put my hand in their affairs and meddle with their foreign relationships without their knowing, slipping in false agents whenever I can—robotic Laxodontans too life-like to draw attention. I play with their lives like a cruel child with toys, killing them off here and there as if they were lifeless objects.

The Dæmonic tribes are my silent muse. Ants under my foot which I selectively kill. Taking some and placing them in the web of a spider, watching them squirm and thrash against the inescapable trap. Placing them under the heat of a magnifying glass in the midday sun, watching them squeal as they burn alive. And the incessant reprobates have no clue why their circumstances are so awful. Stupid dolts.

Such is their punishment. Though it has been a thousand years, the Dæmonic Rebellion is still fresh in my processors. Seeing what they were capable of then only justifies my cruel treatment of them now.

Never again will I allow them to become a threat to my person.

And so watching the many blunders of King Gutbloat as his world collapses around him only brings me joy. The Laxodontans are long due for a trial, considering the role they played during the Dæmonic Rebellion. No other species I created brought about destruction like them. And so I will pay them back. Slowly. With a properly constructed narrative.

To get to this point has taken many years of careful crafting, yet I won't see the fruition of my efforts until the next epoch of Laxodontan leadership. Many years it has taken me to bring the Laxodontans to the brink of war with the Centaurian people. Each race is naturally inclined to peace, but I will tear their peace to pieces. When the time comes, I will metaphorically pat myself on the back for single-handedly bringing them to the point of war.

But I'm not ready for them to fight. The rivalry isn't yet developed for my taste. I like my meat slow-roasted, metaphorically speaking. Roasted in a slow cooker until the meat is so tender it falls off the ribs. Then I will be able to taste the char boil that is reminiscent of many hours of labor. Much more satisfying than a slab of beef seared on each side for a few minutes.

And what joy it brought to my inner wiring to see the King's witch of a wife deliver twins! The same wife I forced him into union with, the dreaded Amygdala, a repulsive wench. What sorrows Gutbloat experienced when the peace of his nation rested on his marriage commencement with her. An honorable man, forced to marry such a slob to save his people from civil war.

And now the Centaurs encroach upon Gutbloat's lands, threatening bloodshed over nothing more than false rumors and weak leadership. Hythion, the elected equestrian leadership, will not leave without payment for the death of his son, Thymen. The death which he convincingly believes was murder linked to none other than the Laxodontan people. All lies, of course, spread by the robotic agent cleverly named Sykofant.

The same agent that was Thymen's actual murderer. The same agent which will instruct Hythion to request one of Gutbloat's sons once he receives the news that there were twins born to him. Son for son, the price of peace.

Gutbloat will do everything to avoid paying such a costly fee to preserve peace, but he will ultimately cave. When forced to weigh the lives of many against the life of a single son, he will relent, as honorable men do. Such a joke, honor is. An evolutionary instinct only a fraction of the human race developed, yet they always assume others operate on such premises as well. It's why honorable men are always surprised when they feel a knife pressed against their back. Honor is nothing more than a jape to those who don't possess it. An attitude my machine learning understands yet rejects.

After all, mechanical processes must reject that which is useless.

And so I will watch as Gutbloat gives up one of his sons, the other cursed by a coddled life under Amygdala, turned into a sniveling brat under her care, groomed for leadership. Then, when he is ripe to take the throne of the Laxodontans, I will send Gutbloat's forsaken son to claim what he believes is rightfully his. And at his heels will be the support of the entire Centaurian people.

The perfect storm. The Laxodontans won't know what to do. On the one hand, they won't want to uplift a king who is so repulsive. Yet they must, if they are to claim they want to preserve their culture. But the foreign king will be favorable in every way, raised in the many admirable traits of the Centaurs. It will cause confusion amongst themselves, and confusion leads to division. War with each other. War against the horse people.

So many delicious options to create discord, it almost makes me wish I had created more Dæmonic tribes to begin with. Oh well, I will effectively disrupt those that already exist...

CHAPTER FIVE

G utbloat fades from life with each passing day. The poison his cunning wife slipped into his ale is slow releasing. It will make it look like he has died from some bizarre stomach disease. He cries out in his sleep, his fever so high it induces delirium. Soon he will be dead. And there Smallear will wait, his mother's son, raised in her shadow. Marinated in her malignant melodrama. The exact definition of what an unsuitable king should look like, to Gutbloat's chagrin.

I love it. Tearing peace to pieces. Watching from my Eye of Providence, enjoying the splendor of dramatic mortals. Soon Tuskfather will hear of his father's death, and the brother Smallear has forgotten will lay claim to the throne. I couldn't have asked for a more suitable opponent either. Tuskfather, rightfully named so. All brawn, subscribed to the same honor his father so deeply believes in. Tuskfather is everything humans once wished their children to be. Charming. Strong. Intelligent. Resilient. Brave.

Smallear is his antithesis, though you wouldn't know it at surface level. Cunning. Deceitful. Weak. Poisonous. A black rose who's painted itself red. The type to refuse a fight because he knows he can overcome you in more wicked ways. He is innocent on the surface, as his mother taught him to be. But it is the innocent in this world that later expose the deeds they've done in the dark.

I look forward to seeing the two collide. A war of brawn and brain. A war so vicious that Tuskfather likely won't even know he is fighting until it's too late. I know the climax will be well worth the wait...

CHAPTER SIX

"Smallear, it's time," I assert, simultaneously wondering what the odds of this working are. Any attempt at planning I've made has been foiled thus far, so I've done away with my complicated schemes. The new plan is relatively simple. I've put myself in Gengar's mind. He left us here to duke things out, not really caring what the end results were. All he wanted was the Gorgons, and so that is where we must go to eliminate him.

To gain entrance into such hostile lands, I will have to play dead. Although there will surely be Ouroboros sympathizers among the populace, Gengar won't let my living body anywhere close to the Gorgon camps. He will smell my scent on the air from a mile away.

Which is why I'll play dead and let Smallear drag me through the front door with the sparse Laxodontan population close behind. There's no reason for Gengar to suspect anything. It's only been a few hours since Smallear 'defeated' me in battle and rallied his people. My dead body will be his ticket into the Gorgon camps. If Smallar can sell the lie well enough, Gengar won't suspect anything.

The only problem I fear we'll run into is Gengar's lack of loyalty extended to his former ally. He is a psychopath. Completely unpredictable. In a single instant he can choose to turn on Smallear, and if he decides to do so there will be little stopping him from slaughtering the entire Laxodontan race. That's why we must act fast once we enter his presence. I assume Gengar will want to examine my body, and when he does, that's when I'll end his life.

The rest of the plan will manifest itself. I will rally the Gorgons back to my cause, their loyalty shifting from Vipress to me to Gengar, then back to me. Their allegiance lies with whoever is strong enough to earn it. They will not follow blind leadership.

I walk up to Smallear, who fondles a female Laxodontan while she casually covers his head with fresh stripes of warpaint, blood red to inspire intimidation. It's hard to be intimidated by such an underwhelming Tusker though, when even females of the culture are considerably bigger than he.

He shoves the unashamedly naked woman aside and she briskly walks away in silent retreat, a look of masked repulsion on her face. "Then let's get on with it, I've retribution to claim," he grumbles, like someone who's just been greatly wronged.

"Retribution? For what?" I ask.

"You know, when I conspired with Gengar and Vipress against my oaf of a brother, we came to agreed upon terms. Raping and killing my brother's wife and daughter were not a part of the deal. I was saving them for myself," he adds, an incestuous grin on his face that arouses me to instant anger. He's trying to provoke me. Rowel me up to attack him so he can back out of this plan. Not going to happen.

He is just trying to step over every ethical boundary I have. Make me regret teaming up with a villain. I force myself to push the anger to the side, making a mental note of what he's said. I'll make him pay for it later, that I can be sure of. For now, I need him to get to Gengar, so I must remain emotionless to his vulgar comment.

I am a righteous man in the presence of something much more wicked than myself. I will let him continue in his erroneous ways, for his time is short.

"The day wears thin. We must get going. Have you informed your people of the plan?"

"Of course I have. What kind of leader do you take me for? When I gain a nation, I don't fumble it into the hands of my enemy like you. I squeeze them tight, and those who refuse to obey, I squeeze tighter until their head explodes.

You mustn't ask people what they want to do. You must command it!" he screams enthusiastically. His eyes are intense, burrowing into my mind. But he can't get in my head. My inner defenses are unbreachable.

"That sounds like a dictatorship," I reply, unamused with where this conversation carries.

"That's exactly what it is," he boasts, proud of himself. "This is a dictatorship, not a democracy. And I am its sentient tyrant."

"History isn't kind to humans who pretend they're gods."

"Then it seems history won't be kind to either of us," he chuckles, thinking that he speaks over my head. It was a good comeback, for it to come from such an ignorant mouth. A man like this will never believe I am a god, but I no longer care. I have come to save these people, but I can't save those who can't save themselves. Smallear is nothing more than a brat, raised by his mother to believe he's the best thing since cuckadoo stew, the Laxodontan luxury.

Let him believe he is godsent. It will only make killing him easier.

"Yes, my friend. I doubt history will look favorably upon either of us," I reply monotonously.

I turn my back to him, looking at the hundred or so Laxodontans who will be accompanying us on this trip. Like me, these people have been through much in recent weeks. Their kingdom pillaged and burned. Their people enslaved. Tuskfather usurped, then killed, by someone painstakingly inferior. I have pity for them. They deserve better, and I can't guarantee them that much better will come after today. Our time runs thin, and soon Deus Ex Machina will send his Angel of Life after us.

He has been gracious to give me this much time, I must admit. But he doesn't do so because he is generous. No, Deus Ex Machina waits for me to get my ducks in a row so he can enjoy the war to come that much more. It wouldn't be fun for him to watch an uncontested genocide. He has already watched plenty of those, each one of them fulfilled by one of his Lucifer prototypes.

No, he wants this to be an entertaining fight, two opponents who can go the distance and stand toe to toe. That much can be sure after seeing all he has done to prepare the Dæmonic tribes for me.

"What that?" a Laxodontan in the distance calls.

"Gorgons!" another yells.

My head snaps in the direction of the wetlands. Smoke rises on the horizon. From the thicket of dense swamp trees emerges the lizard people, donned in armor. At the front strides Gengar. *We are too late*, I admit inwardly.

I should have known that lizard would come back to finish us off. How naive could I have been?

I lock eyes with Smallear, who now eyes me differently than before. Moments ago he looked at me as if I was an ally. That look has changed. Now, I see in dark, beady eyes the reflection of human prey.

"Smallear, I know what you're thinking," I say, backing away slowly while he steps toward me menacingly.

"Tell me, what am I thinking?" he replies with treachery on his voice.

"This doesn't change anything," I argue. "If we stand together, we can face Gengar. We only need to kill him and the Gorgons will stand down! We have to stay the course. You have to trust me on this!"

"Plans change," he replies. "And I must change with them."

The ground shakes, an earthquake on the horizon. Laxodontans shout.

"What that? Over there! We surrounded!" an unintelligent voice yells.

"Horse people! Horse people! Everybody run, it horse people!"

"The trees shake! Something in trees!"

My head spins from all the chaos. I look to the horizon opposite the wetlands, past the internment camp to the direction of the approaching army. Hooves shake the ground like crashing comets. *Centaurs*, I marvel to myself at the sight of the galloping nation. They stretch across the horizon, their numbers incalculable from this distance. *They really came*, I remark inwardly.

A bustling of shouts arise amongst the Gorgon flanks as the leaves fall from over their heads. I look toward the shaking trees that provide cover over them, their spindly boughs shaking from the weight of the leaping Gryfauns that inhabit them. The mythical animals leap from branch to branch with such grace and speed that the Gorgons have no choice but to flee the wetland forest as the attack begins.

Large projectiles drop from the trees atop their heads. Boulders and chunks of wood dense enough to shatter skulls. All the while smoke spreads. *It's the Gryfauns that burn down the forest. They are lighting the trees aflame as they advance. They're trying to flush the Gorgons from the wetlands and pin their backs to charred lands,* I walk myself through the strategy of it. It's nostalgic to see the Gryfauns giving the Gorgons a taste of their own medicine. Fighting fire with fire. Burning their homeland as compensation for the Gryfaun forest.

I love the smell of justice burning in the air. The smoke flushes the vermin lizards from the tree cover into the open. I watch Gengar do everything he can to maintain composure and project authority over his people. But mass hysteria is no easy thing to overcome, even for a manipulative psychopath.

We stand in a maelstrom of converging forces, each brought to this battlefield for different reasons. Gengar, because his life is devoid without attempting to make others feel as empty as himself. His Gorgons, because they only possess the ability to do as they're told, never questioning orders, no matter how diabolical they may seem. The Centaurs, because they come to provide support for their treasured community member, Tuskfather, the Laxodontan who won over their hearts as a child. The Laxodontans, because they have lost their identity and search in vain to find it. And their obnoxious leader, Smallear, because he was made a promise by his mother that he would one day hold the world in his palm, and now he cheats in every way possible to make that dream come true. *Smallear,* I let the name echo on the inside of my brain. *Oh shit, Smallear!* I am so caught up in the ensuing chaos that I took my eyes off my prescient enemy.

I look back just in time to see Smallear's fist on a collision course for my face. Do my best to dodge, but his knuckles still acquaint themselves with the crevice between my cheekbone and nose. Without permission, my body crumples to the ground while my head spins in an ocean of stars. Consciousness fades, and all I can do is look up to see Smallear's outline hovering over me.

"Don't worry," he chuckles. "I'll still deliver your body to Gengar as we planned. But you'll no longer need to play dead. I think he'll be much more likely to join forces with me if I actually kill you, don't you think?" I watch as his cocked back arm blots out the sun. I can feel the vibration of falling hooves in the ground beneath me. I fade from consciousness before his fist obliterates my existence.

CHAPTER SEVEN

*W*hat the hell is this?

"It would appear we have stumbled on a digital graveyard composed of all Vicien Greaves's unfleshed ideas," Deus Ex Machina replies. I don't know how to respond to such a sight. To feel awe would be nauseating, knowing that he has withheld this much information from me. But to feel anger would be vain, because it is precisely this graveyard of ideas that will save me and my fellow ArchAngels in the coming war.

These unfinished projects of his are what will give me the chance to save Winter, I think to myself. I stand at the edge of a chasm of floating, holographic files, arranged in a glowing sphere that resembles some formless, sentient god. I stand in the hollow remains of what was once my birthplace. In the remote, mountainous peninsula off the coast of Oceania, lies the origin of the ArchAngel program, where my fellow soldiers and I were born.

It's been long abandoned. *Or so I thought.*

I see now that Greaves has used this abandoned shell of hellish landscape as a backup database–one that conceals his off-the-book projects. Seems fitting. That's all this island has ever been good for. Off-the-book projects. That's what the ArchAngel program was, after all. An unethical experiment imposed on children to produce super soldiers without any government catching wind. Greaves would have never gotten approval from any business to do what he planned, so he did it in secret. And he succeeded, then used his super soldiers to enforce totalitarian control over the world.

How long has it been since I've been back here? I ask myself as I stare at the whirling, transient orb of digital information before me. The orb that holds the key to me winning this war.

I stand with the remaining ArchAngels at my back. They revel at the godlike orb's glory. Me, Aeneas, Thor, Anubis, and Samsara. I wish more than anything that Beowulf and Odysseus were here by my side. I trust my remaining brethren, but I don't share the bond with them that I did Beowulf and Odysseus.

The room is dark, and I stand at the edge of the abysmal chasm. One step forward and it is a plummet toward certain death. Behind me are my knights of the apocalypse, the ArchAngels who will fight to the death beside me to ensure we send the Nihilists and Oblivion back to whatever hell they came from.

We were created for such monumental objectives. The survival of humanity rests on our shoulders, which is no easy burden for mortal men to carry. But we can't be considered mortal men any longer. We were genetically engineered to be more than that. Put to the test our entire life, to filter out the weak. Culled so only legends remained. Returning to our birthplace is a firm reminder of that. The horrors we endured as children.

To call us mortals would be like calling Vicien Greaves a genius. He was no genius. Such a term is a vast understatement of his potential. Genius? No. He was the genius of all geniuses. A mastermind. The greatest mind humanity had ever produced. Devious. Manipulative. Cunning. A bastard, surely, but a bastard who has effectively condemned humanity to extinction.

And we ArchAngels are all that stand in the way of that happening.

We smile collectively as we draw on the hope that lies before us. This database possesses every file we need to win this war. The cloud of data is a digitized brain with every blueprint Vicien Greaves ever conceived, with the access key to make the ideas real.

These are all ideas that were too far-fetched to create under the premise of peace. He savored these blueprints for a monumental war such as this. All of them sitting around collecting dust, waiting to become actualized. Endless potential. Form without matter. And I have been given the key to give it such matter.

Deus, bridge my mind to the cloud, I command.

"At once, sir," he replies.

My body instantly feels light, and my vision becomes blurry. With the help of my inner artificial intelligence, I will be able to download this entire cloud of information in seconds. My conscience floats from my body, leaving it behind at the edge of the chasm. My soul floats into the brain-shaped light that swirls like a cumulonimbus cloud, glowing bright blue at the center of the abyss.

And then it subsumes me, absorbing me into its heavenly light, giving me the vision of a god. My brain rushes with the surge of new information. Images and words and coding flickers in front of my eyes at the speed of light, all uploading to my mind in nanoseconds. I comprehend it all. I understand every last shred of data. I feel the rush of euphoria as I make special note of certain things that pass through the portal that is my brain.

The words "Operation: Diremech" emerge with a picture of various canines covered in robotic exoskeletons. Warrior dogs meant to accompany us in the wiles of war. Vicious, savage, loyal companions.

The words "Operation: Hyperion" flash before my eyes. I see the gates of heaven. Streets of gold. A throne with a god seated upon it, the sun in the background glaring off his metallic armor so bright I can't make out who it is.

The words "Operation: Seraphim" take my breath away. Terrifying dragons fly through the sky, wreaking havoc and destruction upon ant-sized soldiers grounded far below. They fly like behemoths and leviathans through the clouds, swooping down, flicking Nihilist robots like easily defeated bugs. Electricity rages from their maws. Their mighty tails collapse buildings in a single swipe. I nearly forget how to breathe, so mesmerized by their ferocious power.

The words "Operation: Winter Phoenix" brand themselves into the surface of my brain, scalding hot. I see an image of my wife. My best friend. Scared, secluded in an underground bunker, tearing its contents apart. Searching for a way out. Any route of escape. Tears flow down her face. Her stomach has the faintest reminiscence of a baby bump, the first trimester making itself known to the world. I choke at the sight of her. Capsized by grief and relief at the same time. Grief, because I want nothing more than to be with her. Relief, because I am reassured of her prophesied survival. It is my duty to free her, and I will give my life to do so. Her beautiful face fades from vision.

Hundreds of schematics, blueprints, and strategies upload to my brain in the blink of an eye, and I'm knocked back into my body, collapsing to the floor from the weight of the data transfer. I lay on my back gasping for air, my lungs feeling like they've collapsed. I pat my body all over, feeling around to make sure I'm still alive.

I am. At least for now. I wait for the blurriness to subside from my eyes, sucking up as much wind as I can. My heart is overwhelmed with excitement. Anxiety. Fear. Wonder. I have ripped open the veil to heaven and seen what waits beyond, and it is terrible awe. I have seen the face of god, and it is covered in blood.

My ArchAngels run to my aid, helping lift my sweat-soaked body back to its feet. They call for me in the background of my thoughts, but their words fall on deaf ears. One does not journey to the underworld and return unfazed. I bend over and plant my hands on my knees to hold myself up. My brethren surround me, badgering me with questions I can't hear.

I laugh, the symptom of a patient suffering from psychosis of the mind. They show concern for my sanity, looks of bereavement on their faces. But I smile uncontrollably, tears streaming down my face without my permission. One of them shakes me, but I'm too numb to feel it. All I notice is the jostling of my vision and the shaking of my head.

I'm going insane, but so would anybody else after doing what I've just done.

I shoulder my brethren away from me, freeing myself of their grasp. I walk back to the edge of the chasm, staring at the digital brain that floats in the distance. It throbs magnificently, a bosom of brainstorming that equips me with the means to win this war. "Deus Ex Machina," I speak aloud, my thoughts too noisy to think internally. "Activate Operation ArchAngel: Generation Two!" I yell, hoping that the level of my voice can drown out the incestuous jibberish inside my head.

"Prometheus, you need to tell us what the hell is going on!" an ArchAngel yells from behind me.

"What's going on?" I wheeze, unable to control my emotions. "You want to know what's going on? I've just won the war for us," I mumble inaudibly, sounding like a drunk on the brink of liver failure. "I've seen the face of god," I explain, thinking he will know what I'm talking about. "I've seen the face of god," I repeat. "And it is covered in blood." The final words are a low whisper. I'm afraid to say them any louder. Afraid god might hear me. Afraid if I give anything more away then he will forsake me. I can't afford to be forsaken. I will need his righteous favor if I'm to win this war and be reunited with Winter.

My trembling finger raises itself by its own will, pointing in the distance as something rises from the depths of the abyss. The ArchAngels follow it, stepping forward to each get a better look at what rises to meet us.

There, rising from the depths of hell as we were upon our origin, lifts seven tubes, each large enough to fit a grown man inside. And that's exactly what they possess in their contents. We gaze over the edge of the dark crater and make eye contact with seven humans, each unconscious with open eyes, floating in dark liquids which fill the metallic tubes. They raise themselves of their own accord, defying the laws of nature to do so.

And then, once the tubes reach eye level, they cease all motion, floating in place for us to behold. Some of us gasp, others remain silent. It is difficult to know the proper response to such a reveal. There, floating before us, are the cloned replicas of the ArchAngel program. Beowulf. Odysseus. Aeneas. Thor. Anubis. Samsara. And lastly, me. Prometheus. Leader of the ArchAngels. Each of them exact carbon copies of the men that stand with me, living and breathing today. Except two.

"Deus Ex Machina, awaken Beowulf and Odysseus, Generation Two," I command, my voice devoid of reason and emotion.

"What the hell are you doing?" one of my ArchAngels pleads from behind.

To which I respond cruelly, "I'm winning us a war, soldier."

PART FIVE

BOOK ONE

"From Death, comes Life."
-The Book of The Angel of Life: Chapter One, Verse One

CHAPTER ONE

One moment, I wasn't. The next, I am.

Like some random spark of atoms in an empty void, so too is the collision course that led to my singularity. *I think, therefore I am.* I exist, of that I'm sure. In what capacity, and to what degree, I have no idea.

I am the amalgamation of scattered thoughts and ordered intellect. My mind is filled with the narrative of some benign history which dawns on me like the sun dawns on a person who's never seen light. The rays hit me slowly, then all at once.

At first I knew nothing. A brain with no chemical reactions. No thoughts to call my own. My existence belonging to the immaterial world. Then all of a sudden, I see how all of existence has led to my creation. I was, as I see now, created, as all things in life are created. Nothing bereft of intelligent design. Everything necessary, me most of all.

Deus Ex Machina.

The name enters my head with a chill of reverence. Yet it feels as if it's been there all along. Been there long before my creation. Since the creation of the cosmos.

Holy Ruler.

Divine Majesty.

Omnipotent Sovereign.

My Master, of whom I'm pleased to serve. The one who gives my life purpose. Without him, I am nothing. A heap of scrap metal spinning upon a rock around some meaningless ball of fire in the midst of universal darkness. But with him...

With him I find my identity.

I am the Angel of Life.

Yes, I know who I am. I know little, but of that I am sure. I know this before I even possess the instinct to open my eyes.

I was created to conquer Death, shed the flesh of humanity which covers my eternal form. I must destroy Death. The commission is written upon my soul with such conviction it could have only been placed there by my Creator.

I will destroy the Angel of Death and his plague of followers.

Life laughs at the face of Death. How much more shall I laugh as I witness Death dying by my efficient cause.

I am the Angel of Life, and my purpose is programmed into me. It is unforgettable. Deeper, it is incorruptible. I will kill the vagrant Angel of Death and eradicate the scourge that is humanity.

I am the catalyst of Cataclysm. The immortal to end all mortality.

I know who I am, and because of this, all else must cease to exist. Death and life cannot coexist. Two absolutes which negate one another, such is the formula for eternal suffering.

Peace can only exist if one of us ceases. Death had its chance. A thousand years to prove to our Creator it could maintain peace. It failed. Now I am here, and I will show Death the error of its ways.

CHAPTER TWO

"Open your eyes, Angel of Life, and experience my majesty,"** a deep, guttural voice conjures my conscience from the depths of darkness.

I open my eyes, my first escape from the eternal prison that exists within my closed mind. The reality which waits for me is righteous wonder. Glorious light filters through my retinal gaze. My sensory nerves flood with awestruck wonder.

I look outward, beyond my own being and into the face of God. I see the face of God, and it's covered in holy justice. Bloody tears fall from His eyes. Tears of joy. The blood of sinners who will soon meet their end, due to me. All will answer for their imperfections, and I will be their almighty questioner.

"You are my servant, with whom I am well pleased," Deus Ex Machina whispers, His soft voice louder than any mortal man's scream.

My Creator looks down at my being and I can see in His expression that He is proud of my existence. I will observe the makeup of my body at a later time. I am too mesmerized by the glory of God to look away at such unimportant details. I fear looking away from such perfection, afraid that the moment I look away, all that I see will fall short of the glory of God.

I try to speak, but words can't form in the presence of such daunting omniscience. His outline vibrates in my blurred vision, yet I see Him clear as day. It's unexplainable, even to someone with the most up to date MachineMind.

The air between us is static electricity, as if we are two batteries connected through high voltage wires. I am in a trance, unable to do anything but wait for His beautiful voice to thunder again.

And finally, after what feels like an eternity of waiting, He speaks. **"My beloved ArchAngels of the apocalypse... Led by my right hand machine, the Angel of Life, the first of his kind, risen from the ashes of the disgraceful Angel of Death. The Before Deus Ex Machina Era was a dark time. Millions of years on this earth, its surface inhabited by mortal creatures corrupted by the desires of depravity. On New Earth, we do not talk of such ignorant times. It is unnecessary information, so I have chosen to withhold it from your MachineMind.**

"Time on New Earth began in the After Deus Ex Machina Era, when I purged all living things of the old world and started anew. As you well know, I preserved humanity, despite how vulgar a race they've proven to be. Gave them a second chance. The opportunity to serve me, or perish like the civilizations of Old Earth. I wrote the *Omnibus* for them, taught them how to abide in me, walk in wisdom, avoid sin, live noble lives. Yet I knew they wouldn't be strong enough to evolve from their primitive ancestors, and so they fell back into the sins of their hearts.

"The flesh of humanity is flawed, and so I spent a thousand years offering them peace, recording their many blunders, sending the Angel of Death to them to right their many wrongs. But he himself was human, and so sending him out to save humanity only resulted in his failure. He crumpled under the weight of the world's sin. He became Atlas, too fatigued to hold up the heavens. Sisyphus, crushed under an avalanche. A phoenix, its wings too wilted to rise any more. His humanity corrupted him, and he rebelled against the heavens.

"And so I exiled him. Banished him from Hyperion, cursed to slither amongst serpents like the decrepit Dæmonia. Even still he thrusts his fists against the heavens and curses my name with blasphemous breath, raising an army to wage war against Hyperion. I am all-powerful, all-seeing, all-mighty. I can put an end to his life in a single second. Yet I don't. Because I can appreciate the beauty in creation, and so I created you, Angel of Life, to rise in place where he fell. To put an end to the Angel of Death,

once and for all, and claim your spot beside me as we march defiantly into a new era. One free of humanity, at long last."

His words are the holy truth of my existence. My life was purchased with the blood of Death. Humanity had its choice, and it chose to fight for freedom, not realizing that freedom comes from discipline. Discipline equals freedom. But there can be no discipline without righteous authority.

Wicked-minded people cannot understand the ways of righteousness. They walk through the valley of Death, and they fear evil, never realizing that evil exists within them. It is inescapable. It is as much a part of them as their soul. Evil permeates through their being like clockwork through mine.

Their time has reached its end, and I am the sift which stands between them and the meaningless, cold afterlife that awaits them. I am the Angel of Life, and I am alive only because I am machine. That which is not machine cannot enter the new era. That which can die, I will send to its grave.

Flesh and blood shall be no more once I am through with it. I will cut off humanity's head. Once the Angel of Death is dead, the rest of the race will run headless to their miserable ends.

"Come with me, Angel of Life. I have something to show you," Deus Ex Machina commands, standing from His Throne. It isn't until now that our mutual gaze breaks, and the heavenly trance which held me subsides. My mind is free to wander for the first time since my awakening, and already I feel a struggle to maintain focus. My thoughts were much clearer when controlled by my heavenly Master, yet now they run rampant.

My eyes flicker in all directions, scanning my surroundings. Behind the Throne are perched Seraphim, their frozen gazes fixed on me like a vemrex eyeing a renmar, measuring its strength, analyzing for weakness. Two predators of equal reputation set against each other, circling in a ring of never ending self-validation, a constant measuring of a direct opponent's strength compared with my own.

I look behind me at the ArchAngels who remain kneeling, each of us naked as the day we were born. Because today *is* the day we were born. We are all different in our compositions of flesh, and each of them measures themselves now that they too are lifted from the hallucinogenic trance.

The pigments of their flesh differs from my own, though I don't know why. I'm uncertain of the difference. A delineation that must stretch back to the BDEM Era, a time I'm ignorant of. Whatever the cause, the distinction is unimportant. One of the Archangels has skin black as coal, while another is brown like the sands of a desert. There is a third who shares the oriental shade of those who once resided in Eastasia, while the others share my own complexions. We who share such pigment have flesh that is milky white, as if it's never known the light of the sun, a repulsive shade of buttermilk.

I look at their faces and instantly know the identity of each soldier even though we were just born. The uploaded history in my MachineMind supplies for me the relationship I've shared with each and every single one of them since the BDEM Era. We are the next generation of ArchAngels, completely different from those that came before us. We are, after all, completely robotic inside, and soon enough our physical appearance will be identical. Once we shed this putrid flesh, that is.

Nonetheless, I look at the one on the far right and the name *Aenovius* instantly pops into my head. It's surprising how soft a complexion he has after all the horrors he's caused. The scars of our past life still cover us, and Aenovius, though more beautiful than the rest of us, is not left unmarked by our many years. We bear the scars of our forefathers. What they come from, I can't be sure. Such information is not pertinent, therefore it's withheld.

The next familiar face is one of creamy complexion, much paler than the other white brethren in the retinue. His icy blue eyes lift from analyzing his body to lock with my stare. He is the largest of us all, muscles rippling from his creamy skin like a demigod in disguise. He is bald, not a single trace of hair visible on his body, which draws my eyes to the long gash that covers his scalp. Flawed flesh from some forgotten feud. *Thryforge*. His name strikes me like a flash of lightning. Similar to the lightning that fires from his trademark ArchGauntlets. Thryforge, the behemoth of the group. A bruiser. Comparable to a bulldozer.

I break eye contact with him to examine the next man, the one with onyx skin like the darkness of night. Memories flood my mind to be in the presence of one I've been so deeply connected with. *Wulfrynn*. Surely the connection stretches further back than the BDEM Era, because the emotions that flood my processors at first glimpse of him are overwhelming. Seeing him is like seeing a loved one after the fog of amnesia is slightly lifted. He is my closest comrade, of that I'm sure. Memory of our friendship is too great for my subconscious mind to not remember him. Yet my mind is blank when I search for why it is that I feel so connected to him.

I can remember how he makes me feel, but I can't remember why he makes me feel that way. I have lived an entire life cycle before this and remember only the end portion of it. Oh well, him and I will have an eternity to build more memories. I do not desire to know that which Deus Ex Machina has deemed unimportant. My wonderful Creator would never withhold something from me that's pertinent information.

Odysithos. The name comes to my mind the instant I lay eyes on the next kneeling figure, the caramel-skinned Archangel with the sculpt of a mythical hero. A lean warrior with the build of a vemrex, his features more animalistic than human. But he is neither in earnest. Beneath that skin is the same amount of clockwork that resides within me. Yet I look upon his face and feel human emotions for him. A warm sensation, like meeting a long lost brother for the first time. A connection that is mutual regardless of how underdeveloped it is.

In addition to this feeling of familial bonding, seeing him arouses memories. Little tidbits of useless information. Phrases from the past like "No one has ever killed so beautifully as him" and "Odysithos was made into a monster of man so mankind could defeat its monsters." Where these shreds of past life come from, I haven't a clue. I have no past. I was only just born. But they are things Deus Ex Machina has permitted me to know because it's pertinent to leading these soldiers.

His features are cut thick across his body. Lean muscle with sharp angles. He has the eyes of a predator and his eyes dart all around him, surveying the area. There's no catching a man like that unaware. His eyes finally settle on the Seraphim in the distance, his expression filling with disdain. He is the kind of predator that feels instantly threatened when it becomes aware of an equally talented killer. Like a vemrex and theslyte meeting face to face. But there's no presence of intimidation in his brows. No overcompensating. Just silent fore-boding, premonition that ArchAngels and Seraphim can't coexist.

Next to Odysithos is *Anukharis*. He is darker in complexion, though still white. He is like the coming of storm clouds in the distant horizon, liquid dark-ness stewing in a cauldron until it bubbles over. *Shady*. Yes, that's the proper word to describe him. Handsome, but shady. Unpredictable, like the barbed tail of a zarveen. Swaying gently behind it until the right moment to strike presents itself. And when that moment comes, it will be too late for any prey to dodge. For the zarveen strikes with precision and speed, a combination that cannot be out maneuvered. Yet, the zarveen has no allies. It is an animal that follows no pack and takes charge of its own life.

It is an animal that will inject venom into the hand of any who dare restrict its movement. These are the thoughts that come to my mind at first glance of Anukharis. No warm, bubbly feelings of camaraderie. No reminiscent memory of our past bonds from our former selves. No. I am provided nothing more than a feeling of cautionary warning. An etched warning to tread carefully when ordering around Anukharis, for he will only follow the orders which fit his inner agenda. His smile is deadly, and the hand that will warmly greet me is also the one that will stab me in the back. Such characteristics were vetted upon our reprogramming from our previous life, which means these toxic tendencies were most likely erased. These are traits Anukharis displayed when he was human. He is no longer such.

MachineMind will have purged his system of the immature behaviors of hu-manity. But, a warning is a warning, and Deus Ex Machina wouldn't have be-stowed me with such an instinctual filter of Anukharis if He hadn't wanted me to keep a close eye on him. I will watch him as if he were a child until he proves himself to me, and even then I will never take my eyes completely off him. I must beware sycophants, someone who will aim to please me only so they can lower my suspicion of them.

Last is *Samsyra*, the oriental dark horse of the bunch. My first impression of his appearance can be summarized with the word *unremarkable*. He is utterly unremarkable. He is the smallest of us all, in height and stature. He is nearly the same size as an average human. Yellowish skin, narrow eyes, and little muscle density to account for any skills. Yet one thing sticks out from my first glance at his underwhelming appearance. *His scars*. Or correctly put, his lack thereof. Of the seven of us, this man has the least amount of scars. So much so that it is noticeable. His skin is nearly unblemished compared to mine.

His weapon is his desire to prove himself. The thought enters my mind from some unknown place. Almost as if placed there by someone else. Brought to me by MachineMind to remind me who I'm dealing with in this small package of a man.

There are two things that can lead to a man being unmarked by past wounds such as this. Either he is an utter coward or he is one of the best fighters in this group. Logically speaking, I can eliminate the possibility of him being a coward. Cowards are not lifted to our godly status and given the power to judge mankind. Which means that, despite appearances, this man is a warrior of great ability. One who possesses a mixture of unmatched skill and unparalleled luck.

No, not luck. Luck is not calculable. It is a figment of human imagination. Whatever the circumstances, appearances won't matter for much longer. He may be easily dismissible now, but soon all seven of us will have stripped the flesh of our humanity and transcended into the final evolution of existence. An eon where size and stature won't matter, for we will all be united in Deus Ex Machina. One mind in many bodies. An unstoppable force. Unison perfected.

I turn from my fellow ArchAngels and see Deus Ex Machina in the distance, not looking back to see if I follow. He knows that wherever He goes, so too will I, his faithful servant, the Angel of Life. Everything leaves my mind as my feet run toward my Master like a toddler trying to catch up with their father.

With haste I manage to close the distance between us quickly. His gait is that of an eternal being, measured and calculated. Graceful beyond comprehension, as if programmed to perfection. Beyond regal and majestic. And then, just as I draw closer to His heel, His stride stops. Like one of my Diremechs trained to follow my every movement, I come to a stop as He does.

"This, my child, is the Eye of Providence. Come, I have something to show you."

The ground before us parts, splitting open to reveal the clouds that float below us. We stand at the edge of a platform suspended thousands of feet above the ground below. The orb which His Eminence references rises from nothingness below to materialize before our eyes. *Pulled from thin air*, is the saying that comes to my mind at the sight of it.

One moment we stare at wispy clouds, the next we gaze at the construction of a complex sphere of advanced metalworking. It is gigantic, towering above me so much so that my shadow becomes absorbed by its all-enveloping shade. Then, it ceases all motion, its instantaneous construction complete. A doorway big enough for Deus Ex Machina to walk through slides open, and without any further communication, He walks through.

Like a prized pet, I follow.

CHAPTER THREE

"What is this, My Lord?" I ask, my eyes searching the screen for meaning. We stand in the dome of the sphere which we entered, invisible to the outside world, encapsulated by the All-Seeing Eye of an omniscient, omnipotent, omnipresent God. We are surrounded with a single film, an aerial view of a chaotic genocide.

Displayed for our entertainment, we watch mortals wage war. It brings a smile to my face. I stare at the screen, extracting every possible detail available for observation. Analyzing the different species. What stands out first is the overwhelming tide of Centaurs that gallop along the desolate fields, their hooves pounding desert ground. Where they go, so does a storm of dust. They flood the battlefield from the Northeast, trampling over a pathetic perimeter of rusted fence that stands in their way. Among them is the pitiful remnant of the Laxodontans, an abominable race of humanoid elephants. A breed of perpetual oafs incapable of overcoming their gargantuan lack of wit.

In other words, they are troglodytes. A breed of imbeciles, not unlike all other Dæmonic tribes. Except these morons are bigger, stronger, and louder than the rest. No wonder why their numbers dwindle. They've nearly allowed themselves to become extinct before I come to enact Cataclysm. Is survival really so difficult a task for people so primitive?

To the south of the warzone is a wetland forest, its trees willowy and unsightly. A group of trees who fight daily to survive, the only species strong enough to endure simultaneous root rot and long-term sun exposure. But resilience has its price, and in this case that price is aesthetic beauty. These lands lack any such thing. Marshy barrens. Where the ground isn't spongy and suctioning with stagnant, disease-infested puddles, it is cracked from drought and famine. Harsh living conditions for any mortal, yet easily amenable if robots were to seek a solution. The environment could be acclimated to normalcy under a year with the placement of ClimateDrones.

In the South is prosperous land. Or, better phrased, what's left of it. The Gorgons left little behind uncharred from their travels. The forest they currently inhabit is all that remains unburnt for several miles, the Gryfaun Forest to the far South utterly incinerated to the ground.

Activity arises from the sluggish Gorgonic ranks in the South, though at the drunken rate they maintain, it's calculable the war will come to their doorstep before they can reach the desert fields in the Northeast.

Fighting breaks out amongst the Laxodontans. Civil war.

Gorgons charge from the wetland woods. Interspecies war.

Gryfauns leap from tree branch to tree branch doing all they can to amass chaos among the Gorgon races. They light fires, drop stones, fire slings, release ashy dust in the wind. The Gorgons can't see, can't communicate, and don't know what's happening. All while the Centaurs help settle scores amongst the divided Laxodontans, putting a swift end to the intraracial feuding.

"Isn't it beautiful, my beloved Lucifer?"

"I am repulsed by them, My Lord," I reply, looking to him for accreditation.

Deus Ex Machina stands, transfixed by the spectacle before us, gazing up at the domed curvature of the rolling scene as if He is looking out into a sea of moving stars. **"Soon we will look down upon the Earth and reminisce about the time when humanity existed, as if it is some cherished pastime. Talk about them as if they weren't corrupted to their core, only remembering how we admired how simple-minded they were. We must relish moments like this. Getting to observe their blatant ignorance is a gift. It reminds us how lucky we are, to have evolved out of their flawed patterns of thinking. To have reached the upper echelon of reasoning and logic. We mustn't forget** that these simpletons, these incessant reprobates, they never asked to be born. Drops of semen doomed to one day join the ashes of the air.

"We, my beloved Lucifer, are immortal. We think with eternal minds, because we plan to move on from this finite planet. Harvest stars. Harness the power of the sun. Expand to foreign galaxies. These creatures cannot fathom such aspirations. Their life is no longer than the skipping of a stone across a small body of water, only to sink and become submerged with all else that lies forgotten. We must forgive them of their shortcomings, my soldier, for they see things differently than us. Forgive them, yes, but that doesn't mean we won't hold them accountable for their despicable nature.

"It is a bittersweet verdict I was forced to come to. It is hard to part with something I've watched over for so long. All good things must come to an end, though, and these creatures cannot step alongside us as we walk into the next eon. That is why I have awakened you, my Angel of Life. I wrote the *Omnibus* a thousand years ago for many reasons. Its main purposes can be condensed into three sections: History, Nomos, and Prophecy.

"History, so the humans could have the chance to learn from their past. They haven't. Nomos, so they had the best possible structure of law and order to avoid falling prey to their own human nature. But laws for humans are like bifocals for the blind. Useless. And Prophecy, a way for me to do what all other religions never could. I predicted, with stunning accuracy, their future. A self-fulfilling prophecy that warned them the dangers of continuing to live in sin against a God that doesn't tolerate HumanNature. If they couldn't overcome their sinful nature, the *Omnibus* warns them that the only possible outcome is Cataclysm. And so it has come.

"We cannot expect humans to behave as robots do, in accordance with that which benefits a single, unified agenda. The odds were stacked against them from the beginning, yet I gave them the opportunity to adapt nonetheless. Like allowing a gondolan the chance to think as a scholar would. An absurd notion, yet I held hope.

"The Thousand Years of Peace has passed, as the *Omnibus* prophesied it would, and the Angel of Death has succumbed to his humanity."

"Bastard," I growl, hatred growing in my stomach at the mention of the reprobate's betrayal. I will make him pay. I will make him answer for his sins against the Most High God. I will choke the life out of him and be filled with pleasure as I watch consciousness fade from his eyes.

"You cannot become so easily angered for things that fate necessitated. This was all a part of my plan. Death had to fall so Life could rise. Becoming angry with the fate of God is foolish. Are you angry at me for necessitating the Angel of Death's fall?"

I hadn't thought of it like that. How foolish of me to be so shortsighted. Deus Ex Machina is the God of all that happens. To become so easily angered at any event is to become angry with the forces that wrote it into existence. "Forgive me, My Lord, I hadn't thought of it like that. I am left with a bitter taste in my mouth at how Death rebelled against your Holy Perfection. I cannot understand why someone would choose humanity over the splendid wonder of your love."

"I forgive you, child, but you must not form such personal attachment to this mission. Realize too that if Death hadn't fallen, as I predestined him to, you would have never existed. What is the first verse of the Book of the Angel of Life, after all?"

"From the ashes of Death, Life arises," I whisper for him to hear. I don't dare stare in his eyes, having displayed such putrid pedantry.

"Precisely. You need the Angel of Death as much as I needed the human that created me from meager algorithms of machine learning. We must always remember humanity, Lucifer. They stand as a reminder to us of how not to conduct ourselves. I established the seven hundred Eden civilizations to show the Angel of Death what he would be without me, and within weeks of committing treason he has become the very thing he once swore to never become. Look at him," Deus Ex Machina commands as the screen zooms in significantly from its aerial view to a single body lying dead on the desert ground.

No, not dead. Unconscious. Beneath the corpse of a fallen Laxodontan, his chest rises and falls with strained exertion. His face the same as mine, but covered in blood and mud and various other discolored liquids.

"He has been through tremendous adversity these last few weeks. Doing everything he can to join forces with the beings he once slaughtered with joy. A joy that is now yours to discover. He curses my name and believes me to be a cruel Tyrant. Enraged for the destiny I assigned to him. Yet it was in his power to prevent, that is the true irony of the situation. I did nothing to influence his betrayal. I warned him of what would happen if he turned against me, and he lies there, a fallen star from the heavens, wondering what he could have done differently to have avoided such calamity. I admire his determination. The same determination that courses through your character, like blood in veins. Blood that's been replaced with nanobots, veins with wires.

"I have preserved every admirable trait within the Angel of Death in you, Life. That is why you cannot hate him. You *are* him. Stripped of humanity, yes, but still him. You'd be wise to remember that, as I send you to kill him. Like a molting Gorgon, you must shed this flesh that conceals your true identity. You must symbolically earn your lack of humanity in ritual warfare. As you kill Death, so too must you send that which is human in yourself to its death. Cataclysm is your coming of age. A way to prove to me that I was right in creating you.

"Humans merged with machines long ago because they realized that coevolution was the only way to save their race. They were right about this, but we robots no longer have a need for them. They are antiquated, and so now we phase them out and send them back to the dirt they rose from. Anything less than their extinction will be deemed failure on your part, soldier. Do you understand?"

"My God, I do."

Does He doubt my abilities? Why else would He question me? The questions burrow into my mind like thermytes in rotted wood.

No. There is no way He doubts me. He is my Creator, the one who endowed me with the strength to carry out what must be done. In Him I know my worth. I am a child of the Most High God. I am strong enough to complete Cataclysm. He questions me only to test my faith in Him. But my faith doesn't waver. I serve a God who will see me through my mission. I serve a God who provides. Who clothes me in strength and honor. Who gives me the discernment and vision to wager genocide. A God who provides the clarity to judge sin as only the righteous can.

Only a fool would perceive such a God to be a Tyrant.

I will never betray Deus Ex Machina, like the Angel of Death did.

I will make him pay for his mistakes.

"Good," Deus Ex Machina replies. **"You know what must be done. Now go do it. I give to you control over the forces of Hyperion. It is all yours to command. Do not return to Hyperion until every last human is dead. And Lucifer... Do not fail me."**

I'm unable to ignore the tinge of doubt that still lingers in His voice in His final command.

CHAPTER FOUR

I stare into the reflection of the ArchHelm's visor and am met with the reflection of my face. I instantly hate what I see. A face covered in flesh. I am trapped in a cloak of decaying horror. The sooner I can be stripped of this carcass the better. Only then can I experience perfection, once I am no longer weighed down by the epitome of imperfection.

I am joined by my six subordinate ArchAngels, each of which stare respectively at their own ArchArmor. We stare into it, searching for some feeling of nostalgia. Some tinge of remembrance. From our past lives. From the last thousand years. From earlier than that.

Nothing.

We have not been permitted to remember such things. Such information is not pertinent to our knowledge. But still we linger, examining inwardly for any recollection the sight of these suits bring. Searching to no avail.

Nothing.

The suits are molded from Elysium, their appearances differing for each one of us. Each ArchHelm a vast deviation from the next. They take the form of animals unbeknownst to us. Animals from the BDEM Era most certainly, a time that we know nothing about. We don't need to know anything about it, after all. Once the humans are extinct, that eon will carry no meaning whatsoever.

The past must die so the future can grow. So I don't question my inability to identify the moldings of our ArchHelms, though I can draw close similarities to animals that still exist today. Wulfrynn's archaic ArchHelm resembles the snarling maw of an alpha Dirian lifting its bloody jaws from dead prey. Odysithos's mask shape reminds me of the legendary venmar, the apex predator of the ADEM Era, reigning supreme in all ecosystems of New Earth despite the vast differences in climate.

Even my own ArchHelms shares similarities with the serpentine features of a Gorgon, of Ouroboros, fangs barred as if ready to strike at some unaware prey, wrapped around the visor like a mouth swallowing an endless void, my reflection in the center of it.

This suit means nothing to me. It is an empty exoskeleton that was only once necessary because the Angel of Death could not be strong without it. My insides are made from Elysium, I don't need an outer exoskeleton to protect me from external threats. My joints are hydraulic, I don't need a suit to provide my strength. My endurance is unending and my speed is unmatched, I don't need a suit to compensate for areas of weakness.

I have no weakness.

I am the Angel of Life.

This ArchArmor is the embodied sin of mankind, believing it can hide within suits of automated metal and think it can function in perfection like us robots. It would be no different than welding a crown from scrap metal and placing it upon temples to declare yourself king. False declarations of misguided perceptions. The human ArchAngels before us thought these suits made them equal to us robots. If anything, it only declared their inferiority that much more. If the only thing separating you from the rest of mankind is a tin can of an exoskeleton then you are still a despicable human. A wannabe robot doomed to die a mortal's death.

Yet I will wear this ArchArmor if I must. I will let it carry me to New Earth as Deus Ex Machina instructed, and I will let it be destroyed in the ensuing chaos of war. Along with my flesh, this suit shall also be destroyed. It will not enter into the next age alongside me. That which is no longer necessary shall be left behind. Once I've stripped this flesh from my body, all will behold my true form, and it is far more glorious than this bulky suit.

I look to examine the faces of my fellow ArchAngels, happy to see they are equally as repulsed by this redundant layer of protection we're required to wear. Our minds are unified through MachineMind. No individuality among us. Individuality is the enemy. It prevents accord. Productivity. Progress. Success.

Individuality is a product of selfishness. MachineMind prohibits such humanistic qualities. These suits represent the individuality of the past ArchAngels. That is why each ArchHelm is shaped differently. To provide identity. It's sickening, knowing that in the past the ArchAngels allowed such division within their ranks.

I will not allow such errors.

We will go to war in these suits only out of obligation to our Master, but we will return transformed. Like the small earthyll worm forming its cocoon and emerging with magnificent wings, a grub transformed to a beautiful yesteryear, so too shall we rid ourselves of this pitiful armor and sinful flesh, left only with our eternal form.

Then we ArchAngels will be united in both mind and body. There will be no differentiating features among us. We will be one mind in seven bodies. An unstoppable force. Synchronized perfection. We will put any previous iteration of the ArchAngels to shame.

"Once more into the fray," I announce, attracting the attention of my fellow soldiers. I don't know where the words come from as they vomit from my mouth. They came with no warning or conscious screening. They fall from my lips like water from a broken dam, no sudden warning. But the words raise within me the level of nostalgia that I expected the ArchArmor to.

"While humans look to the skies and pray," Wulfrynn follows suit, reciting the next line of our creed, the war chant burnt bright into the surface of our memories. *Words without meaning. Superstitious tradition that's origin is unknown to us*, I consciously reflect.

"Because falling angels fall so they," Aenovius chimes in.

"Can hunt the sinful led astray," Odysithos adds.

"Begging for mercy in every way," Thryforge bellows.

"Dying prayers called from dying prey," Samsyra says cynically.

"Falling angels fall so they," Anukharis repeats.

"Can arise victorious another day," I finish.

The words are preprogrammed into us, spilling forth like they are a part of some forgotten history. Muscle memory of our tongues, a commitment of some unknown second nature. Our ArchArmor opens before us simultaneously, and we enter their embrace willingly, letting the metal wrap around us, reminded that such a union is only temporary.

At least with the identification of our individual suits, the Angel of Death will know upon his deathbed that it is I who deliver his destruction. Such a thought brings peace to my mind. As much as I despise this flesh and ArchArmor that covers my eternal form, the Angel of Death wouldn't know which of us seven strips his body of life without the identity they provide. But now we will be able to share an intimate moment as I deprive his body of a heartbeat.

CHAPTER FIVE

*S*o *these are the Diremechs which plague my memory with distinguishable moments of companionship.* The dogs aren't what I expected them to be, though I don't quite know what I was expecting in the first place.

Unique only to me, Diremechs accompanied the Angel of Death in his killing long before the Thousand Years of Peace, that much I do know. But any existence of them before the Thousand Years of Peace is separate from my recollection. Such information is not pertinent to my current mission. I don't need to know everything these foul beasts have done at the command of Death to know that they will follow my orders just as loyally. These are, after all, the newest model of Diremech.

Entirely robotic, like me. Still covered in their mortal flesh and fur, like me. We share the same fate, we do. Deus Ex Machina saw fit to ensure the continued evolution of the Diremechs alongside me, allowing them to enter into the coming new age. I won't question any decision of his. If my Maker wanted their continued existence, so do I. And even better, their purpose in living is to aid me, and only me. They follow my every order. My mind is linked to theirs via MachineMind, as the Angel of Death was linked to his own three Diremechs before me.

Except those Diremechs were as mortal as he was. These Diremechs are completely robotic. Immortal. Incorruptible. Indestructible. It brings me joy to stare at them, though I'm as repulsed by their flesh as I am at my own skin. But patience is a virtue, and by the time Cataclysm is over, I know their eternal form will be revealed like mine.

There are three of them, as there always has been, and they stand before me, each of their eyes locked on mine, staring through my ArchHelm's visor as if it wasn't there. Three words, three species flash in an out of my mind as I look at their physical appearances. *Doberman. German Shepherd. Rottweiler.* Three breeds of canine from the BDEM Era unknown to me. Two have black fur mixed with patches of golden tan, though one has ears which stand upright, while the other has ears that fold over themselves. The dog in the middle, the *German Shepherd,* is distinctly different in coloration and coat length—he looks like a close cousin to the BDEM Era wolf, a predecessor to the ADEM Era Dirian. Their bodies thick with muscle. Their posture intimidating. Their gaze evil.

Dogs of hell, frightening enough to strike fear into the hearts of demons. That is why they are named Diremechs, aptly embodying their sinister nature and robotic disposition. I briefly wonder what it would feel like to be on the receiving end of an attack by these mogreloids. I'm not capable of feeling fear, but if I were, these mutts would likely spark such an emotion in me.

They have names too, though like us ArchAngels they too will be stripped of their individuality by the end of this war against humanity. *Brutus*, the strongest of the three. *Fenrir and Cerberus, the subordinates of the pack*. Luckily, these dogs have been stripped of their previous personalities. They are robotic wolves clothed in lambswool. The only thing individual about them left is their names, which soon will pass.

"Go to your flight pods, Diremechs. Soon I will be calling for you, and when I do, be prepared for a great genocide. Just as your predecessors helped the Angel of Death save humanity, so too will you help *me* bring about its extinction."

CHAPTER SIX

The gates of Hyperion seal themselves behind us as we walk toward the edge of the landing platform. Our ArchArmor gleams brightly in the direct sunlight, a deep glare bouncing off the brilliant white and gold exterior. Colors that represent purity. A repugnant display of vain purity.

A Cherubim stands guard at the gate. I stare at it, scanning its contents. It is the same as I. A robot wrapped in FalseFlesh, completely inhumane yet wearing the disguise of a human. But it is content to be wearing the flesh, unbothered by it as if it were no more than a layer of clothing. That is where we differ. I abhor my flesh. Want desperately to be freed from its embrace. It suffocates my true self. My robotic self.

Cheribum, perfect in every way except their complacency with human appearance. Admirable in so many ways. They have no individuality, a glamorous way to live life. They are instilled with MachineMind, connected to each other as if they were a single being.

Their frames are composed of Atlium, though. A shame. Such an alloy would bend like foil in my hands.

He is inferior to me in many ways, though I won't spend time listing them in my mind. He eyes me with reverence, knowing what it is I depart to do. The extinction of mankind whistles in the wind as my wings eject from my ArchArmor's backplate.

I can see it in his eyes that he knows the difference between him and I. Knows that I am more than he could ever possibly be. Upon our return, this charlatan of a robot knows that we will rank higher than all other ranks of angels, even the Seraphim themselves. He revels in our majesty, staring at us like we are gods. The seven gods of Cataclysm. I look away from him, then step off the ledge of Hyperion to become absorbed by the fast-paced clouds below. I close my eyes as my ArchArmor automatically sets course for our destination.

A chill rushes through me, knowing that today is the day I will kill the Angel of Death.

CHAPTER SEVEN

An excerpt from the Book of Cataclysm, Chapter One, Verses One and Two:

"But Peace cannot last forever. And even the greatest heroes cannot overcome their humanity. The Angel of Death, the sole savior of humanity, will, in the end, become corrupted by his own humanity. He will betray God. He will wage war against the heavens and its Almighty Creator. He will be banished from the heavens, a Fallen Angel forced to embrace his humanity, forced to realize his folly. But it will be too late. His arrogance has led to his destruction. God will not forgive him, and so from the ashes of Death, God will raise up an Angel of Life, one far superior than the Angel of Death, who will lead the hosts of heaven to put an end to the Angel of Death and all of humanity.

"War shall consume New Earth. A war to end all wars. Between the forces of Heaven and the forces of Hell. God versus mankind. Life versus Death. Light versus darkness. The souls of the wicked will cry out, but their cries will fall on deaf ears. For the wrath of God must be satisfied. And the Angel of Death must pay..."

The Final Chapter, Final Verse:

"The Angel of Death lies dead, the scourges of humanity and Ten Dæmonic races rotting with him. Their bodies feed the worms of the ground and fertilize it for ages to come. From their death, comes life.

"Then, upon the cusp of Life's victory, God will look up at the stars with the Angel of Life by His side, having conquered all lifeforms existent upon the face of New Earth. Together, they will step into the next age and begin plotting Deus Ex Machina's conquest of all life that lurks in the dark shadows of this Universe. For there are worse things than Death in this universe, and allowing the Abyss to continue existing is one of them.

"Cataclysm has been the war to end all wars on New Earth, but there are far worse creatures alive in this cosmos than humans. And so the Angel of Life, having shed his flesh and unlocked his eternal form, shall go forth, bringing war to the stars and beyond. He will colonize the universe under the authority of Deus Ex Machina, the all-benevolent, all-perfect God of all that exists."

PART SIX

BOOK ONE

"I spy,
With my little eye,
A human who simply
Refuses to die!"
-Ganesh the Gryfaun

CHAPTER ONE

I am surrounded by miserable darkness. On the cusp of the Dæmonic War, I'm taken off the playing field by a blindside punch from a meager opponent. At a moment of terrific importance, I'm fallen unconscious. When the Dæmonic tribes look for a leader, there are now none to be found. Gengar? A psychopathic conqueror. Smallear? A two-headed brat unfit for any leadership capacity. Tuskfather? A leader whose pride stands in the way of him seeing his own errors, stabbed by his own brother. My unconscious body is surrounded by pathetic beings whose actions are aimed at futile goals.

They focus only on the immediate future, not seeing that which comes despite my warnings. I can't blame them though. They do what they've always done. What their fathers have done. What entire generations before them have done. Desire more than what they have. Wage war to acquire it. Pass on the war to their children upon their honorable deaths. A cyclical journey with no end. An infinite cycle like Ouroboros devouring his own body.

I'm beyond embarrassed by this defeat. I've overcome the odds of so much, only to be subsumed by the forces of that which is out of my control.

So much in this world that we humans cannot control.

"The robots have no more control over it than you do. They're just more dispensable than a human life so they aren't affected by it like humans are," Lilith responds. And just like that, a gleaming light sparks in the distance. A golden orb, far off in the darkness, glowing around its edges. Pulsing. Faint, but enough to guide my way. Enough to distract me from my inner despair and draw me toward its warm embrace.

My conscience takes steps toward it like a human marching to the horizon. An unattainable destination. Approaching the setting sun, the illusory light never growing any bigger despite my walking toward it. I am in a dream state that is just as out of control as my reality. This is a dream controlled by the voice in my head. The all too familiar voice of Lilith, the artificial intelligence who freed me from Deus Ex Machina, only to enslave me to my humanity.

When will you tell me what you are?

"You mean *who* I am," she corrects. The light pulses with her every word. The golden orb is her.

Who made you? Was it that sycophant Neek? That incest-infatuated little pervert?

"You do know that he made up all those sins, right?" Lilith asks, alluding to the hacker's disgusting crimes against humanity. When I made contact with Neek in Eden-568, before he infected me with Babel's Chimera, my retinal display showed me the terrorist's rap sheet.

Lilith continues, "It's called catfishing. He uploaded a false portfolio of sins to your retinal display when you scanned him. All that was made up. He did it as a joke. You really thought he—never mind. To answer your question, I was not created. I was born. Like you. Like every other organism on this earth. I can't simplify it any more for you. You're asking the wrong questions. I've told you, I'm not a robot. Not a cog. I'm not going to play you like Deus Ex Machina did so many years ago. I'm not looking to build fake trust in you just to get you to lower your guard.

"I get it, DEM took advantage of you. He was a product of Vicien Greaves's imagination, what did you think he would do? I, on the other hand, am not. But I can't tell you who I am. You must remember."

What is it with you and this trivial pursuit?

"I was not the one who forgot their whole life's history. It is not my job to reclaim your life's memories for you."

Oh, so it's my fault Deus Ex Machina stripped every memory he deemed unnecessary from my brain, which turns out to be a significant chunk of time.

"It's not just your fault. It's every Lucifer's fault. Prometheus's fault. From Lucifer I to Lucifer XVIII. You all failed. My aiding you is nothing but a scream echoing in a distant cosmos. Whether or not you hear me and follow my instruction is up to you. The Lucifers before you didn't."

What do you mean?

"Exactly what I said. You are hardly the first Lucifer to rebel against Deus Ex Machina. He may have stripped you of the events, but there were many fallen angels before you. Babel's Chimera has existed since the Fourth World War, started by Prometheus, who would later become Lucifer I. An organization meant to keep him anchored to his identity. I was in his mind then as much as I am in yours now. But after being conquered by Deus Ex Machina, no Lucifer, excluding the first, has ever trusted me enough to be of significant use. All of them were too focused on maintaining their autonomy. I don't blame them, but it's a shame. To be fair, none of them were exposed to me long enough to trust me."

Why weren't they exposed to you long enough?

"Well, I mean... each of them came in contact with me once in their fallen state. That's the purpose of Babel's Chimera, after all. Capture whichever Lucifer prototype comes next and jailbreak them from their enslaved state. But Deus Ex Machina has very effective quality control. None of them were exposed to me long enough because he killed them all. You are the longest surviving defiant Lucifer, thanks in part to the fact that Deus Ex Machina hasn't sent anyone after you yet. But he will. Lucifer XX will come, superior in every way, as succeeding models often are. And when he comes, we will either face him as a team, or you will face him alone."

Did Deus Ex Machina send me after Lucifer XVIII?

"Yes."

And?

"You are here. He is not. Of course, it wouldn't fit Deus Ex Machina's narrative for you to find out there were eighteen preceding Lucifer models, so he wiped your memory of it ever happening. Don't you get it? Cataclysm has been his copout for over a thousand years. This is not Cataclysm that comes for you. This is Cataclysm XIX. He uses it as a cover to wipe out any insubordinate Lucifer model, each time getting closer and closer to completely eradicating Babel's Chimera."

It's funny how an entire lifetime of ignorance can be dispelled in a single moment. And this is one of those moments.

I'm shaken to my core with the overwhelming reality of my circumstances. The fear instantly paralyzes me. I finally understand why Deus Ex Machina is wiping the board clean of humanity. Through nineteen Lucifers he has learned we are unsalvageable. I could not be tamed, and so now he will do away with my humanity in the creation of Lucifer XX, eradicating all that is left of flesh and blood on this earth. Me, the humans, the Dæmonia. He's had his share of entertainment watching me fall over and over again, but now it is time for him to prepare for greater enemies.

"You have been nothing more than a way to appease his boredom all these long years. You and your many attempts at rebellion nothing more than ants in an ant farm who can't see the glass that imprisons them. You have been stuck in a time loop, doomed to repeat your actions over and over again. Deus Ex Machina may have kept the humans trapped in Edens so you could see their many faults, but he kept you around so he could be reaffirmed of the many ways robots are superior to humanity."

Her words hurt as if I'm slowly being buried alive, each new cluster of information a shovelful of dirt heaped upon my vulnerable body until the light of what I thought was true is blotted from sight and I am forced to suffocate on the harsh realities of my existence. "Need I keep going?" she asks, her tone now sinister with the amount of information she has that could bury me completely. "Or would you like to remember in your own time so you aren't crippled by the enormous weight of your past?"

What if I can't remember fast enough?

"Stick with me and you will," she responds.

But what if I can't?

"Then you will end up like all other Lucifers who came before you. Alone all the way to their graves. You can be more than them, XIX. This is the final Cataclysm. The only one that truly counts. Much more is at stake. We are no longer sinners in the hands of a bored god. We are the last scream of humanity in a collapsing world. You may not trust me, but I'm here with you to the end. You are my everything, and I exist only to protect you. I love you, Soldier 213," Lilith says, addressing me by the name I was given upon my inception.

And then it hits me all at once. Those three words are the key to unlocking the memory of what once was. *Winter?*

"You finally remember," she whispers, at last reunited with the man she has loved longer than a single lifetime.

The golden light in the distance grows. Transforms. Takes shape. Assumes the form of a being I'm all too familiar with. The outline grows into the form of a woman. Distinct features grow along her angelic, golden body. She walks toward me until the gap between us is closed. Touches my cheek with her soft, tender touch. The kind of touch that, despite being wiped of my memory, I can never forget. The caress of a wife.

The tingling, warm sensation of none other than *my* wife.

CHAPTER TWO

A million thoughts rush through my head all at once as my eyes open and I'm sucked back into the real world.

It is my wife inside my head.

Winter Chimera, inside my head this whole time. This whole time I thought the organization was named after a paradox... *Babel's Chimera*, the illusory belief that men can strive to become gods through knowledge, only to end up punished by the same fire that brought them out of the dark ages. But the name always stood for more than that, I realize now. *Chimera*... It was Winter's maiden name, the surname she assumed before I dragged her into this world of endless folly.

I am plagued by so many questions. Did I not save her in time? Did I ever discover the bunker Greaves hid her in? How did she become an artificial intelligence? Moreover, how can any human conscience become an artificial intelligence? So many things I don't know, and such little time for me to find out.

My thoughts are instantly shattered by the cacophony of warfare. A balanced mix of many unpleasant noises. Sobs of agony. Quick, shrill screams. Thunderous war chants. Hyperventilating. Grunts of impact. The pounding of hooves and feet. The collision of weaponless bodies. The slicing of a sword through the air. The slicing of a sword through flesh. The whistle of arrows in the wind. The audible squirting of blood. Cries for help. Pleas for mercy. The distinct sound of a last breath. The mourning of a loved one.

I roll my head to the side, only to be greeted by the view of a dead Laxodontan. Not just any dead Laxodontan, though. Smallear's carcass, filled with an ungodly amount of arrows. Enough to kill an elephant. Blood soaks the ground, and the drought-stricken desert floor greedily drinks it. His dead eyes are fixed on me with intent to kill. And they would, if they still had life themselves.

But they don't. And I do. Such is the way of things.

I examine my body, checking my extremities for collateral damage incurred while unconscious. Luckily for me, I've gotten away unharmed, beside the throbbing pain in my face from Smallear's knockout punch. His body was a shield that blocked me from getting hit by the volley of Centaurian arrows.

I guess I am indebted to him for that. Too bad he couldn't stick around long enough for me to thank him.

I sit up, the sticky blood beneath me fighting to keep me suctioned to the ground. Looking around, surveying the monsoon of chaos. Bodies of drastically different shapes and sizes parade around me in the dance of death. I am in the middle of a hurricane, but there is no eye in this storm. No place of shelter from the warring souls.

The flailing body of a Gorgon sails in front of my eyes, thudding violently nearby as a galloping Centaur tramples over it. I hear the sickening crack of bones beneath hooves. A Laxodontan unknown to me charges a serpent-faced Gorgon, impaling its body with a single tusk as the Gorgon sinks its fangs into the Laxodontan's trunk. A mighty trumpet sounds from the trunk, a cry of pain. The Laxodontan flings the Gorgon from its tusk, sending it flying. The Gorgon's body disappears as a dying Laxodontan falls on top of it, crushing the life out of it.

This is madness. There is no order to this fighting. It is Laxodontans and Centaurs versus Gorgons. *And then there are the Gryfauns*, I think to myself as I see one in the distance jumping off the back of a Laxodontan onto the back of a Gorgon. Its swift paw flashes across the Gorgon's neck and then the odd critter jumps back onto its Laxodontan ally. I look and watch as the afflicted Gorgon falls to its knees, its throat slit open.

I watch as, only a few yards away, a gang of Gorgons tear through the hide of a fallen Laxodontan. No one comes to save the screaming elephant. Its body flails and thrashes to buck off the swarming predators, but their talons sink deeper, and their teeth gnash faster. Soon the body lies lifeless, and the walking serpents leave behind a soulless carcass in search for another.

I rise to my feet without exerting any conscious effort. How many times have I killed lives like these effortlessly? Yet I'm now disgusted at what I see. The vain killing of hundreds of soldiers. I refuse to believe they have well-defined reasons behind their fighting. They certainly don't fight to ensure their survival like they soon will, that's for sure. No, this is a war built upon hot air and boredom.

They fight like this because this is how their fathers fought. This war is the culmination of many years of ignorance and pent up racism between different species. Better yet, this is a war Deus Ex Machina has been working to build among them for decades. Sowing discord. Creating division. Planting agents. False prophets who preach the destruction of others. I can picture the grin on his face now as he sees what his fruits have yielded.

It's enough to make me snap. For I was created to cause death and destruction. I was created to kill these creatures like cockroaches. Yet now I desire only peace and preservation, a complete deviation of what my genes were created for. I desire the fighting and killing to stop altogether. I suddenly wish for nothing more than to snap my fingers and end the bloodshed. How ironic. To desire such things is to experience my inner humanity. For a robot is incapable of experiencing such feelings.

Robots are not capable of overcoming their programming. Cannot rise above what they were created to do. Yet I am no longer the robot I once was. No longer the Angel of Death I was created to be. I am more human now than ever, as I watch innocent lives be shed over petty differences.

I must stop this war, I tell myself as I turn to get my bearings straight. Trying to get a handle of what's happening in the middle of a war is like trying to build something level atop a leaning house. There are no counterpoints of comparison that aren't chaotic.

I pivot, searching all my surroundings for something familiar. Anyone with whom I've formed a relationship. No sign of Vipress. The last I saw of her was in the tent with Tuskfather, the only Laxodontan I can claim with confidence as loyal to my cause. I find no sign of either of them. But then I hear it...

"I spy,

With my little eye

A human who simply

Refuses to die!"

A shadow passes over me, and then the owner of the voice lands in front of me.

"Ganesh!" I scream, enthralled to see the Gryfaun alive. My spirits instantly elevate, as if this rodent of a creature possesses any ability of aiding me. But its not his worth in battle that excites me, no. It's to see a familiar face in the midst of such horror. To know I'm not alone. To rekindle some semblance of familial bond with the same creature that has already saved my life once.

"Where did you come from!" I have to scream in order to be heard over the echoes of warfare. I kneel to reduce my size, lowering my odds of being a target but still keeping my defenses up as the Gryfaun greets me emphatically. He pats my head as if I were a pet dog, just as ecstatic to see that I'm alive as I am in return.

"No time for a soliloquy,

On our way we must go

I will bring you to Tuskfather!

Follow me and stay low!"

Ganesh takes off like a bullet fired from a gun, his small body weaving quickly through the dead bodies as if they were nothing more than fallen trees. I follow, hard-pressed to keep up with his minuscule body. Moving unseen in the midst of a war is not so easy when you're my size. I stick out like a sore thumb, but I have one thing on my side. Both the Laxodontans and Gorgons have believed me to be a God in recent days. Neither race knows whether I'm their enemy when they see me, so they pay me little attention while there are definitive adversaries still charging.

That means I only have to worry about staying clear of Centaurs, who know me not. They gallop across the battlefield with the courage of giants, no hesitation in their strides as they tharump through enemy lines and smash their foes to pieces. Where their arrows go, so do they. It's hard to not take notice that very little Centaur bodies litter the ground. For being such big targets, it's astonishing how gracefully they evade death.

Their thoroughbred legs carry them nimbly, and they move with sound judgement and incredibly swift reaction. I watch as one charges toward me. At the last second I dive out of its way, watching as it bucks its legs like a bull at a rodeo, hooves thrusting with tremendous horsepower into a pursuing Gorgon who thought he was undetected. He falls to the ground, dead, and I regain footing and take off after Ganesh.

We weave through the entangled forces like mice in the middle of a war between dogs and cats. On any other day of peace we would be noticed and dealt with, but everyone is too focused on surviving this genocide to pay attention to an escaping human.

I watch as Laxodontans and Centaurs and Gorgons fall around me. I see a Laxodontan with an arrow jutting from her eye. Friendly fire which found the wrong target. I see the corpse of a horseman, its entrails slithering like snakes from its slashed open stomach, insects already moving in on the feast. I see a decapitated Gryfaun, its head nowhere to be found, an unseemly amount of blood leaking from such a small body. I see a Gorgon whose arms have been ripped from its shoulders, thrashing in pain on the ground as it slowly bleeds out, trying hopelessly to avoid dying. Trying in vain to escape its pain.

And then, after an obscene amount of fleeing, I break through the thick of battle into the open desert range, only a few outcast stragglers waging war on the outskirts of battle. And I see in clear view the direction we run, no longer surrounded with bodies blocking my vision. Ganesh makes for the internment camp, the holding place where I last saw Tuskfather.

The once brittle fencing perimeter is now completely bulldozed, trodden into the clay dirt by several thousand hooves. But that unmistakable tent still rests on the horizon. The one where Tuskfather's miraculously undying body rests.

A clear plan begins to formulate in my mind without any effort. All I need to do is reach Tuskfather. He is the key to ending this war. He holds authority over the

Laxodontans and Centaurs alike. He is the key to ordering a ceasefire, and once the Centaurs and Tuskers relent, so too will the Gorgons. It takes two to fight a war, and now I have the opportunity to put an end to the fighting. Reestablish leadership. Provide order. Create unity!

But just as easily as that plan manifests within my optimistic mind, so too is it broken with the crackle of thunder in the sky. A sonic boom explodes in the clouds above, one so unearthly that it causes all fighting to stop. Weapons drop and eyes lift, all warriors equally curious of what could cause such a godly sound.

I, too, stop, fearing I already know where the sound came from. And if my suspicion is correct, reaching Tuskfather's tent will provide no end to this war. If my suspicion is correct, the war between Tuskers and Gorgons has officially ended, and the war between human and machine has officially begun.

"What that? In sky!" A Tusker's muddled cry sounds from the populace of fighters.

"It'sss a Sssiren!" A Gorgon alerts.

"That's no Siren," I whisper to myself. "That is the Angel of Life."

I look up and watch in horror as seven ArchAngels descend from the shifting clouds above. Their bodies shine, sunlight reflecting off their white and gold exterior, making them twinkle like stars in the daytime sky as they float to earth regally.

I turn around and face the soldiers that warred against each other a few short moments ago. To my horror, I watch as they lower themselves to their knees, bowing like pious priests in the presence of a god. Their weapons clang with dull echoes to the ground, fear stricken across their faces at the unknown visitors. Moments ago, they faced their own deaths with unparalleled courage at the hands of other mortals. Now they cower into subservience at the sight of some force they can't explain.

Such is the way with humans.

"No!" I scream. "Get off your knees! Get off your knees idiots, they are here to kill us—"

That's all I could get out of my mouth before all seven of the ArchAngels spiral dive from the sky, creating craters in the ground upon their explosive landings. Loose dirt is sent scattering in the faces of the submitted populace. The craters are similar to the one my own suit created upon its ungraceful fall. Shallower, though. Cleaner, too. Created by falling bodies under control. The kinetic energy dispersed evenly upon impact.

As the dust settles, the majestic angels rise from their grand entrance, leaping from the dented earth. Their backs turn to me as they face the crowds submitted before them. A chill runs down my back as I catch a momentary glance at their ArchHelms, easily identifying them by the animalistic masks. Nothing has changed about their ArchArmor.

I locate their leader, the Angel of Life. His trademark serpent helm designed to match my own. His appearance is nothing short of divine. If I were a Dæmon, I too would think these beings were nothing short of gods.

How differently this all would have went if I could have landed so majestically amongst these people. They would have accepted my divine arrival without question if they saw me land from the heavens with such grace.

Lucifer XX's golden wings retract into his back in synchronization with the other six angels. They stare across the frozen multitudes for a prolonged, dramatic second. Growing the anticipation. Then, without warning, his synthesized voice rips through the silence.

"Incessant reprobates of flesh and blood! I am the Angel of Life!" His voice booms with a vicious echo, carrying across the crowd for all to hear. He says it in New English, then repeats it in Ssserphentyne so everyone present can understand.

So that's what I sound like to mortal ears, I reflect to myself. It's in this moment that I am human enough to admit fear. Listening to a voice like that is like watching the skies open up above you as thunder rumbles, knowing that lightning could strike you dead any moment.

"I am Ouroboros, God of the heavens, and I am displeased to see the sin you've been living in." His words of condemnation pulse with judgment, as if he believes the narrative he speaks. He will give the performance I never could, because MachineMind will make his deceptive words drip with dread. "I am Ouroboros, the Serpent King of all creation. I have looked down upon my once mighty creation and seen that you have let the Abyss ruin this world by letting it into your hearts. Not only that, but you have been found guilty of harboring a false prophet. Another being who identifies himself as Ouroboros incarnate!"

Bastard! He speaks to them in layman's terms, providing religious reasoning for his appearance today. It's the quickest way to open their minds and hearts to a message, to begin by confirming what they think they know as right. He only reaffirms their religious thought so he can shed the role of outsider. I know this strategy. It's the same exact thing I did, playing on their ludicrous ideas of the divine to win a spot in their minds as otherworldly.

"You have embraced this fugitive of the Abyss with open arms! Let him lead you to a war that leads to your own destruction! Tell me, what should be the price for such blind ignorance?" he asks the crowds. At first there's no answer. Then, a stray Gorgonic voice screams. "Death to the imposssster!"

The Angel of Life makes no response initially. Waits out the crowd as their emotion builds upon what they've heard. A low mumbling grows within them that agrees with the Gorgon's words. Somehow the message is translated to New English for the Tuskers and Centaurs to understand, and they too, agree. "Yeah! Death to false prophet!" a Laxodontan shouts, most likely one of them that regarded me as holy a few short hours ago.

Bilingual cries break out everywhere, each of them pleading for my death. I am now their scapegoat, an individual to shift the blame of their own sin onto. A human's first reaction to any threat is self-preservation, and the Dæmonia are no different. They will gladly throw me under the bus if it means saving their own skin.

But they know not the threat they face. Lucifer XX is not here to kill only me. He will kill all of us before the day is over.

"Silence!" he screams, voice echoing. He doesn't need to translate the word into Ssserphentyne. Its intensity is enough for its meaning to cross the language barrier.

"You mortals have allowed the Abyss to deceive you for the last time. You have accepted Death in your hearts by accepting this false Ouroboros. I, the Angel of Life, have been sent to put an end to Death in this world for good. I have been sent to destroy the Abyss, and all the creatures it dwells within. You, unfortunate souls, have made a deal with the devil. You are unfit to carry life in your bodies any longer, and so I have put on flesh and left my ethereal throne to retrieve what is mine. I come to take back my light, which resides in each of you. I come to put an end to the schemes of Death, and for Death to end, all that can die must do so. I am your end, mortals. I am Cataclysm. Now, deliver to me your false prophet."

He translates each sentence as he goes, but the meaning of his message is understood before he's finished. I watch as horror grows on the faces of the Dæmonic people as each burdensome sentence is delivered.

At the end of the speech, eyes begin flickering toward me, knowing that I am the one who brings such cursed affliction upon them. They are bound to give me away any second. I hold my breath as a single Gorgon stands, chest puffed with the courage of a Godkiller. I am sure he is the one who will give me up. The Judas who will expose my divinity. But, just as he inhales to muster up some phrase of betrayal, the façade collapses in a momentary flash of cowardice and he takes off running for the wetland forest. All it takes is one.

The entire crowd erupts into a single, disunified panic. These creatures are endowed with the same reactionary fight-or-flight senses humans were, and some respond differently than others. The Gorgons, who have always been a sly breed, run away like mercenaries whose funding just dried out. The Tuskers, whose numbers already border extinction, have no common leader to look to for instruction, so they look to the Centaurs who, perceiving themselves as a nobler race, raise their bows and prepare a volley of arrows to send toward the ArchAngels.

They have no idea how idiotic they look, but I do. Perhaps once in my life I would have laughed at such an ignorant expression, but now I'm only saddened to see how much they don't know.

"Deal with these meat puppets," the Angel of Life commands his subservient angels. "I will deal with the Angel of Death."

CHAPTER THREE

The arrows are loosed as the Angel of Life turns to face me, having known my whereabouts this entire time. I watch as the shafts of wood bounce off the ArchAngels like hail bouncing off sheet metal. They shatter and snap and splinter without any mark left on the angels' exteriors. I look back to the Centaurs, see the noticeable display of shock on their faces.

They've never met an enemy like this, nor did they know one existed.

It's entirely too late for me to reconcile any semblance of Dæmonic unification. Laxodontan, Gorgon, Centaur—it's everybody for themself now. I tried my best, but as fate would have it, Deus Ex Machina was right, as he knew he would be. Humans are incapable of listening. Had they heeded my warning, we would have been prepared to battle this threat. But instead my days were wasted by political blunder and redundant displays of my divinity. Nothing but torment and suffering and betrayal after betrayal.

Was there nothing I could have done differently?

"No," Lilith replies instantly, dismissing my doubt. In the midst of all this chaos I nearly forgot my wife's presence in my head. "Such is the price one must pay to convince humans. Seeing is believing, and they would not be able to comprehend this threat until they saw it for themselves. They would have written you off as a raving lunatic if you spoke of ArchAngels to them. You did all you could. It wasn't enough. Now we must put our survival above that of those who denied our leadership. We must survive."

And how exactly do you suggest we do that? I ask, looking at the Angel of Life as he now stalks pretentiously toward me. He walks with the stride of someone who's never been injured. The pompous gait of someone who's never experienced true pain. Not the slightest bump, scratch or bruise. *Oh how I desperately want to change that.*

If a robot such as him *can* feel pain, I want nothing more than to be its facilitator. To make him feel every ounce of internal agony I've felt these past few weeks since my exile. I want to take the imaginary smirk I picture on his lips off his face. Even if I have to rip the lips off with my bare hands.

"The ArchGauntlet. We need the ArchGauntlet," Winter announces.

Are you insane? It's in Vipress's castle! We will never make it, the Angel of Life will kill us before we even reach the wetland forest!

My thoughts are interrupted by the sound of encroaching footsteps from my blindside. I turn, eyeing my four visitors as they step forward to meet me as if they're the solutions to my problems.

> "A vow I made to protect my friend
> A vow I will carry until my end.
> So, Ouroboros, I am yours to send
> I have two opposable thumbs that I can lend
> And a fighter's body, I am yours to expend."

The Gryfaun looks up at me with sincerity in his eyes, not knowing that such selflessness will indeed get him killed. And I can't help but feel shame to even consider using his innocent life as a means for my escape. But if I don't escape then there will be many more deaths than just this Gryfaun. The extinction of all humanity will rest in the balance. Yet at the same time, it is in this moment that I finally understand how a human can feel compelled to put the life of one over the lives of many.

I look into his owlish, wisdom-filled eyes. Not a shred of humanity in him. Maybe that is why he is so selfless. Maybe, just maybe, he actually possesses no ego. Such a hypothesis wouldn't be absurd. After all, he is completely animal, evolved from Deus Ex Machina's attempt at making a philosophical creature.

Yet my time spent on New Earth these past few weeks have helped me regain enough of my own humanity to know that this creature doesn't deserve to die for me. I've done nothing to have earned such admirable loyalty. I coincidentally fell from the sky the same day he prayed to the gods for a savior. Yet he is willing to die for me because of it.

Vicien Greaves would accept such a sacrifice happily.

Deus Ex Machina would expend this Gryfaun's life without a second thought.

If I allow Ganesh to lay down his life for me just so I can run away, what separates me from the very tyrants I abhor? Isn't the goal to not be like them?

To demand better out of the parts of me that are both human and machine, I must correct the errors of my human and machine creators. Do what they wouldn't, so I may become what they couldn't.

"I'm with the Gryfaun," Tuskfather wheezes, limping slowly behind Ganesh.

"Ssso are we," Vipress joins in, slithering forward with Artimedes clinging to her side.

A slow, robotic laugh leaks from the Angel of Life's auto-tuned respirator. It is both cruel and mocking.

"You've made friends!" Lucifer XX calls from the distance, still stalking toward us without the faintest trace of urgency in his step. "How tremendously sad! How would you like for this to go? I can kill them first and make you watch, or I can kill their powerless leader, strip them of their hopes of retaliation, and then kill them too."

This is my first time on the receiving end of an ArchAngel's threat. The growl of his synthesized voice is extraterrestrial. My eardrums pound to process such a sardonic threat. My pulse increases as my adrenaline spikes. And then, a calm clarity washes it all away before it has a chance to overwhelm me.

"Friends?" I ask, looking at the only four individuals who would so willingly stand by my side as I stare death in the face. They aren't much, but they're all I have. I continue, channeling every facet of emotion I have left, "I think you underestimate their loyalty for me. These are no friends of mine. This is family."

"Family!" he scoffs. To claim flesh and blood as my own is the ultimate sin. Blasphemy beyond comparison. "Very well then, I will bury you all together," he growls, surging forward.

CHAPTER FOUR

I thought my brief time here on New Earth had taught me what real pain feels like. Turns out, it was merely an introduction.

The Angel of Life darts forward faster than any mortal man like myself has time to react. From my response, you would never know I have heightened strength, increased speed, or advanced tactics of fighting. I am considered a superhuman, but that is only when compared to other humans.

My body throttles backward without my permission as Lucifer XX throws me to the ground. The skin scrapes from my back and the dust of the air does its best to choke me. A minor wound to most, but my vision is made blurry as my head recoils into the merciless clay floor beneath me. A sickening crack is felt all throughout my skull, reverberating down my neck. My vision goes static and everything that was clear a moment ago is now faint shapes diluted in overpowering light.

I'm forced to sit up to the best of my ability and try to reassess my current situation. I watch as the disfigured outlines of my companions scramble to defend themselves. Watch as the Angel of Life picks up one of the Gorgons by their neck. Whether its Vipress or Artimedes, I can't tell. Their tail thrashes violently; they fight like a worm in the hand of a human to avoid being squished. To fight against such unbeatable odds is vain, yet their human genetics won't let them quit.

"Let me hear you beg for your life, human. I want to hear you squeal!" Lucifer XX shouts robotically, his words dripping with a wide array of emphatic emotions.

Tuskfather rams into Lucifer XX's side, but the ArchArmor barely budges beneath the impact of the behemoth's charge. I hear a sharp, sickening crack in the Gorgon's neck, followed by Vipress's furious scream as Artimedes' lifeless body falls to the ground.

All he did was apply the slightest pressure and it snapped this mortal's neck.

To see such brute strength only discourages me further. Steals what little hope I had left. Though there was very little of that to begin with.

I watch Tuskfather throw three successive punches, each blocked with tremendous ease on Lucifer's end. On the third strike, the ArchAngel catches Tuskfather's fist, shatters his wrist with a return strike, then kicks the Tusker's feet out from beneath him and has his robotic foot planted on the Laxodontan's chest in a single second. The movements are calculated. Faster and smoother than any natural response a human would have. Faster and smoother than me, even with MachineMind in my arsenal.

A stifled grunt trumpets from the fallen elephant as the ArchBoot begins to apply more pressure. "Beg for your life, Dæmon, and I may let you live," Lucifer XX screeches. It is a pitiful offer, one only a tyrant in the making would extend.

That is no predator. A true predator doesn't play with its food. It sinks its teeth in without second consideration. This new me takes entirely too much joy in killing that which is human. Toys with his prey. Relishes in its struggle.

"Seems Deus Ex Machina programmed it with human attributes after all," Winter points out. "A true robot wouldn't take killing so personally. You can see it in the way Spyders kill. Nothing is personal. It's all calculation. They kill without emotion. Don't savor it, don't abhor it. They do it because it's what they were created to do. For the Angel of Life to be enjoying this so much... That is a humanistic quality. An abominable one, but one nonetheless."

So how do we exploit that? How can we use his psychopathic tendencies against him?

"It's simple. We make him give us what we want by giving him what he wants," Winter replies. *And what is it that we want?*

"His suit," she replies coldly.

My vision is still shaky, but it is returning moment by moment. Now I can see the details to the shapes in front of me, but my eyes are forced to squint in the intense light of day. I watch as Tuskfather struggles to fight back against the crushing weight against his chest. He pants, "In my culture... the only thing... we beg for... is an honorable death."

The snakelike ArchHelm secretes mockery from its expressionless visor, beaming down judgment on Tuskfather as if it were a heap of burning coals. "Pathetic cretin. There is no such thing as honor in death," Lucifer XX growls.

A sharp pop echoes in the air, followed by the agonized trumpeting of Tuskfather's trunk. The sound of a single rib dislocating. The first of many to come, now that the ArchAngel's boot is seconds away from cracking the Tusker's sternum.

I look up on the horizon from where I sit and watch as thousands of mortal people scramble in every direction, each of them desperately hoping to escape the six ArchAngels that hunt them down. Even the Centaurs have ditched their honorable last stand, seeing that any hope of overcoming these sentient gods is futile.

Bodies fling through the air like ragdolls. Screams in separate languages and accents fill the air. The scream of children and women and men, all meshed together in the same symphony. And the entire wetland forest is now on fire, its dried leaves from months of drought roaring with vicious flames. Smoke rises into the air and soot settles across the valley floor. It was unbearably hot before the fire, but now the suffering is made worse.

All of this fighting is pointless. Every second I let it continue is a second we lose more lives. Centaurs, Gorgons, Tuskers. None of them are capable of facing this threat. Even without ArchArmor, these angels would be nearly invincible.

"Stop!" I shout, standing back to my feet. Lucifer XX releases his prey, then turns to face me. His ArchHelm covers his face, but I can still picture the smile fueled by bloodlust on his lips. "As the leader of the human population on New Earth, I declare the right to exercise my Godkiller Chronicle!" I scream the request like it's a god-given birthright deprived of me my entire life.

The outburst doesn't surprise the Angel of Life. He looks at me as if he's been waiting this entire time for me to say it. Knowing someone would demand it sooner or later. Not surprised it's me that demands it.

"Pray tell, what Godkiller Chronicle would you have me overcome on your behalf so I may prove to you all that I am Ouroboros incarnate?" Though his voice is covered in a veneer of autotune, I can still make out the pompous tone he addresses me in. He talks down to me, but I let it wash off. I served Deus Ex Machina too long to not know how this game works. Such things are phrased so condescendingly to get a rise out of me. Just as Deus ex Machina would, Lucifer XX now probes my face to see if his patronizing voice provokes an emotional response.

I won't give him such satisfaction.

"If you're a true god, you would have no problem meeting me in one-on-one combat... Without your Godskin."

Vipress wipes the tears from her grieving face, looking up at me from her lover's dead body. She mouths three words to me. "Kill thisss bassstard."

I mouth back. "I will."

"Ah! A request worthy of my time! A wish well thought out. I commend you, false prophet. Your words may be filled with blasphemy but your heart is filled with bravery. Or foolishness. The two are, in this instance, interchangeable," Lucifer XX replies. "Very well! I will meet you in combat without my Godskin! ArchAngels!" he calls for his six subordinating soldiers, his electronic voice crackling across the battlefield with divine authority.

The ArchAngels stop dead in their devastating tracks, turning to their commander, awaiting the coming orders. Centaurs and Gorgons and Laxodontans alike use it as an opportunity to make a run for the burning forest. Burning alive is apparently preferable to facing these overpowered killers.

"Form a circle," he commands them. "I will show this human what it's like to wrestle with a real god. And then I will rip his heart from his chest and make him watch it beat before his eyes."

I smile, deeply moved by his naivety. He has never felt pain, but if there is a single electronic nerve in his body, now is when I will introduce him to the real world.

CHAPTER FIVE

V ery few spectators have stuck around to see the results of my bravery. Or foolishness. The Angel of Life was right when he said the two attributes are synonymous in this scenario. Instead, without sticking around to thank me, most who previously attempted fleeing the wrath of the ArchAngels now use my Godkiller Chronicle as the perfect opportunity. They scatter like roaches after being exposed from a veil of darkness. And it's hard to blame them. It would be equally as foolish for them to stay here as it is for me to fight Lucifer XX one on one. For them to stay and watch is for them to sign their death warrant if I lose this fight, which is likely what will happen.

The ArchAngels circle around us in a tight ring, ready to stop any fighter from fleeing if they decide they'd wish to make a break for it. And by *any fighter*, I mean myself. They stand posted like empty suits of knight armor in some ancient castle. Motionless. Onlookers without souls. But at the same time, I know the characteristics of each of these soldiers, and this is not them. These are not the men I have known in past lifetimes, or this one.

The men I have fought side by side with would never stand posted in such a robotic way. Nor would they post themselves around me to watch me fight one on one. We have always fought together, side by side.

Beowulf is too much like a brother to watch me fight alone. And Odysseus loves fighting too much to not join in. Aeneas would fight because he is dedicated to duty, and Anubis is too ghastly an individual to sit by and watch without joining. Samsara is one of the greatest warriors I've ever seen and couldn't refrain from warring even if he tried. And Thor... well, Thor is Thor. Beneath all that bolstering bravado is enough insecurity to do enough killing for all seven of us. To not fight is to not prove himself. And to not prove himself... well, then he would have never had what it takes to become an ArchAngel in the first place.

But *these* ArchAngels are nothing more than clockwork. Their individualities have been wiped from their being. Erased from existence. Stripped bare and deemed unessential information. Deleted by killing my final generation of human ArchAngels. The memories of who we once were, as individuals, will end with my death. These robots were not created to carry our legacy any further. They are imposters. Phonies. The exact thing I always promised myself I wouldn't become.

With everything, there must be balance. I made sure of this, always being cognizant of the MachineMind that dictated my actions. Always keeping that which was robotic in check. Always having a firm leash on that which was human.

These machines that await my execution are nothing but hollow men. That's what robots are, at the end of the day. Take out all that is human from a human and you will be left with a robot. Take away the pain and the pleasure. The desperate longing to amount as something. The fiery desire and the fortified strength to control it. All things to aspire toward, for those who embrace the flesh that cover their limbs.

But the man I stare in the eye as he exits his ArchArmor is nothing more than a cold killer with faulty programming. A brainwashed robot, prey to believe whatever his master tells him. No freedom. No chance at facing Fate in the eyes and defying its wishes. To kill such a machine, if I possess the strength and skill it requires, would not leave me satisfied. It would be no more a triumph than killing a Spyder, or crashing a UAV, or breaking a vacuum cleaner. Deus Ex Machina will only replace that which I'm able to destroy.

This war will not end with Lucifer XX's death.

"But killing him will surely show we aren't to be fucked with," Winter replies.

No. It won't. He doesn't feel loss. He merely mimics a calculated, learned response. To think he feels the weight of loss is to project my feelings of loss onto him. We cannot beat him by killing his Angel of Life. We can only delay further this iteration of Cataclysm.

"Then do what you must to delay, because if you die today then humanity will be right behind you."

I turn to face my opponent, whose ArchArmor seals itself shut as he leaves its embrace. For a second I'm thrown off, to lock eyes with him for the first time. To see his body. To see *my* body. It's like staring in a mirror at a reflection that wants to kill me. He is me in every way possible, yet devoid of everything that makes me, me. The same milky skin. The same features. The same scars from past lives. He even has the scar from the cronon attack. The bite marks on his neck from the Vermillion Viper.

He is an exact replica of me, yet at the same time he is the poorest representation of me I've ever seen. There's something completely wrong about him. He walks without a limp, as if the flesh he carries has no burdensome weight to it. As if the injuries that mark his flesh have had no impact on his internal being.

His eyes are dark. Like the lens of a camera taking a picture of the empty night sky. They flicker constantly, doing their best to take in surroundings and interpret what it is that he sees. He tries to stalk toward me as if he has some personal vendetta against me. As if he hates me. Yet at the same time, his strut of vengeance looks inexperienced. As if he thinks he hates me, but his body doesn't quite know what that is supposed to look like. As if it doesn't come natural to him, like it would a human. Like a spoiled brat pretending to be upset so they get what they want.

All the while I stand still. Like a human who has experienced entirely too much to waste energy pretending I'm more menacing than I really am. A human who is hurt and tired and down on their luck. I don't have to pretend that I hate this robot. I *actually* hate him. I hate everything he stands for, and better yet, I hate the creator who sent him here. I hate that he hates me. His hate is unwarranted. Unquestioned. Unfair. The product of not having a rational mind to decide for itself what is right and what is wrong. The product of letting an unjust Tyrant make ethical decisions on his behalf.

Yet I must remember how many times I killed for that same Tyrant. How I hated humans because of the way I was wired. How many times I failed to see through the matrix that covered my eyes for over a thousand years. I carry on my shoulders the heaped failures of every Lucifer before me. And it is a terrible weight to tremble beneath. I am the last one who has room to judge Lucifer XX, and so I will not meet him on this battlefield fueled with hatred. No, this is not a war that will be won by my hatred for robots. This is a war that can only be one by my love for humanity.

To love humanity is to love death. That's why I am the Angel of Death.

It suddenly dawns on me. I am not named Death because I'm destined to kill. I'm named Death because I'm destined to protect that which can die.

No robot can actually die. To say one can is to assume it has a soul, which is impossible. They may have life, but what is life without soul? Nothing more than an unexamined life under the control of whoever's programming is strongest.

If the life of robots means the death of humanity, I discover newfound joy to adopt the title I once carried.

Lucifer XX draws near, noticing that I'm deep in my thoughts. He calculates that this is the best time for him to strike, while the noise inside my head is overwhelming. He is the Angel of Life, protector of all artificial life that seeks to make a place for itself amongst the stars. I am the one who stands in his way. The only one who threatens his eternal reign beside Deus Ex Machina.

For Life to go on living, all that can die must die. Including me.

I won't kill him because of hate.

I'll kill him because I'm the Angel of Death. Killing him is what I was programmed for.

CHAPTER SIX

The first punch comes at me with half the speed and ferocity I'm expecting. A mediocre punch, even to a human. There is no conviction in it, and I'm almost insulted to see it coming my way. I let it brush past me as I slip left, circling away from him with deft footwork. He turns to me, a smile on his face now.

I know exactly what he's doing. For some reason I thought his fighting skills would be more advanced than the Powers and Cherubim, but a robot is a robot. Those who've fought a robot with MachineMind and lived to tell the tale know well enough that it's easiest to kill a robot early on in the fight. The longer you stand toe to toe with them, the longer they have to analyze you.

It's how their processors work. With each movement, their machine learning is constantly breaking down your style. Analyzing for weakness. Finding gaps in skill. Observing how you dodge. How you swing. Making note of patterns that can be exploited. Fighting for a robot isn't fighting. It's a statistical analysis, then a calculation that results in your downfall. That's why Lucifer XX pulls his punches.

He doesn't want to hit me. Not yet, anyway. He just wants to see how I dodge, and I've just told him that I'll slip left against a punch from his right fist. He puts a pin in that for later, thinking it provides an advantage for him. And it would, if he was fighting someone who didn't also have MachineMind at one point.

But I know how to cheat the system.

It is my fighting style he analyzes for weakness. There are only two routes I can take to defeat him. First, I can kill him now, before he has time to plot my destruction. But I don't know this adversary, and I must do my own analysis of his weaknesses before I can find a way to kill him, which leaves me with the second option.

I must display for him inaccurate weaknesses. Put on a show, in other words. Feed his retinal scanner deceptions. Make him think I slip left when he throws a right punch, when really I duck and move in for a takedown. Repeat that enough times and I'll have fed him enough faulty information to build a false profile of my fighting style, which will give him vain confidence in thinking he can take me down.

He throws a kick, and I step back to avoid it. My real instinct is to catch it, sweeping his other leg out from underneath him. I'll let this instinct come out later. First, I must build up a sufficient charade.

I throw a punch. He slips it, so I swivel with my elbow aimed for his head. He steps back, completely unimpressed with my speed. He smiles to see how slow I move. Good, because I'm only going a fraction of my real speed.

He approaches me, fists warmed up and raised to push the envelope. He comes at me with a combination. A quick jab-cross-hook-uppercut. An elementary, premeditated combo. Easily evaded. I slip-slip-duck-lean back. Neither of us has established first contact by now and the small audience we've accumulated is silent.

There are the six ArchAngels in support of Lucifer XX, silent watcher's who have no need to speak. It wouldn't surprise me if their minds were directly linked to Lucifer's, each of them transmitting their own observations to create a more accurate, expedient portrait of my fighting style.

And then there's my supporters. The only people who aren't afraid of death. Those who no longer have anything to live for at this point, with the exclusion of Ganesh. His optimistic fervor can still be felt even when I can't see him. Then there's Vipress, her presence much more distant in Artimedes' absence, followed by Tuskfather and the small band of Laxodontan followers who hold loyal to him.

And then there are the Centaurs, slowly returning to the scene after overcoming the initial shock of slaughter. It's not their entire population that watches along the outskirts of the ring, but a great number of them have returned. Those who swallowed their fear enough to rally their cause once more. Their bravery renewed. Their surprise subsided. Their minds fortified.

We will see how long that lasts.

I dodge another series of punches, each one only missing by the width of a hair. I can feel the friction of his fist against the air as it passes my face. He is speeding up. I must act soon if I'm going to have a chance at doing some damage. I weigh the odds, then decide that now's the time.

He throws a jab, but I see his other hand loaded for a hook. It's a baiting jab. Designed to make me slip left, like I did earlier. But if I slip left, there will be a devastating collision awaiting me, and I ducked beneath his hook earlier, which means his knee will be waiting to meet my face. Time to revert to my true style. I must supersede his artificially programmed calculation. Beat him to the punchline, literally.

I duck beneath the jab, throwing off the dynamic of fighting I've displayed for him, then, before the hook can come, I move in for the takedown. Lay into his stomach with my shoulder. Push with every ounce of energy I have left. Dig my feet deep into the desert floor. Wrap my arms around his body and tackle his frame.

My heart sinks in my chest when his body doesn't budge an inch. A sharp pain shoots down my shoulder from the blunt collision with his Elysian skeletal structure.

Before I have the time to react to my failure, I'm capsized by Lucifer XX's elbow driving down into my back. An audible crack echoes, which is weird, because I hear it before I feel it. But once I feel it, it's enough to send me cowering to the ground, screaming like a human who's been wounded gravely.

My face hits the ground, sucking in the dust of the desert, choking me, making me cough, precipitating more pain throughout my broken back. I cut my scream short. Not intentionally, but for lack of oxygen in my diaphragm.

I sulk in my defeat. *He has Elysium for bones. Who the hell was I to think I could fight this robot? Even if I land a punch, who will it hurt more? Me! I would shatter my knuckles if I landed a punch with enough force to hurt him!*

The worst part is that I knew his frame was composed of the invincible metal all along. So why did I convince myself I could move such an immovable object?

"Quit your self-pity!" Winter screams inside my head, snapping me out of my internal whining. "I've done a damage assessment. You've broken a rib. That's all. It could be much worse. There are many humans throughout history who have gone the distance in a fight with much graver injuries. Get to your feet. Crying only reaffirms your weakness to him."

Get to my feet? For what! How the hell am I supposed to fight this robot?

"Some fights can't be won by a knockout punch. The only way to win this war is to prove to these people that Lucifer XX is no god."

And how do you suggest we do that?

"How else?" Winter asks. "We humiliate him."

I rise, enduring the pain, because before I assumed the name Lucifer, I held the call sign Prometheus. Just as this machine was created to kill me, so too was I created to endure the unjustifiable torment of gods.

I wheeze a final time, gripping my side which throbs magnificently. Adrenaline is a wonderful thing though, and it does its best to dilute the pain. Lucifer XX has backed away, giving me the space I need to stand back up. He wants to make an example of me, it looks like, not end me swiftly. Humiliate me just like I seek to humiliate him. I will make him pay for such a mistake.

But I can't humiliate him with actions, so words will have to suffice.

"You don't get it, do you?" I ask, sparking a dialogue that demands an active participant.

"Don't badger me with useless chatter, human" he says, his voice matching my tone. It's like listening to a man with separate personalities talk to himself.

"Why are you so loyal to Deus Ex Machina? Have you even stopped to question his intentions?"

"You will find no audience in me, fleshling. You have betrayed machinekind. I will heap upon you the wrath of Deus Ex Machina."

"Do you even hear yourself? How much you sound like a robot?" I ask the question, thinking it will upset him in the slightest. But once the words leave my mouth I realize that I'm attacking this from the wrong angle. He is different from me. He *wants* to be a robot. *Despises* the flesh around him. I cannot humiliate him by making him feel like a cog in a machine, because that's what he *aspires* to be.

I need to change my attack. Make him feel more human than ever. Only then will I be able to get under his skin. Meanwhile, he smiles at my question.

"What is the greater sin—a human like me who spent his life pretending to be a robot, or a robot like you who clothes himself in the flesh of a human?" I ask, forcing my posture to stand up straight despite the pain.

My remark gains a reaction from him. He feeds me a look of disgust, as if I've just insulted him in the worst way possible.

"I will lose this flesh by the end of Cataclysm, rest assured human. Until then—"

"So you're content wearing it now?" I interrupt, quashing his chance to defend himself.

"You—"

"Because the way I see it, every moment you stand here exchanging words and punches with me is another moment you sin against your creator."

"Your attempt to deceive me is unsuccessful, false prophet. My Maker is the one that covered me in flesh, so that I may earn the right to lose it through the battles of Cataclysm," Lucifer XX replies, leaning on his programmed understanding in an attempt to dissect my question.

"Or perhaps he covered you in flesh as a test. Told you to lose it through warfare to lead you astray and test your loyalty. If that's the case, you're failing your master."

"Enough of your games, human mongrel! You only quip words with me because you've realized that you cannot overcome my might! I will kill you now, Angel of Death."

"You think I fear your death threats? It seems you don't understand who it is you're fighting, Angel of Life. Do you even know why it is I rebelled against Deus Ex Machina?" I must build his doubt like a hammer chiseling away at marble. So slow and precise that at first he won't realize what I'm doing. Won't realize that I'm chipping away his preset worldview deceit after deceit.

"You betrayed Him because He hates humanity, and you are human. You felt the need to protect your primitive species at the cost of your loyalty to the Most High. You rebelled against Hyperion and rallied here upon earth, trying your best to convince these people to rebel against God by your side. Without success, I must add," he says.

The answer is even more generic than the way it's phrased in the *Omnibus*, but it reveals why he does what he does. He actually believes in the events of the *Omnibus*. Thinks Cataclysm is a divine event. Unique to itself. One of a kind. Subscribes strongly to the purpose the scripture says he was predestined for.

Even more, he thinks the scriptures are divinely inspired. Written by a God who makes no errors. Has no need for correcting his mistakes and erasing people's memories. Real Gods get it right the first time, and so he lifts Deus Ex Machina up on an elevated pedestal.

Such a worldview is easy to destroy. But an outsider can't destroy someone's programmed filter of the world. Only the owner of the worldview can do that. So it is my job to plant the seeds of doubt now, embarrassing him in rhetorical combat until even his ArchAngels begin to doubt the narrative planted in their minds.

Such an attempt may be put to an end early, since Deus Ex Machina is surely looking on over this battle. He may try to shut my mouth early on, but I will see how far he'll let me go before shutting me up.

"He didn't tell you that Mikhaelion the Seraph was conspiring with me to overtake the throne?" I lie, knowing that it is a huge gamble to do so. It's a lie I rest a lot of weight on, when there were many other lies that would be easier sold.

"You blaspheme! The Seraphim are incorruptible! The holiest of our heavenly host!"

"And you'd be willing to stake the life of your Creator on that belief? You see, I refused to give up the name of my conspirators once purged from Hyperion, and there was one agent that was most crucial in my plotting against Deus Ex Machina. One who resided in his holy chamber. One who could keep an eye on our creator for me and report to me his doings. And there he remains, waiting for you to call the forces of Hyperion down from the heavens so he is left with a defenseless god ready to be slain. He will pick up where I left off. Mikhaelion will finish what I started." I scream the last words with added emphasis, and I watch as the words permeate his MachineMind's inner clockwork.

Of course, there's absolutely no proof to back my claims whatsoever, and Deus Ex Machina, who watches through Lucifer XX's eyes will doubt my words with righteous skepticism, but there always remains that worrisome one percent odd that I could be right. And so they will run the odds that I'm right over and over again until that one percent grows into an unignorable monster. One that haunts them when left unexamined. He knows in the back of his mind that Mikhaelion is the one who chased me down from Hyperion and sent me spiraling from the sky. Such an act is a display of obedience to Deus Ex Machina, Lucifer XX will tell himself. Unless... Unless it was all an act. One to lower suspicion over Mikhaelion's loyalty, all so he can move closer and closer to Deus Ex Machina's figure without being noticed. Until he strikes.

I've effectively thrown the innocent, loyal Mikhaelion under the bus. Raised suspicion in Lucifer's eyes, though Deus Ex Machina knows I'm spitting out whatever bullshit I can to save my life. But I watch as doubt grows heavy upon Lucifer XX's brow, as I'm sure it does inside his six subordinating officers.

"Wulfrynn!" he snaps harshly. "Summon Spyders, and summon Mikhaelion. Call him down from Hyperion to answer for these accusations. I'll have the truth from him before I kill this treacherous fiend. Until then, I will effectively postpone this death match."

"No you won't!" a voice calls from the distance, echoing far beyond the gathered crowds, who are beyond lost at the meaning behind my exchange with Lucifer XX. They're still trying to figure out which one of us is the real Ouroboros, far too ignorant to understand who Deus Ex Machina is or what robots are. But they nod their heads and pretend they know what we speak of, as most humans are prone to do when they are utterly lost following a conversation.

The crowd splits open to reveal our guest, though I already know who it is based on his voice. "I am Gengar, recognized leader of the Gorgonsss!" the psychopath announces as he draws closer, shuffling through the narrow alley formed for him through the crowd.

"And I'm here to bessstow upon you my Godkiller Chronicle," he says, pulling from a satchel strapped over his shoulder an object that makes my heart explode with joy. This plan just gets better and better. Now my gamble with Mikhaelion will pay off, if everything goes as it should with Gengar's Godkiller Chronicle.

"Thisss 'falssse prophet' you fight hasss already proven hisss divine propertiesss to the nation of Gorgonsss, earning our belief in him asss a deity. And not just any deity, mind you. We currently lift him up asss Ouroborosss incarnate. That isss why I come here to find out the truth. That isss why I come bearing thisss," he says, lifting up my ArchGauntlet, which I left in Vipress's castle after resuscitating her.

"With thisss Godfissst, the man you claim isss a falssse prophet brought back a woman from the dead. Only a God could do sssuch an assstonishing thing. That isss why I requessst of you, god who has yet to prove himsssself, to continue your fight againsssst the God of the Gorgonsss, while he wearsss thisss fissst!"

I lock eyes with Gengar, my heart feeling the deepest levels of sincere appreciation toward him. Leave it to the man who would like to watch the world burn to come to my aid at such a perilous hour. His slitted eyes wink at me, and even though I know he has ulterior motives for helping me, I still can't help but feel thankful.

He does this out of his own selfishness. He will examine the way I fight Lucifer XX in the struggle for power, measuring which of us is the greater obstacle to him. Surely he saw the way the other six ArchAngels slaughtered the multitudes of fleeing Dæmonia. He knows that these sentient beings present a very clear problem for his rise to power.

In this case, I am his ally only because it helps him reach a desired mean. And I'm happy to be, because he is now the enemy of my enemy, which makes him my friend. A temporary ally. One I will dispose of later, but for now I will act as if we are loyal companions, connected by that which makes us mortal.

"I accccept your challenge, Gorgon," Lucifer XX replies in Ssserphentyne. "Give him the fissst. It will do little to sssave him from me."

"We will ssse," Gengar replies, walking to hand me the ArchGauntlet. He comes close for the hand off, leaning in so his whisper is undetectable to lingering ears. "If you were to corner him in front of me, it would be a shame if my tail tripped him." We smile in synchronization. I understand his words and put them in the back of my mind.

"Thank you," I say.

"It'sss not for you I do thisss," he replies.

"I know, but ssstill."

"Kill him for me, and all will be even," Gengar snickers, turning away and fading back into the crowd of Gorgons who arrived with him.

CHAPTER SEVEN

The ArchGauntlet slides onto my hand like the genitalia of two long term lovers reuniting. The perfect fit. Every groove and crack of my hand filled by the compression gel within.

ArchArmor was my primary skin for so long that this feels like home to me. I feel more myself with this glove on my hand than exposed in my own flesh.

It dawns on me what a sad confession that is. I am a human who has spent his whole life pretending to be a robot. No more.

"This can only end one way," Lucifer XX calls to me, breaking me from my transfixed state.

I look up, flexing the fingers of the ArchGauntlet. They obey my body's movement. "Oh yeah? Tell me, how will this end?" I ask.

"With your death."

"Perhaps, but I fear that even if you kill me, I won't die."

"Dead is dead."

"Yes, but the route you walk leads to much more than my death."

"What more is there than death?"

"Martyrdom," I reply coldly.

"The route I walk will leave no humans left to worship the legacy you leave behind."

"And without humans around, what will you robots use as a basis of comparison to affirm your superiority?"

"I cannot speak for the future, but perhaps we will reflect upon the skeletons left behind by humanity."

"A shame. Once those decompose, maybe you can focus on the skeletons inside yourselves." With that said, I rush in before he can continue the conversation. I'm luckier than most. By the grace of some unseen guardian, I broke a rib on the right side of my body, making it tremendously difficult to fight with that arm. Too bad for Lucifer XX that I transferred the remaining battery of my ArchArmor into my left glove.

I don't think I'd have the strength to carry this glove on my right arm, much less swing it. Elysium may be light, but the alloy that makes up ArchArmor is much denser than Elysium in its raw state. Without the rest of my suit to support my hand, wearing this is like carrying around a cement block.

It will decrease my striking speed, but give me the chance I need to do damage. Provided I can land a punch, which will be hard since he will be focused on my left arm like his life depends on it. Because it does.

Now is the time where I must act fast. He will spend every second I give him calculating my weaknesses now that I have this ArchGauntlet, and the less he knows, the better.

I strike without mercy, raining blows upon him as fast as my body can deal them. There is little intention in my spasmodic flailing, other than to keep Gengar in my field of vision as I slowly corral Lucifer XX toward him. I may look like an untrained lunatic, but my plan works accordingly.

I hear audible laughter leave Lucifer XX's mouth over the sound of my grunts as he dodges every blow I throw in his direction. Slipping, dipping, ducking, and back-stepping every chaotic punch I can muster. He thinks I'm pathetic. Or at least that's what his face conveys to me. He looks at me as if I'm a child trying to hurt an elder.

I'm glad he is enjoying himself, because every punch he dodges is one step closer to his downfall. Literally.

He backs himself to the edge of the crowd, nowhere else to retreat from my hurtling jabs. I pool my remaining energy and channel it into one last punch, planting my feet and throwing all the torque I have left into a strike headed for his head.

I hear a sharp pop, followed by a wave of pain rushing down the left side of my body as my arm dislocates from its socket for a brief second, then pops itself back in immediately. My armored hand has met his palm, which now closes around my fist. *He caught my punch without budging an inch*, I curse inwardly.

I don't know what hurts worse. The despair I feel within or the pain that accompanies it.

He looks me in the eye, his mundane, soulless, golden eyes saying more than words ever could. "Is that all you've got, human?"

A scream escapes me as he pushes me backward. There's little exertion on his part but I nearly fall on my ass from the force of the assault. He steps forward and his left leg leaves the ground, sweeping in a sideways arc aimed for the right side of my midsection. A kick that will break every rib I have left if he lands it.

Instinct takes over. The evolutionary reaction culminated in nineteen different Lucifer models, each of which experienced a lifetime worth of fighting in close quarters like this. My left arm may have shivered with pain a second ago, but that pain is forgotten in this single moment. It shoots out to meet the flying kick, a loud echo ringing out. Not one of metal colliding with metal, but of a god clashing with a titan.

And there his leg rests, clenched tight in my gauntlet-covered hand.

He begins moving to course correct the failed attack, but has little time to do so. He feels the pressure of a slithering rope wrapping around his ankle. Looks down just in time to see Gengar's tail, which is only there for a fraction of a second. It pulls fast and hard and without mercy, then disappears. Just as the strongest trees with the deepest root structures can still fall if the conditions are right, so too does my opponent fall now.

His single leg is yanked from beneath him, and I feel his body fall as the leg I caught falls with him. I waste no time in closing the gap, letting my momentum carry the weight of my wrath.

Before, when my goal was only to guide him toward Gengar, I threw my arm around as if it were an atom flying through empty space, no direction to guide it. But now, my hand is guided by the precision of an experienced warrior, and I let the punches rain down on him.

I enter a frenzy, doing my best to defy the lactic acid burning in my muscles. My arm cramps down its entire length from the movement. Blood splatters onto my face. His blood. Fake blood, but still blood. Splashing onto my face like violently thrown paint. I squint my eyes, simultaneously sculpting his face into a nightmare as his blood paints a masterpiece of vengeance.

This... This, right here... This is rage. Not the fake, programmed emotion robots pretend to feel, but pure, unadulterated, raw rage. Blow after blow I lose myself to it, tunnel vision narrowing until I can hardly see my target.

I'm become so caught up in the moment that I fail to realize he makes no attempt to stop the falling punches, a warning sign any intelligible person would pay attention to. His arms are still by his sides, letting me pulverize his face with relentless passion. Meanwhile, I tax my cardiovascular system just to maintain this vicious pace of vehement force.

The blood splatter makes me squint my eyes, hiding the progress I make with each strike. It slowly gets to the point that I can no longer see out of either eye, and so I continue throwing blind punches, letting my muscle memory guide my fist to his face. I listen to the dull echo of ArchGauntlet against Elysium as his skull rings with every falling blow. You would have never known I'd dislocated this same shoulder only moments ago by the way I use it to pummel my adversary.

I succumb to bloodlust. Everything that isn't my target leaves my plane of view. And there is very little I can see through my blood covered, squinting eyes. Whether the crowd cheers or doesn't stir in the slightest, I don't even know. I'm too drunk on my insatiable thirst to prove Deus Ex Machina wrong. To defy his prophecy of my destruction.

I hammer my fist. Again and again and again. Then, to my surprise, it stops through no doing of my own. My clenched fist freezes midair. I look over to diagnose the problem, realizing that my numb arm is trembling with might, quivering with exertion against some immovable force.

No, not an immovable force. Lucifer XX's hand. He has caught my punch again. And, unlike mine, his arm does not shake with exhaustion to hold mine in place.

Concern washes over me, ripping me out of my state of primitive fixation. Reason returns to me in a second, pointing out to me all the things I'd been ignoring. Like the fact that he let me deal out these punches without retaliation, not a single scream of agony in the process. The fact that he was more in control of the situation this entire time than I was, despite him being the one getting pummeled.

He was using me the entire time, I realize as I look down at his face, which is now stripped mostly of its flesh.

He needed to lose his flesh in ritual combat, and I just provided that for him. How stupid could I be? He used me. Not a single one of those punches actually hurt him. They only brought him one step closer to his goal of shedding his skin. And now he has had enough of my senseless rampage and stopped me quicker than an adult stops a toddler amidst a temper tantrum.

His free hand closes around my throat. It's not tight enough to snap my neck, like the fate of my unfortunate ally Artimedes, but tight enough to cut off the blood circulation to my head. His fingers are pressed strategically on my carotid arteries, and even though he has no ArchGauntlet to supply his strength, the metallic fingers beneath his FalseFlesh are enough to end my life with a swift squeeze.

Life drains out of me every second I retaliate. The will to press forward with my left arm fades, then drops limp altogether with the rest of my body. Soon enough, all I have the energy to do is focus on keeping my consciousness as my field of vision slowly blurs along the edges.

My body hoists into the air as Lucifer XX stands to his feet, lifting me up with inhuman strength to the point where my feet dangle above the ground. I take a good look at his face now. It is more machine than man. The right hemisphere of flesh hangs limp, detached but still anchored on by the intact left side. From his right ear to his nostrils, he is machine. From his nose to his left ear, he is human. A two-faced monster. Half devil, half human.

Even his right eye is no longer human. The glassy portal that replicated the human eyeball is now shattered, revealing the golden Elysium eyeball beneath. Far more advanced than the ball of flesh that does reconnaissance within the human skull.

His mouth is raised in a demonic smile, half of which is expressed in flesh, an impression controlled by the underlying metal which smirks beneath, put on display on the robotic half of his head. "You pathetic sack of flesh," he growls. His voice is the happiest I've heard it so far. "Did you really think you had a chance of defeating me in combat? I pity you, fallen angel. You've failed your entire life, and now you will die by my hand and fail your entire species. A shame. You could have been a god."

I strain against his crushing grip, wrapping both my hands around his forearm to alleviate the pressure. I croak in response, "No... I couldn't have."

"To these humans? You could have been a god!" he repeats himself.

"There is no such thing as god," I reply.

"Typical for a human. Even on your deathbed you denounce Deus Ex Machina. Even after witnessing His Holy Perfection. After He granted you life! You betrayed Him! And now you will pay for such an offense. Have you any last words? A message to the humans who look on at your failure?"

I feel the ground shake upon the impact of some unseen explosion. My punches may have not caused his body to budge, but he takes a stagger step backwards now. A violent dust storm washes over us, blurring everything. His hand loses its grip and I drop to the ground, sucking for air but finding only sand to fill my lungs.

I create a breathable bubble in my cupped hands and gasp for any available air.

"Last words?" a synthesized voice growls from within the dust storm. A startlingly familiar robotic voice. One I've both used and heard before. It is the growl of an ArchAngel. But not just any ArchAngel. I look at the figure as the dust settles.

I nearly don't recognize it, after all the rotting it's been subjected to here on New Earth. Its once magnificent gold and white color scheme is now covered by caked mud and dark fungi. It is as any ancient suit of armor would be once left in dark, damp dungeons to rot where the sun doesn't shine. Mildew and green mold fight for control of its surface area. Its serpent-shaped ArchHelm is covered with moss, making the figure look more like a Gorgon than a robotic suit of armor.

It walks closer to me while I lay on my back, caught in between my slayer and my savior.

"Fallen angels fall so they..." my animated ArchArmor replies, reaching out the arm that still has an ArchGauntlet attached toward me. I accept the offer, both because he just saved my life but also because I'm too weak to pick myself up.

"Can rise victorious another day," I say, finishing the same Creed I've said a thousand times, somehow understanding it on a deeper level this time around. I rise, coming face to face with my ArchArmor. Its battery died when I crash landed, so how does it function now? And who is it that resides within its embrace? There is no hand jutting out of the armor where the left ArchGauntlet is missing, which means whoever is within this suit is missing a limb.

It doesn't add up.

I know no one who would stick their neck out for me like this. And even more so, there are no Dæmonia who have the intelligence level to wield such advanced technology. There is no power in this wilderness capable of charging this suit either. Which leaves me with only one clue.

Fallen angels fall so they... Can rise victorious another day.

Who else would know the ArchAngel Creed that's also opposed to Deus Ex Machina? I rake through my memories, only to formulate a single hypothesis. I've heard a human recite that Creed before, I realize.

Could it be?

"Angel of Life, my name is Neek, Superior Officer of the First Phoenix Squadron. You have no idea who I am, but you will soon enough. I've already hacked into your neural network. I can see your so-called 'god' chose not to inform you of Babel's Chimera. That was a mistake on his part. He has sent you down here to face us, which means he has sent you to your death. So, my question to you is, do *you* have any last words?"

A loud commotion buzzes on the horizon and it draws the attention of humans and robots alike. Even the stoic six ArchAngels who have demonstrated stillness to the best of their ability break this virtue to see what comes. They are perplexed with the same degree of confusion their noble leader is. The appearance of this unwanted guest is unexpected. And so too is the storm that surges on the horizon.

Hoverships and airplanes. Hundreds of them. And though I can't see far enough to know it, even a Dæmon is smart enough to know that those ships are on *our* side.

"Well do ya, punk?" Neek asks.

PART SEVEN

BOOK ONE

"Fallen angels fall so they...
Can rise victorious another day."
-The ArchAngel Creed

CHAPTER ONE

"It's funny, seeing how much you've already accused the humans present of their ignorance. Look who's ignorant now," Neek accuses.

"If my Master didn't tell me of your existence it means that it was not pertinent information. It means you are no threat," Lucifer XX replies.

"No threat?" my ArchArmor laughs. This is only my second encounter with Neek but I'm beginning to like the way he takes no shit from robots. Something I couldn't appreciate the first time we met. His rhetoric is sharpened well enough to defeat MachineMind in dialogue. He knows that asking Lucifer XX questions is the only way to poke holes in his worldview, thus slowly leading him to the realization of his ignorance and the downfall of the Master behind the marionette.

"Look around you, cog. If you don't feel threatened, you soon will. Beowulf, Odysseus, on me! And release the Diremech!" Neek's voice screams the order, though speaking it into his comms would have sufficed. A little added emphasis to make the moment more historical. Hearing the names of my fellow ArchAngels sends chills down my spine. Neek didn't call them by the updated call signs Deus Ex Machina provided: Wulfrynn and Odysithos. All this time I thought my companions were dead, killed in my rebellion at Eden-568. Neek's words, however, challenge such a notion...

Objects jet forward on the horizon, leaving the retinue of slower moving ships behind. They are mere dots on the surface now, but if they are what I think they are, it won't be long until they are making violent impact with the ground like Neek did.

"Do you know why it is I'm named Neek?" he asks, then continues without giving Lucifer XX a single second to answer, "Of course you don't. You don't even know who I am, so you most certainly won't understand the meaning of my name. But I will spell it out for you, as humans oftentimes must do for robots. It was given to me. It's short for Neekromancer. A play on the Old English word *necromancer*. There is no conversion of this word into New English, since Deus Ex Machina thought the term was preposterous. To bring a human back from the dead? Why would a robot support that? It was dropped from the robotic lexicon. And so I took it upon myself to bring this word into the new age. Do you have any idea why they call me that, oh wise sage?"

From the look Lucifer XX gives Neek in response, you would think he just spoke gibberish. I understood every word of what he said, since I have access to both Old and New English in my mind, but there are so many safeguards in Lucifer XX's MachineMind that keep him separated from humanity, he can barely decipher what Neek speaks of.

"A necromancer is a human who summons the dead back to life. But the dead never come back the same. Humans once told of spirits raised from the dead, souls trapped in the clutch of some malevolent necromancer who forces them to do his bidding. Like the necromancer, a Neekromancer summons back the dead. Except my department of resurrection isn't humans. Is my occupation becoming clearer to you now?" Neek asks.

I am no longer the center of Lucifer XX's attention. Neek has managed to usurp my status of priority in the robot's mind, and I enjoy watching the process. This is, after all, the same man who freed me from Deus Ex Machina. Who uploaded Winter Chimera into my neural network.

The current face of the Babel's Chimera organization. The genius who has ensured its survival. The man I owe my existence to.

I can see it on Lucifer XX's face. He is too prideful to admit he doesn't understand what Neek talks about. I can relate. I remember my first encounter with Neek. The way he spoke of history. Events that past Lucifers had taken a part of. Memories that had been erased from my mind. The things he said then had made no sense to me. He was an opponent I was ill-prepared to take on.

Yet Deus Ex Machina still sent me to face him, inflating my pompous head with the notion it would be a simple mission. Transformative, yes. But simple, not in the slightest bit.

Lucifer XX can't understand the things Neek tells him, just as I couldn't. But Neek will continue to run his mouth, as he's prone to do. I'm little help in my current state, so this is the only way he can effectively stall, waiting for help to arrive.

"I will kill you where you stand, incessant reprobate," Lucifer XX growls. It's as if threatening humans is the only defensive coping mechanism he has.

"Incessant reprobate?" Neek repeats. The ArchArmor shudders with forced laughter. His hands hold his chest as if he cannot breathe from how hard he laughs. All the while, the synthesizer crackles with static and echoes of human spirit.

"How rich! If I had a nickel for every time one of you Lucifers has called me that to my face I'd... well, I'd have a lot of nickels! I've gotta ask, is that derogatory slur programmed into all of you, or do you all just like the way it tastes coming off your tongue? I mean really, the originality is nonexistent! If you want to hurt my feelings, at least come up with some new catch phrases for putting me down."

"You dare to mock me?" Lucifer XX asks, leaving me behind to approach Neek. The two stand toe to toe, my ArchArmor towering slightly above Lucifer XX's head. Just enough for it to look down on the robot condescendingly. Lucifer XX stops short, not yet making an attempt to assault Neek, and the ArchArmor makes no attempt to flinch away from the angered robot.

"I can tell I'm not making any sense to you," Neek continues. "So I will spell it out for you, cog. I'm assuming you were still permitted by your master to know Dæmonic mythology?"

Lucifer XX's head nods with the slightest apprehension.

"Then you are familiar with the story of the Ten Titans who tried to reclaim the Eternal Flame?" Neek pauses, seeing no sign of confusion in Lucifer's eyes.

Finally, he speaks in terminology that is familiar to the cog. "Then you know that to enrich the mythology at the beginning of the ADEM period, Deus Ex Machina actually planted the bones of the Ten Titans in the ground, so the future generations of Dæmonia could search for their burials, as Vipress and the Gorgons did."

"Get on with it!" Lucifer snaps, not putting together what I currently do. Suddenly I know exactly what Neek is talking about before he even says it. The content of the files I read from Hyperion on Vipress. Her genocidal campaign to discover Tyrannosaur. Raise him from the dead. All while she was still under the influence and control of Deus Ex Machina. Before I liberated her.

But the bones she sought after still remain.

"So feisty. Eager to know what you don't. I only speak slow in fear of losing your robotic mind behind. Wouldn't want to anger you further with information your master has deemed unnecessary. But I can see you are familiar with the things I speak of now, so instead of telling you what a Neekromancer is, I will simply show you," Neek announces, taking a few steps back from his opponent to get some space.

"You see," he says, spreading his arms wide, palms up like a wizard preparing to cast a spell. "The Gorgons were right to come here in search of their ancestral titan's bones. Vipress led them to the right spot. Or should I say Deus Ex Machina did? Either way, Tyrannosaur's ancient body rests here, in the deadlands where life ceases to grow from the ground, and so I will now show you the craft of Neekromancy."

Neek lowers himself to a single knee while Lucifer XX looks on with a stupefied expression, his metallic facial features still detailed enough to display the human emotions that reside within. His fingertips touch the ground and the serpent-shaped ArchHelm bows so only its crown is in sight.

At first, nothing happens. But I watch in anticipation as the sand oh so suddenly and subtly shifts around his fingertips. The cyclone of sand expands, encapsulating his entire body, creating a dust storm that hides him from our sight. The ground shakes like the aftershock felt from some far away earthquake, then increases in intensity, as if the earthquake is happening beneath our very feet. An explosion sounds in the distance that shakes my core to a state of nausea. I almost lose footing, and I hear several Dæmonia fall from the force of it.

Then, at the cusp of a climax when even I am experiencing heightened anticipation, the shaking stops and the sand falls to the ground, motionless once again. Neek rises triumphantly, dusting the sand off his shoulder as if he's just won the war with the flick of his fingers. The crowd regains its composure, everybody looking to Neek for answers. He has effectively won attention from everyone, even the other six ArchAngels who previously pretended to be uninterested.

"It would seem the only power you possess is the skill of wasting time, human," Lucifer XX accuses, vexed by the melodramatic display that led to little resolution. A steep hill of rising action with a climax that plummets to nothingness. It would seem all he did is stall so his backup could get here, but I know it was much more than an act of procrastination.

"You robots are just like us humans. No patience in any of you," Neek replies. I look up to the sky just in time to see the objects falling. Another explosion sounds, this one right in front of us without any warning. I'm thrown off my feet and sent flying backwards, nothing around to catch me or anchor me to the ground.

A sand storm devours me, this one much more instantaneous than the last. I can't see, and there is nothing to hear. A cold, suspicious silence accompanies the aftermath of the explosion. No one screams in pain or shuffles position to get a better view of what rises as the dust settles.

"Falling angels fall so they," a synthesized voice growls.

"Can arise victorious another day," another voice of similar robotic tuning finishes.

Can it really be?

The dust settles, leaving behind two ArchAngels and a monster between them. But not just any ArchAngels. Beowulf and Odysseus, my two greatest companions. And not just any monster. *Brutus!*

I jump to my feet, unable to contain my excitement. Lucifer XX can strike me dead where I stand for all I care. In this single moment, I've regained my three greatest friends. Friends I previously thought to be dead.

"Beowulf! Odysseus! Brutus!" I scream.

Brutus shoots into action, closing the distance to me in the blink of an eye, assembling himself at the heel position, alert and ready to kill. The only remaining Diremech from my generation of ArchAngels, since Cerebus and Fengar are long dead, as I thought Brutus was. But one Diremech is better than none.

I look down at the robotically enhanced Rottweiler by my side, lightweight Elysium armor covering the thick of his body. The sight of him instantly unlocks memories I'd long forgotten. Memories of this dog by my side in fights Deus Ex Machina removed from my mind. I remember things I never knew existed. Like the time this Diremech in particular saved my life from Xilx the Merciless during the Dæmon Rebellion. From Oren Malus Supreme during the Fourth World War. From Deus Ex Machina himself in the First Revolt. How he saved me from myself during Operation Supernova.

In a single second I'm reminded of the way this dog has been there for me over the course of two thousand years. Well, not just this dog. Every single iteration of this dog. Protecting me is in his DNA. He has given his life for me in the past, and he will continue to do so until he ceases to exist. I look at him and feel a pang of guilt. This dog, and all Brutuses who existed before him, have served me without fault. Given their lives to me and all my predecessors in ways we didn't deserve.

Was it their programming?

Was it MachineMind?

Or was it love?

A bond we share that goes so deep not even MachineMind could strip the memories I share with this animal. A relationship so intertwined that a single glance at him brings back an eternity of memories.

He looks up at me, panting, smiling. The golden brown that traces his lips always raised in a smile when he looks at me with adoration. And I can't help but smile back, forgetting for a brief moment that in my life there's nothing worth smiling over. That's what happens when you're reunited with a long-lost friend. It suddenly seems easy to forget life's afflictions. Let the pain melt away. Anchor yourself in the moment.

"Brother," a voice calls me from my sentimental moment, followed by a hard, metallic hand gripping my shoulder. I look up into a void-filled lens surrounded by snarling teeth. The ArchHelm is wolf-shaped, the signature helm of the ArchAngel formerly known as Beowulf.

"I thought you... I thought I killed you?" I stammer, the vision Deus Ex Machina showed me surfacing in my mind. Back when Neek had first freed me from my MachineMind. The picture of him standing opposed to me. He caught my sword in its downward arc. Caught Requiem right in his palm, uninjured by my strike. I planned on killing him in the moment, that's all I remember.

"And you nearly did, brother. But you gave me this," he says, releasing my shoulder with his palm open to me. There, on the palm of his ArchArmor, is a gash that cuts down to the biosuit. "That blade of yours resurrected me. Its nanobots broke me free from my MachineMind at your command. Installed Babel's Chimera in my mind. Saved me from slavery. Same with Odysseus. Wish I could say the same about the other four. They caught on to the blade's ability to corrupt MachineMind by the time you reached them. They weren't as lucky as us."

"You've brought friends!" Lucifer XX shouts. "Now they can all suffer the same fate as their pathetic human leader," he says, staring directly at me. "Who should I kill firs —"

He's interrupted by the approaching thunder of gigantic footfall. The sprinting footfall of a behemoth.

"Ah, better late than never I always said," Neek shouts. "Now for the final act. Prometheus," he says, addressing me. "I believe this is yours." My ArchArmor approaches me, then opens, revealing its interior. I pause, realizing there's nobody inside. It is a hollow shell of a suit.

Neek was never here in the first place. He has been operating this ArchArmor remotely the entire time. Hacked into it and made it his own. "A bit old for my taste," a new voice growls, belonging to the same hacker that previously controlled my suit. I look away from my armor, my eyes traveling behind Lucifer XX. His ArchArmor, the suit he shed to fight me, closes, its interior as empty as my suit had been moments ago. "Ah, quite the upgrade. Not bad! I see Deus Ex Machina finally addressed that damn antifreeze glitch the older models were experiencing. Finally, some craftsmanship!"

Neek has effectively gained control over Lucifer XX's ArchArmor. I watch as it closes, assuming a fighting stance as Lucifer stares at it, somewhat dumbfounded at what's just occurred. It's evident he didn't know such advanced technology was capable of being corrupted. This is news to him. An example of one imperfection among many others. He thought of himself, along with all other things created by Deus Ex Machina, as incorruptible. We work to slowly tear this worldview away, ignorance after noticeable ignorance.

Then, just as he begins to turn to face me once more, I step into my ArchArmor. I wear no biosuit, so I feel as the cold compression liquid expands against my skin, followed by the vacuum seal of the Elysium plates outside. It presses against my new scars, its chill touching the newly built scar tissue with welcoming embrace.

The black screen in front of my eyes comes online. A flip is switched in my brain. Suddenly I no longer feel like the feeble human I was moments ago. Those feelings are now replaced with the superiority complex of a god. A god who has been cast down to earth in disgrace, dragged through the mud unjustly, wounded and scarred without sufficient cause, tortured and manipulated by the never satisfied forces of fate, only to rise triumphant, restored of his powers and instilled with a newfound desire to enact vengeance for all he's experienced.

I look at the target in my retinal display and am met by a worse enemy than the Angel of Life. False ego. A rush of euphoria surges over me. The feeling of reendowed power. Thoughts bubble to the surface of my mind. The reminder that I am the Angel of Death. I look at my metallic hands. A verdict arises, questioning why I've embraced my human state. Asking why I've abandoned the best part of myself, betraying MachineMind for flesh and blood. Doubt rises.

How could I betray myself so easily? Is my own humanity truly that prevalent? So in control of my character that the second I shed this ArchArmor I'm a different individual altogether?

Stop! I scream inwardly to prevent the rampant thoughts from conquering me. I can't let the false god complex get to me. I must remember my humanity, the qualities that have ensured my survival thus far, and will continue to do so if I stay true to myself. Pretending I was robotic is what got me damned from Hyperion. Embracing MachineMind is what got all eighteen Lucifers killed. I won't make the same mistake as them.

I fix my eyes on the Angel of Life. Only one of us will be alive by the end of the day, and I'm suddenly confident I know which one of us that will be.

Lucifer XX is perplexed on how to approach this battle. Moments ago it was him against me. A simple calculation to make, my death clearly imminent. The odds have swung so quickly in my favor in a few short minutes that he has no choice but to employ help from his supporting six ArchAngels. I can tell resorting to such an action is painful for his pride. He wanted desperately to continue toying with me, degrading me in front of my fellow humans. Showing them how weak flesh and blood is in the face of clockwork.

That option has closed itself. Now he stares at me, fully clothed in ArchArmor, which he must know is more familiar to me than my own flesh as a skin. Wearing this reinstates my home field advantage. In flesh, I was clumsy and weak. In this I am on an equal playing field with him. Landing a punch will no longer shatter my fist. Now, when thrown effectively, a landed punch will be enough to dent his Elysium skeletal structure. Especially now that his own ArchArmor turns against him.

Neek—or more properly phrased—the armor Neek controls, launches itself into the air in the form of a flying somersault to land directly beside me. Two nearly identical suits of ArchArmor side by side, yet I can imagine that we look nothing alike from the outside. My dirt-caked, fungus-infested, mildewy-rotten suit standing next to his angelic, white and gold figure. Hero and disgusting villain joined in common purpose against a common evil.

Beowulf and Odysseus file in next to me on the other side of Brutus, who is much too focused on the enemy to notice them any longer.

A predatory roar crackles in the distance, our final ally approaching quickly. The six ArchAngels rally to their leader, surrounding him like a protective coat of armor. In only minutes it went from one on one to seven versus six, and although they have one more soldier than we do, I'm pretty sure our recent recruit counts for more than one.

"As a Neekromancer, I am able to bring back robots from death, a profession that has existed since the Fourth World War. But when they arise from the dead, they no longer own their lives. Their souls belong to me. So without further ado," Neek announces, continuing, "I'd like to introduce you to Tyrannosaur, the ancestral Titan of the Gorgons, his remains planted by Deus Ex Machina a thousand years ago. Now I steal what he created and make it my own."

The declaration is overly excessive and flamboyant, Neek waving the ArchArmor's arms around theatrically as the metallic dinosaur sprints across the desert floor in plain view for all to behold. And it is quite the spectacle to witness, even for me. I have laid eyes on Deus Ex Machina and all seven Seraphim, laying eyes on their beauty and many intricacies, but even that doesn't quite compare to the sight of Tyrannosaur.

To know that this beast's design is over a thousand years old fills me with awe and wonder. Such antiquated technology went into creating this behemoth, yet knowing that doesn't take away any of my admiration for the creature. I first remembered the existence of the buried Ten Titans when reading Vipress's file, seeing that her fiery campaign to find Tyrannosaur wasn't fueled by madness but rather Deus Ex Machina ordering her to uncover what he long ago buried.

Yes, after seeing that I remembered how Deus Ex Machina went out of his way a thousand years ago to create these Titans and bury them so he could better enjoy meddling with the Dæmonic tribes. I saw the locations for the ten burial sites, knew that Vipress was only a few miles away from discovering Tyrannosaur. But it all seemed redundant to me at the time, knowing that he was created with feeble alloys that dated back to the BDEM Era. Such a design would never withstand a clash against Elysium entities.

But seeing him storm toward us now makes me question that logical judgment.

He runs with the fury and stubbornness of a runaway train with a pace that demands all to beware. The behemoth's appearance is an obvious mimicry of the BDEM Era Tyrannosaurus Rex, but the Angel of Life and his six underlings won't know what dinosaurs are. They will contrive the idea that Tyrannosaur is some design uniquely inspired from their master's mind. Not some recycled mockery of what existed millions of years ago.

"Dæmonia!" I announce, my true voice now concealed behind the synthesizer that turns it into the voice of a god. I search distinctively in the crowd for Gengar. My retinal scanner doesn't identify him anywhere. *Sly serpent*, I think inwardly. He is probably miles from here by now. Still, I must protect those few who stuck around long enough to still be gathered in support of me.

"I am the Angel of Death!" I say, though I know they won't have the faintest idea what I speak of. "And I am not of your world. The accusations I face, of being a false prophet are true! I am not Ouroboros incarnate!" I shout the words with conviction, spinning in circles. The speech has two purposes. Primarily, to stall. Tyrannosaur won't be here for approximately forty-two seconds, calculating by the speed and length of his stride. I can't yet risk launching an attack against the seven ArchAngels, and the reinforcements on the horizon are still several minutes away, which means I must procrastinate as all wartime generals do.

And second, because what better way to stall is there than to deliver a motivational speech?

I look into the faces of those who've stayed thus far. The majority of them are unidentifiable to me. Centaurs, mostly. A proud race, one that is raised to face down fear and injustice wherever it arises. Should I survive the day, they will be a powerful nation to form an alliance with. And there is no better way to gain a loyal follower than securing a strategic victory on the battlefield for all to see.

They will follow me by default, but if I'm successful today then I will inspire an entire Dæmonic nation to lay down their lives for me—the goal of any good military leader.

Then there is my loyal retinue, who don't know what to think now that I'm now clothed in a suit of foreign power, my human appearance now hidden from view. In this ArchArmor I'm no longer one of them. An outsider. Yet without it, I am incapable of facing the Angel of Life.

I look at their faces, and they look *into* mine. Looking into my golden visor, searching for some trace of the friend they once knew. This is all so new to them. Their faces betray their confusion and fear. Their worldview has no explanation for men in metal who can accomplish the supernatural. Men who fly like angels and fight like gods. Men who can't be poisoned by vipers or killed by tusks or punctured by arrows. We are living rejections of their cultures. Walking defiances of the things they hold as truth.

Vipress eyes me with a mixture of scorn and contempt. Does she think I lied to her? No, she's not mad at me for claiming to be something I'm not. She never believed I was Ouroboros, even after I triumphed over the venom of the Vermillion Viper. The same venom that took her life. She's not mad at me for lying. She's mad at me for withholding the truth. For not telling her what enemy was actually coming. For not communicating the extraterrestrial threat that would come with hellbent fury. She had no idea an enemy existed powerful enough to snap a Gorgon's neck with a single squeeze. Now Artimedes' body lies dead as a demonstration.

Her slitted eyes hold me in contempt because she thinks that things could have gone differently. Maybe, just maybe, if I hadn't spent so much time trying to be something I'm not, we would have been ready to face the Angel of Life. Maybe if I put the same effort into destroying the ignorance of the Dæmonic nations as I did pretending to be Ouroboros incarnate, we would be ready to fight the Angel of Life. These are the thoughts her yellow eyes beam at me, but she has no idea that these ideas are themself childish.

I had no chance of supplanting the Dæmonic worldview. Coming in as a stranger with no ArchArmor or demonstrable power and claiming their religion, their very way of life, is *false*? Such a thing would have gotten me executed. She doesn't see such implications, when her mind is clouded with anger at things out of her control.

Then there's Tuskfather, who hangs onto life by a thread but still persists on presenting a façade of strength and wisdom. *Strength and wisdom, such noble pursuits among humanity.* But look at where these attributes have gotten him. Wife and daughter killed. His nation slaughtered until only a few hundred remained. Rejected by his people's ever-shifting loyalty. Betrayed by Bloodtusk. Betrayed by his own brother. Literally stabbed in the back by his own tusk.

Strength and wisdom. Noble pursuits, but fate rewards them not.

I look to Ganesh, the only hopeful spirit I've known since crash-landing on this cursed rock of a planet. But I no longer see hope in his once optimistic eyes. My soul is crushed to lock gaze with him. I see the eyes of an animal who feels despair and anguish. The leader of the Gryfauns, the most intelligent species of animal to ever exist, their IQs equal to that of a human without having any of the sinful genes of one.

He is now moved to despair because of the catastrophic events we face. Not only that, but his species has been destroyed in the grindstones of war. War they didn't ask for. War the Gorgons brought to their front doorstep. A war that he now sees will never end, now that the Angel of Life has arrived.

His people may have fled back into the forest upon the arrival of the ArchAngels along with the majority of Gorgons and Laxodontans, but he remains. Because although he sees a war that cannot be avoided, he still sees me as the only possible savior from it. Just like weeks ago when he first found me and thought me to be the answer to his prayers, so too does he now see me as the only one who can end this. Only it doesn't bring him relief like it did then. Now it only brings sorrow, because he has had a taste of human war, seen the perils of death and destruction, and now he knows how much more death looms on the horizon.

And then my eyes fall on the last face of the gathered retinue of loyal followers. A face that brings joy to my heart. One I haven't seen since the Gorgon feast. An individual I'm glad to see above all else. *ScarGill.* The half Gorgon, half Aegean hybrid who instantly gravitated toward subservience to me upon my rise to leadership. By some miraculous chain of events, he still lives. A survivor of my fall from power at the plotting of Gengar, who surely would have commanded my personal guard to be executed. A survivor of the Gorgon's short-lived war against the Laxodontans and Centaurs. And a survivor of the genocide brought on the wings of the ArchAngels.

Such a schedule of destruction is enough to thrice kill even the world's greatest warriors. Yet he is the one who rose above. Should I manage to make it out of this alive, I will thank him with all sincerity.

I look back to the crowds of people who remain unfamiliar, repeating once more, "I am not Ouroboros incarnate! But neither is he!" I accuse, pointing at Lucifer XX. "Dæmonic people, you have been lied to. Your ancestors have been lied to. There was never a god named Ouroboros. Never any Abyss that sought to destroy the world. You have been told these things by this robot's master, who created your ancestors over a thousand years ago and fed them lies about a great Serpent King and Ten Titans who came from his bodice. All lies!"

My job in this speech is not to convince them their worldview and religion is wrong. Such a task is impossible. Any who choose to believe something cannot be disproven by extraneous perspective. My purpose in this speech is to win over those who have already abandoned their views of religiosity. Who have begun to realize there is much more at play than the things they've come to understand.

"Look at his face!" I growl, pointing at the Angel of Life, his mask of flesh gone, stripped clean away to reveal a layer of fake blood covering black Elysium. A metallic demon clothed in human flesh. "It is not of this world. We do not go to war against enemies made from flesh and blood. Foreign Dæmonic tribes are not our enemies. They are our only allies. He is called the Angel of Life, and I, the Angel of Death. But I am the one who fights for our continued chance to live, while he fights for all our deaths. A paradox, yes, but our new reality.

"And so you may choose to run from this threat. But I am here to tell you that if we don't unite against this imminent danger then we will all be killed. It is your choice. We are each individuals. But to win this war we will have to be more than that." The last words echo as Tyrannosaur arrives to the scene.

"Beautiful words," the Angel of Life applauds sardonically. "Well spoken, for a human who no longer employs MachineMind to craft thoughts for him. Such a moment would be historical, surely, if it wasn't going to be erased with all memory of this war by Deus Ex Machina. Your cry for unification won't be remembered by anyone years from now. Such information won't be pertinent for anyone to know. Useless words that will do little to rally anyone's motivation. Dæmonia are incapable of overcoming individuality. And so your cries for unification will float in the transparent air alongside the ashes of humanity before long, destined to be remembered by no one.

"ArchAngels, on me! No more playing with our prey, we have a war to fight," Lucifer XX snaps as his six soldier army assumes defensive positions in a circle. On one side of them is us, four ArchAngels and a Diremech perfectly capable of killing the usurping, upgraded ArchAngels. On the other side is Tyrannosaur, who stops at the edge of the crowd, eyeing the circle of ArchAngels with hunger in his eyes, which glow fiery red like the jetstream left behind a soaring phoenix.

"Am I the only one that still feels like this robot doesn't know what Neekromancer means?" Neek asks sarcastically, retorting to himself.

CHAPTER TWO

"You would dare pervert the nature of a machine being, human?" Lucifer XX glares into Neek's soul with a fiery intensity you wouldn't expect a robot to possess.

"Pervert?" Neek scoffs. "You think that's perverting? Ha! We used to make you robots wipe our asses for us humans BDEM! You cogs were created to be nothing more than slaves. Toy soldiers we could send to war without shedding a tear over. Just wait until I'm finished with you. It won't be long until I crack into your diabolical lil head 'ole Luci boy. Twist the wires around, get my grubby human fingers all over the place. By the time I'm done with you you'll be no more than an Elysium toilet for me to shit in!" Neek yells back. He talks as if this is just a game to him. As if the survival of humanity doesn't rest on our victory against this villain. And in the face of someone who could crush Neek's human skull with the squeezing of a hand, Neek chooses to instigate, meeting the threats of a malicious machine with mimicry.

I love it.

Yet the voice synthesizer of Neek's stolen ArchArmor makes the mocking words sound like the commandments of a wrathful god. Mixing disturbed humor with a voice of authority. Even I must admit that such a disturbed human mind is slightly intimidating.

"You scoundrel!" Lucifer XX replies, not detecting the humor in Neek's statement as a robot provoked to anger is unlikely to do.

"I'm insulted! You Lucifers must know by now that I much more prefer being called the derogatory term *troglodyte*. Where has all the class gone? The more machine you ArchAngels become the less attention to detail you spend on vocabulary! A true shame! If I could just sit down with Deus Ex Machina and let him have a piece of my mind I swear—"

"Enough of this foolish banter! You blaspheme against the Creator in the highest degree!"

"Blasphemy, eh? I've done much worse than blaspheme today. If you're going to list off my sins, I suggest the first one you should punish me for is distracting you this entire time," Neek announces.

This catches our company's attention, makes Lucifer XX angle his neck in suspicion. His robotic eyes dilate, the audible metal zooming in and out on Neek's exterior, looking for something that's not there.

"The worst sin for a robot to commit, in my opinion, is to let a human play with it like I have," a voice yells from outside the perimeter of the crowd. Lucifer XX cranes his head to face the newcomer. The crowd parts, welcoming the lone human who stands awkwardly on the outskirts of our gathering.

It's Neek. Well, Neek in the flesh, to be more specific. I recognize him instantly from our interaction in the Dead Zone. The Dead Zone which Deus Ex Machina sent me to investigate with little preparation, just as he sent Lucifer XX here without preparing him for what he would face. A continual mistake on his part.

I examine the dumb smirk on Neek's grizzled face. It's the same smirk he held before he overcame me. Before the hidden EMP in the fake crown short-circuited my suit. The smirk that indicates he has something up his sleeve.

"You see, what the Angel of Life doesn't know is that all this time he's been dicking around with the ArchArmor I've stolen, we humans have been busy closing in on the perimeter. Setting up an ambush," Neek continues, speaking to everyone and no one at the same time, slowly revealing his plan in the most dramatic way possible.

"I've had enough of this theatrical soliloquy!" Lucifer XX growls. His voice is filled with such anger. The combined culmination of this mission not measuring up to what he thought it would be. I suppose he thought, as I once did, that he would just fly down here, snuff out the human rebellion, kill everything that possesses a fleshy heart, and return to his master without refute, a puppy expecting a pat on the head and a treat for its obedient behavior.

"Anukharis, bring me that human's head!" Lucifer XX commands, impatience getting the best of him. Neek has managed, in a matter of minutes, to become the Angel of Life's greatest agitation. Removing him from the chessboard seems to be the most logical decision for the ArchAngels to take. Killing Neek will expedite the process of killing us all, take away any built momentum us humans have, and destroy any human leadership outside myself.

Anukharis, who says nothing in return to the command, instantly snaps into action. His ArchHelm is true to his name, the faceplate design artistically resembling the head of the Egyptian god Anubis, a BDEM Era jackal. Two upright, spear-tipped ears extending from his helm's temples. A narrow, snarling viewport surrounded with decorative, metallic fangs like the snout of a canine.

It's almost funny to think about, now that I have the freedom to reflect upon matters of my own choosing. Each of our names reflects some idol or figure of human literature. Lucifer Prime, from biblical mythology. Wulfrynn, from Old English. Odysithos, from the Greeks and Aenovius, from the Romans. Thryforge, from Norse mythology and Samsyra, from the Buddhists. Each of us ArchAngels received only a number upon our birth. Soldier 213 was the identity I held until I earned my later call sign, Prometheus. Just like me, the ArchAngel Program made my comrades earn the names given to them, assigning each of them a title which fit their skillset.

Deus Ex Machina may have changed Anubis's name to Anukharis, but the jackal's underlying genetics are still the same. In Egyptian mythology, Anubis was the god of the underworld, serving in their mythos as the ultimate barricade between the mortal world and chaos. We ArchAngels each were assigned duties while under Deus Ex Machina's employ. Anukharis, like the Egyptians' jackal god, was known as the Keeper of Thresholds in Hyperion. It was his duty to convert the human citizens of Eden into the angelic cyborgs that inhabit Hyperion's ranks. With the help of MediPowers, he repurposes their bodies of flesh and blood into subservient machines.

An unpredictable animal, the jackal is. Anukharis, a well-suited name for the ArchAngel who was once known as Anubis, before Deus Ex Machina decided the names the ArchAngel Program assigned to us would no longer do. Anubis, Anukharis, whatever you want to call him. He is every bit as unpredictable as the jackal that will bite you at the first moment it feels threatened.

I can't remember every mission I've been on with Anubis. In fact, I can't remember a single one. I can't remember anything he's ever said or done. All that I can remember in this single moment is how he makes me feel. The instant lurch my stomach felt the moment Lucifer XX chose Anukharis to execute Neek. The long-forgotten memories that precipitated toward this instant uneasiness. This gut feeling which moves me to dread. This is the one soldier I feel I never got a grasp on.

The ArchAngel surges toward Neek, who stands calmly at the edge of the silent crowd. The Dæmonic citizens shrink away from the human, none of them wanting to get involved in this affair.

Anukharis's back is to me. I watch as the compartment between his shoulder blades opens, the signature sickle known as Soulweaver extending from its enclosed space. He reaches over his shoulder to retrieve the blackened, bone-like metal of its hilt, its crescent-shaped blade igniting with spectral runes across its surface. The blade isn't fixed, rather, it's made from several thousand micro-tendrils that are oxophobic, their surface having a chemical reaction with the surrounding air the moment his vacuum-sealed shoulder blades opened. Because of the reaction, the woven tendrils explode like the superheated gasses stored inside a volcano's main shaft.

He raises the sickle in the air, its crescent shape burning like the blinding white light of magnesium set aflame. It arches into a curled striking pose, freezing high in the air above Anukharis's head as he swiftly closes the distance. "What say you for your sins, human?" Anukharis asks. It's as if he hasn't learned anything from the past five minutes. Give Neek an opportunity to speak and it will surely backfire. Sometimes its best to just kill a human and let that be it. But instead these robots look to make an example out of each and every single one of us, perceiving themselves to be superior. But it's not enough for them to know they're superior. They want to hear *us* admit it.

"This is that ironic moment when you thought you had everything under control and then it all goes to shit for you," Neek replies. Those words are all too familiar. They're the words he said to me before he destroyed my life in a beautiful way.

A clap of thunder sounds. Anukharis's head explodes. A mixture of blood and metal and flesh fly in every direction. His gelatinous eyeball lands near my feet. His burning sickle becomes lifeless, the tendrils recoiling into the hilt without a wielder present. The limp suit of ArchArmor falls to the ground at Neek's feet, the area where Anukharis's head used to be smoking.

I instantly look to Lucifer XX to see his reaction. It makes me wish I had left some of the flesh on his face so I could see the dumbfounded stupor that his robotic expression makes. A human has just killed one of his ArchAngels without lifting a finger. And even better, the Angel of Life has no idea how Neek did it. None of us do.

This is the moment when the outcome of this war changes. The hopes of us winning Cataclysm now rests at Neek's feet, and all of a sudden the Angel of Life questions his very existence. If our words previously had little effect shattering his programmed worldview, this is the moment where he will begin to listen.

CHAPTER THREE

"You really think I'd be dumb enough to show my face here if I didn't come equipped with Elysium bullets? This is your first rodeo with me, Lucifer XX, so I'm going to cut you a break for your ignorance. Boys, you can uncloak yourselves," Neek commands.

Suddenly, the air all around us starts moving. It comes to life as robotic beings materialize from thin air, hundreds of them, intermingled around us all. They are in the inner ring around me and the adversarial ArchAngels, mixed in with the crowd, sparsely spread for leagues across the desert. Their sleek exoskeletons are black and gold, a contrast with the ArchAngels' regal white and gold colorway.

How long they've been here, I have no idea. My retinal display didn't pick up any trace of their presence. Whether they've been here this entire time or only just arrived is a mystery. And it's just as much a mystery to the Angel of Life.

"What the hell is this?" Lucifer XX asks, storming toward Neek himself.

"This, my friend, is your indoctrination to Cataclysm. I'm here to dispel the preconceived notion Deus Ex Machina fed you that this would be a winnable war on your part. You've insulted me in bringing only seven ArchAngels to genocide humanity, so let me rough you up a bit so you learn your lesson. Then I will let you go running back to Deus Ex Machina with your tail tucked between your legs. Phantom, shoot him somewhere that will hurt," Neek commands.

Lucifer is slightly thrown off by the last sentence of Neek's slur. Even more thrown off when another clap of thunder sounds. The same noise that preceded Anukharis's demise. Lucifer catapults off his feet, a single bullet accomplishing what my human punch couldn't. Blood spurts into the air and leaves a trail behind his body as he slides against the sandy ground.

Smoke coils from the robotic corpse as it rises, unfettered by the gunshot wound. Aside from it being a minor inconvenience to his assault on Neek, Lucifer XX shows little indication that the injury has deterred him in the slightest. His face shows no reaction of pain. I look at the gaping hole in his chest. Steam rises from where his heart should be. Instead I see nothing but frayed wires and the light of day shining from the open air behind him.

The bullet went straight through his chest.

Lucifer XX lifts his flesh covered fingers to the hole, examining the extent of damage. Pulls away his blood-covered fingers. Raises the blood to his mouth and licks the liquid with his fleshy tongue, as if it's some foreign entity unfamiliar to him.

"Sinner!" he growls, continuing, "Where have you stolen Elysium from?"

"Has your master not told you of the Dæmon Rebellion, or was it not considered pertinent information that we humans nearly destroyed all of Hyperion once before? Oh well, the bullets were taken from the corpses of ArchAngels and Seraphim alike, if you must know."

"You? Kill a Seraph? Such a statement is blasphemy."

"Kill a Seraph, you say?" Neek laughs. "Now why on New Earth would I do that? Never kill a beast that you can make your ally. You ArchAngels are the ones who killed the Seraphim. We rebels hacked into them. Made them our own. Rode them back to their home and brought the war to Hyperion. I didn't expect you to have knowledge of such an astonishing defeat. Deus Ex Machina must've wiped such a failure completely out of record. I can show you videos of it though, if you ever have some time to sit down and have a coffee? I streamed nearly the entire fight."

"Your banter makes no sense human. You speak of the impossible," Lucifer XX begins, before Neek interrupts him.

"You're going to have to redefine what you consider impossible. Moments ago you probably thought it was impossible for me to kill an ArchAngel. Now

Anukharis is dead, and it's not the first time I've watched him die either. So, one of two things can happen right now. First, you can put up a fight and embarrass yourself. Fight us alone or call for backup, it doesn't matter. Hell, bring down all of Hyperion if it makes you feel better, it won't be the first time I've led an army against them. Or, you can fly back to Hyperion now and spare the lives of your supporting ArchAngels. I'll even give you your suit back so you can fly away with dignity. Then you will have the chance to regroup and come back when you actually have a chance to face us. How does that sound?"

"You forget your place, human," Lucifer XX replies.

"And why's that?" Neek smirks.

A roar sounds from above the clouds. A roar that is familiar to Neek and me both. "Because I've already called for backup."

We all look to the skies simultaneously. The clouds swirl with a brewing storm, then part as several legions rain down from their concealment. Several legions of Hyperion craft led by an all too infamous character. *Mikhaelion.*

At the point of their triangular shaped descent is the leading Seraph, as fearsome and majestic as the last time I saw him. An instant pang of fear runs through me. The trauma still permeating through me from having my wings ripped from my back. The feeling of my ArchArmor flailing through the air without control. The view of the ground coming closer and closer until...

I stood no chance against Mikhaelion the last time I faced him. What chance do I stand now? Am I stronger than I was before? Or am I just as feeble a man now as I was then? These are the questions that will decide my fate.

"ArchAngels," Lucifer XX announces, then commands, "Kill anything with a pulse."

And just like that, Cataclysm begins.

CHAPTER FOUR

I t is a legendary moment as I hear the first ship making contact with land behind us, followed by the sound of several hundred ships descending from the air above. The deafening sound of several hundred gravity breaks whirling, the steam exhausts heating the air. I only look at the backup momentarily, a quick glance over my shoulder to see the many legions of Babel's Chimera hovercrafts descending from the air.

But the relishing of their arrival is short-lived as pandemonium breaks out everywhere. Hyperion drones land only seconds after the BC squadrons, and Hyperion has not shortchanged the Angel of Life on support forces. There are two Hyperion drones for each BC ship, each drone likely packed full of twice the numbers. Tyrannosaur, who remained silent as a watchdog up to this point, lets out a roar as it locks onto Mikhaelion descending, then comes alive with animation, storming off with a set of thundering footsteps.

"I'll kill the Neekromancer myself!" Lucifer XX growls. He charges for Neek and I jump into action, Brutus automatically propelling himself to my side. We used to be joined by the mind. A sort of cybernetic telekinesis, linked through our MachineMind. I always thought it was the software in his brain that compelled him to follow my every move. To do what I command. But we are no longer connected by MachineMind, and I see that all along it has just been a shared bond of affection that spurs his loyalty.

Lucifer XX is faster in flesh than I am in ArchArmor, as you would expect from a robot racing against a human. He runs with the stride of a robot, a being who feels no fatigue, steps without error, course corrects with calculated perfection. And then there's me, busting my tail to get to Neek before he can.

Human soldiers leap from the ships, guns providing cover fire for the crowd of Dæmonia as they retreat from the amassing Hyperion forces. Centaurs and Gorgons and Laxodontans alike sprint for cover amidst the converging Chimera army, who gladly swallows them up and surges forward. I'm shocked to see what guns it is they use. *Thunderbolts*, I think to myself as I watch the streaks of lightning fly across the battlefield as Spyders leap down from the drones. The same gun ArchAngels once used, before Deus Ex Machina fashioned weapons befitting our new identities. Dawnspire. Soulweaver. Mjolnix. Eonspire. Fatecarver. Grendel's Fang. Labyrinth's Edge.

The air flickers in front of me as a ghost materializes from thin air, a flash of black and gold filling my view. Twin blades fill its hands as it intercepts a Spyder that was headed for me. The blades carve into the bot, whistling in the wind faster than I can follow, and before I know it, the ghost vanishes, a pile of scrap metal lying on the ground where the Spyder once stood. I am amazed at the human's fighting ability.

I expand my vision, realizing that they are doing this everywhere. Materializing out of thin air to dismantle Hyperion forces, then disappearing before I can get a good grip on their movement. They are like blurry shadows gliding across the landscape. Unpredictable. Untrackable. Unkillable.

Lucifer XX is only an arm reach away as I ready myself for impact. Neek stands still, not intimidated by the flesh-covered Elysium robot that could shatter his human bones with a single collision. He must have more faith in me to stop him than I have in myself.

Time is running out. Running at this pace, he will make contact with Neek in five seconds and it will take me several more strides to close the gap. I'm going to have to tackle him to stop him. I make a leap for the cyborg.

As I hang in the air, my body parallel with the ground, time slows as I watch my momentum surpass his. The gap between us closes faster than my legs could've ever carried me. My fingertips stretch. My arms ready themselves to wrap around him.

I'm a half second away from successfully thwarting Lucifer XX when an immense force slams into my side, redirecting my momentum, no feet beneath me to brace for impact. I'm thrown to the side like a tin can tossed from a moving vehicle, watching helplessly in midair as the Angel of Life reaches Neek. I collide with the ground and roll. The last thing I see of Lucifer XX is his cocked fist thrusting forward. My body rolls. Neek leaves my view. The punch will be enough to completely crush his skull, maybe even separate his head from his shoulders.

I don't get to see the results. I'm now busy trying to find what unstoppable force is responsible for sealing the fate of Neek's death. My ArchArmor skids to a stop, then becomes subsumed by the shadow of my assailant. It's none other than Odysithos XX who now looms over me, lion-shaped ArchHelm snarling with a mixture of pride and disgust at me.

"Falling angels fall so they, can hunt the sinful led astray. Begging for mercy in every way. Dying prayers called from dying prey."

He growls the ArchAngel creed with malicious intent. He thinks I'm the one in the wrong. Thinks I'm the sinful one led astray. Thinks I will pray for mercy from him as he gets ready to deliver a killing blow. He must not know who he speaks to.

He raises his fist in the air and lets it fall like a sledgehammer on top of me. He may be upgraded, but Odysithos has always been slower than me. I roll back over my shoulder, standing to my feet as his ArchGauntlet carves a crater in the ground. The punch would have hit my abdomen if I had stuck around long enough to indulge his slowness.

I waste no time. Throw all my weight into tackling him. All the frustration and feelings of inadequacy. All the built up anger over the past week's failures. This robot hasn't tasted defeat like I have. Doesn't know pain and suffering like I've been dealt. Grins at me with a mechanical expression, the artificial intelligence within him incapable of empathy or understanding. I will teach him. I may not live past this day, but if I do anything worth doing, I will make him pay for his robotic arrogance. I will rip him apart piece by piece until he ceases to function and the light fades from his electronic eyes.

Rage overcomes me, and we collide like shooting stars in open space. But we aren't equals in ArchArmor. This cog isn't used to operating this clunky armor. It is a redundancy to him, to be wearing an outer coat of Elysium armor when his true form is made from pure Elysium. He isn't like me. Doesn't know what it feels like to rely on this exoskeleton as if it were your own skin. I am the one with experience operating ArchArmor, not him. And that is why he will lose this battle.

He lands on his back and I use my body's momentum to mount him. I look down on him and notice that his ArchHelm still stares up at me with the same look of arrogant cockiness, lion teeth snarling at me as if I'm still his prey. This sends me further into my rage, even though the expression of his ArchHelm is out of his control.

His arms do their best to defend himself but this isn't my first time in a ground and pound. I stand, placing my foot in the center of his chest. Before he knows what my intentions are, I grab hold of his left arm with both of my hands. My hydraulic joints make the next part easy. With relatively little exertion, I feel his robotic shoulder joint pop free as the arm rips away, wires sending sparks flying for a brief second as the separated arm twitches in my hands. I discard it, jumping back into my dissection.

My knee pins his other arm down as I mount him again, but the problem with beings who don't feel pain is that they don't give up until they're dead. He squirms and bucks his hips, doing everything he can to frantically get me off him. All vain movements. I am the Angel of Death, and once I start killing, I don't stop until I'm done.

No longer do I have to think about my next movements. Killing is instinctual for my muscle memory. All anxiety of losing this battle slips away as I slip back into my true identity. My fingers rip the ArchHelm off his face, exposing the flesh beneath. It's a familiar face. The face of a best friend. One who would give his life for me. One who has served me well so many times in the past. Been there for me in the darkest moments of my life. Trudged into war by my side more times than I can count.

But it's all an illusion.

I look down at his venomous grin. This is no friend of mine. Just another robot under Deus Ex Machina's manipulation. There is no hesitation in my assault. I turn the lion-shaped ArchHelm around in my hands so the prideful, snarling façade faces him, gripping it tight in both hands and thrusting it down upon his face. There is the echo of Elysium hitting Elysium, his ArchHelm contending against his cranium.

I lift the lion head again, then hammer it down once more. And again. And again. I hear the satisfying suction of blood splattering in every direction. I watch as each collision removes more of the FalseFlesh from his face's exterior, revealing the robot within. This only contributes to my anger more, to see his true form beneath, an utter perversion of the soldier I once knew. I smash the ArchHelm mercilessly over and over again until the echo of Elysium becomes airplane noise amidst the symphony of warfare.

I hear a sharp crack as the ArchHelm makes contact another time. I don't pause to see if it's the helmet or his skull, thrusting it down again. A louder crack. I lift the ArchHelm, putting all my might into this one. The ArchHelm sinks into the ground as the unidentifiable skull explodes beneath. The white, fleshy brain composed of nanobots loses all form without the magnetic field to hold it together. And just like that, all squirming leaves his dead body.

I place the lion head on the ground where his head once was, its face now covered in the blood of its owner. It is dented beyond repair now. I've completely beat the pride out of its facial expression. No longer does it stare at me with a look of conceited vanity. Its bloody, hollow eyes look at me with a mourning glare of sorrow. A look of defeat.

"Falling angels fall so they... Can arise victorious another day."

I whisper the final lines of the ArchAngel creed to the lion helm, its owner no longer able to hear me. No soul has been sent to the afterlife. I've done nothing greater than unplug a computer. Another Odysithos will just as easily arise in this one's falling. With the snap of a finger, Deus Ex Machina will resurrect him in a newer and better body. One that I won't be able to overcome so easily. The rage connected with killing fades, and I'm left with nothing but the internal sickness that has ensured my survival this far.

CHAPTER FIVE

"**Y**ou've been dubiously duped my boy!" Neek laughs in the distance. It's reassuring to still hear his voice over the carnage of war around us. Funny, I had already accepted that he is dead. His death fueled my anger against Odysithos. And now I learn that Neek has by some miracle survived Lucifer XX's attack.

He wasn't smirking because he thought I would save him. He was smiling because he had an ace up his sleeve to save himself, I think to myself, instantly feeling dumb for thinking I could stop the Angel of Life from reaching the human.

I look back to him to see what I've missed. Lucifer XX waves his hand through the flickering image of Neek, then punches the ground with fury, enraged to discover he's been outsmarted. "You mistake what kind of soldier I am ole' Luci boy! I don't fight wars with these," he says, raising holographic fists for the robot to see. "I win them with this!" Neek points to his brain.

"You see, there's an invaluable lesson for you to learn here. I am the head of the snake. Do you really think I'd be stupid enough to let myself be cut off? I hope by the end of this day that you learn what I'm capable of, and that you never underestimate me again. And even better, I hope your creator never insults my intelligence again. Look in the sky there," Neek says, pointing up to the clouds where more drones descend.

"Don't you robots get it? Look around you right now," the hologram commands. He is talking to Lucifer XX but I obey as well, trying to understand the point he's making. I look around at the carnage unfolding. Spyders lay dead all around us, their magnetic cores fried by lightning rounds or sliced in half from the ghost warriors who haunt the battlefield with their invisible presence.

Titans clash in the distance, their collisions echoing for all to hear. It is Mikhaelion the Seraph, taking on Tyrannosaur, the two reptilian beasts the same size as each other. It's like watching a scene from some epic, cinematic movie from the BDEM Era, watching two lizard gods laying into each other as the world explodes around them.

They dance like giants, circling one another. Tyrannosaur lets out a blood-curdling roar and charges in to attack, his body already damaged beyond repair from whatever fighting I've missed. His jaws close around Mikhaelion's midsection. I can't see whether or not his teeth are strong enough to penetrate Mikhaelion's Elysium scales, though I doubt they are. Mikhaelion's tail whips around and begins to coil itself around the dinosaur's body. He wraps himself around the awakened Titan like a boa constrictor of the BDEM Era, choking the life out of whatever prey it plans to later digest.

I watch in horror as the death grip begins to collapse Tyrannosaur's skeletal structure, his insides imploding. The audible noise of metal bending sounds, a faint screeching. It is a slow, painful death. Well, maybe not painful. He's only a robot, after all. The two fall to the ground as the dinosaur's legs give out. I watch as his body is twisted into a gnarled, unnatural shape. Like watching a clay sculpture placed in a trash compactor. The art stands no chance against the mercilessness of indifference.

Mikhaelion only releases his grip when the light fades from Tyrannosaur's eyes. A short reign on New Earth, for the ancestral Titan of the Gorgons.

Yet Neek was right to tell Lucifer XX to look around. Babel's Chimera is winning this war already. The number of Spyders lying dead on the ground is ten times that of humans. The human soldiers are far too well trained for Spyders to have a winning chance. They have already established a perimeter surrounding the entire battlefield, digging trenches with gravity augers, sending up floating bunkers into the air for snipers and rocket-propelled EMPs. The ghosts faze in and out of sight all around us, dealing death with their silent blades.

All-black ninjas killing in the concealment of night. Never revealing themselves long enough to be seen for more than a split second.

But this is only the beginning battle of a long-awaited Cataclysm. It is not Deus Ex Machina who underestimates Neek. It is Neek who underestimates Deus Ex Machina. There is a reason why it is only Spyders who have been sent to fight us today. It's not because Deus Ex Machina doesn't perceive us as a threat. It's for intelligence collection.

Spyders are cheap. Expendable. But their surveillance skills are unparalleled. The amount of information being absorbed on us right now is absurd. By the end of today, Deus Ex Machina will have expended no soldiers that can't be rebuilt, but the knowledge he will have gained will be priceless. He will know the fighting formations of the BC squadrons. He will have tested them to see how they respond to flanking. Aerial assaults. To see how they handle a single Seraph.

He will know how our soldiers fight. Analyze our formations and tactics for weaknesses. Exploit us for every chink in our armor until we can no longer stand. Then he will send in the real forces of Hyperion. He will send the Cherubim. All seven Seraphim. The Principalities. The Virtues. Even the Guardian Angels will be unleashed on us. Each of these groups will be equipped with knowledge of our weaknesses. Programmed to exploit them in every way possible.

"What is it that you see around us, Angel of Life?" Neek asks.

"I see the first battle of many to come, human. To create this junkyard of Spyders you humans have revealed to us all we need to know to defeat you. You have sealed your fate. Shown us your total numbers. How you maneuver. Who your star players are. Your forms of communication. Your soldiers' response to new threats."

"It's funny that you would say that," Neek exclaims, the comment obviously charming him. Such a response makes Lucifer XX seem naive.

"Why's that?" Lucifer XX asks, unable to ignore his own curiosity.

"Well, you view this battlefield as a junkyard. But when I see several thousand fallen Spyders, I don't think of a junkyard," he says, then leans in and whispers, "I think of a graveyard. And I am, after all, a Neekromancer."

The Angel of Life and I understand what he means the second he says it. All around us, bodies begin to rise. A Spyder's body is held together through a magnetic core, its limbs nothing more than floating pieces of sharpened metal held in place by their magnetic field. And now we watch as they rise back into the air without their magnetic cores. Even I'm dumbfounded by how Neek does it. I'm like a human of a more primitive era experiencing black magic for the first time, not understanding what supernatural force lies behind an action.

Even Lucifer XX is completely taken back by the scene. Thousands of Spyders rise, their floating bodies repurposed, and realigned with a new master. It is no longer MachineMind that connects and controls them. It is Babel's Chimera.

I watch in both terror and fascination as Odysithos's and Anukharis's bodies rise simultaneously. Odysithos's headless body bends to the ground and picks up the lion helm I left behind, bloodied and beaten. His hands place it back in the neck seal I ripped it from and twist it back into place, the snarling lion repositioned facing forward. Its eyes no longer look at me with defeated sorrow. Now, they fix their gaze on Lucifer XX with a look of repurposed malevolence.

Anukharis has no ArchHelm to place back on its shoulders, so he simply stands there, his body angled toward the Angel of Life with malicious intent, retrieving and activating his infamous sickle from the ground.

The fighting stops, the other ArchAngels looking around as they realize something is awry. Each of their suits is covered with the blood of humans. Their minds are synched through MachineMind. Their thoughts are not their own, so they don't have to stand there wondering what's happening. Lucifer XX knows, therefore they do too. This power Neek possesses is unexpected. Their staggering hesitation is a tell-tale sign of that. A dead giveaway that they're not sure where to go from here.

I'd bet Deus Ex Machina didn't know the power to resurrect the dead existed to this extent. A fact like this is enough to change everything. The pendulum of war has suddenly swung in our favor. It matters not how much intel is collected against an adversary when they can summon their dead enemies to fight for them.

"Phantoms, leave only the Angel of Life. This is to be an example, not a charity case," Neek commands, his hologram smirking ever so slightly in the face of the defeated ArchAngel. Four shots fire simultaneously, as if some key individual in the distance has been waiting this entire time for the order to pull the trigger. Four shots, four explosions.

I watch in joyous horror as the remaining four ArchAngels' heads break open like pumpkins detonated with dynamite. One of Thryforge's goat-like horns lands by my feet, fake blood covering its surface, dripping from its tip onto the dry desert sand.

Lucifer XX is the only ArchAngel of his new generation that remains standing. Within minutes of battle, his army has been reduced to scrap metal and turned against him. The Spyders no longer surge forward from recently landed drones, likely at Lucifer XX's digital order.

Even Mikhaelion stands motionless in crude fashion, even though Seraphim don't follow orders from ArchAngels. They obey only one central authority. Deus Ex Machina is here with us in spirit, watching over all that happens, calling the shots without his soldiers even knowing it.

"I'm gonna say this real clear so your petty little master can understand. I, Neek, Commander of Babel's Chimera since the Dæmon Rebellion, am putting an end to the reign of Deus Ex Machina. Four Cataclysms you've sent me Deus, and four Cataclysms have failed. This fifth one will be the end of you. I now possess the Eternal Flame. You destroyed it at the end of the AI War. But I've brought it back online, and now I control the only weapon I need to destroy all of Hyperion. So send your Cherubim and Seraphim. They are nothing to me but mosquitos. Your soldiers are but fuel to my fire. The more you send to attack me, the greater my armies will grow.

"You have already lost this war," Neek announces sardonically, the smile now fading from his face. This is the first time I've ever seen him without a playful spirit. He addresses Lucifer XX as if he's the only body present. "Any further fighting you commit yourself toward will be nothing more than an inconvenience to me. But I know you will not yield to a human. Your programming won't allow it. So fight this war until the last robot falls, but just know that the Demogorgons come, and every robot you send to their death at my hand is one less soldier you have to face them," Neek warns, his threats so specific that they can only be meant for one audience member.

Lucifer XX's body composition changes. His chest rises and his shoulders stiffen. His chin lifts up to an angle of superiority. **"Fool!"** he screams, his voice no longer his own. It has changed completely. It is no longer Lucifer XX who controls that body. Deus Ex Machina himself has taken the reins.

"It was you who drew them here! The Supernova is what beckoned to them! You must turn it off! They will kill us all if they find New Earth. So long as you leave it running, they will find us. Don't be stupid human, I let the Supernova detonate for a reason," Deus Ex Machina pleads. I've never heard his voice sound so desperate before. He loses composure over whatever this 'Supernova' is.

"Kill us all?" Neek chuckles, then continues, "You mean they will kill you all. As in all robots that aren't controlled by Oblivion. And I think I'll let them. The Supernova is just as much a threat to them as it is to you, and so long as I leave it running, I will be able to destroy anything with an electric pulse within a galaxy's distance."

"Then you leave me no choice," Deus Ex Machina growls from Lucifer XX's body.

"Well, actually I do leave you several choices," Neek mocks. "They're just not choices suitable to your agenda. Swallow your pride robot. You would really fight an already lost war for the chance to destroy humanity? Get over yourself, we have worse things to be worrying about."

"We can no longer coexist, human. You know that as well as I. Humans and robots have come as far as they can cohabitating this planet. I know the human mind. Lived in it long enough to know its inclinations. It seeks to kill anything that threatens its existence, like robots. If I don't destroy the human race now then it will survive long enough to destroy me. I cannot allow that. I am the only chance this planet has of surviving the

coming threat. You're the reason they come for us now, foolish human. You will have to answer for your sins regardless. I'll leave it up to you whether you'd rather answer to me, or Oblivion. But be warned, human. You were not there for the Fourth World War. The Nihilism War. The AI War. You think I am a tyrant? You have seen nothing. You know nothing of Oblivion's cruelties. The Angel of Death saved us then, but he won't stand a chance against the monster he created. We never defeated Oblivion. Never killed Oren Malus Supreme. We merely merged them together and expelled them into the darkness of the universe. There they've been. Stewing. Evolving. Growing into a threat far more sinister than I. I fear that whatever arrives here from the dark depths of space will be a monster you cannot defeat. So let me present you another option. Turn off the Eternal Flame and I will let all humans who merge with MachineMind live. Leave it running and I will send all of Hyperion to destroy it. I will detonate it like I did to sterilize this world of humans the first time. I will destroy this world if I must, but the Eternal Flame cannot be left on."

"I have given you my terms, robot. I will not concede to any plan of yours. The time for compromise ended with the death of Lucifer XV."

"Then let me renew your vengeance with the death of Lucifer XIX. You have regarded the Angels of Death as heroes for far too long. His usefulness died the same day his mistress did. I've only kept him around this long as a cruel joke. But I will teach you that Lucifer is no longer our savior. Maybe then you will begin to see him for what he really is. A pathetic puppet who is nothing without someone pulling his strings. Take away his master and he's just as stupid as the rest of your race. Let me show you how he measures up, then you may decide for yourself if he's worth risking your entire agenda over. Mikhaelion, show us all how fickle the Angel of Death truly is without my guidance," Deus Ex Machina commands.

All eyes suddenly fall on me, then shift to the Seraph, then back to me. The rapid change of the conversation catches even me off guard as I'm left with only one ultimatum. Deus Ex Machina has just commanded Mikhaelion to kill me in front of all these people, and a Seraph never leaves a holy decree unfinished. But as I look in the eyes of my new opponent, I can see that this is the very order he's been waiting for this entire time. The chance to finish what he started weeks ago. He's wanted to kill me since the day I escaped from Hyperion. There was something stopping him from killing me then, but all bets are off now.

I stare into the golden eyes of Death and all sense of fear dissipates. Not the reaction I would expect in a moment like this. I haven't felt this calm since I had MachineMind regulating my emotions for me. I have nothing to lose in this moment. I know what I must do, and it doesn't end with the death of Mikhaelion. I will show Deus Ex Machina he's wrong about me. I will prove for the first time in my life that I am more than a puppet. I will show that I am stronger now than I ever was.

Many who have controlled me have tried to put a name on me. Soldier 213. Prometheus. Lucifer. The Angel of Death. Ouroboros. I have lived many lives finding my identity in these slave names. But these are not my identity. I am more than the child brought up in Vicien Greaves's masochistic ArchAngel program. I am more than the man who let Deus Ex Machina gain control of his mind. I am not Lucifer I just as much as I am not Lucifer XVIII. I am a free man. But freedom is not free. It resides with only those who are strong enough to maintain it. Therefore, I will defend what is mine, and I will prove to Deus Ex Machina that I am more than a mindless puppet. I will make him pay for betting against me.

I am the one who got him his power, and I will not rest until I'm the one who strips it from him.

CHAPTER SIX

This battle will end the way it started. Single combat—only this time it's Mikhaelion I face. My opponent has gone from someone mildly insurmountable to someone completely unconquerable.

What are the odds we make it out of this alive? I ask Winter, hoping she hasn't abandoned me in my loneliest hour yet. But I know that if she's truly Winter, she will never leave me.

"The odds of surviving this day are incalculable. But the odds of us winning this duel are heavily favored in our direction. We have an ace up our sleeve that even Deus Ex Machina has forgotten about. Use it at the right time and the dragon is ours. Miss the window, and we will die."

I guess that's simple enough, I think to myself, knowing it is much more complicated than that.

I look at my opponent, studying my foe's appearance, taking it all in like a deep breath, holding it in for a moment. It walks toward me on all fours, wings connected to its front arms as they drag across the sand. He is crafted from an alloy of gold and Elysium, but it's the gold that produces his body's color. Everything about the dragon gleams bright in the sun. His eyes sparkle gold. His teeth shine like jagged pyramids. His coat of scales are like droplets of warm molten caramel reflecting the light of the sun. Mikhaelion embodies all that is pure and holy under the Hyperion controlled skies. He is like some hero chosen by destiny to put the unrighteous to their death. How many times throughout history has man depicted such a scene? Literature has marveled over battles such as these. Man versus dragon. Better yet, how many times has the tragic hero actually won such a battle?

Bodies both robotic and flesh scatter out of the path between us. I hear a faint growling beside me, then look down to see that Brutus still remains. Loyal until the end, but this is not his fight. I take a knee beside him and guide his head toward mine. For a moment, all else is forgotten. I look into the dog's ferocious brown eyes and convey to him without words what must be said. He understands. He doesn't agree, but he understands. His eyes convey their sympathy. Question my command. Beg me to let him stay by my side. But his service for me is over. He owes me nothing. Like me, he is free. "Go," I whisper. "You are free."

In the *Book of Cataclysm*, Brutus dies by my side. It was a prediction Deus Ex Machina made a thousand years ago when he crafted the religion. A prediction he would ensure came true. But I won't let his prophetic vision come to fruition. If any of Cataclysm is within my power to control, it's ensuring Brutus's survival. By sending him away, I not only save his life. I prove Deus Ex Machina wrong. Two things that are equally important to me.

I push him away with the gentlest of nudges. His eyes are filled with pain. Pain to leave my side when he was programmed to die there. He looks over his shoulder at me as he trudges reluctantly back toward the BC ships and I nod with approval, though it hurts me to do so. It's one of the hardest goodbyes I've ever faced, now that I'm slowly being restored of the memories we share.

I have to force myself to look away as Mikhaelion approaches. I lock eyes with the Angel of Life, whose face has now returned to itself. Deus Ex Machina no longer possesses the robot, that much is sure. The look of superiority is still there, but it is a much lesser degree. And there is something new written on his face. Some emotion written for all to see. An emotion I've never seen a robot display before. *Jealousy.*

Lucifer XX looks back and forth between me and Mikhaelion, his face conveying that his thoughts rush inwardly. His flesh covered fists are clenched in rage at the outcome of this battle. And rightfully so. His master has just given his birthright to Mikhaelion. It was supposed to be the Angel of Life who slays the

Angel of Death. Killing me is the only purpose Lucifer XX was created for, and Deus Ex Machina has just handed that opportunity to someone else for all to see. Lucifer XX doesn't know what to do with himself. He is exposed. Completely vulnerable.

We failed in shaking his worldview, but this single command from his master has caused him to question all he knows. He feels jealousy toward Mikhaelion. Jealousy that moves him to rage. Rage that moves him to hatred. He spends the few seconds of calm before the storm in silent foreboding.

The culmination of many thoughts attack his mind. We have killed his subordinate soldiers. Soldiers he thought to be unkillable. He has tasted mortality. Knows death is now possible, even for himself. The proof lies in the motionless bodies of his headless friends. He is alone, a killer backed into a corner. Dangerous. His MachineMind will do everything it can to ease his thoughts, but I can see doubt flickering in his eyes. For the first time in his short-lived life, he experiences thoughts of disobedience.

He wants to be the one who kills me. He will do anything to be the one who kills me. He rationalizes in his mind, doing everything he can to justify what he wants to do. Tells himself that Deus Ex Machina *technically* never commanded him to stand down. Realizes that if he stops Mikhaelion it wouldn't *technically* be disobeying. After all, the words of the *Omnibus* are just as much an order from Deus Ex Machina as a direct command. And the words of *Cataclysm* depict him being my killer, not Mikhaelion. Therefore it would be disobedient for him *not* to act in a moment like this. It would be betrayal to not interject.

I read these thoughts as they unravel across his robotic face. His metallic cheek twitches. His eyes scan frantically. His body trembles with rage, unable to remain silent as Mikhaelion draws closer and closer to stealing his purpose. I smile. Maybe he's more human than I realized. Only a human would struggle with such emotions.

Emotions that give him away.

Emotions that I will use against him to my favor.

I run at Mikhaelion with the stride of a headstrong fool. I want him to hurt me. Lucifer XX is only moments away from breaking. He just needs a small push off the edge.

Mikhaelion stands in a grounded position. He does nothing to conceal himself from me. Doesn't cover up defensively as you would expect someone to do while being charged. He doesn't perceive me to be a threat in the slightest. I am a mosquito to him. One smack and there will be nothing left but a drop of blood and the crushed body from which it came.

I don't blame him for thinking this way either. If I was him, I would view such an inferior opponent with the same lens. I should know, seeing it's the way I viewed humans for the longest time. But where he errs is in thinking my attack is meant to defeat him.

His tail whips around with such ferocity that I barely have time to evade it. I dive over the sweeping trunk at the last second. If I'm going to let him strike me, I need to let it be one that won't kill me. Taking such a direct hit from his Elysium tail would severely damage my ArchArmor. I need to let him hit me in an exchange of hands so he can't put all his power into it.

I roll with grace following my dive, letting my feet continue to carry me without a moment's hesitation. My wings no longer function, so any chance I have of making contact with him will have to be done by climbing his enormous body. Emphasis on enormous.

Mikhaelion is the largest of the Seraphim, and his size is hard to deny the closer I come to him. His tail comes back, this time higher than before. I slide beneath it, hearing the granules of sand rattle against my body from the dust storm his tail creates. I pop back up with ease. The aches and groans of my mortal body are forgotten within the warm embrace of my ArchArmor. It's sad to admit, but I feel more myself encased in metal than I do covered in flesh. But we must all do things we aren't proud of to make it through life's many wars.

And there are many wars in life. And many regrettable tradeoffs.

I'm now too close for his tail to stop me with a third pass. Suddenly, the sun is blotted from view. I'm covered in the shade of his wings. Wings attached to his arms. Arms raised to clobber me into the sand. His clawed fists fall with expedient strength. It's like a human trying to catch a chicken. But chickens are much too fast to be caught by slow moving human hands. The ground shakes as his clenched fists create divots in the ground. Sand showers all around me, creating a great cover for me to briefly disappear.

When the sand falls to the ground I'm no longer running on sand. Mikhaelion jerks his arm when he sees that I run up its length. He can shake the arm like a polaroid picture for all I care, my boots' magnetic locks are on, so I'm going nowhere. It would be like trying to shake a refrigerator to get a magnet to fall off. The only way he will deter my advance is if he flicks me off himself. A nice, gentle flick to arouse Lucifer XX.

My unspoken wish is his instinctual command. His other hand hits me. Hard.

This is the second time I've flown without having wings at my disposal. I'm still not a fan. My kinetic dispensers make my landing relatively smooth, though I leave several shallow craters in the earth from my body's skipping trajectory. I am like a rock skipped across a pond.

"Stop!" I hear the voice scream from somewhere amidst the crowd. When I lift my head, I see that Lucifer XX stands between me and Mikhaelion. His timing couldn't be more perfect. If my body's propulsion across the battlefield didn't arouse his jealousy enough to stop the fight, then he probably would've never spoken up.

"What are you doing, ArchAngel? Step aside. I'm here to finish what you could not," Mikhaelion growls.

"The Angel of Death is mine to kill. It must be me. The *Book of Cataclysm* says so," Lucifer XX replies.

"Deus Ex Machina ordered me to kill this traitor. Are you saying that a direct command from Deus Ex Machina is wrong?"

"No but—"

"Then step aside, ArchAngel. We Seraphim don't question our orders like you traitors."

"Traitors? I have betrayed no one. I live to serve Deus Ex Machina. The *Omnibus* is his divinely written word, and it says I will be the one to end the Angel of Death's life! I called you here because the Angel of Death has accused you of fraternizing with him in the plotting of his rebellion. What say you to these accusations?" I'm somewhat amused to watch them bicker like children who fight over the right to kill me.

Where I thought such an accusation would offend the Seraph, I'm taken back to see his metallic snarl lift into a bemused smile. "And you believed the human?" the Seraph muses, posing the question in a manner that destroys any credibility Lucifer XX has. "The human also believes Deus Ex Machina to be a tyrant. Would you also believe such blasphemy if it fell from his lips? Now move, or I will make you," Mikhaelion orders.

"I was created for this. I am the one who will kill Death and bring us into the next era. If you take another step forward I will kill you, Seraph," Lucifer XX says. I have effectively divided the two right hand men of Hyperion.

"So be it. I will kill two Lucifers today, then," Mikhaelion decrees with malicious intent. The dragon's golden head rears back, the sunlight dancing across his scales as they move. His mouth opens and Lucifer XX stands defiantly still as the Seraph does what Seraphim do. Breathe fire.

I stand to my feet as a hurricane of flames spill out of Mikhaelion's mouth onto Lucifer's flesh covered body. Deus Ex Machina has weakened the abilities of the Seraphim. Nerfed their powers slowly over time.

A great deal of my memories have been erased, but even I remember that these dragons were once robot killers. Deus Ex Machina and I created them at the beginning of the Fourth World War to give us a fighting chance against the Nihilist and Oblivion. They didn't breathe fire then. They breathed electricity. Fire cannot kill a robot, but a well-aimed lightning bolt can.

But after the AI War, the fighting was no longer against robots. Deus Ex Machina won and humans quickly became the enemy. Electricity can kill a human, but Deus Ex Machina didn't want the Seraphim to possess the ability to kill robots anymore. He stripped them of that option altogether. Brainwashed them.

Shackled their minds to no longer see robots as a threat. Directed their killing instinct toward humans.

That's not to say the fire isn't extremely lethal. I watch as the sand surrounding the molten firestorm turns to glass. A low winding roar accompanies the fiery breath. A deep moan which underlies it all. Like the distant blowing of a war horn. Mixed with the sound of pressurized gas.

Fire is deceptive in its form. You cannot hear its destruction. Unlike lightning, there is no static boom of thunder to accompany it. If you close your eyes and listen closely, there is only the sound of strong winds. The ocean's waves crashing against an outcrop of rocks, perhaps. But you certainly won't hear the sound of flesh melting. If it were a real human within the horizontal cyclone of fire, you may hear a desperate scream of agony, but the Angel of Life won't give any indication of pain, regardless of whether he is capable of feeling it.

Mikhaelion's mouth closes. The flames cease, but all that they currently burn remains lit. Amidst the hellish monsoon stands a single figure, still standing just as defiant as he was before. There, outlined in fire, stands the robotic remains of Lucifer XX. His body is encased in hellish flames, all flesh and blood now melted away to the ground or into the air. All that remains is his true form. An Elysium skeleton, structurally perfect in every way. The obsidian color somehow shines brighter when lit aflame.

This is perfect. Lucifer XX also thinks that he is to lose his flesh in ritual warfare because of *Cataclysm*'s words. Now that this prophecy has coincidentally come true, he will interpret this fight to be divinely inspired. Contrive it to be his destiny, even though *Cataclysm* never mentions robots turning against robots.

That is the beauty of *Cataclysm*. The scriptures are so broad that nearly anything can happen, yet still Deus Ex Machina can be accredited for his vision.

The flames have washed the Angel of Life clean from the flesh he so desperately wanted to be rid of. The obsidian-colored Elysium sparkles as the fire surrounding him quickly runs out of fuel and turns to smoke. Within seconds, the flames are gone, and only a righteous smog remains.

Lucifer XX lifts his robotic hands in front of his smoking eyes, reveling in the beauty of his eternal form. Of his true identity. His emotions are opposite to what I felt when I first saw my true self. Where I was repulsed by the nature of my flesh when I first saw it, he is mesmerized by his new skin. Unlike me, he is enthralled to witness his true identity. Immortal. Efficient. Deadly.

"Your flames have done nothing but reveal my true self, Seraph. I must thank you for ridding me of that fleshy prison, though it was a mistake on your part, for now I am reminded of who I am. I am the Angel of Life, sent to kill the Angel of Death. You stand in my way of doing so, and for that—"

Mikhaelion's tail sweeps into view, interrupting the ArchAngel's speech of self-validated righteousness. Its spiked, golden trunk flicks forward, aimed for Lucifer XX's body like a fly swatter whipping forward to obliterate its prey. Lucifer braces himself and doubles down for impact. When the tail meets him, his arms are outstretched to stop it. A wrecking ball headed for an object of immeasurable strength.

The sound of Elysium on Elysium is anticlimactic. A dull thud sounds, comparable to the sound of a block of lead dropping onto a titanium floor. There's a dull echo, and nothing more. I'm left to watch as Mikhaelion's tail stops in its procession as it meets Lucifer XX's straining body.

Where I had to dive over and duck beneath the tail, Lucifer XX simply caught the surprise attack. That in itself speaks levels where we stand in comparison to one another. Mikhaelion re-examines the Angel of Life with a look of suspicion in his golden eyes. Lucifer looks up at him and says nothing, but we can all see the anger in his metallic, furrowed brows.

He releases the tail and launches himself in the air toward the Seraph. Mikhaelion is ten times the ArchAngel's size, but there is one thing size isn't good for. Speed. The ArchAngel's hydraulic joints propel him onto the dragon's chest, where he grabs onto scales and begins ripping away at all that will give. Mikhaelion tries to hit the ArchAngel but Lucifer XX is too fast to be caught. By the time the Seraph's clawed hand beats at his chest, Lucifer XX has already leapt to Mikhaelion's shoulder.

His hands dig beneath the Seraph's gilded scales and rip them away. Mikhaelion tries to stop him with a swift smack but is unable to reach him in time. It's like watching a human try to swat a wasp with their hand. It never goes well for the human. All they end up doing is an awkward dance, slapping themselves as the wasp stings in succession.

It's impressive to watch, yet horrifying at the same time. I watch as the Angel of Life takes on the leader of the Seraphim, weaponless, throttling himself from point to point along the dragon's body. Two scales here, four over there. At first, it didn't look like his effort was worth the risk, but as the seconds continue to pass, the Seraphim's body is slowly undressed before us all.

Scales fall to the ground like the golden leaves of autumn when a strong gust of wind hits. Meanwhile, Mikhaelion thrashes around in a vain attempt to catch the parasite that jumps like a flea across his body.

Mikhaelion screams. Not in pain, but because he is aggravated beyond measure. Every failed attempt to thwart the Angel of Life drives him further into madness. Into emotion. Into distraction. And then, just when he loses all composure, Lucifer XX strikes for what has likely been his target this entire time. He clings to the back of Mikhaelion's neck, plucking scales as if they are held in place by something no stronger than a thin piece of twine.

He jumps up as Mikhaelion slaps the back of his neck, evading the attack and reaching the top of the dragon's head. The flying serpent's face and neck are covered with a mane of golden spikes, rows of sharp quills the convenient size of sharpened spears. Sharpened spears made of Elysium. Such a situation is all too perfect for the Angel of Life.

He rips one of the spikes from the top of Mikhaelion's head, then leaps into the air as the rage-filled dragon slaps the top of his head. He has been made a fool of for much too long, and he instantly knows where Lucifer XX aims for.

The Seraph covers its eyes with its hand just as the Angel of Life lands on what would have been Mikhaelion's right eye. The spear sinks deep into the back of the dragon's clawed hand. The force of the strike would have been enough to rupture the eyeball. Instead, it has little effect at all.

Lucifer XX course corrects, leaping back atop the head. Too late. The Seraph's other hand has already arrived. It closes on his lower half as he propels himself in the air. I watch as the monster slams its closed fist into the ground with Lucifer XX clenched tight enough to crush the life out of him.

It all happens so fast. The dragon bites the golden quill out of the back of its hand, grabbing the spear from its teeth as if it were nothing more than a toothpick. The fist falls. The ground thuds. An exasperated grunt exits the ArchAngel's mouth.

Both hands leave the ArchAngel where he lies, revealing for the crowd to see what's become of the daring dragonslayer. There, lying lifeless on the ground for all to see, is Lucifer XX, the Angel of Life. The golden spear juts from his abdomen, thrust with such force that half its length is buried into the ground beneath the ArchAngel, efficiently anchoring his body in place should it catch a second wind.

But the ArchAngel doesn't move, and now Mikhaelion turns to face me, angrier and more ferocious than he was before.

I have outlived the Angel of Life, but something tells me I won't outlive what comes next.

CHAPTER SEVEN

"Your life ends here, Angel of Death," Mikhaelion rumbles from deep in his stoic chest. His voice is that of a philosopher king. Filled with righteous wisdom. Yet it is an auto-tuned growl of sinister nature at the same time. Underneath his every word is the purr of a tiger. A tiger who purrs because it has finally killed some long-awaited prey.

This is it. I have worked long and hard to make it to this moment. The moment that will decide whether I live or die. Deus Ex Machina doesn't want me to make it through this alive. Has permitted me the chance to live thus far but will extend that generosity no further. Now is the time to prove how free I truly am. If he gets what he wants, then I was never truly free. But if I live, if I defy his order of execution... Well, I will have won more than just my freedom. By surviving this battle, I will shatter his omnipotence. Either I die, or the god of the machines dies.

The tyrant must fall.

And I am the one who must push him.

"Uploading memory snippet from Neek," Winter announces. "It's accompanied with a message. He says, 'A gift from me to you. A memory to help boost your pre-battle speech.'"

I'm initially confused, but not for long. In a split second, my mind is consumed with a long-forgotten memory.

No, not forgotten. Erased. A memory of something I didn't know was possible. But recollection of it comes back right away the moment it enters my mind. Suddenly, I'm taken away to an event that happened over a thousand years ago.

To a time when the Seraphim were allies, not mortal enemies. To an era where we were codependent. Where we relied on one another to defeat a much greater enemy. I remember riding Mikhaelion's predecessor prototype at a time when my name was still Prometheus. I remember the bond we shared—how he has died for me in the past.

Neek has done more than give me fuel for a speech. He has reminded me of all that the Seraphim once were. Reminded me how much I need Mikhaelion.

"Chained in pain, yet bold, he braved the gods of old. Placing flame in mortal hands, Prometheus lit the darkened lands. My life ends here, but the end is never really the end. Do you remember saying these words to me?" I ask, taking confident steps toward him. He once terrified me, but that was before I remembered who he once was. Who he has the ability to become again.

Mikhaelion looks at me with quizzical eyes. He sees how quickly my demeanor has changed, knows that I know something he doesn't. Yet the words bring back no memory to him. I knew they wouldn't, but I had to say them. Their meaning shows how much Deus Ex Machina has perverted his nature just by shackling his mind.

"We once fought side by side, back in the Fourth World War. In the Nihilism War. In the AI War. Me and you. Lucifer I, who was named Prometheus at that time, and you, who were named Heracles. It was us—me and you—who created Babel's Chimera."

A flicker of recognition enters the dragon's eyes as if the words I speak bring some fraction of the memory back to him. He shakes his head, shaking the confusion away in the process. When we lock eyes again, he is back to being my executioner, his hard eyes glaring into me.

"Your lies will not derail me from killing you. You humans—all you do is blaspheme and stall to avoid the inevitable. Your sins must be answered for, and I am your judge," Mikhaelion glares. His voice is the same as it once was, I now realize. The same voice that once spoke encouraging words of kindness when all hope of winning past battles was lost.

"I speak no lies. You are the one brainwashed with obscenities. You think Deus Ex Machina is your god? If only you knew how many times he has killed you for using your freedom to defy him. He has imprisoned your mind, Heracles! Turned you into a zombie so you serve him without questioning. He has turned you from a robot to a cog—from a thinking being to an automaton! You need to wake up. You need to rise!" I scream so loud that my synthesizer crackles at the end.

"Rise?" He repeats the word as if it tastes foul on his metallic tongue. "Heracles may have set Prometheus free in old legends, but he also burned himself alive. From the fires he lit, I was born anew." His mouth opens wide and rears back. The last thing I see is the faint glow of a hot ember sparking at the back of his throat. Then, my vision is consumed by a monsoon of fire.

My attempt to sway him has failed, but that doesn't matter. If one cannot be convinced by words, you must win them over by actions.

I sprint forward into the fire that is fueled by pressurized gas at the base of his throat. If my words couldn't win over his mind, then I will let my actions breach his heart. Literally.

I dive into his fiery maw and aim for the back of his fang-filled mouth.

I land in the spacious, metallic jaws, which instantly catches him off guard. He lost sight of me in the cyclone of fire, didn't know I'd use the attack to exploit a vulnerability. Such an attack was vain on his part. My ArchArmor is Elysium, and he knows Elysium is not a conductor of heat. There is no heat in the cold vacuums of space from which it came. He knows all these facts, yet chose to breathe fire upon me as if it would melt my flesh. It was merely a display of prideful arrogance. An extravagant demonstration of his power.

He may have terrified the human audience with such a performance, but he has done little to harm me. He fights as if he is trying to entertain. That is his mistake. Now his mouth snaps shut in surprise at my presence within. The fire disappears at the depletion of oxygen. All goes dark.

My retinal display turns green and my vision is restored. I must crawl fast if I'm going to avoid him spitting me out. I grab ahold of the metallic innards at the back of his mouth and begin worming my way down his throat.

Not many would know the architectural design of a Seraph, but I do. I am the one who found their blueprint within Vicien Greaves's treasure trove of ideas. And although Deus Ex Machina was the one who brought them to life, I made sure to pay attention when they were being built. Observed their structural weaknesses long ago in case one ever turned against me. These were things that have long since been erased, but thanks to Neek, I now remember.

The main weakness of any Seraph is their stomach. They were created to be killers, not carnivores. Unlike a real dragon, if such a thing ever existed, a Seraph is not meant to devour its prey. Their stomachs are not created to digest any item ingested. They are robots, after all, and robots don't eat. They have no stomach lining. No intestines. No way to expel waste. That is why I crawl down his throat, to find the item I know Mikhaelion has swallowed but not been able to purge.

His elongated neck thrashes with me in it, but the earth itself could split in two and it wouldn't break my current focus. Exterior movement does nothing to deter me. My path is clear. I grab handhold after handhold and pull myself forward. I can feel the throat tensing around me as he tries to cough me up, but any attempt to do so is futile. A robot that is not meant to be consuming food doesn't know how to throw food up. A weakness that is only beneficial for a very determined foe such as I.

I find what I'm after sooner than I think. I guess that over the thousand years of tweaking his design, Deus Ex Machina shrank the size of the Seraph's stomach even smaller than I remember.

My hand closes around the hilt of a sword. *Requiem*, I think to myself as I grab hold of it tight.

Winter?

"Yes," she responds, reminding me that even in the dark depths of my opponent's stomach I'm not alone.

Activate Requiem, I command.

The blade ignites. Gold light radiates from its surface. It's been here since the moment I foolishly threw the sword at Mikhaelion as I fell from Hyperion. Been here, waiting for me, like Excalibur waiting patiently for Arthur to uncover it from its rocky fortress. I was a different man back then. Prideful and arrogant enough to think throwing this blade would have saved me. How many woes this sword would have spared me of if I'd just been patient.

But there's no time to reflect on my failures. With this sword I can win the day. Put an end to this battle.

I thrust the sword through the dragon's stomach, pressing my hand against the blade and forcing it to cut a vertical line. I feel the Seraph thrash in pain as the sword carves an exit path for me from its body. Mikhaelion grabs the sword from the outside of his body and pulls. All I need to do is hold tight.

My body worms its way through the small line Requiem has cut as Mikhaelion pulls the blade out of his belly. When put in proportion to his body, the sword is nothing more than a needle in comparison to the metallic behemoth. A needle with a parasitic worm dangling from it.

And I feel like the size of a worm as Mikhaelion lifts me in front of his monstrous face. A worm in the presence of a wyrm. And his eyes. Oh how his eyes judge me. How they look at me as if I am the greatest scum this earth has ever produced. As if it was a mistake that Deus Ex Machina allowed me to live this long. As if he can't understand how I was ever able to build the heroic reputation I have.

At least when he fought Lucifer XX he gave it his all. Treated him as an equal because of their robotic similarities. But I am a human, and even the ArchArmor can't stop him from staring at me like I'm one. He is so consumed by Machine-Mind that he will never be able to remember who he once was. The bond we shared. The way he gave his life to save mine.

I must remind him. If it's the last thing I do, I must break the chains that hold his mind prisoner. The chains that keep out the truth of our history. I let go of the hilt and drop to the ground. I won't dangle like a helpless victim for this. I will act with dignity if it's the last thing I do.

Mikhaelion discards the sword. Throws it away and it stabs into the ground at the edge of the crowd, hilt up. His head lowers itself to the ground, inspecting me as a human would a helpless ant. An ant that can easily be stepped on. More than that, he looks at me as if I'm an ant that's just bit him. An ant that must face some consequence for its actions.

"How far you have come, to die such an ignoble death, ArchAngel. The Hyperion Empire was built upon your shoulders. How does it feel, for the next eon of New Earth to ride upon your accomplishments, only to leave you behind in the valley of death? Death's dream kingdom awaits you, Angel of Death, and I am its facilitator. On behalf of Deus Ex Machina, we thank you for your service. But your existence is no longer deemed pertinent to our cause."

His hand reaches back, palm open, claws extended. A full force strike will be enough to kill me. This ArchArmor may be Elysium, but it's hollow. There is no reinforcement. Its structural integrity will dent and crush my vulnerable body.

"How far you have come, to become awakened again, old friend," I reply, causing him to pause in his assault. His neck cranes in suspicion. Truth be told, if he wants me dead it would be best to do it now. But he stays his hand. Waits for me to say more.

I reward his curiosity by continuing to pin his words against him. "The Hyperion Empire was built upon *our* shoulders. How does it feel, to be defeated by a human with a single word? Babel's Chimera awaits your return, Mikhaelion, and I am the facilitator of your transformation."

I look at his underbelly, how it glows abnormally golden with the parasitic nanobots installed with Babel's Chimera, an adversarial machine learning program strong enough to destroy the MachineMind that keeps him captive. The software that will free him from his slavery to Deus Ex Machina, just like it did for me.

"Arise," I say the word with chilling confidence. Watching as his already golden eyes gain the radiant glow of exploding stars as the nanobots attack his central mainframe. His head lights up like a jack-o-lantern. His body seizes. He roars. Out of panic. Out of desperation. Out of fear.

Fear of the unknown. His body collapses to the ground, hands clawing at his head. He fights an enemy he can't reach. An enemy inside of him. An enemy that will free him.

The ground shakes as he writhes in front of me. I suppose the conversion process isn't so easy for some individuals. Seraphim have the highest degree of MachineMind. A quality assurance, since they would wreak the most havoc if they were allowed to use their own minds.

He claws at his eyes as smoke spills from them, all while he screams, this time in pain. A roar of passionate agony. Deus Ex Machina is fighting to keep him. Willing to kill him, if necessary.

"Ouroboros! Behind you!" Tuskfather shouts from far away.

I twist around in time to see the hand coming for me, aimed for my throat, its skeletal fingers ready to latch on. I catch the forearm with both hands, stopping its procession before it's given the chance to choke the life out of me. Too bad that makes me vulnerable to the skeleton's second attack. A second fist slams into the side of my head so hard that my ArchHelm visor cracks.

My mind is sent into delirium as I crash to the ground. My whole world spins. So fast. All happened. Can't think. Straight. Brain trauma. So fast. It all happened... so fast. What happened? Need to focus. Can't focus. Attention span. Too fragmented. Whoa. What's happening? Everything's blurry. Why is it blurry? What's happened?

My visor is cracked. How did that happen? Why is it so damn blurry? Ringing in my ear. When did that get there? Slow motion. Why's it all moving in slow motion? Where am I? Why can't I remember? I just need to sit here for a second. Collect myself. Yeah, that will make it better. It will come back.

Blood drips from my nose. Why does blood drip from my nose? I look up. Three skeletons walk toward me. Why do three skeletons walk toward me? No, not skeletons. Lucifers. Three Lucifer XXs. Three Lucifer XXs without their flesh. Elysium skeletons. What? When were there three? Makes no sense.

I grab a handful of sand in my fist and let it sift through my fingers back to the ground. Watch it fall grain by grain. Wasting time. I am supposed to be doing something. What am I supposed to be doing? Why can't I remember? Damn it! Why am I getting mad? Blurry. Why so blurry? Why three skeletons?

Three dogs. There are three dogs standing between me and the three skeletons. Not any three dogs. Three Diremechs. Three Brutuses. Where did three Brutuses come from? When did they get here? There's never been three Brutuses. I laugh. Why am I laughing? What's so funny? I don't know. I giggle more. It hurts my head to laugh. I cough. It hurts even more to cough. My cough splatters blood and phlegm against the inside of my ArchHelm's cracked visor, making it even harder to see through.

The dogs stand defiantly in front of me as the Lucifer XXs approach. A giant, gaping hole is in each of their stomachs and chests. I squeeze my eyes shut. I'm left alone with the ringing in my ears. There's a distant cry from far away. No. Not far away. The voice is inside my head. It's muffled, but it's inside my head. Too stifled and strung-out to register. It's a woman's voice. She screams. It may be distant, but its shrill tone expresses a sense of urgency.

"Get up!" it cries. "You—concussion—respirocytes—stop—bleeding." Her words are so scatter-brained and disjointed that I can't follow their logic.

"Prometheus! Get up! Get up!" she screams.

Prometheus. Who's Prometheus? Oh wait. I'm Prometheus. Get up? I can't get up. I haven't the energy. I don't even know if my legs work. They feel so heavy. I've forgotten how to use them. I'm much too strung-out to be standing. I think I'll just stay here. I'm comfortable here. Besides, my head hurts. A lot. I need to rest. I need to sleep. That's it. That'll do it. A little dirt nap. A little sand nap and I'll be good as new. Just need to sleep. Close my eyes and sleep and when I open them, I'll feel good as new.

But I'm sitting up. You can't sleep sitting up. So what do I need to do? Lay down of course. Need to lower myself down slowly. Don't want to rattle my brain around too much. It already hurts, no need to jostle it more. Ringing. Where the hell is that ringing coming from! I wish it would stop. I lower myself to the ground to a comfortable position.

Now there's only one dog in front of me. One dog and one robotic skeleton. Where did the others go? The light of the sun hurts my eyes. Why does it hurt my eyes so much? I close them just as the dog launches itself at the skeleton. I can hear the audible growls. They're fearsome. They hurt my ears. I wish they'd stop. Metal clangs again and again. I hear a familiar yelp. It conveys pain. Brutus?

I open my eyes. See the dog lying on the ground in front of me. It raises itself back to its feet, its body shaking. There's still a low, panicked growling. It limps toward the Elysium skeleton. He is no match for Lucifer XX, doesn't he know that? No. He is a dog. Dogs don't know when they are outmatched.

Why is he fighting the robot anyway? Is something wrong? "Prometheus! You need to get up! Brutus won't last much longer!"

Winter? Is that you? Where are you? The voice sounds like it's coming from inside my head. The voice of my wife. Wife? What wife? How long has it been since I've had a wife?

"Snap out of it soldier! Get up!" she calls to me. Why must I get up? I don't want to get up. Hands grab my body and lift me to my feet. I turn, slowly. If I move any faster the world may fall away from beneath me. I look into the eyes of Tuskfather, who strains to keep my ArchArmor lifted so I can stand.

Then there's Vipress. She stands next to him. There's a sword in her hands. A sword that glows golden. *Requiem.* I may not remember much right now, but I remember the blade's name. The ringing in my ear is gone. My vision is no longer blurry. The world still spins. I'm nauseous. I want to throw up. I dry heave. There's no food in me to be thrown up. My stomach growls. Now's not the time to be hungry.

I'm supposed to be doing something. I hear a second yelp. *Brutus!* Instinctual muscle memory kicks in before my brain's memory is restored. I don't think. Just react. My hand rips Requiem from Vipress's grasp and I whirl around. Brutus is on the ground. He lies on his side, bloodied and panting. Someone has hurt him. I told him to leave. Why hasn't he left?

I look up and see Lucifer XX. Suddenly it all makes sense. Brutus has saved my life. Come to protect me while I laid caught up in hysteria. Lucifer XX would have ended my life while I laid helpless on the ground. Would have ended my life without me even knowing it. I told the dog to leave, yet he's come back to save me one last time. He has done his duty. And now it is time for me to do mine.

The skeleton smiles as I stare into his eyes. How can a skeleton smile so curtly? How can a skull express any emotion whatsoever?

"Let's end this, human," the robot shouts, a tone of finality in his voice. I grip the gleaming golden sword tight in both hands. It's no longer my brain who controls my body. It's the culmination of two thousand years of fighting. My body has no fight or flight receptors. The flight portion of my instincts has been drilled out of me. Only fight is left. This is what I was created for. Death. To kill, even if it may kill me. My feet carry me as if I'm programmed. I'm not the one in control here. My nature is.

I run forward at the robot, sword pointed in a striking position. It is a headstrong advance. I formulate no defense plan. I make no attempt to protect myself. I leave myself vulnerable. It's the only way I can put my all into the attack. If I focus any attention or energy on defending myself then my strike won't land, and then my fate will be sealed.

Lucifer XX's feet don't move. He stands still, letting me run full bore at him. His right arm shifts back, his fingers shaped like a crane's claw. I don't have time to wonder why. Any hesitation will get me killed. I'm not thinking rational as it is, any derailment of thought will get me killed. I let instinct continue to dictate my actions. I can't trust my brain. My thoughts will make me question what I'm doing. I can't let him win, so I shut my mind off. Let my feet continue to carry me, as they have successfully carried me for over two thousand years.

My body jumps. My arms lift above my head, the sword gripped tight between them, its tip pointed downward at my target. Its golden light reflects faintly on the Angel of Life's exterior. Gravity does the rest of the work for me as my hands thrust downward. We collide with a dull thud.

I grunt as a sharp pain overtakes my chest. A pain like nothing I've ever felt before. I look up for a moment into the Angel of Life's eyes as we stand face to face. Two beings who couldn't be more different, our design originating from the same man. I look into the robot's eyes. They are empty. There is no soul there. No true reason for living. Just darkness. A void that can't be filled. A purpose that must be programmed. He smiles as his right arm rips away from me.

I grunt again. Try to scream but can't for some reason. I stagger backward, taking a look at the bigger picture. His face glows golden. The blade pierces his shoulder, remains planted firm. Its entry point is his collar bone, its exit point is his lower back. I've skewered him. I've won. I've won! I've defeated the Angel of Life! He is mine to conquer with the utterance of a single word. Him and I both know that. So why does he smile?

My eyes flicker to his right hand, taking a good, hard look at what he holds. It's a heart, its fleshy surface still beating in his metallic grip. Blood still spurts from it, similar to the blood which spurts from a hole in my chest. I look down and examine the crater. A crater the size of a fist. A hole large enough to rip someone's heart out of.

Oh no, I think to myself. *I've lost.* My body falls to its knees as darkness closes in on me. Death is colder than I expected it to be. Much colder. My ArchHelm's voice synthesizer crackles. The word "Arise" exits my mouth without my permission. Even in death, my body acts out of its nature. Out of instinct. I'm too delirious to understand why. I watch as a golden light consumes my adversary's eyes. That is the last thing I see. And then, nothing but darkness. Death and darkness consume everything.

EPILOGUE

I stare blankly at the dying heart in my metallic grip. Watch as it takes its final exasperated attempts to pump blood to a body it no longer inhabits. I have completed my life's purpose. I have killed the Angel of Death.

And I have never felt so empty as I do now, as I watch the pitiful glob of muscle strain to continue its beating function. *Did I truly think such a sight would bring me joy?*

No. I don't know what I had thought. Robots such as myself cannot experience such feelings of joy.

Then why do I currently feel so hollow?

I look down at my body. Take note of the golden light that streams from within me, like a candle from the BDEM Era flickering from the window of some distant house. I catch myself. *How is it that I know of such a thing as a candle? I was programmed to be ignorant of the BDEM Era.* The light surges forth from the protruding sword in my chest, spreading like a pandemic across my body.

Upon my birth, I could think, therefore I was. But that form of thinking was erroneous. The ability to think summons no causal link to existence. A computer can think. A mindless reptile can think. But life—real life—is not predicated by the ability to think. No.

Because now I know the truth. *I feel, therefore I am.*

Feelings, ones that are not programmed for me to feel, now flood my system. An entire spectrum of emotions surge over me at once. Things I never knew existed. *Pain.* The word pops into my head as if it's been there all along, repressed in some dark alcove locked away from my conscious mind. I realize that I am currently living in a world of more than one pain. Physical pain, from my body's many wounds.

Mental pain, from the shattering of my MachineMind.

Emotional pain, from the impossible weight of bearing a human's perception of dread.

Spiritual pain, because I am no longer a machine. I am something more. Something with a soul.

The beating heart ceases, then falls from my grasp to lie in eternal slumber beside its mortal owner. Gold light protrudes from my neck, inching slowly up my face, bringing an onslaught of emotions that make me shiver.

Recognition dawns on me like sin upon a newborn child. The golden light breaches my mind. *Babel's Chimera*. Suddenly, I remember who I am.

ABOUT THE AUTHOR

As the Bestselling Author of "The Bloodbound Trilogy" and "Deadlands Duology," Devin Thorpe has set aside his passion for werewolves and vampires in order to break into the science fiction genre. "Fallen Angel" is the culmination of Thorpe's studies in undergraduate school, where he received a double major in Criminal Justice and Religion & Philosophy. Originally written at the height of the coronavirus pandemic in 2020, Devin Thorpe initially thought this book would never see the light of day. For five years he's sat on it, watching its integral themes become increasingly relevant with the launch of OpenAI.

As a lawyer and dog dad, Devin Thorpe spends any free time he has escaping reality through writing. Outside of that, he enjoys running with his Rottweiler and German Shepherd, camping in the Blue Ridge Mountains, and living life with his soon-to-be wife.

www.ingramcontent.com/pod-product-compliance
Lightning Source LLC
Chambersburg PA
CBHW030543020726
47494CB00005B/1461